Final Kill

Leslie McKelvey

ISBN 978-1-936556-07-6

Published 2016

Published by Black Velvet Seductions Publishing

Printed by Black Velvet Seductions Publishing
A division of Savage Publications

Visit us at:
www.blackvelvetseductions.com

Dedication

This work of fiction is dedicated to all men and women in uniform, a family of which I am proud to be a part. They sacrifice, run toward what most would run away from, and die to protect the freedoms we all enjoy. May they never be forgotten, and may they always be honored as the heroes they are.

Military Terms and Acronyms

AQ – Al Qaeda

B&E – breaking and entering

BOQ – base officers' quarters

BUD/S – Basic underwater demolition/SEALs, training candidates undertake to become SEALs.

Cas-evac – casualty evacuation

Chinook, Blackhawk – types of helicopters

CIA – Central Intelligence Agency

CO – Commanding Officer

Comms – communication devices, usually earpieces that transmit and receive sound

CONEX – large, metal shipping container

CQB – close quarters battle, hand-to-hand combat

DHS – Department of Homeland Security

Digitals – digital camouflage, can be Arctic (white/gray), desert (brown/tan/gray), jungle (green, black, gray) or naval (blue/gray/black) colors

EMP – electromagnetic pulse

ETA – estimated time of arrival

Evac – evacuate or evacuation

FOB – Forward Operating Base

Helo – helicopter (aka chopper)

Klick – kilometer

Laser-trip – laser used to detonate a bomb or another explosive. Laser trip-wire.

LT – lieutenant, informally pronounced el-tee

LZ – landing zone

M16, M4, .416 – different types of rifles

MOS – military operational specialty. In other words, one's military job.

Military Terms and Acronyms

MWR – Morale, Welfare, and Recreation. All bases have an MWR office where soldiers and their families can buy discounted tickets to anything from airlines to amusement parks. MWR also provides for basic entertainment such as movies, television, and even Internet service. It's like a military YMCA.

NSA – National Security Agency

NVB – night vision binoculars

NVG – night vision goggles

OCS – Officer Candidate School

On my six – right behind me, on my ass. Think of it as points on a clock face.

PX – post exchange, aka military Wal-Mart

Recon – reconnaissance

RFID – radio frequency identification

ROTC – Reserve officers' training corps

RPG – rocket propelled grenade

S&R or SAR – search and rescue

SF – Special Forces

Sitrep – situation report. In other words, what the hell's going on?

SOCOM – Special Operations Command

SOP – standard operating procedure

SP – security police, formerly known as MPs or military police

TAC – short for *tactical*, usually referring to articles of clothing worn by police and military personnel with pockets designed to hold extra ammunition, magazines, and other weapons related items.

Tarmac – runway

Transpo – transportation

UCMJ – Uniform Code of Military Justice

Willco – will comply

Chapter One

She remembered the face of the first man she'd ever killed: the rest of them... not so much.

Regulating her breathing, Cat peered through the scope of the .416 rifle as snow fell fitfully, almost as if it didn't want to reach the ground. The snap of AK fire interspersed with the shouts of the Taliban firing the Russian-made weapons bounced around the ravine below her. She scowled.

Half an hour ago, she'd been sitting in a hidden mountain cave, relatively warm, monitoring two-way radio and cell chatter with a pair of specially designed headphones, using very expensive, top-secret, brand new, state-of-the-art technology. Now, because of what she'd heard she was lying on a ledge in the snow with her rifle, more than a kilometer from her relatively warm cave.

"Do you have them?" she whispered as the crosshairs found one turban-clad head.

"The SEALs are less than half a klick in front of them and losing ground." Tripp grunted. "What the hell are they doing out here?"

"Dying," she replied in a solemn voice. "But we're not going to let that happen, are we?"

Cat listened carefully as Tripp rattled off the firing solution, and she adjusted her scope as he did so. In all, she'd counted seven pursuers, but the only one she was concerned with at that moment was the one in her sights. Cat exhaled completely, held her breath, and squeezed the trigger.

The rifle recoiled, and before the first bullet reached its target she had retracted the bolt, dropped a round in the chamber, and closed the bolt. Less than four seconds and she was honing in on terrorist number two.

"Hit," Tripp reported.

She squeezed the trigger again, cycled the bolt, found her next target, and fired a third round as Tripp confirmed a hit on the second shot. She cycled the bolt again and paused.

"And number three is down." Tripp chuckled. "Keep 'em coming, Tiger."

It was then the rest of the group realized three of their compatriots were dead. Cat watched the four remaining men scramble for cover as they tried to discern her location. The clap of the .416 echoed off the hills, bouncing back and forth between the walls of the ravine, making it impossible for them to figure out where the deadly shots were coming from. Her fourth shot hit the target in the upper chest, dead center at the base of the neck. His head went spinning through the air like a macabre Frisbee, the blood-spattered turban flapping wildly. After that the extremists went to ground in the thick, mountain brush.

"Nice!" Tripp said. "He really lost his head with that one."

"Very funny." Cat scrutinized the distant hillside and smiled grimly when she spotted a turban. She adjusted her aim again, but the turban disappeared. "Does Tonto have them?"

She could hear Tripp breathing as he scanned the gorge below. "Affirmative. He's leading them up the back way. We're good."

"Not yet," she said. "If any of these guys get back to whatever hole they crawled out of they'll be right back here, messing my shit up."

"They'll be back anyway," Tripp replied. "Not them, I mean, but more like them."

"I know," she agreed, "but eliminating these last three will give me a little more time to pack. I have a lot of expensive equipment to evac."

"Always thinking ahead." There was a brief pause. "Maybe you should leave just one so there's someone to tell the tale."

"Nah," she replied with a smirk. "Let 'em wonder."

Several minutes passed with no movement, but Cat knew *terrorist* wasn't a synonym for *dumb*. Snow continued to fall and a deathly quiet descended over the ravine. It seemed even the wind had died; not a twig, branch, or bush moved. A shiver traversed her spine, but Cat shook it off and stared through the scope.

"Anything?" she asked in a whisper.

"No... wait, hold on." He moved his spotting scope a fraction. "Got one."

He did some quick calculations and then read her the numbers. Cat smiled when she focused in on her fifth extremist. He was half-hidden behind a pine tree, and the only part of him she could get a clean shot at was his right leg. She squeezed the trigger and less than a second later the man's hip exploded, his leg launching like a missile as the force of the impact spun him around. He landed face-first on the bloody snow and never moved again.

This was enough to send the last two into a panic. They started scurrying back the way they'd come, obviously overwhelmed by their fear. Survival instinct had kicked in, effectively silencing any common sense. Instead of staying hidden, they had decided their only option was to run. She felt a spurt of pity for them then took aim.

Despite the zigzag pattern they ran, she picked them off with relative ease.

"Hit."

"Not even Superman can *outrun* a bullet," Cat said in a low voice. She reloaded and peered through the scope. "Superman can only *stop* a bullet. Turns out a terrorist can, too... *once.*" Another squeeze on the trigger.

"And last one is down," Tripp said shortly after her final shot. "Can we go now?"

"Yep," she said. She capped her scope, folded the bipod, and quickly gathered her empty casings. After scooting back from the edge, she stood and swung her rifle over her shoulder. "Let's get back to the cave. We need to finish packing."

"You realize it won't matter you saved a SEAL team," Tripp commented. "The boss is gonna be *pissed* at you for doing this again."

"*I* didn't do anything," she said with a roll of her eyes. "This was a team effort, and if it really upsets him that much he should send us stateside." She glanced at Tripp. "He should know by now we're not going to sit around and listen to our boys in uniform get killed, especially if we can stop it. After the last two incidents, you'd think he'd have figured that out."

Tripp grinned. "You'd think."

"Besides," she continued, "it's almost time for us to be out of here anyway. We just advanced the timetable."

"You really *do* enjoy getting his jock strap in a twist, don't you?"

Cat chuckled. "It's almost as much fun as sniping bad guys and babysitting all of you, Tripp. *Almost.*"

***

Lieutenant Ryan Heller, US Navy SEAL, followed the stranger dressed in snow-cammies deeper into the tunnel. Digger leaned heavily into Ryan's side. His other teammates followed behind loaded down with their weapons. Ryan had no idea who the stranger was or how he had materialized out of the snow, but he didn't really care. All he cared about was getting Digger to a medic.

Gradually he detected noise and light, and his eyes widened when they entered a large cavern packed with computer monitors and illuminated by electric lights. Apparently, the stranger was accustomed to finding electricity and advanced technology in mountain caves because he kept walking. Ryan counted five other people all dressed the same as their quiet counterpart, but they were busy taking apart the computers and packing up the various components. He glanced over his shoulder at Mack, who shrugged in reply and continued on.

On the far side of the cavern was another tunnel. Ryan and his team followed the stranger silently. After about 20 meters the tunnel opened up again with several smaller caverns formed off the main passage. The guy led them to one outfitted with a gurney, an overhead light, and a small cabinet for medical supplies. As Ryan and Mack lay Digger on the bed their rescuer finally spoke.

"Wait here," he said. "Doc will be with you in a moment." His message delivered, the stranger turned on his heel and disappeared down the passageway.

Ryan looked at Grady who had dropped the weapons and was examining the supply cabinet. Then Ryan focused on Digger who was barely conscious.

"Great," he said, "not even a Better Homes & Gardens to flip through." He shook his head and started to unbutton Digger's jacket. "What are doctor's offices coming to these days?"

"Who cares?" Mack said, leaning against the rough stone wall. "I want to know who was manning that rifle. That first shot had to be... what? Fifteen hundred meters?"

"At least," Ryan replied as he pulled a knife from his belt and sliced through the material of Digger's clothes. "Whoever the guy was, I plan to buy him a case of beer when we get back to Bagram. There's a Brit who owes me one for kicking his ass in poker."

"A *case*?" Grady repeated. "I was thinking my firstborn would be a good start on payment." He grabbed a nearby metal chair, spun it around and straddled it. "Don't like kids much, so it'll be a win-win."

"Are they military?" Mack asked.

"I don't think so," Ryan replied. "There are no rank or MOS insignias, no unit patches, and no identifying marks on their uniforms aside from last names, and who knows if those are even real." He scratched his beard. "No, these guys aren't military."

"Then what?" Grady asked. "Private security, NSA, CIA?"

"Pick one," Ryan said. "We have an entire bowl of alphabet soup to choose from." He heard footsteps coming from the direction of the tunnel. "It's not important now. Zip it."

"Sorry to keep you gents waiting." A man dressed in snow-cammies entered the medical bay and walked up to the gurney. He was young, mid to late twenties Ryan guessed, with blonde hair and blue eyes, and a tall, lanky build. He snapped on a pair of latex gloves then bent over Digger. "I'm Corpsman Tom Massey, but everyone calls me Doc. What have we here?"

"Took one round to the chest," Ryan replied, watching closely as Doc examined the wound. At least the guy *seemed* to know what he was doing. After a thorough inspection, the corpsman donned a stethoscope and listened carefully to Digger's chest. He then checked Digger's visual acuity and blood pressure. Ryan leaned closer. "What's the verdict, Doc?"

Massey straightened, his expression neither grim nor hopeful. "Well," he began, "there are decreased breath sounds on the left. The bleeding has stopped, but without an x-ray there's no way to tell what's going on inside, and trying to get the bullet out could do more harm than good." He met Ryan's gaze briefly then turned his attention back to Digger. "I can keep him stable for a while, and, provided we get him to a surgical unit in the next couple of hours, I think he'll be okay, but I'm only a corpsman. I'm not equipped for this."

Ryan nodded. "Good enough for me." He turned to Grady and Mack. "You guys stay here. I'm going to see if I can find out who's in charge and get a timetable."

Ryan strode back down the tunnel and entered the main cavern as two more people walked in from the opposite side. These, too, wore Arctic camouflage, both of their heads wrapped in turbans, their faces covered by scarves. The one in front was about 5'10" with a lean build and Ryan's brows rose when he saw the .416 rifle over his shoulder.

The name stitched on the front of the jacket read Beckett. The guy in back was an inch or so taller than Ryan, roughly 6'4" and powerfully built, but it was obvious the shorter man was in charge. Beckett walked around a table in the center of the room that was draped with a map, presenting Ryan with his back. He pulled the scarf from his face and leaned his hands on the edge of the table.

"Sitrep," Beckett said.

At least he *sounded* military. That gave Ryan a small measure of comfort.

An Asian guy with a fancy looking laptop and a headset spun in his chair and rolled over to the table. "There's definitely been an uptake in chatter," he said, "and I've triangulated their position to... here." He marked a spot on the map. Ryan edged closer as the man continued. "They probably realize the ambush didn't go down as planned, and once they decide to send out a recon team it'll take them less than half an hour to reach the kill zone."

"Perfect," Beckett said, his voice laced with sarcasm. He peered at the map. "Once they get *there* it won't take them long to locate us, especially if they find the spot Tonto picked up the SEALs. Our Injun didn't try to cover their tracks so it won't be hard to follow them."

"Hey, you said move fast so we moved fast," said the man who had led them to the caves. "That would preclude hiding our trail, boss."

"Doesn't matter anyway," Beckett said. "It's still snowing, so that will help." He straightened, put his hands on his hips and exhaled slowly. "Well, don't stand there looking at me. Finish packing." He pointed to a tall, beefy man with the distinctive features and large build of a Pacific Islander. "Techno, forget about loading it all. Get the important stuff: hard drives, scanners, mikes, dishes. You know what is and isn't necessary. If it's not important, top-secret, or insanely expensive, leave it."

"You got it, boss."

"Burgess."

A man sitting at a computer monitor turned around to face Beckett. "Yeah, boss."

"Coordinate with Techno. Make sure we've got all the important stuff out, then start wiping hard drives and prepping the rest of the equipment for evac."

Burgess nodded. "You got it, boss."

Beckett checked his watch. "Bam-Bam."

Another man, with sandy brown hair and eyes had a flat, monochromatic appearance, until he looked at Beckett. When the two locked gazes, a predatory gleam entered Bam-Bam's eyes that made his whole face come to life. Ryan blinked.

"Whatcha need, boss?" Bam-Bam asked. He fidgeted, obviously anxious to be about his master's bidding.

"It's not Christmas," Beckett began, "so the only gift I want those assholes to get when they find these caves is a really, *really* warm welcome, if you get my drift." As Bam-Bam scurried off, Beckett leaned on the edge of the table again. "Lee, double check that the cas-evac they were prepping for the SEALs is still on the way. Bagram can consider it requisitioned. Contact base and let them know how much gear we've got, how many personnel, and that we have wounded. Be certain they have the right coordinates for the LZ this time so we don't have to play radio tag in the mountains again."

The Asian man with the fancy laptop laughed softly and started tapping on the keyboard. "On it."

Ryan watched as people scurried around. While it was frenetic, there was nothing unorganized or panicked about the evacuation. Everyone seemed to know exactly what to do, and they were doing it without having to be told or directly supervised. Impressive.

Beckett and the tall man he'd come in with were conversing quietly, looking at the map. The .416 still hung over Beckett's shoulder. Ryan watched them for a moment then approached slowly, not wanting to interrupt. As he did, Beckett reached for his turban and pulled it off and Ryan froze. A long, thick, red braid fell down Beckett's back. His jaw dropped and he stared, but in his periphery he saw Beckett's companion had noticed him and was tapping Beckett on the shoulder. Ryan managed to close his mouth as Beckett turned to face him.

Ryan found himself looking into the most beautiful green eyes he'd ever seen. They were large, lined with thick lashes, and had a distinctly feline appearance with tipped up outer corners and a vivid, unwavering gaze. His pulse jumped. He saw the surprise there, as if she'd just remembered why she needed a rifle. She smiled and something in his chest melted.

"Lieutenant," she said. "How is your man?"

It took him a second to find his voice. "Your corpsman thinks he'll make it to Bagram, ma'am," he finally replied.

"Then he'll make it," Beckett said. "Doc is the best I've ever worked with." She waited a moment. "Is there something you need, food or water maybe? We're a little busy but I can get you something to eat or drink if you need it."

"Um, no, ma'am, we're good," he ground out. "I wanted to say thanks for saving our asses back there. That was some pretty impressive marksmanship."

"Yeah," agreed the taller man whose jacket read Trippler. He had dark hair cut in a high-and-tight and pale blue eyes. "She does okay... for a *girl*." He chuckled and looked at Beckett. "Need to get my stuff, darling," he said, affecting an awful British accent. "You can tend to our guests without me, can you not?"

Beckett looked at him out of the corner of her eye and fought a smile. "Get out." She turned back to Ryan. "Sorry, Lieutenant. Tripp likes to infuse humor into tense situations. It's a coping mechanism, and a character flaw."

"He your spotter, ma'am?" Ryan asked.

She had a generous mouth with full curves, and that mouth widened into a *you-have-a-gift-for-stating-the-obvious* smile. He noted the gentle features, the slender nose, and the elegant brows. She was stunning which, oddly enough, irritated him. SEALs weren't supposed to be *stunned* by anything, or anyone.

"Indeed he is," she replied. "And stop calling me ma'am. Now, I'd love to chat but we have to get out of here."

"Can I help?" he asked, a bit too quickly.

Her smile deepened, revealing a set of dimples that transformed her from cover-girl beauty to girl-next-door approachable, an unnerving and fascinating combination. His heart did an uncharacteristic flip but Ryan schooled his features into what he hoped was an impassive mask and waited for a reply. Thankfully, she had pity on him.

"See to your men, LT," she said. "When we bug out you're going to have to help your wounded to the helo, but thankfully the terrain isn't as rough on the *other* side of the hill from where you met your new and, sadly, deceased friends. Should be a relatively easy trek." She turned and started to walk away.

"What's your name?" he asked, again, a little too quickly.

She lifted one brow and glanced down at her name stitched so neatly on the Arctic camouflage.

Ryan frowned. "I *can* read," he said. "What's your *name?*"

She studied him for a moment, her gaze sharp and probing but still friendly. "Catharine," she finally replied, "but you can call me Cat."

"I'm Lieutenant Ryan Heller," Ryan said, "and you can call me whatever you want, but the guys call me Reaper."

"We call her Tiger," Lee said without once looking up from his computer, "but you're not qualified for that yet, Lieutenant."

"Nope," said Techno as he walked by with an armload of what looked like computer hard drives. "She has to like you first."

"Maybe she *does* like him," Bam-Bam commented as he affixed a round, black disc to the wall with a metal spike. There was a circle of red dots blinking on the front of the disc, and Ryan realized it was some type of explosive, a type, oddly enough, he'd never seen before. Bam-Bam continued speaking, his expression fierce as he concentrated on setting another charge. "After all, she was actually polite to this one. The others she hardly even glanced at, and when they questioned her she showed them why we call her Tiger."

With that everyone went still and silent and turned to stare at him. It would have been comical if the situation hadn't been so serious.

"Get back to work," Cat snapped. Immediately the noise resumed and she looked at him. "My apologies, Lieutenant. We rarely get guests so the children are quite unsure how to behave."

Ryan smiled for what felt like the first time in days. "It's okay. I'm just glad you're on our side." He paused, leaned toward her, and lowered his voice. "You *are* on our side, right?"

Cat laughed softly and put a hand on his shoulder. "Cut us and we bleed red, white, and blue, LT." She turned him toward the tunnel. "Now, wait with your men, please. When it's time to go, I'll come get you."

"And how long will that be, ma'am?" he asked with a mischievous grin.

Cat frowned, but when she saw his smile she chuckled and shook her head. The change in expression was dramatic and Ryan had no trouble understanding why they called her Tiger. When she scowled he had almost expected fangs. Her appearance was fierce, primal, and her stare was just as arresting as that of an angry Bengal.

Ryan knew snipers were a solitary lot who associated mostly with other snipers or their spotters. Their line of work required an entirely different skill set than what was needed to be part of a regimental combat unit, and camaraderie wasn't top of that priority list. Snipers were lone hunters. He was friends with a few of the military marksmen, though not a close friend. Often, they were regarded with a mystical reverence bordering on fear. Her first four shots had taken less than a minute, and while he had no way to know if she'd hit all her targets the fact their pursuit had stopped told him she probably had. But, unlike some snipers he'd met, he didn't get the hair-raising vibe from her. Nevertheless, he'd just met her. Perhaps a woman sharpshooter had a different disposition from the men he was familiar with. Until he knew her better, he thought it wise to allow himself to feel some of that reverent fear. After all, discretion was the better part of valor and if he pissed her off she could probably kill him from a mile away. Ryan shook himself as that creepy vibe finally registered.

"We'll be out in less than an hour, Lieutenant," she replied, breaking his train of thought. "Don't worry about your comrade, either. Doc will make sure he's ready to travel. He's aware of the time constraints."

Ryan snapped to attention and extended his hand. She looked at it for a moment then wrapped her fingers firmly around his. A faint tingle crept up his arm and he cleared his throat. "I feel like I should salute you or something," he said, "but since you're not a military officer, a handshake and my sincere thanks will have to do until we get back to Bagram."

Cat tipped her head to the side. "And what happens when we get back to Bagram?"

Unexpected heat burst inside him as he pictured what he'd *want* to happen, but he managed *not* to say anything. Pushing those mental photos aside he thought about her question for a moment, choosing his words carefully. "Whatever you want," he said at last. "If it's within my means it's yours. You deserve it after what you did for us. We wouldn't have made it out of that canyon if you weren't such a crack shot. We owe you our lives."

He thought he saw a hint of pink creep into her cheeks, but in the half-light of low wattage bulbs it was hard to say for sure. What he did know was she was still holding his hand, and that tingle grew stronger. It was strange, but he found he quite liked it.

"Why don't you buy me a cup of coffee when we get back to base and we'll call it even?"

His brows rose. "Really? That's it? I would have thought dinner at the mess hall would be your *first* choice, but hey, if coffee's your thing...." He frowned. "I did say whatever you want, right?" She chuckled and released his hand, much to his disappointment.

"Well," she began, "if we make it to the helo perhaps I'll give it some thought on the ride to base." She met his gaze. "Can I get back to you?"

"Of course, and I have a feeling no matter where I am on base you can find me," he replied. He gestured toward the rifle. "Just use that scope... finger *off* the trigger preferably."

A smile curved her mouth. "Deal."

"Great." He turned and started to walk away then looked at her over his shoulder. "Now I'll go wait with my men. Thanks again... Cate." He gave her a wink then turned away.

Cat blinked and watched the tall sailor walk confidently down the tunnel, feeling warmth and a strange tingling at the base of her spine. She didn't like it one bit. His demeanor, his manner, his genuineness was so unlike many Special Forces soldiers she'd met. That particular breed of men possessed a certain type of arrogance that often bordered on narcissism. She recognized it was necessary but she didn't usually like it. The utter confidence in oneself and one's abilities exhibited by most SEALs, Green Berets, and the like usually triggered a negative response in her, but not with this one. She remembered the shock of surprise that had registered when she'd met those crystalline blue eyes and the unwelcome jump in her heart rate. Cat crossed her arms over her chest and stared down the tunnel.

He was older than his men, probably mid-thirties, taller and bigger than most SEALs, about as tall and nearly as broad as Tripp. That was roughly four inches taller than her. She knew there was no set standard for the height and weight of SEALs, but shorter, wirier, lighter men usually performed better in the arenas SEAL teams worked in. This meant Lieutenant Heller possessed some impressive physical abilities that allowed him to overcome the disadvantage his size had presented during the qualification process. And while he wasn't as muscle-bound as Tripp he was muscular in an athletic, beefy way, like Russell Crowe in all his Gladiator glory. His eyes were dark blue, his black hair longer than the typical military cut because of his current location, and even the full beard did nothing to lessen his appeal. Lieutenant Heller was a very attractive man, and it annoyed her that she found herself attracted.

This wasn't the time or the place, and yet she couldn't remember the last time a man had affected her like he did.

"Admit it, you like him," Lee said from behind her.

Cat turned a sharp gaze on the man and he immediately returned to what he was doing. With a huff, she set off down one of the side tunnels toward her quarters.

Since she traveled light she didn't have much to pack, and in less than five minutes she was finished in the small alcove off the secondary tunnel that served as her "bedroom." Cat hefted her backpack over the shoulder opposite the rifle and walked back toward the main cavern. Everyone was there except Techno, who was no doubt gathering all the top-secret listening equipment from outside. She glanced at her watch and saw 25 minutes had passed since initial contact, but nearly everything was done. Bam-Bam sat on a crate near the entrance tunnel, and she approached him.

"Ready to welcome our guests?" she asked.

Bam-Bam nodded. "All that's left is to laser-trip the entrance. After everyone else is out I'll laser-trip the exit tunnel in case anyone makes it through the first car of the welcome wagon." He pulled a monitor the size of a small cell phone out of his pocket and grinned.

"What's that?" Cat asked, almost afraid of the answer. Although Bam-Bam was the best at what he did, sometimes his enthusiasm for explosives bordered on the disturbing.

He stroked the smooth, black surface as if it was a lover's hand. "If I don't *hear* the charges, this little baby will tell me when both sets of explosives have been tripped." He gave her a look that was slightly maniacal. "When *that* happens...." He reached into his other pocket and pulled out what looked like a dead-man switch. "When that happens, I push *this*... and the whole top of the mountain explodes. Thanks to me this hill will be a couple hundred feet shorter by close of business today."

Cat smiled and clapped him on the shoulder. "You *really* like keeping the geologists busy, don't you?"

He grinned, an expression that would send children scurrying to hide behind their mothers. "It provides job security for them and hours of amusement for me. It's a symbiotic relationship ensuring a positive outcome for all, like those little fish who eat parasites off sharks."

Cat stepped back and shook her head. "You worry me, Bam-Bam. You really do."

Techno strode by with an ammo box in each hand. "You're up, blast-man."

"Don't set the laser until I've had a chance to go look out front," Cat reminded him.

Bam-Bam nodded and his face lit up like a child on Christmas. He rubbed his hands together and disappeared down the tunnel. Cat grabbed Techno's arm.

"How many boxes do we have?" she asked.

He wiggled dark brows at her. "Well, I worked my magic so one each, boss. Lee will carry two since he doesn't carry a weapon, and two can be loaded on the stretcher with our injured SEAL. That will free you, Tripp, and the Bam-master up. I already cleared it with Doc."

"Did you magnetize everything else?" she asked.

"Of course." He smiled and patted her hand. "You can thank me later."

"I may just kiss you later," Cat replied. "Thanks, Tech."

"Anything for you, Tiger."

Cat watched him disappear down the exit tunnel then took a deep breath and stood on a crate to address the room. "All right," she began, "is there anyone who's *not* ready to leave?" She scanned the cavern, but the men stood there, silent and resolute. Cat smiled. "Good." She glanced at Lee. "What's the ETA on the helo?"

Lee looked at his computer then at her. "Five-zero minutes," he replied.

Cat glanced at her watch. "It's less than a klick to the LZ, which means we should get there right before the chopper does." She paused when Lieutenant Heller, his uninjured men, and Doc entered the room. Her eyes met those of the SEAL and again her pulse did a split-second leap. He and his men looked ready to go, their weapons slung over their shoulders. She took another breath and continued. "Techno has the boxes by the back door so grab what you can carry on your way, minimum of one each."

Lieutenant Heller stepped forward. "My men and I can help."

"Doc?" she asked, looking at the corpsman.

"I need one guy to help me with the stretcher," Doc replied. "Other than that, we're good and ready to go."

"Okay," Cat said with a nod. "Lieutenant, pick someone to help Doc carry your guy, and whoever is left can help with cargo."

"Roger that," Heller replied with a small smile.

"All right, people," she said, clasping her hands behind her back. "You all know the way to the landing zone so move like you have a purpose. Aside from our Navy guests, the most important cargo are those boxes, so I expect all of them to reach the LZ in the same condition you found them. Techno will take point and Tripp, Bam-Bam, and I will bring up the rear. No matter what you hear, gunfire, explosions, Toby Keith singing, *do not stop*. Get your asses and that equipment to the helo and back to base. Understood?"

"Understood," was the unified reply.

Cat put her hands on her hips and dropped her chin. "Move out."

Chapter Two

Ryan stood to the side as people filed past him, moving quickly down the exit tunnel. He looked at Grady. "Go with the Doc," he said. "Mack and I will hang back and help out."

Grady nodded. "Yes, sir. See you at the LZ."

"Be safe."

"Always," Grady replied with a grin. "You, too."

Grady and the Doc disappeared down the passage and Ryan turned back toward the main cavern. Cat and Bam-Bam stood at the map table, checking weapons and stacking empty M16 magazines as Tripp grabbed a box of ammunition, obviously the large-caliber bullets for Cat's rifle. He grunted to get her attention and tossed the bullets to her. She put aside one cartridge and then emptied the box into an ammo bag attached to her belt. The tinkling of brass was almost musical. She closed the Velcro seal on the ammo bag and turned her attention to her rifle. Ryan watched her, admiring the efficient grace with which she handled the weapon. Her movements were easy, practiced, almost sensual, and his thoughts started to drift. After inspecting the rifle, she dropped the single 4 1/2 inch shell into the open chamber and slammed the bolt home with the ease and confidence of someone who worked with the four-foot, 23 pound weapon on a frequent basis. She propped the rifle against the table and reached for a box of normal ammunition.

"She's obviously done this before," Mack said under his breath.

Ryan shook himself and glanced at his teammate. "Y'think?" When she began loading the M16 magazines he walked toward her. "If you have some more 5.56, Mack and I can help. I may not be able to take out a target at 1500 meters, but I'm not a bad shot."

"Yeah," Mack affirmed. "I'm pretty good in a firefight, too."

Tripp reached under the table and came up with four boxes of 5.56

cartridges in his huge, meaty hands. "Here you go, gentlemen. The more the merrier."

"Thanks," Ryan said, taking the boxes and handing two to Mack. They joined the others at the table and started filling empty magazines. Ryan glanced under the table and then looked at Cat. "You've got a lot of ammunition here. Expecting an army?"

A grim smile curved her mouth as she looked at him out of the corner of her eye. She picked up an empty M16 magazine. "Better to have it and not need it than the other way around, don't you agree?"

Ryan chuckled ruefully. "Yes, ma'am, I would definitely have to agree with that."

Silence prevailed for a few minutes, broken only by the click of bullets being inserted into magazines. When Cat had loaded a dozen or so she stacked them in front of her and leaned her elbows on the table.

"Lieutenant," she began, "I've been meaning to ask you something."

"Well, Cate," Ryan said, "since you saved my life I think you can ask me just about anything."

She turned toward him. "What the hell were you and your team doing out here?"

"To be honest, I'm kind of wondering that myself now." Ryan frowned and continued to load his magazines. "It was supposed to be a light mission. A truckload of weapons and ammo was hijacked from a convoy about a week ago. RPGs, rocket launchers, M16s." His scowl deepened. "We received intel that part of the hijacked weapons had been stashed in a village not far from where the convoy was hit, about 40 klicks north of here." He looked at Cat. "We got sent out, and the objective was simple. Recon the village to determine whether or not the weapons were there, and if they were, destroy them. Easy, right?"

"What happened?" Cat asked.

"We weren't even halfway there when we got ambushed," Mack said with an angry huff. He stuffed his now full magazines in his TAC vest and looked at Ryan. "It's almost like they knew we were coming."

Ryan flashed Mack a warning look. "Mack, zip it."

Cat's eyes narrowed and she straightened. "You think it was a set up?"

Ryan met her gaze and said nothing.

"Wow." She blinked and exhaled slowly then looked at Tripp. "And they ran straight this way." Tripp nodded, but remained mute.

"We didn't have much choice," Ryan said. "This was the only direction bullets *weren't* coming from." He paused and frowned. "Wait, do you think something bigger is going on here?"

Cat planted her hands on her hips, a scowl on her brow. "I don't know," she replied. "I've never liked coincidences, but in this country, it's almost impossible to tell if something was planned or the bad guys got lucky. I've seen both happen."

"Me, too," Ryan said. "So, what do we do now?"

Cat chewed her lip for a moment then loaded an M16 and handed it to him. "We need to finish this conversation," she said at last, "but not now." She turned to Bam-Bam. "You ready?" The demolitionist nodded and stood. Cat glanced over her shoulder at Tripp. "Tripp, you and the SEALs grab whatever boxes are left outside and hightail it for the helo. Bam and I will be right on your heels." Tripp walked over to her and held out a hand. Cat slung her rifle over her shoulder and handed over her backpack. The huge man shrugged into it and turned toward the exit tunnel. Bam-Bam and Cat started walking the opposite direction.

Ryan frowned, slung the M16 across his back and shouldered his M4. "Wait," he said, "where are you guys going?"

Cat stopped, turned, and gave him a tolerant look. "I'm going out front to see if anyone's coming this way. If they are, I'm going to try and convince them to rethink that plan of action."

"And once she's done convincing I'm going to activate the lasers," Bam-Bam added.

"We'll be right behind you, LT," she said.

Ryan crossed his arms over his chest. "Mack, go with Trippler. I'm staying here."

Cat lifted one arched brow. "Lieutenant...."

"Go on, Mack," Ryan said. "I'll be on your six."

Mack grabbed his rifle and nodded. "You got it, Reaper."

Cat waited until Tripp and Mack had left the cavern then she sighed. "Have it your way, LT. Grab as much ammo as you can carry and Bam and I will be back in five." A jaunty smile tipped the corners of her mouth. "Then again, depending on how close they are it may be sooner, so, be ready to go."

"I'll be ready," Ryan replied. "Just make sure you come back."

"Oh, I'll be back," she said, a mischievous sparkle in those vivid green eyes. "I fully intend to collect on that cup of coffee."

The heat in his chest expanded even as his throat tightened in anxious anticipation, and it took everything inside of him not to follow her. He was accustomed to running *toward* danger not waiting around for it to come to him, especially when there was a woman in the middle of it all. *Yeah, I'm a caveman.* Ryan scowled and started grabbing boxes of ammunition from under the table. When he could carry no more he stood and looked around the deserted cavern. There was still a lot of equipment in the room, but nothing they seemed overly concerned with leaving behind. He walked over to a blank computer monitor and turned it off as several pops came from the direction of the tunnel. Ryan's head snapped up and he started toward the passage. Before he could take another step, Cat ran into the cavern.

"Time to go, Lieutenant."

Ryan stared at her for a second. She was smiling and her cheeks were pink. In fact, she actually seemed to be *enjoying* this.

"Where's Bam-Bam?" he asked.

"On my six," she replied.

"I take it we're going to have company?"

"They're not here yet, but they're coming."

At that moment, Bam-Bam materialized out of the tunnel. "Let's move," he said. "After you, Lieutenant. Once you and Cat are out I have to arm the lasers on this side."

Cat sprinted across the cavern and Ryan followed on her heels. They ran down the tunnel, past the alcoves where the medical bay had been and others Ryan hadn't seen before now. He ignored it all and concentrated on following her. She moved like a feline, lithe and quick. The tunnel wound through the mountain for another hundred meters or so before he saw light. About a minute later they emerged into the frigid mountain air.

They were on a semi-circular landing with a narrow trail leading down from the western edge to his right. Ryan immediately knelt and raised his weapon, peering through the scope at the surrounding countryside. Although their enemies had been on the other side of the peak, that didn't mean there weren't bad guys on this side. However, the air was cold and still, the silence oddly reassuring. If there were Taliban on this side of the mountain no doubt a firefight would be raging between them and the people who had already evacuated.

"How far back are they?" Ryan asked. He glanced at Cat and saw she had assumed a similar stance, her eyes peering into the brush.

"I got two at about 500 meters," she replied, her cheek resting on the stock of the rifle. "I saw a total of six, but I'm sure more are coming. They'll pause for a few, gather their wits and their dead, and then continue to follow us."

Ryan chuckled grimly. "That would be their worst decision today."

She smiled and continued to survey the countryside. "No, their worst decision was going after you guys in the first place."

"And so, the Tiger came out," Ryan said. "Good for us, bad for them."

Bam-Bam exited the tunnel and gave Cat a thumbs-up then followed the trail down the western slope. Cat took another look through her scope, rose, and inclined her head.

"After you, Lieutenant," she said.

Ryan stood and shook his head. "Nope. We go together."

She pursed her lips. "The trail is only big enough to go single file."

"Then humor me," he said, planting the butt of his rifle on his hip, "and give me something to follow. Call me a caveman if you want, but chasing something pretty provides me with incentive to move faster." In the light of day, the faint flush that stained her cheeks was much easier to see, despite the overcast skies and light snowfall. She scowled and Ryan grinned. "After you, Cate. I always bring up the rear. Call it a coping mechanism, or a character flaw."

There was a mutinous set to her chin and an angry glint in her eyes that made his smile widen, and her scowl turned darker.

"Fine," she said at last, jogging past him, "but only because we don't have time to argue right now."

He gave her a small head start, then followed and matched her pace. "Whenever you want to argue, ma'am," he said with a low chuckle, "I will be happy to oblige you."

The terrain was easier on this side of the peak, but it was still a mountain in Afghanistan, so easier was a relative term. Between the topography and the altitude, Ryan knew even the most physically fit individuals would have difficulty. But he was a Navy SEAL. He *lived* for this type of stuff. It seemed Cat, too, was accustomed to the difficult landscape. She was quick and sure on her feet as the trail continued on a downward angle. Occasionally she glanced at him over her shoulder, and he gave her a cheerful salute in response. He had a feeling it annoyed her and that made him grin.

They'd been moving for about twenty minutes when the mountain shook and the sound of an explosion reached them. The three skidded to a halt and looked back. The peak itself was obscured by trees and brush, but the cloud of smoke rising into the sky was much easier to see.

"Looks like they found the entrance," Ryan commented.

"Which means we need to pick up the pace," Cat said. "It'll slow them down, but I don't want to give them a chance to shoot that helicopter out of the sky once we get airborne."

"Hear, hear," Bam-Bam said. "Picking up the pace, boss."

They continued at a speed just beneath a dead run and even Ryan started to feel it. Cat's breathing became more labored, and Ryan could hear Bam-Bam at the front sucking wind from where he was at the rear. The scenery blurred by in a smear of black, gray, white, and tan, all the muted colors of the snow-covered mountains. Ryan had often admired the stark beauty of the Hindu-Kush, but now was not the time to sightsee.

"I hope we're already in the helo before that second charge goes, Bam-Bam," Cat said, "but if not... blow that mountain."

Bam-Bam glanced over his shoulder. "You sure, boss? That'll probably trigger an avalanche, and we'll be right in its path."

"I know," Cat replied. "The objective is to get that equipment out. If we can give them a few more minutes to do that, that's what we need to do. Besides, if we don't make the helo they can always send another one." She looked back at Ryan. "You okay with that, Lieutenant?"

Ryan respected her for asking, even though his answer would affect the outcome very little. He nodded. "I'm all for completing the objective, ma'am."

That tiger scowl was back. "*Stop* calling me ma'am."

"Sorry," he replied. "Force of habit."

"Change that," she said flatly, "or when I *do* find you with my scope there will *definitely* be a finger on the trigger." Suddenly she held up a hand and skidded to a stop. "Hold up."

"What is it?" Bam-Bam asked.

"Ssh."

Ryan regulated his breathing and watched her as she closed her eyes and listened. A few seconds later her eyes snapped open and she smiled. Ryan started to ask why she was smiling when the faint "thump thump" of helicopter blades reached him.

"What?" Bam-Bam asked.

Cat shook her head and gestured for him to continue. "Bird's on schedule, but I suppose there's a first time for everything."

They ran on for another minute or so, and with each meter that ticked off, the sound of the helo grew louder until even Bam-Bam could hear it.

"Chopper's here!" he announced.

"Think we'll make it before Bam-Bam has to bring that mountain down?" Ryan asked.

"We're almost to the finish line," Cat replied, leaping over a log that had fallen across the trail. "I think we can risk it."

Another explosion roared behind them, but this time they didn't stop.

"Want me to bring it down, boss?" Bam-Bam called over his shoulder.

The trail took a sudden upward turn, and a moment later they crested a small ridge onto a wide, rocky plateau. The Chinook helicopter sat in the center with blades whirling, and the last of the evacuated personnel were loading into the back. Mack, Grady, and Tripp stood outside the helo, weapons ready, and Tripp raised an arm when he saw them at the edge of the field. Ryan looked at Cat and she grinned at him.

"We made it, Lieutenant," she said. She turned to Bam-Bam. "You can blow it now, Bam, or wait until we're airborne. The latter will give you a better view."

"Woohoo!" Bam-Bam shouted. He ran for the helo. "Move over boys, I need a window seat!"

Cat chuckled and started after him and Ryan brought up the rear. When he reached Grady the two grasped arms and Grady grinned.

"If you'd been another minute Mack and I were going to head back looking for you," Grady said as they entered the helicopter and took up defensive positions on the end of the ramp.

"Another minute and you'd have seen the top of that mountain come down," Ryan replied. "Digger okay?"

"He's stable for now and a med team will be waiting on the tarmac," Grady replied. "Mack and the Doc are with him. We were just saying this was about the easiest extraction we've ever done."

As soon as the words were out of his mouth, there was a whistling, a plinking sound, and Ryan felt the bullet zip past his left cheek. He turned around and stared at the hole in the side of the helicopter not six inches above Lee's head.

"Get down!" Ryan shouted. "We're taking fire!"

"Tripp, tell the pilots to get the hell out of here!" Cat said from behind him.

Ryan and Grady flattened out on the ramp, their weapons pointed out the back of the helicopter. A second later Cat joined them as the pilots spun up the helo's engines.

"And I'll bet you thought this was going to be an easy evac," she yelled.

Ryan shook his head and sighted down the barrel of his M4. "Should've known better."

He scanned the hills and saw a flash of movement as Cat said:

"Ten o'clock, gentlemen, 30 meters south-southwest of that huge conifer. See 'em?"

Ryan adjusted his aim. "Roger that. Grady, you got eyes?"

"Affirmative, Reaper. Locked and loaded."

"Fire at will," he said.

He started firing, and a grim smile curved his mouth when he saw a splash of blood on the snow behind the man he'd taken aim at. The target went down, but like roaches, another took his place, and this one had a bigger weapon.

"RPG!" he called out.

The helicopter shuddered and left the ground.

"Got him," Cat said, in a low, calm voice.

After the boom of the .416 it seemed like forever before the bullet hit home, even though Ryan knew less than a second had passed. He whooped as the extremist with the grenade launcher took aim at the chopper at the same moment his chest blew apart. The body remained standing for a few seconds. Then the weapon fell to the ground and the dead man toppled over.

"Nice," Ryan said, firing in rapid succession as terrorists continued to stream over the rocks and down the trail like ants on a mission. There were more than a dozen, and probably more than that behind them. "That puts you in double-digits today, doesn't it? Not bad."

The .416 roared again. "For a *girl*?"

"Hey," Ryan began, "just because the US military thinks a sniper has to have a penis doesn't mean I do." He paused, gave her a sidelong glance, and then lied through his teeth. "And I hardly noticed you were a woman."

Cat reloaded, giving him a wry look as she did so. "Of course you didn't. And this is just another day at the office. At least that's the way it's gone recently." She looked over her shoulder and shouted, "Bam-Bam, you can blow that mountain anytime!"

Even from half a mile away, the shockwave rolled over them like water and Ryan heard the collective gasp from inside the chopper. The vibrations reverberated through him and the helicopter, and his mouth dropped open when the top of the mountain literally mushroomed out, hung suspended there, and then collapsed in on itself. Smoke and debris were thrust high into the air and the rumbling continued for another fifteen seconds or so. He glanced at Cat and Grady, but they were as transfixed by the sight as him.

The explosion started a chain reaction as half of the front of the mountain fell away. Ryan looked through his scope and saw the Taliban still scrambling over the rocks toward them, but now they were running for an entirely different reason. He lowered his rifle and leaned on his elbows. It was an awesome sight as the jagged peak shed part of itself and pursued the extremists with a churning wall of snow, rock, and vegetation more than five meters high. The helo continued to move away, but the avalanche was moving faster than the chopper was. The cascade of snow overwhelmed the terrorists and continued its relentless course.

"You may want to get some altitude on this bird!" Ryan yelled over his shoulder.

He doubted the pilots had heard him but someone must have relayed a message because the helo started a straight vertical climb. They were roughly 50 meters up when the avalanche hit the berm at the edge of the plateau and exploded like an ocean tsunami hitting shore. Ryan instinctively shielded Cat as dirt, snow, and rocks burst upwards towards the chopper. It sounded like machine gun fire as stones and debris peppered the underside of the Chinook. Then everything went quiet except for the drone of the engines.

Ryan suddenly realized he and Cat were facing each other, cheeks pressed together, and strange electric pulses fanned over his skin. He pulled back so he could look at her out of the corner of his eye. There was a small smile on her mouth, and one red brow rose skyward.

"Gotta protect the girl, eh?" she asked softly.

He met that vivid green gaze, fought the urge to kiss her, and shrugged. "Sorry. Force of habit."

The dimples appeared and she looked at the floor of the chopper.

"Don't change that, Lieutenant." She lifted her eyes to his. "It's nice to know chivalry isn't completely dead."

With that she pulled away from him, got to her feet, and made her way quickly toward the cockpit. Ryan watched her go, then sat up and made his weapon safe.

"Wow," Grady said under his breath. "I heard the electricity snapping between you two over the *engines*. Reaper and Beckett sittin' in a tree, k-i-s-s—"

"Shut it, Mouth," Ryan warned. "You've been pretty quiet until now, and I find I like it. I like it a lot."

Grady laughed, got to his feet, and shouldered his weapon. "All right, all right," he said, extending a hand. "I'll wait till we get back to base to give you shit."

Ryan took his comrade's hand and stood. "Why is that?"

"Because I know *you* won't shoot me," Grady said. He jerked a thumb toward the front of the helo and grinned. "Her... I'm not so sure about."

Ryan chuckled and shook his head. "That, Mouth, is the first smart thing you've said since we met." He clapped the younger man on the shoulder. "Don't make it a habit or I won't know it's you."

***

Cat finished speaking with the pilot then returned to the cabin of the Chinook and sat down next to Tripp in one of the cloth jump seats. With a sigh, she closed her eyes and leaned her head against his muscled shoulder.

"You did good today, Tiger," Tripp said, plopping her pack in her lap. "You got everyone out, no casualties, and Command will be real happy the equipment is intact and accounted for."

Cat wrapped her arms around the bag. "Thanks, Tripp. You weren't so bad yourself. I was afraid you and the SEALs would wind up in a pissing match toward the end there, but you were oddly gracious." She opened one eye a crack and looked at him. "You feeling okay?"

Tripp laughed. "Yeah, Cat. I'm good. And I like SEALs. My cousin's a SEAL."

"Ah," she said. "So, if your cousin *wasn't* a SEAL you would have been your normal, obnoxious, confrontational self?"

"That's affirmative," he replied, "*especially* if they were Air Force Para-rescue. Can't stand those guys." He leaned his head back and closed his eyes. "So, what are you going to do when we get back to base? Me,

I'm going to ask Mitchell if he can get us some USDA prime beef. A 24-ounce rib-eye steak with all the trimmings sounds about like heaven right now."

"Mm," Cat said. "Yes it does, but *I* would prefer a hot bubble bath and a cold bottle of Riesling." She sighed again. "Yep, that would be it for me. Bubbles and wine."

"You know you're not going to get either one of those, right?" Tripp asked with a low chuckle.

"I know, but one can dream, can't one?"

"Cat?"

She recognized the voice immediately and looked up into those dark blue eyes. A quiver went through her. "Yes, Lieutenant. What can I do for you?"

"You can start by calling me Ryan unless we're in an official setting," he said with a wry twist of his lips.

Cat's heart jumped and she smiled. "All right... Ryan. What can I do for you?"

His gaze wandered over her face for a few moments then he shook his head and smiled. "Nothing," he replied. "I wanted to thank you again. We owe you, big time."

Cate handed her pack to Tripp, rose, and faced the SEAL, tipping her head back so she could look him in the eye. "You don't owe me anything, Lieutenant... I mean, Ryan." She glanced into the cabin and spotted Mack and Grady sitting near Digger, their expressions grave, and then returned her gaze to Ryan's face. "You guys are the ones who sweat and hurt and bleed and die out here. Every American, me included, owes *you*, big time. Because of what you and your guys do Americans get to sleep warm, safe, and blithely unaware in their beds, only to bitch about how bad it is when they wake up."

She paused and took a breath. The way he was staring at her made her oddly nervous and it took her a moment to find her voice.

"You guys *know* how bad it is because you're face to face with it every day." She looked down at the floor and shook her head. "You don't owe me a damn thing, Ryan, except to stay alive."

Ryan put a finger under her chin and tipped her face up. "Does that mean that cup of coffee is off?"

Her skin tingled where he'd touched it and Cat gulped. "No," she replied, fighting a smile. "I told you I fully intend to collect on that."

His expression was pensive and he studied her for a moment before nodding. "Good," he said at last. He looked at her for a few more seconds, then turned and walked over to where Digger lay on his stretcher.

Cat watched him and smiled as he crouched down beside his injured comrade.

"Admit it. You like him."

"Shut up, Lee," Cat said, her eyes still on the tall sailor.

"It's not a crime, Tiger," Lee said with a chuckle. When she turned on him he held up his hands and retreated to the cockpit, where he'd run after nearly getting shot earlier. "Okay, boss, okay. Shutting up now."

Cat growled and plopped back into her seat next to Tripp.

"He's right, you know," Tripp said absently.

She clenched her teeth. "About *what?*"

"You like him," Tripp replied, "and it's not a crime." He deposited her pack on the empty seat beside him and gave her a knowing look. "Live a little, Cat. It won't kill you to feel something other than the intense satisfaction of sniping bad guys and pissing off Mitchell."

"What is *that* supposed to mean?"

"It means... go have a cup of coffee with the guy." Tripp glanced at Ryan. "Sit down and eat a meal with him, go to a movie together, take him back to your quarters and fuck his brains out. That would *really* get Mitchell's jock in a twist, by the way. Just... tread carefully, Cat. I'd hate to see you get hurt." He rose and looked down at her with brotherly affection. "Y'know, despite this... *superhuman* persona you put on for the rest of us, we all know you're not bulletproof, no matter how much you try to prove otherwise." He smiled. "Have some fun, Tiger. None of us will think any less of you if you do."

Chapter Three

"Beckett," said the copilot as he sat down opposite her.

Cat was stretched out across several jump seats, her pack masquerading badly as a pillow. She immediately sat up.

"Yes, Major?"

"We're five out," the co-pilot said. "Get your people ready for landing. An ambulance is standing by for the SEALs, and transpo will meet you and your people on the tarmac."

"Roger that, Major," Cat replied. "Thanks for picking us up, by the way. Your timing was impeccable."

The co-pilot nodded and gave her a smile. "Anytime, Tiger. Anytime. That was quite a show back there."

"Bam-Bam's doing, not mine," Cat said. "I tell him to make sure none of our stuff is salvageable and he interprets that as *bring down the mountain.* What can you do?"

The major chuckled. "As far as I'm concerned, a little overkill is a good thing, especially in this situation."

"Yeah, well, thanks again."

The man nodded and returned to the cockpit. Cat stretched then stood, faced the cabin, and clapped her hands several times.

"All right people, listen up." She waited until the conversation died down and she had everyone's attention. "We are on the ground in five, so stow your gear and prep for landing. Transpo will pick us up on the tarmac, but the SEALs are the first off so stay in your seats until they're out. Got it?" A chorus of "Yes" went up. "Good. And nice job today. You all did what you were supposed to do, and we got out with our equipment and personnel intact. Kudos, everyone. I plan to make sure you all get a few days off after this."

A cheer went up and Cat smiled. While her team talked excitedly about what they would do with their time off, she made her way over to where the stretcher was laid out. Ryan rose and faced her.

"An ambulance is waiting for you and your team." She glanced at Digger. "How is he?"

"He's stable for now, thanks to your corpsman," Ryan replied. He sighed and rubbed his eyes. "I thought we were going to lose him for a minute there."

Cat remembered when the SEAL had flat-lined during the evac flight, and Doc had pulled out every weapon in his arsenal to stabilize the injured man. It had been close, too close. "I told you, Doc is the best I've ever worked with. Digger's going to be okay."

"I know," Ryan replied, "but they may have to evac him to Ramstein. The base hospital is good but Digger may need a specialist, which they *don't* have. Doc says they'll know more once they get him to the medical center."

He didn't show it, but Cat knew he was worried about his friend. In the field, combat soldiers relied on their unit corpsmen and trusted them completely, more so than doctors with whom they were unfamiliar. Doc wasn't the SEAL's corpsman but he was the first to treat Digger and had saved his life, which was good enough. She looked at Massey.

"Doc." When his blue eyes swiveled her way she smiled. "How'd you like to stay with your patient?"

Doc rose and looked at her strangely. "What?"

"You want to stay with him, don't you," Cat asked, "at least until he makes it into surgery?"

Doc seemed taken aback. "Yeah, Cat, I do, but if he needs a specialist they'll probably fly him to Ramstein."

Cat shrugged. "So, you'll go to Germany."

"Really?" Doc blinked at her. "Can you... do that?"

"Consider it done," she replied. "You go with Digger and I'll send someone to debrief you at the hospital. The report can wait until you get back... if you really want to go with him." Doc nodded emphatically and Cat smiled. "Good. Have a nice flight." She met Ryan's gaze, gave him a wink, and the SEAL gaped at her. When she turned to walk away he grasped her arm lightly.

"Cate, you didn't have to do that," he said in a low voice. "I don't want you getting into any trouble."

"Would you feel better if Doc stayed with him?"

He blinked at her. "If Digger has to make the trip he'll have a full medical team with him," he said. "It's not necessary."

Cat crossed her arms over her chest and lifted one brow. "Answer the question, LT."

He glared at her for a moment then dropped his gaze. "Yeah, I'd feel better."

"Well, there you go." She planted her hands on his broad shoulders and the musculature there made her abdominals tighten. "Now prepare for landing." Taking a quick breath, she patted his arm and walked toward the back of the helo. She hadn't taken two steps before his voice stopped her.

"Looks like I owe you an entire pot of coffee," he said softly.

Cat looked at him over her shoulder and smiled. "Maybe you do. We'll talk about it once we're safely on the ground." The intensity of his stare was unsettling, and she found herself unable to look away. After a few moments, a smile lifted the corners of his mouth.

"Yes, we will, Cate. We certainly will."

***

When the helo touched down the ramp immediately started to descend. Ryan motioned for Mack to grab the foot of Digger's stretcher while he took the head, and they walked toward the rear of the chopper. Doc walked beside Digger, and Grady, once again, brought up the rear.

It was near dusk at Bagram, and when a foot of sky was visible the red and yellow flashing lights of the ambulance invaded the cabin of the Chinook with obnoxious splashes of color. Ryan tapped his foot on the floor of the chopper. Once there was enough room for them to exit the helo he told Mack to move. Almost as soon as his feet hit the tarmac, the waiting corpsmen took the stretcher and rushed Digger into the ambulance, Doc on their heels.

"Go with him," Ryan said to Mack and Grady. "I'll join you guys as soon as I can."

"Roger that," Mack said. A sly grin split his face. "And tell Red we said thanks."

"Yeah," Grady agreed, "if y'all aren't too busy k-i-s-s—"

Ryan frowned. "Grady."

Grady laughed, slapped him on the back, and started jogging backwards toward the ambulance. "I told you I'd wait till we were back on base to give you shit." He flung his arms wide. "Well, we're back on base, Reaper, and it is open season."

"I was going to tell you to keep it down," Ryan called out. "Like you said, you don't have to worry about *me* shooting you, but *she's* still within earshot."

Grady's eyes widened a bit and he looked toward the Chinook quickly. "Good advice, Reap. Good advice." He gave Ryan a salute, then hopped into the back of the ambulance and closed the doors. Ryan sighed and ran a hand over his face.

Since he knew the base general would send a car for him Ryan eased down on the tarmac and dropped his gear. He looked toward the helicopter and watched as Cat directed traffic. She stood to the side talking with Tripp while the rest of her team offloaded the cargo, though they needed little direction. He wondered briefly what was so important inside those boxes, but wisdom told him it was better he not know.

A moment later three black SUV's drove onto the flight line and lined up close to the chopper, the drivers hopping out to open doors and tailgates. The boxes were loaded carefully into the vehicles then the personnel got in. Tripp and Cat approached the lead SUV. From where he was he couldn't hear their conversation, but obviously Cat had said something that didn't sit well with Tripp and he scowled. He opened the front passenger door of the Yukon and gestured for her to get in, but she backed up and shook her head. Tripp said something else, but she only crossed her arms over her chest. He finally got into the black car, with obvious annoyance, and the convoy pulled away leaving Cat standing there by herself.

She glanced around the flight line, and her brows went up when she spotted him. Ryan stood, lifted one hand in lame salute, and smiled as she walked toward him.

"What was all that about?" he asked, looking in the direction the SUV's had gone.

"Nothing." Cat rolled her eyes. "He just wasn't happy that I decided to walk back to my quarters. You waiting for a ride? You should've said something and we could've dropped you wherever you need to be."

"The base general will send a car for me," Ryan said. "Standard operating procedure. He always wants a fresh debrief when things go south." His eyes narrowed on two pinpricks of light at the end of the flight line. "In fact, that's probably my ride." He paused and his head snapped back around. "Wait. You're going to *walk* back to your quarters? I'm assuming you're in transient housing on the base's north end."

"Yep," she said with a nod.

"That's about four miles," he said flatly.

"I know."

"It's going to be freezing once it gets dark."

"I know." She gave him a pointed look and gestured to her attire. "Arctic camouflage? It's not only fashionable, but functional as well. Hypothermia is not a concern."

Ryan looked down his nose at her. "If I were Tripp I would've picked you up and tossed you into that SUV."

Her cheeks dimpled. "Tripp knows better."

"I see." He crossed his arms over his chest. "I've seen you take out a target at 1500 meters, but how are you at close-quarters-battle?"

Her eyes narrowed slightly and she took a step toward him. "You could take your best shot and find out if I'm any good at CQB," she suggested with a wry grin. "Just keep in mind a gun is not the only weapon I carry... or that I know how to use."

He fought a smile as he briefly entertained the thought of taking her up on her challenge. The idea wasn't entirely without merit. "So, you've had extensive training in self-defense?"

"Yes," she replied. "I'm also the youngest of six children, and the only girl. My brothers taught me a lot before I hit puberty."

Ryan threw his head back and laughed as the picture of her in pigtails chasing her brothers around with a .50 caliber weapon flashed in his mind. "Outstanding. Now I know why you're so comfortable in this predominantly male environment."

Her head turned as a Humvee stopped about a dozen paces away. "Your ride is here, Lieutenant. I guess this is goodbye."

"Hey," he began, "it's not *goodbye*. It's... until next time. And I said 'official setting,' remember? The *name* is *Ryan*."

"Well, *Ryan*, this sort of *is* an official setting." She gestured toward the hangars. "This is a military base and you are a military officer, so that makes it pretty official, don't you think?"

His brows drew together. "I meant 'official' in the sense that anyone else present would raise an eyebrow in disapproval were you not to address me by my rank." He glanced around. "I don't see any of those sorts of people here."

She grinned and shook her head. "You win." The door on the Humvee opened and the driver stepped out. "That's your cue, Ryan. Your superiors must be anxious to speak with you."

Ryan met her gaze and something in her eyes pulled at him. "Are you sure you don't want a ride?" he asked, hoping she would say yes. "I can drop you anywhere." She seemed to think about it for a moment then she stuffed her hands in her pockets and looked toward the mountains.

"Thanks, but no," she replied after a brief silence. "It's been a tough day and walking helps me clear my head." She smiled ruefully and scuffed the toe of her boot against the tarmac. "It gives me a chance to mentally sort through everything that happened...." Her voice trailed off, her expression sobered, and her chin dropped to her chest, ". . . and to ask God to forgive me for ending eleven lives today."

"Hey," Ryan began, scowling as he took her chin gently between his thumb and forefinger and forced her to look at him, "you *saved* a dozen lives today and countless others in the future by eliminating a very real threat." His hand dropped back to his side. "We're at war, and those men were the enemy. If given the opportunity they would *kill us all,* everyone on this base, on *every* base, our families, our friends, *everyone.* Don't for one second feel guilty about what you did today."

A poignant smile curved her mouth and she glanced at the Humvee again. "I don't feel guilty," she said, "just... sad. They weren't always the enemy. They were somebody's little boys once, and someone somewhere will mourn for them."

"Cate...."

She put a hand on his chest. "It's okay, Ryan. It's not the first time I've done this... not even close." She chuckled softly. "I always pray it will be the last, but if I was put in that position again I would do exactly the same thing... without a second thought."

And just like that the Bengal was back. The pull of attraction that surged through him made him gulp.

"Lieutenant Heller," the driver said.

Ryan looked at the man sharply. "A minute," he said. When he looked at Cat again her expression had returned to normal, and he saw neither the sadness she'd just shown, nor the ferocity that had earned her such an appropriate nickname. "Cate—"

"Why do you call me Cate?" she interrupted, tipping her head to the side. "Everyone else calls me Cat or Tiger and my father calls me Catharine. What's different about you?"

"I don't call you Tiger because that's what everyone else calls you, and I didn't think I was qualified for that yet," Ryan replied with a wiggle of his brows. "Catharine is too formal, and Cat... well, I don't think Cat suits you other than it's a description of your speed and sureness of foot. *Feline* would be more appropriate, but Cat? It's...." He paused and searched for the word, ". . . inelegant."

She blinked and her eyes widened slightly. "That's... that's actually the nicest thing anyone's said to me in a very long time."

"You're beautiful." Ryan didn't know where that had come from, regardless that he thought it was true.

Her brows shot up. "Okay... *second* nicest."

"Lieutenant Heller, *sir.*"

"You need to go," Cat said with a smile.

"I don't want to," Ryan replied in a low voice.

"And I don't want you to."

His heart thrummed at her simple reply. "Coffee?"

"We're still on."

Ryan searched those emerald eyes and warred against the anxiety rising in him. "When?" She smiled, and his heart melted a little more.

"Whenever you're free," she said, "I'll make time. Now go, before you get in trouble."

He didn't want to leave. "You sure you don't want a ride?"

Cat laughed softly then grabbed his shoulders, turned him toward the Humvee, and gave him a small shove. "I'm sure. Now get out of here before the base commander comes looking for you personally. My superiors I can face down. A two-star? Rather not go there."

Ryan paused and looked at her over his shoulder, and she gestured for him to keep moving. He gave her a smile and walked to the Humvee. After getting in he rolled the window down and leaned his head out.

"Last chance," he said. "It's really not such a bad ride."

Cat crossed her arms over her chest. "Ryan, what rank is your driver?"

Ryan glanced to his left. "Lieutenant, why?"

"Lieutenant!"

The driver had returned to his seat behind the wheel, and he leaned forward a little so he could see her. "Ma'am?"

"Get him out of here, please."

The lieutenant smiled and gave her a two-finger salute. "Yes, ma'am."

Ryan scowled at her, but he was also smiling. "No fair."

"Women don't fight fair," she called out as the Humvee pulled away.

"Remember that, Lieutenant!"

I'll remember it, Ryan thought as he settled into his seat. He moved the side-view mirror so he could watch her as they drove away. *Just like I'll remember you.*

***

It took her just under an hour to walk the four miles to her quarters, and she felt much better when she arrived. On Bagram, her quarters were actually a 12'X16' construction of wooden 2"X4" beams and insulated half-inch plywood, fitted with a single door on either end of the building that opened into the room and security screen doors that opened outward. An air conditioner/heater took up one of the four windows, and the others were covered by light-blocking curtains she'd put up herself. Grey indoor/outdoor carpet softened the wooden floor and the walls were bare except for a few coat hooks and a ¾ length mirror against the back wall. She had a locker, a foot locker, a mini-fridge, an electric teapot, a bed, a desk with a metal chair, and little else. There were nearly 30 such buildings on this patch of earth, with a community bathroom in the center of the compound. It wasn't much, but at least she didn't have a roommate. She knew many of these same structures housed up to six military personnel at once. Because of whom she worked for and her gender, she was allowed her own little piece of Bagram Airbase heaven.

Cat paused in front of the tiny house and looked into the sky. The one thing she loved about Afghanistan was the sky at night. Nowhere in the world could a person see more stars than from where she was except, perhaps, from the mountain cave they'd just evacuated. The sky there had been absolutely spectacular. As she watched a meteor zipped across the heavens, leaving a quickly fading slash of white in the darkness. She smiled, unlocked the door, and stepped inside. As the door clicked shut the hairs on the back of her neck prickled. Cat turned toward the interior of the cabin and reached for the light switch.

"Why do you always do this?" a familiar male voice asked. "You're *supposed* to return to our offices with your team for debrief. Why is it that huge spotter of yours can't keep you in line?"

Cat flipped on the light. Sitting on her bed was her supervisor, Peter Mitchell. She leaned the .416 against the wall and scowled.

He was tall, nicely built, and handsome with aristocratic, chiseled features, but he was a politician through and through. His wavy brown hair was cut neatly, and he had eyes the color of melted milk chocolate, eyes that had melted her years ago. Their affair had been passionate but brief, lasting only long enough for them to sleep together twice, and for her to find out he was very married.

"Why do you insist on breaking and entering?" she countered, hands on hips. "I could call the SPs you know."

He snorted derisively. "They can't do anything to me."

Cat crossed her arms over her chest and wondered vaguely what she'd ever seen in him. "They *can* remove you from my quarters," she pointed out.

Mitchell stood and took a step toward her. "We both know I'd be back in an hour, only I'd be slightly more pissed than I am now."

A thrum of anger warmed her. "Hmm." She tipped her head to the side. "I could shoot you." When he chuckled and rolled his eyes, Cat felt a stab of heat in her chest. Her eyes narrowed and she unzipped her jacket with one quick, angry jerk.

"I understand you enjoy risking your ass for our men and women in uniform," he began, pacing in front of her, "but I know you well enough to know you'd never risk yourself on my account. You enjoy what you do too much. You wouldn't be able to put your life and career on the line if you were in prison."

Cat hung up her jacket. "Didn't say I was going to shoot you *now*," she said flatly, "or *here*." She tossed him a grim smile. "You could be leaving your house in that lovely D.C. suburb you live in when you're not in New York with your wife, and I could kill you from *Virginia*."

Mitchell stopped pacing and stared at her. Her expression was carefully neutral, and he couldn't tell if she was joking or not. A sliver of fear started up his back, but a shudder of excitement wound through him as well.

"Are you... *threatening* me?" he asked. The idea was oddly exciting.

Cat lifted one brow and plopped down in a nearby chair. Her lack of a reply was a reply in itself.

A tingle of eager anticipation ran through him and settled in his groin. "You don't want to make me angry, Catharine," he informed her in an imperious tone. "You really don't."

"Why? You gonna turn green and grow out of your pants?"

She rose in one fluid motion and stood toe to toe with him. The faint aroma of her scent, the one that was uniquely hers, wafted past him.

The desire for her he always kept banked burned a little hotter and he had to concentrate to maintain his calm, even expression.

"Look at this face," she said, pointing at her own head. "Do I look like I give a shit whether you're angry or not? I killed eleven men today, Peter. *Eleven.* Do you honestly think I care if *you're* pissed off?"

Eleven men. The enemy seemed to be legion, but a dozen dead bodies would most definitely be noticed. A contradictory swirl of pride and concern simultaneously warmed and chilled him. *I wonder if they've connected the dots yet.*

"So," he began in a low voice, "your team wasn't exaggerating."

"My team doesn't exaggerate," she replied, turning her back to him. "You should know that by now."

He was silent for a few moments then he sighed heavily. "I'm sorry it was such a bad day, Cath, but you know how this works."

She whirled on him. "You're right, I do. So, can we skip to the part where you sorely chastise me, I pretend I'm sorely chastised, and we move on?"

Part of him wanted to strangle her for her insolence, to feel her throat beneath his fingers as, bit by bit, her struggles slowed and then ceased. However, a bigger, stronger part of him wanted even more to feel her body writhing beneath his as they became one. He pictured it: flaming hair spread out over the pillow, pale breasts heaving with each labored breath, her hot, tight flesh wrapping around him. The image always bolstered him when his temper flared, allowing him to maintain control. She would fight him, he knew, but that only made him want her more. Oh, yes, he would have her, but until the time was right he would content himself with the pictures in his mind.

"Cath," he began, "the base commander is waiting for your report. A SEAL team was ambushed and this is the third BETA test we've had to abort because of unexpected insurgent activity in an area that was supposedly cleared."

"Really? Is *that* what happened?" She pressed a hand to her heart and looked at him with wide, mocking eyes. "I would *never* have guessed." She walked over to her jacket and grabbed it off the hook.

His irritation bubbled hotter. "Cath—"

"No, you're right, Peter." She shrugged into the coat. "I need to make my report, and maybe the guys at Langley will see a pattern to all of this. It's obvious you don't. I mean once, okay, the bad guys got lucky. The second time... hmm, the chances aren't as good, but in this country it's still possible luck favored the Taliban." She zipped up the jacket and glared at him. "But three times in a row? I don't think even *Vegas* would take those odds."

Mitchell was taken aback. *Has she figured it out?* He cleared his throat and squared his shoulders. "What are you insinuating, Catharine?"

"I'm not insinuating anything," she spat. "I'm saying it flat out. Six weeks ago, it was a team of Green Berets in the area north of Kunduz that got ambushed and driven toward us by enemy fire. Two weeks ago, a group of Army Rangers in the mountains south of Kandahar, and now this." She walked up to him, hands on hips. "Each team leader I spoke with told me the same thing when they reached our hideout: *'This was the only direction bullets weren't coming from.'*" She pointed toward the door. "Somebody out there has information they shouldn't have, Peter, and I think you need to look into that before you send us out on another futile BETA test."

Again, he was both proud and worried. If she *had* figured it out he doubted he'd still be breathing. Even so, she was putting the pieces together and it was only a matter of time before she completed this particular puzzle. When she did it would not bode well for him. Best to keep up the charade for the time being, so he affected a haughty look. "Well, if there *is* a leak it's none of *my* people. Perhaps someone on *your* team—"

Pain blossomed in his chest as Cat punched him with both fists and shoved as hard as she could. He toppled backward onto the bed and stared at her. He hoped his expression revealed only surprise and not the electric desire pushing through him. God, she was beautiful when she was angry! His hands itched to grab hold of her and jerk her down on the bed with him. Her response to such an action would no doubt be violent, which only made him more eager. He felt himself hardening and realized his excitement would only fuel Cat's ire and suspicion. Focusing on the mental images of his wife he kept at the ready, he stayed silent and kept his eyes on Cat as his erection waned.

"*Don't* you dare!" she seethed. "Don't you dare accuse any member of my team!"

"Cath—"

"No!" She pointed a finger in his face. "Not another word about someone on my team being a traitor or, as *God* is my witness I *will* shoot you, *right* here, *right* now."

Mitchell held up his hands as if in surrender, and gingerly got to his feet. He knew better than to provoke her further, so he maintained a safe distance and straightened his shirt. "Fine," he said in a low voice. "I'll initiate an investigation."

"Quietly."

He nodded. "Of course," he agreed. "Wouldn't want to spook the leak, if there is one."

Cat gave him a mirthless smile. "Good."

Mitchell gave her a long, assessing look. "So, you done?"

"I was done with you a long time ago," she replied.

His heart twisted and he approached her slowly. "That was *your* choice."

Cat's eyes narrowed. "Actually, that decision was made for me years before I even met you," she said, "when you exchanged marriage vows with your rich, Hampton-born, living on Fifth Avenue, going to inherit Daddy's money, wife."

"You must know I still care about you," he said softly. He reached a hand toward her.

She dropped her chin and clenched her teeth. "*Don't* touch me."

His fingers hovered about an inch from her cheek. He studied her for several seconds, and her expression told him all he needed to know. Deciding it was better to err on the side of caution, he dropped his arm back to his side. "You enjoyed my touch once."

Cat scowled. "That was years ago," she said, "and it was a mistake I won't make again."

"C'mon, Cath," he cajoled. "Afghanistan is a lonely, desolate place. What's the harm in old lovers enjoying a night of each other's company?" He gave her a look filled with hidden promise. "No one needs to know."

Her lips pursed and her nose wrinkled as if in distaste. His temper fought to be unleashed, but he pictured her again, naked beneath him, their limbs entwined, and he managed to pull it back.

"*I'd* know," she said in a voice laced with disgust. "And don't give me this loneliness crap. I know for a fact you're doing that little airman the Air Force assigned as your assistant, so why don't you go shovel this shit for someone who'll believe it?"

Well, that didn't work, time for a different tack. Mitchell looked at her silently for a long, long moment, then shook his head and sighed. "You've changed, Catharine. You seem harder, jaded. Perhaps it's all this killing you've done, but you're not the same woman I made love to back in D.C."

Cat rolled her eyes and groaned. "I'll take that as a compliment." She gave him a bored look. "Now, can we go, or do you want to continue this pointless romp down memory lane?"

"Have it your way," Mitchell grumbled, his anger bubbling dangerously high in spite of his favorite mental movie. "C'mon. My car is around the corner."

"Didn't want me to know you were here?" she asked as she walked to the door and opened it.

Mitchell walked past her and into the cold, dark night. "Like I said," he replied as she followed behind him, "I know you. If you'd seen my car you'd have kept right on walking."

Cat locked her door then faced him. "You're right. Now let's get this over with. I have a shower to take and a hospital to visit."

Chapter Four

Ryan finished his written report, signed it, and handed it to the General's aide. It had taken nearly three hours to finish his debrief and write up his statement, and a glance at his watch told him it was nearly eight o'clock. His stomach growled loudly, reminding him he hadn't eaten in more than 16 hours, but it wasn't food that was his primary focus. He was worried about Digger.

"The general said once you were finished here you were dismissed, Lieutenant," the young officer said. "Do you need a ride to the Special Forces compound?"

Ryan stood. "Actually, I need to get to the hospital."

The lieutenant nodded. "Of course. Let me give this report to my assistant and I'll drive you over myself."

Ten minutes later Ryan strode through the doors of the Heathe N. Craig Joint Theater Hospital. After speaking briefly to a nurse at the reception desk, Ryan realized he wasn't going to get any meaningful information from her, so he followed her directions to the waiting room. Mack and Grady were sitting there, and when they saw him they jumped to their feet.

"How is he?" Ryan asked. "Is Doc with him?"

"Digger's in surgery," Mack replied, "but they wouldn't let Doc go in with him. Doc's being debriefed somewhere. Red sent someone here to get his report so he wouldn't have to leave."

A half-smile curved his mouth. "Yeah, she said she was going to do that. How long has Digger been in?"

Grady twisted his cap in his hands. "They took him in as soon as we arrived, and that was more than three hours ago." The younger man threw his cover across the room in frustration. "Damn it, Reaper. Why doesn't somebody give us an update or something?"

"Easy, petty officer," Ryan said. He sighed and tried to think of something that would distract the agitated sailor. "Have you guys eaten yet?"

"No," Grady said, sullen. He pointed a finger at Ryan. "And I'm *not* leaving until I find out something."

"You don't have to," a familiar voice said from behind them. "Dinner is served, gentlemen. We have pizza, Coke, and beer. I hope you like Heineken. I paid some Polish sergeant $20 to get this six-pack."

Ryan half-turned toward the door and tried not to stare. She looked amazing. It was obvious she had showered, her hair hung in damp waves around her shoulders. She wore blue jeans and a cable-knit sweater, and now that the arctic camouflage was off he saw the magnificent curves the thick, insulated garments had kept hidden. She walked past them to deposit the large pizza boxes and the drinks on the wooden coffee table, bending over and giving him a great view of her backside as she did so. It was a very, very nice backside. Ryan gulped, and an arctic wave of guilt washed over him as his attraction for her pushed thoughts of his injured comrade aside. He looked at the ground for a moment to regain his composure then gave her a small smile.

"Thanks, Cate," he said.

"Yeah, thanks, Red," Mack said as he walked around her, sat down, and opened one of the boxes.

An amused smile danced on her lips, but she wasn't looking at him. Ryan groaned inwardly when he saw Grady with his jaw hanging slack as he stared at her. Mack, wisely, had turned his attention to the pizza, but he was fighting a grin. Ryan snapped his fingers in front of Grady's face.

"Petty officer," he barked. "Eat."

Grady shook himself and immediately sat down next to Mack. He picked up a slice of pizza, and when Ryan saw him glance toward Cat he growled. Grady looked at him and then turned his eyes to the pizza box, his expression contrite.

Ryan moved to the waiting room door and leaned against the jamb. Cat walked over, faced him, and leaned her shoulder against the opposite side of the door frame.

"How is he?" she asked.

"Don't know," Ryan replied, looking at the floor. "I got here five minutes ago and apparently there has been no news. All the nurse would say was he was in surgery and I would have to wait for the doctor." Ryan clenched his jaw and slammed his fist backwards into the wall. "I fucking *hate* hospitals."

"Me, too."

Something in her voice made him look up, and when their eyes met he instantly regretted it. He had more important things to focus on than this charged current shooting through him. She blinked and turned her face away, and he wondered if she had felt it, too.

"There's plenty of pizza," she said, watching Mack and Grady devour the huge pie. She looked at him out of the corner of her eye. "When was the last time you ate, Ryan, 0400?"

"About then," Ryan admitted. He glanced at his two teammates and smiled. "My stomach is growling but right now the food would just be a distraction. I don't think I'd be able to get a piece down, if you want to know the truth."

"I get it," she said in a low voice, a shadow dancing in those emerald eyes. "I know what it's like to sit in a hospital waiting room for hours, praying for someone to come tell you something, *anything*." She sighed. "It sucks."

"Yes, it does," he agreed.

Silence prevailed for a few seconds, and he dared another look at her. She wasn't looking at him; she was still watching Mack and Grady.

"Tell you what," she began, "why don't you sit down, have a Coke, and I'll go see if I can get any information on your teammate."

Ryan's brows rose. "Why would they talk to you if they won't talk to us?"

She gave him a sultry smile and batted her eyelashes, her cheeks dimpling prettily. "Because I'm going to go find a male nurse," she replied, "and I'm going to ask *very* nicely." She laughed softly and shrugged. "My father always told me to use what I had."

Ryan shook his head and fought the tingle of lust that pulsed through him. "Well, with what you've got you could probably sweet talk the Commander in Chief out of the launch codes." He exhaled slowly and rubbed his forehead. "Glad I'm not in your sights, actual or... otherwise. I'd probably lose my Trident."

"I doubt that, Lieutenant," she said with a chuckle, "but thank you... I think. Now, why don't you sit down and put your feet up? I'll be back in five."

After she left the waiting room it took all his SEAL training not to lean his head out into the hall and watch her walk away. He could clearly picture her lushly rounded backside and gave himself a mental slap. "Get it together, Ryan," he said to himself. "Get it together."

His feet dragged across the floor as he moved to a cushioned chair across from Mack and Grady. With a heavy sigh, he dropped down onto the padded seat and took the can of Coke Mack handed him.

"Cleans up well," Mack commented, grabbing another slice of pizza. He gave Ryan a guarded look. "Never would've guessed it under all that insulated camo."

"I know," Grady agreed heartily, unaware that Mack's comment had been directed at Ryan. The younger man let out a low whistle. "Did you see the rack on her?"

"Grady!" Ryan snapped. Grady, his mouth full of pizza, looked at him in surprise and Ryan leaned toward him. "You can talk like that about a porn star all you want, but you *will not* talk like that about the person who saved all our asses today. Show a little respect, petty officer."

The younger man swallowed his mouthful. "Aye aye, sir," Grady said, dropping his eyes to his lap. "Sorry, LT. Won't happen again."

"You're right," Mack said flatly, "because if you say another disrespectful thing about Red, or *any* woman for that matter, if Reaper doesn't put a fist through your teeth, *I* will."

Ryan leaned back in his chair and looked at Mack, and Mack gave him a nod as he took a swig of Coke. They'd been teammates for eight years now, and despite his rough appearance Mack was one of the finest, most dedicated men Ryan had ever worked with. He was a couple inches shy of six feet and weighed in at about 180, but it was six feet and 180 pounds of solid, powerful muscle. His beard and eyebrows were a reddish-brown color and he was bald as a cue ball, and not because he shaved his head. His face was square with heavy features and small, piercing brown eyes that saw *everything*. More than once Mack's sharp gaze had saved their lives, and he couldn't wish for a better partner.

Grady, on the other hand, was relatively new to their team. He was a replacement for a comrade they'd lost in battle 14 months ago, but in the time they'd worked together Ryan had grown to like and trust him. He was a handsome kid, with brown hair, blue eyes, and a dazzling grin that had ladies swooning whenever he flashed it, which was often. Grady was taller than Mack by a couple of inches, with the lean, efficient build of a long-distance athlete. The boy could shoot like Wild Bill Hickok and run at near supersonic speeds, and Ryan ruefully recalled several times when he'd had to work extra hard to keep up with the youngster. Brash, confident, and always talking, he was settling into the team as a true member. Now if Ryan could just reign in the kid's mouth, all would be well.

Ryan thought of Digger and his gut clenched. He took a sip of Coke and pressed his thumb and forefinger into his eyes as he pondered losing another man, a man he'd trained with, partied with, been roommates with, and nearly died with. He'd earned the nickname Digger because he looked like Taye Diggs, the actor, and often their fellow SEALs would call him "Hollywood" to get under his skin. Digger was the hardest working SEAL Ryan had ever teamed up with, and one of the smartest. They joked he was the token black guy, but Digger took it all in stride. In the end skin color was unimportant. They were brothers, and Ryan knew that if Digger died it would be a huge loss, both personally and professionally. He was the team mascot, always upbeat, always encouraging, always there. Frustration rose up in him and Ryan slammed his can of Coke down on the table. Mack and Grady looked at him in surprise as he jumped to his feet and stalked to the window. That was when he saw Cat's reflection.

He turned as she walked in and stood next to the seat he'd vacated. He took a step toward her, almost afraid to ask. Mack and Grady were equally transfixed, and not because she was working those jeans.

"Well?" he asked at last.

She stuffed her hands in her pockets. "He's out of surgery," she began, her voice subdued, "but he's not out of the woods yet. Apparently, the bullet did some internal damage and he lost a lot of blood, but..." she took a deep breath, ". . . they *think* he's going to be okay." When they let out a whoop of excitement she held up her hands to silence them and continued, smiling widely. "And, he doesn't need to make the trip to Ramstein. He'll be able to stay right here. Doc's with him right now in recovery and you can see him as soon as he wakes up."

Mack and Grady leapt to their feet, cheered, and started dancing around the waiting room. Relief washed over Ryan so completely he nearly dropped to his knees. He planted his hands on his thighs and took several deep breaths as the floor opened up beneath him. Then he straightened, walked over to Cat, and engulfed her in a bear hug. A small cry of surprise escaped her when he lifted her against his chest, his arms tightening around her slender form and her feet dangling above the floor.

"Thank you," he whispered. "Thank you for everything." His eyes stung and he closed them. "Now I owe you an entire Starbuck's."

Slowly, her arms wound around his neck, her chin resting on his shoulder. "I already told you, you don't owe me anything." She chuckled. "To be honest, I don't even drink coffee."

He pulled back and looked at her. "Really?"

"Really," she replied with a grin. "I'm more of a tea or hot chocolate kind of girl."

Ryan stared at her, painfully aware that those lips with the full, generous curves were only a couple inches away. He really, *really* wanted to kiss her, but he'd never do that while in uniform, and especially not in front of his men. Her eyelids fluttered and she looked at his mouth for a split second, but that was enough to tell him he wasn't the only one thinking about kissing. Color rose in her cheeks and he realized he could feel her heartbeat against his chest.

"You can put me down now," she said in a hushed, breathless voice.

"Don't want to."

She blinked and he saw the trembling of her pulse beneath the pale skin of her throat.

"And I don't want you to," she said softly, "but you're in uniform and your men are watching."

Ryan cursed silently and put her back on her feet. She stepped away and as soon as she did she was scooped up first by Grady, who spun her around, and then by Mack, who did the same as they continued to hoot and holler. Then the two men started dancing a jig, and Cat laughed as she was whirled between them.

A nurse, obviously hearing the ruckus, walked in and looked at them like they were crazy. Before she could tell them to be quiet Grady picked *her* up, spun her around, and kissed her squarely on the lips. Ryan groaned. Digger may have survived, but now it looked like a sexual harassment charge was coming their way.

"He's going to make it!" Grady told the shocked nurse. He released her, turned to Mack, and clapped him on the shoulder. "Digger's going to make it!" With that movie-star smile blazing, Grady sat down and dove into the pizza. Mack joined him and pulled two beers from the six-pack.

Ryan quickly moved to the stunned woman's side. "You'll have to forgive him, ma'am. We just found out our buddy made it through surgery."

Cat put an arm around the nurse's shoulders and walked her into the hallway. "Sorry about that," Ryan heard her say. "It's been a really tough day and he's overly excited. They weren't sure their friend would survive."

"Oh, I understand," the nurse replied. The woman glanced over her shoulder at Grady and Ryan smiled when he saw the blatant female appreciation in her eyes. "He *is* kind of cute."

Cat chuckled. "Yes, he is. If you want, I'll give him your number."

The nurse gaped at her. "Would you?"

Ryan didn't hear Cat's reply as she walked the nurse down the hall and out of sight.

Now that he knew Digger was going to survive the weariness crashed over him. Drained, Ryan sat down, leaned his head back, and closed his eyes. Mack and Grady continued to chat excitedly and he heard the clink of bottles, but he was too tired to care. Only when he got a whiff of shampoo and felt movement as someone sat next to him did he open his eyes.

"You look beat," Cat said with a pensive smile.

"*You* look great," he replied.

She ran a hand over her hair and a faint flush stained her cheeks. "A shower does work wonders, doesn't it?"

Ryan closed his eyes again. "I wouldn't know."

"There are showers here," she said. "I could send someone by your quarters to pick up a change of clothes for you."

"They'd never get in the compound," he replied. "Not even *you* would get past the gate."

"*I* wouldn't try."

"Hey, guys."

Ryan's eyes popped open and he jumped to his feet when he heard the corpsman's voice. He walked over to the younger man.

"Hey, Doc," he said. "How is he?"

Doc ran a hand over his face then gave them a weary smile. "He's awake, and he's asking for you."

Ryan stared at him for a moment, then grinned and clapped him on both shoulders.

"C'mon," Doc said, stepping backwards into the hallway and gesturing to his left. "I'll take you to him."

Ryan stood to the side as Mack and Grady fell into step behind the corpsman. He moved to follow them, then paused and looked back over his shoulder. Cat stood in the middle of the room, hands in her pockets and a smile on her face.

"C'mon," Ryan said, gesturing for her to come with. "I want to introduce you."

The dimples appeared and she shook her head. "You go. This is *your* reunion."

His expression sobered. "If it weren't for you it would be a funeral."

"No," she corrected him, "if it wasn't for Doc and the surgeons *here* it would be a funeral. I simply provided transport."

"Cate...."

"Go," she insisted. "He's not going anywhere, so you can introduce me later." She walked up to him. "I have to get back. My superiors weren't done chewing my ass when I left."

"Is there anything I can do?" he asked. "The General likes me."

Cat chuckled. "I'm good, Ryan. If they're not yelling at me at least once a week something's wrong." She patted his arm. "Go see your friend. I'm not going anywhere, not for a while anyway."

"Good," he said. "We have to figure out how I'm going to get you that Starbuck's."

"Lieutenant," she said, putting her hands on her hips, "stop. The fact you and your team are alive is all the reward I need. And who knows? Because I saved you, maybe that means you'll save *me* at some point in the future. Karma *does* have a way of balancing those scales, you know." She looked at him for a moment, then stood on tiptoe and kissed his cheek. "I'll see you later, Ryan. Give Digger my best."

***

Cat was helping Lee inventory one of the boxes they'd evacuated from their mountain hideaway when Tripp tapped her on the shoulder. She looked up at him, and his expression immediately made her wary.

"What?" she asked flatly.

"You have a visitor," he said, a grin twitching about his mouth.

"Who?"

Tripp picked up a nearby clipboard. "Who do you think?" He glanced at Lee. "It's been nearly 48 hours since we got back. I'm surprised he waited that long."

"Me, too," Lee said under his breath.

Cat's pulse notched up and she bit the inside of her cheek to keep from smiling. "Where is he?"

"Your office," Tripp replied. He leaned against a nearby crate. "Should I assume you're going to take a long lunch?"

Cat ignored the remark and handed him the laptop she held. "Help Lee finish up here. Once the inventory is complete compare it against the original so we know what we left behind."

"Anything else?" Tripp asked with a wry twist of his lips.

"Yeah," she said, lifting one brow. "When you're done tell the team you all have the next three days off. Be back in here Monday at zero-seven."

Tripp looked surprised. "Really? Mitchell agreed to that?" He let out a low whistle. "What did *that* cost you?"

Cat rolled her eyes and started walking across the hangar. "Don't worry about it," she said over her shoulder. "Just finish up, and then enjoy your time off."

"Hey, Tiger!" Tripp called.

She paused and turned to him. "What?"

His grin widened. "Better wipe that smile off your face or Lee and I won't be the only ones who know you like him." He crossed his arms over his broad chest. "You sure don't want Mitchell knowing. He won't be happy with another dog sniffing around his cat."

Cat glared at him, but she really couldn't say much. Tripp was right. Despite the fact she and Mitchell were long finished, the man seemed fixated on her. Even after their affair was over and done, Mitchell had managed to maneuver himself into being her supervisor on almost every mission she'd been assigned. Somehow, she had to put an end to that.

The closer she got to her office the less she thought about Peter Mitchell and the more she thought about a tall, blue-eyed SEAL. Her heart thumped. Although she and her team had been busy since their return to base, she had found herself looking up every time she'd heard a door open. When she'd returned to her quarters that second night, a knock on her door had sent her falling over her own feet to answer. It had been Tripp asking if she wanted to join him at the mess hall. She'd hidden her disappointment and gone with him, hoping to catch a glimpse of the SEAL at dinner. She had returned to her plywood home afterwards, disheartened.

Now Ryan was in her office, waiting on her, and a wave of uncertainty suddenly rolled over her. Cat paused about a half dozen paces from her door and took a deep breath. Fear was an emotion she had learned to control and channel, but it was rearing its head now and she wasn't sure what to do about it. This wasn't a combat zone. This conflict was being waged in the heart, more dangerous territory in her opinion. Who did she take aim at on *this* battlefield?

"Catharine."

Cat squeezed her eyes shut and groaned inwardly. "Seriously?" she said under her breath. Making her face a blank slate, she spun 180 degrees to face Mitchell. Then the thought she'd acquired a target on her proverbial battlefield almost made her smile.

"Yes, Peter?"

"When can I expect those inventories?" he asked, his gaze focused on the manila folder in his hand.

"Lee and Tripp are finishing them up now," she replied. "I was going to take off early and go by the hospital to check on that SEAL we pulled out of the mountains, but if you want me to stay and help them...?"

"No," he said, never looking up from his papers. "I'm waiting on that one report. The rest of your team has already finished theirs and turned them in." He finally made eye contact with her. "Did you tell them they have a 72 hour pass?" When she nodded he smiled. "Good. I'll let you know when you can buy me dinner." With that, he spun on his heel and walked back the direction he'd come.

Cat exhaled slowly and leaned against the wall. She was really starting to hate that man. She scowled in the direction he'd gone, then straightened and walked three doors down to her office.

She paused in the doorway for a moment and allowed herself to look at Ryan. He stood next to a bookshelf near the window that overlooked the flight line, holding a picture of her with her brothers. He was dressed in desert camouflage, but it was clean and pressed and fit him perfectly. Warmth blossomed inside her as she admired the long, powerful lines of his body, the cut of his uniform accentuating the length of his legs and the width of his shoulders. Cat gulped, closed her eyes briefly, and smiled. As if sensing her presence Ryan turned toward her, and the grin he gave her made her palms go clammy.

"Hey," he said, crossing the distance between them in two long strides. He stuffed his hands in his pockets and, to her secret surprise, he actually seemed nervous. "I hope I'm not bothering you. Doc told me where you guys worked, and I do still owe you a cup of coffee so I thought I'd stop by."

Cat leaned against the door frame and crossed her arms over her chest. "What? No Starbuck's franchise? I'm disappointed."

Ryan chuckled. He'd trimmed his beard, and now she saw the square jaw and nicely shaped lips the whiskers had effectively hidden. He was better looking than she remembered.

"Maybe once I retire from the Navy I can use some of my pension to get you one," he offered. "Until then, a cup at Green Beans will have to do." He dropped his gaze and kicked the baseboard with the toe of his boot. "Are you... are you free? They have tea and hot chocolate and smoothies since you don't drink coffee." He glanced at her. "I checked."

Cat tried to fight the grin, but it was impossible so she went with it. "Then let's go. We can stop by the hospital on the way and you can introduce me to Digger." She spun around and gestured for him to precede her into the hallway. "Lead the way, Ryan. This time *you* can give *me* something to look at."

* * *

"I've wanted to be a SEAL for as long as I can remember," Ryan said, stirring his coffee absently. "In high school I played every sport, football, baseball, basketball, track, you name it, and once I graduated I got into the ROTC program at Purdue. Next came OCS, and as soon as I could I applied for BUD/S. The rest is history."

Cat leaned back in her chair and sipped her tea. The Green Beans Coffee shop was bustling, but it was one of the busiest shops on Bagram. Troops could get a cup coffee that had already been paid for by donations from people back in the States, so it was a very popular hangout.

"I think your history is still being written, Ryan," she said with a small smile. "And, one day, you will be able to share some of the extraordinary stories you have with the next generation."

"I'm sure you have stories you could tell, too," he countered. "I know *I'd* like to hear some of them."

She chuckled. "Well, if I told you I'd have to kill you, and that would be *such* a waste."

"So, you *are* a spook."

Her brows rose, and he grinned.

"There are rumors your hangar is home to the CIA," he continued.

Cat gave him an assessing look. "Do you believe every rumor you hear, Lieutenant?"

His smile widened. "No, but I hit a nerve because you just reverted to my rank."

He was right. Cat mentally kicked herself, but she couldn't stop the smile. "I can see I'm going to have to tread very carefully around you. Are you always so observant?"

"I'd have been dead a long time ago if I wasn't," he replied.

"Then I'm glad your eyes are so sharp," she said, reaching across the table to take his hand. "Make sure you keep them that way."

Ryan squeezed her fingers. "Yes, ma'am."

Electricity pulsed up her arm from her hand. His skin was warm and slightly rough, and the thought of his hands moving over her body sent a bolt of lust through her. She felt the heat in her face and gently disentangled her fingers from his.

"So, you've been a SEAL for how long?" she asked, hating the breathlessness she heard in her voice. She cleared her throat and took a sip of tea.

"Nine years," he said.

"How much longer do you plan to stay in this particular MOS?"

He ran his fingers over his beard. "Oh, I think I'm about done," he said with a wry smile. "It gets harder each year. Time to leave all this shit to the younger guys."

"Speaking of younger guys," Cat began, leaning toward him, "why is it you're still a lieutenant? You should be a commander by now."

"Yeah, my dad tells me that every time I go home," he replied. He looked out the window toward the flight line and shrugged. "It's simple; if I make rank they'll pull me from active rotation. I didn't go through 30 months of the toughest training in the world so I could stay behind and work a desk. Pull me from the field and you might as well take my Trident." He met her gaze. "Sorry if that disappoints you."

Cat frowned and indignation flared. "I'm not interested in your rank, Ryan," she said flatly, putting her cup on the table between them. "Rank is simply another pin, bar, stripe, or chevron, and a pay raise, nothing more."

"What *are* you interested in, Cate?"

His gaze challenged her and she suddenly felt like *she* was in the spotlight. Not one to shrink from a challenge she returned his stare. "The man *behind* the rank," she replied. "You're one of the *good* ones, Ryan. I've seen you lead. Your men respect you, they listen to you, they *like* you. When you say jump, they say 'how high, which direction, and how long should I stay airborne, sir?'"

Ryan chuckled. "It's the guys, not me."

"Bullshit." Cat sighed. "Ryan, the military *needs* leaders like you. It takes men of integrity to counteract the effect of all the worthless suck-ups who are in positions of power. Put an asshole in charge, and everyone underneath them suffers for it."

"Sounds like you have personal experience with that," he observed quietly.

Cat thought about the dinner she'd had to agree to with Mitchell to get her team some time off and her stomach lurched. "Yeah, I do." She glanced at him. "I think we all have."

Ryan sipped his coffee and looked at her over the rim of his cup. The mood had darkened considerably and Cat felt like an ass.

"Digger seemed in good spirits," she blurted, hoping to lighten things up. "I'm really glad he's going to be okay."

"Me, too," Ryan agreed. "Y'know, he didn't believe me when I said our savior was a woman. Even with Mack and Grady backing me up, he still doesn't believe a girl could make those kinds of shots." He chuckled. "He told me he won't believe it until he sees it."

Cat smiled, thankful the mood had lifted. "Well, if I ever have to demonstrate my skills for him it will be on a shooting range, and not a place where someone is firing back."

"Amen," Ryan said, raising his cup to her. "Although, there have been whispers around the Special Forces Compound that my team isn't the first to witness your particular skill set." He sat up and leaned his elbows on the table. "In fact, Grady was talking to a couple of Rangers who said a woman provided cover fire for *them* during an ambush a couple of weeks ago down south." His eyes sparkled. "You sure get around, Cate."

Cat remained mute and sipped her tea.

"Doesn't really matter, though," Ryan continued. "I think we've done enough talking about work anyway." He finished his coffee and tossed the cup into a nearby trashcan. "How'd you like to take a walk with me? It's Thursday, so the Afghan bazaar is happening by the south gate. We could go buy some pirated movies... or a genuine Rolex." He wiggled his eyebrows.

The warmth she'd felt the first time she'd glimpsed him expanded through her and Cat laughed. "Sounds like a plan." She rose and gestured toward the stairs. "After you."

He grinned and then offered her his arm. "Nope. This time, we go together."

Chapter Five

Ryan strolled beside Cat through the maze of stalls. The local vendors who had been vetted by the military were allowed to set up this bazaar every Thursday, selling everything from hand-woven baskets and jewelry to "antique" firearms supposedly left in country by the British in the 18th and 19th centuries. Cat stopped near one vendor who sat on a plush, brilliantly colored cushion on the ground, his back up against a big wooden crate. Next to him on the ground lay a large wool blanket on which the man displayed his wares. The vendor was old and wizened with sharp black eyes, dark skin creased with age, and a snowy white beard. When Ryan saw the items for sale, he shook his head and chuckled.

"I should've known," he said as Cat crouched down and picked up what looked like an 18th century flintlock pistol. "I'm going to tell Mack and Grady I've found the perfect woman: beautiful, smart, shoots like Annie Oakley, and...." He crouched beside her, ". . . take her shopping and she goes straight for the guns. What more could a guy ask for?"

Cat chuckled and turned the weapon over in her hands, examining it closely. "When you're raised by a father who's a Marine Corps colonel and five brothers, Barbie dolls are *really* impractical. Shooting, for us, was a family activity."

"So, which one you gonna buy?" Ryan asked.

Cat put the pistol down and examined a musket. "None of these," she said, peering down the barrel of the rifle. She returned the musket to its place on the blanket. "These aren't antiques; they're just made to look like them. Most people don't know the difference."

She said something he didn't understand to the vendor, who shook his head and said something back. Cat and the old man conversed easily back and forth, and Ryan stared. It appeared she was bartering, but Ryan didn't have a clue what she was saying other than it sounded like

Dari. After about a minute the conversation ended because Cat rose and turned to walk away. She met Ryan's questioning gaze, winked, and took a couple steps. The old man called out to her and slowly gained his feet.

She faced the man and watched him with those vivid eyes as he moved behind the crate, rummaged around, and reappeared with a long-barreled musket. A smile curved her mouth as she held out her hands and the vendor laid the gun across her upturned palms.

Ryan looked from the vendor to Cat and back. She inspected the weapon, sliding a fingernail along the areas where the wood of the stock and the metal of the mechanisms met, sighting down the barrel, scrutinizing every inch of the musket. The vendor watched her also, and he seemed anxious for her decision. After about a minute of this, Ryan, too, wanted to hear what she had to say. Finally, she smiled and nodded. The old man's face split into a grin.

Cat reached into her pocket, pulled out some bills, and peeled off several C-notes. The man took the money, talking quickly and bowing repeatedly. She replied, returned his bow, and turned to Ryan. Laying the gun across her palms again, she held it out as if presenting it to him.

"Now *this*... is an antique," she said. "It won't appraise for any grand sum, but it's still a beautiful piece." When he didn't move, she stepped closer. "Go on, it's not loaded, I promise."

Ryan took the musket from her and looked down at it, awed. He admired the beautiful and elaborate hand-carvings, the graceful lines, and the gorgeous patina of the wood. The craftsmanship which had gone into making such a weapon was clearly evident. Aside from Cat, Ryan didn't think he'd ever seen anything so beautiful.

"This is remarkable, Cate," he said. He met her eyes. "How did you know he had it hidden back there?"

She shrugged and they started walking. "You have to know the right questions to ask," she replied. "They'll sell crap as long as people buy it, but they always keep something that's actually valuable close by in case a customer comes along who knows what they're looking for and can pay for it."

"Speaking of knowing what questions to ask," he began, "you speak Dari?" He looked down at her, but she was admiring some locally made jewelry.

"And Pashtu, Farsi, Arabic, and several other local dialects," she replied absently. "Technically, that's why I'm here."

Ryan digested that for a moment and they continued on. "So, *technically*, you're an interpreter." She nodded and gave him a sidelong glance. The light in her eyes sparked something in him and he smiled. "Let me guess... sharpshooting is a hobby."

A faint smile hovered on her lips. "Exactly."

"But," he continued, "given the status of women in this country, what purpose would a female translator serve? The men would never talk to you, and they'd never tell the women anything worth repeating."

She chuckled and fingered a bolt of burgundy silk velvet. "True, but they don't employ me to *translate*. They employ me to ensure the local translators are translating *accurately*." Cat looped her arm through his and leaned into his shoulder as they continued to stroll through the bazaar. "You'd be amazed what the men in this country will say in front of a woman, especially when they don't know she speaks the language. It's *almost* like being invisible."

He tried to concentrate on something *other* than the pressure of her hand on his arm. "Clever," Ryan said with a soft laugh. "Very clever."

"Catharine?"

Ryan felt her tense up. He looked down as she masked the angry scowl and pasted a serene, somewhat blank expression on her face. She met his eyes briefly, then released his arm and turned toward the sound of the voice.

"Peter," she said in a cool voice. "Fancy meeting you here."

Ryan faced the stranger and formed an immediate dislike. He'd seen politicians in his day and he despised them. This guy could be nothing more. He was handsome, a couple inches shorter than Ryan, and quite fit, but Ryan doubted the guy ever exerted himself physically outside a high-dollar gym. He was polished, and looked out of place in his slacks and button-up shirt. It surprised Ryan that the man wasn't wearing a tie.

"Peter," Cat said formally, "this is Lieutenant Ryan Heller, one of the SEALs we evaced the other day." She glanced at Ryan, and he fought a smile when he saw the annoyed flash in her eyes. "Lieutenant, this is Peter Mitchell, my supervisor."

The man's gaze swept over him dismissively, as if he'd already deemed himself superior. Ryan merely smiled and gave him a nod. Mitchell lifted his chin and stuck his hand out, and Ryan grasped it. No surprise, it felt like a politician's handshake. It was neither firm nor limp, but somewhere in between so it would be safe to use on little old ladies as well as younger constituents. The dislike intensified but Ryan kept it hidden. He knew the best way to get under a narcissist's skin was to be gracious, friendly, and act as if they were best friends and equals.

"Mr. Mitchell," Ryan said. "I want to thank you for putting Cate in those mountains. Without her...." He paused and gave her a smile, ". . . none of my team would have made it out alive."

"Yes, well," Mitchell intoned, "she's not *supposed* to be shooting people." He chuckled but even that didn't seem genuine. "Lucky for you, when she *does* pick up a rifle she rarely misses." He paused when he caught sight of the musket and his brows rose a good inch. "My, my, lieutenant, that is a fine piece of weaponry you have there." He admired it for another second or two and then met Ryan's gaze. "May I?"

Ryan smiled and looked down at the gun. "Actually, it's Cate's. I'm just carrying it for her, so she's the one you should ask."

The man looked at Cat. Ryan saw the muscle twitch in her cheek before she gave Mitchell a terse nod. Ryan immediately handed the weapon over.

"Beautiful," Mitchell breathed, caressing the barrel of the musket as if it was a woman. "You've a very good eye, Catharine." He laughed shortly and looked at Ryan. "Good thing, too, eh?" He laughed again as if he'd just said something very funny, and turned his attention back to the gun. "Boy, those Brits sure knew how to make beautiful weapons. If you see another of this quality, Catharine, I'd very much appreciate it if you could pick it up for me, or let me know. I would reimburse you, plus add on a 20% finder's fee." He ran his hand over the stock and sighed. "I would love to put one of these on my wall."

Cat held out her hands. "I'm sure your wife would like that, too," she said, her voice laced with sarcasm.

Mitchell didn't seem to notice. He looked at the Enfield with what appeared to be longing, and then returned it to her.

"What are you doing here?" Cat asked. "You've always turned up your nose at the mere suggestion of visiting the weekly market."

Mitchell gave her a look Ryan couldn't decipher, then pasted a typical election-year smile on his face and shrugged.

"We've been here three months," Mitchell replied. "I thought it time I taste the local culture. Besides, my assistant said she bought some beautiful hand-woven baskets here, and I thought Gretchen would like a set."

Cat chuckled, but it was a mirthless sound. "Of course. I'm sure your wife is *dying* to decorate her Upper East Side penthouse apartment with hand-woven baskets from *Afghanistan.*"

Mitchell's smile faltered a bit, but he managed to keep it in place when he glanced at Ryan.

"Yes, well, she asked me to bring back souvenirs," Mitchell said in a tightly controlled voice. "She loves to have mementos of the places I've been. Has a whole room full."

"Then you should definitely get her some," Ryan said. "I got a nice set for my mother at that booth right over there." He paused and pointed over Mitchell's shoulder to a distant stall displaying baskets of every size and shape. "She liked them so much she asked me to get a second set for my Aunt Judy. You should check it out."

Mitchell set his jaw and looked at him for a moment before the fake smile returned. The man glanced at Cat, then turned to Ryan and extended his hand again.

"I most definitely will," Mitchell said, pumping his hand once and releasing him. "Thank you for the tip, and it was a pleasure meeting you, Lieutenant."

"Anytime," Ryan said easily, even though he wanted to wash his hands. "The pleasure was mine. I've been here a while, so I know the best places to get keepsakes. Just ask."

"I'll remember that," Mitchell said. He looked at Cat. "I'll see *you* Monday morning at 0700."

Cat nodded, but her eyes remained fixed on him as he turned and walked in the direction of the vendor Ryan had pointed out. She didn't relax until Mitchell disappeared into the crowd. Ryan took the rifle, looped the strap over his shoulder, and stood in front of her.

"You okay?" he asked quietly. When she wouldn't look at him he put his hands on her shoulders and used his thumbs to nudge her chin up. "Are you okay?" Her eyes were shadowed, haunted, and a spark of anger ignited in his chest. "Is he one of the assholes in charge?"

"Yeah," she replied. "Can we go now? I'm tired of shopping."

"Of course," Ryan said, concerned. "You bet."

They walked silently out of the bazaar and north, back towards the heart of Bagram. Cat said nothing, but after about a quarter mile she put her hand in the crook of his elbow and leaned against him. Ryan smiled to himself.

"I'm curious," he said.

"About what?" Cat asked.

"You said only your father calls you Catharine."

She chuckled darkly. "Right. I should amend that to my father and people I dislike."

He glanced down and watched her face. "So, I assume you'd rather not talk about him?"

The muscle in her cheek twitched again. "You assume correctly."

Ryan let it go, content to walk with her next to him, her hand warm on his arm. The faint scent of her shampoo drifted up to him, and he resisted the urge to bury his face in her hair.

"What's your favorite color?" he asked, breaking the silence.

Cat glanced up at him. "Burgundy, why?"

Ryan shrugged. "Just curious." He liked the feel of her hand in the crook of his elbow and the pressure of her head against his shoulder. It took all of his willpower not to turn his head and kiss her, but he hadn't made it through SEAL training because he lacked self-discipline.

"What's yours?" she countered.

He looked down and felt himself being pulled under by that vibrant gaze. "Green," he said softly, "like your amazing eyes."

She blinked and he saw the pink rush into her cheeks before she turned her face away. "Thank you."

They strolled for a half mile or so before another word was spoken.

"Have dinner with me," he blurted, unable to hold it in any longer.

She stopped and looked up at him. "What?"

"Have dinner with me," he repeated before he lost his nerve. He glanced at his watch, which read 3:30 p.m. "I have some errands I have to run but I could pick you up at your quarters at 1730." He smiled. "There are several fine dining establishments on base to choose from, and I believe it is Italian night at the chow hall. I hear the lasagna actually has *real* cheese."

"Ryan—"

"Or, there's Pizza Hut, Burger King, or Taco Bell." Pausing, he searched her face but saw only mild amusement there. "I'll pay. I'll even let you pick where we eat, and I'll throw in a movie at the MWR. They're showing that remake of True Grit tonight. Just... say yes." It took nearly half a minute, but when he saw the dimples emerge he almost shouted out loud.

"Yes," she finally said, "but how do you know where my quarters are?"

"I don't," he replied, giving her a cheery smile, "but I do know they're located in the northern end of the base. I figure once we get there you'll lead the rest of the way." He leaned closer to her. "Remember me? I *like* to walk behind you."

She colored again and looked away. "But your errands... it'll take us at least an hour to walk that far. Will you have time to get them done?"

Cat paused, bit her lip, and then slowly lifted her eyes to his. What he saw there made him blink: longing. So, she *did* feel like he did. Excitement raced through him, but he did his best to keep it hidden.

"Yes," he said. "What I need to do won't take long."

"Okay, then," she started, "it's a date." She took a step then stopped, turned, and poked a finger in his chest. "If you stand me up, I know where to find you."

Ryan thought his face would split he was smiling so widely. "Don't worry, Cate. If I stood you up Mack and Grady would kick the shit out of me." He chuckled. "And you could watch them do it from a mile away."

***

Cat watched from a distance as Ryan walked quickly toward the PX. Once he had disappeared inside, she grasped the Enfield musket by the barrel and made her way to the front gate of the Special Forces Compound.

The SF Compound was almost like a base within a base. Inside the chain link, sandbagged, razor-wired enclosure stood dozens of double-stacked CONEX containers customized to form surprisingly comfortable barracks. Inside these modified metal shipping containers lived America's elite military personnel. Navy SEALs, Air Force Para-rescue, Army Rangers, Marine Corps Force Recon, among others, all called the SF Compound home.

A small guard shack stood at the entrance and Cat walked over to it. The gunnery sergeant standing watch stepped outside, his sharp gaze raking her from head to toe.

"Can I help you ma'am?" he asked, a frown darkening his brow when he saw the musket.

"Um, I hope so," she replied. "I want to speak with Mack. He's with the SEAL teams." She scuffed the toe of her boot in the gravel. "I don't have a last name for him."

The guard's eyes narrowed a bit. "Are you... Red?"

Cat's brows rose. "That's not my name, but it's what Mack calls me."

"So, you're the one."

"I'm sorry?" she countered.

"You're the sharpshooter."

Cat's mouth formed a silent 'O' and she dropped her chin. "That would be me."

The gunnery sergeant looked at her for another moment then gave her a slight smile. "Wait here, please."

Cat nodded as the marine walked back to the guard shack. He picked up a two-way radio and keyed it.

"Mouth this is Zeus at the gate, copy?"

The radio squawked.

"Go ahead, Zeus."

"Is Mack in the compound?"

"I'm looking at him. What do you need?"

The gunnery sergeant gave her a nod and a little more smile. "Would you be so kind as to inform him he has a visitor? And he'd better double-time it before one of the Para-rescue guys tries to charm her. I know for a fact that Peltier loves redheads, copy?"

"Roger that."

Cat looked at the sergeant and he nodded his head toward her right. Several men sat at a picnic table nearby playing cards, and they were eyeing her with more than a little bit of interest. One seemed particularly fascinated by her, and Cat groaned inwardly. The walkie crackled.

"He is on the move, Zeus. I repeat he is on the move."

"Roger that, Mouth. Zeus out." The sergeant put the radio back in the shack.

Before he could speak, Cat said, "Thanks. I heard."

The sergeant nodded and returned to his post. Less than 30 seconds later Mack appeared and Cat almost sighed with relief.

His sharp brown eyes roved over her and he grinned. "Good to see you again, Red. Want me to save you from those Air Force guys?"

Cat wanted to be done and gone before Ryan saw her so she cut straight to the chase. "Actually," she began, "I need a favor."

Reddish-brown eyebrows shot skyward. "*You* need a favor from *me*?" He tugged on his beard. "Lots of people needing favors recently."

Cat blinked at him. "What?"

Mack chuckled. "Nothing, Red. What do you need?"

Instead of replying, Cat handed him the musket. Mack looked startled for a moment before he let out a long, low whistle. A couple of the men playing cards half rose from their seats when they saw the Enfield, but Mack tossed them one sharp glance and they returned to their game.

"Now *that* is a thing of beauty," he said, turning the weapon over and examining it. "Reaper would *love* this."

"I want him to have it," Cat explained, "but I don't think he'll take it from me."

"Yeah," Mack mused. "He'll spout some bullshit about not taking gifts and chivalry and integrity and blah, blah, blah." He gave Cat an amused grin. "He's old school, Reaper is, but he's good old school."

"I know," Cat agreed, stuffing her hands in her pockets as the familiar warmth spread through her chest. "Do you think you can... I don't know... get it in his foot locker maybe?"

"Too big."

"Put it on his rack?" she suggested.

Mack shouldered the Enfield and then patted her arm. "You don't worry about it, Red," he said. "I'll take care of it."

Cat gave him a grateful smile. "Thanks, Mack. I owe you one."

"Hell no, you don't," he replied. "This little job ain't even a down payment on what we owe you." His expression sobered. "So, when you need a favor that's actually going to require a little effort, you know where I am." He patted her arm again. "I'll make sure he gets it."

"You're the best, Mack." On impulse, she leaned forward and kissed his cheek, eliciting whoops and catcalls from the group at the picnic table. Mack turned the same color as his beard and Cat chuckled. "If there's anything you guys need, you let me know. And I mean *anything*."

"Well," Mack drawled, tugging on his beard again, "the next time we head out we could use some extra ammo. I saw that stash you had in the cave. What I wouldn't give to get my hands on a *tenth* of that."

Sudden inspiration hit and she narrowed her eyes on his face. "You know what? You get me a list of what you need, and I'll make sure you get it."

"I think I love you, Red," Mack said, pretending to tear up. "Reaper is one lucky son of a bitch." He paused and gave her a knowing smile. "Y'know, Reap is real excited about taking you to dinner tonight, more excited than I've ever seen him, even before a mission. You'd think it was his high school prom or something."

Cat laughed. "God, I hope not. My prom was a disaster, and that's the last thing I want with Ryan."

"Well, keep in mind if he's not much of a talker... it's because he's nervous."

"I will, and thanks again," Cat said. "I better head out. I don't want him to see me."

Mack's gaze slid past her. "Then you'd better move, sweetheart, because he's coming this way."

Cat looked over her shoulder and, sure enough, Ryan had just exited the PX. "Shit."

Mack grabbed her hand. "No worries, darlin', I'll get you out of here." He turned and pointed at the picnic table guys. "And as far as *you're* concerned, she was never here, got that? This here is a surprise for Reaper, so the guy who ruins that surprise is the guy who's going to volunteer his head to be my new basketball, am I clear?" The tone of his voice was threat enough, and the men nodded. He looked at her and grinned. "Follow me, my lady."

***

Cat leaned her head against Ryan's shoulder as the closing credits rolled. The people stood, waiting patiently for their turn to file out of the makeshift theater.

"Let's wait until everybody else leaves," Ryan suggested.

Cat closed her eyes and smiled. "Okay. I'm all for that."

Ryan chuckled softly and laid his cheek against her hair. "Y'know, for someone who's accustomed to telling people what to do, you're awfully compliant tonight."

"Would you prefer I argue?" she asked. "I can, if you want."

"That's quite all right," he replied. "I can think of several things I'd rather do than argue with you."

"Such as?"

Cat turned her head slightly so she could look at him and gulped. His mouth was so close she felt his breath on her cheek. His expression sobered and his gaze wandered over her face, as if memorizing her. Just then the lights came on and the hairs on the back of her neck stood up. She looked past Ryan and focused on a lone figure seated several rows behind them on the end. A flash of irritation warmed her chest. *What are you doing here, Airman? You're not the type who does* anything *solo, unless you're doing your master's bidding.*

She'd recognized Peter's assistant easily enough, she saw the young woman every time she went to work. Granted, it could be a complete coincidence that Airman Avery went to the movies the same night and time as she and Ryan, but Cat didn't believe in coincidence, especially if Peter's fingerprints were *anywhere* in the vicinity. She frowned and apparently the change of expression was not lost on Ryan.

"What is it?" he asked.

His voice seemed muted as she stared at Airman Avery, her anger building as the young woman continued to watch the slowly rolling list of cast and crew. To Ryan's credit he didn't turn to look. She felt his gaze locked on her.

"Cate?"

There was no way she could answer his question, even if she wanted to. How do you tell the guy you're hot for that another guy *might* be having you followed?

Avery being at the theater could have nothing to do with Peter, or it could have *everything* to do with Peter. She'd bet on the latter. However, at the moment all she had was a gut feeling, and that wasn't much to go on. Her chest went taut with frustration and she sat straight up in her seat. When she did, Avery rose and made their way quickly toward the exit, eyes averted. "It's nothing," she said, following the airman's progress. "Just thought I saw someone I knew."

"I'm glad I'm not them," he commented. "Easy, Tiger."

She chuckled and gave him a sheepish look. "Sorry," she said, dropping her chin. "A little paranoia comes with the job, I guess."

"Seems like you could do with some R&R," he observed.

Oh, you have no *idea.*

He rose and Cat followed his lead. "Yeah," she agreed, looping her arm through his as they shuffled toward the aisle and to the exit. "I've got a couple months of vacation stacked up. I just haven't had a chance to use any."

Ryan pushed open the exit door, held it for her, and followed her into the frigid night air. "Where would you go, if you could take vacation?"

Cat smiled up at him as he draped his arm over her shoulders and they started walking. "The South Pacific," she replied with a wistful smile. "Techno is from there, the island of Ofu in American Samoa to be exact. His family has property on the northeast side of the island with a large main family house and an adorable little cottage right on the beach." She slid her arm around Ryan's waist and hooked a thumb through one of his belt loops. "We all went there once, the whole team, for a week." She sighed. "That was the best week *ever.*"

"What did you do?" Ryan asked.

"Everything," she answered, "and nothing. We went hiking and swimming and surfing and fishing and kayaking. I worked on my tan, not very hard since redheads *don't* tan. I slept in, drank too much, ate too much, and basically had a *fantastic* time." She closed her eyes as images of spectacular, deserted beaches and volcanic jungles filled her mind. "Tech's parents let me use it a couple of times when I needed to get away by myself for a while. It's a great place to... decompress."

The hairs on her neck were dancing, and it took all her strength not to look over her shoulder.

"Where would *you* go?" she asked, looking up into that ruggedly planed face and ignoring the tingles dancing up her spine.

"If I could go anywhere?"

"Yep, anywhere."

His expression turned thoughtful and he glanced into the sky. It was several moments before he spoke, and when he did his voice was low and velvety. "It wouldn't matter where," he paused and looked down at her, "as long as you went with me."

Her heart thudded and then stopped. For a moment, she thought he was going to kiss her, then he smiled and faced forward as they continued on their way. Disappointment pooled beneath her heart, although she realized it was probably better this way. They *had* just met, after all, and given their diverse careers a relationship would be difficult, if not impossible, to maintain.

"Sorry," he said softly. "That was out of line."

"Only if it wasn't true."

He stopped walking and turned to face her, his expression solemn, his eyes focused on the ground. "It was true, but we've only known each other a couple of days." Ryan shook his head and wound his fingers through hers. "I shouldn't be talking like that, not yet." A few silent moments passed before he lifted his gaze to hers. "I really like you, Cate, and I don't want to move too fast, not with you."

Uncertainty shivered through her. "What do you mean, 'not with me'?" He sighed, and it was a melancholy sound that made her gulp.

"I mean I've moved too fast before," he replied, "and it always ended in disaster." His eyes searched hers, pleading with her to understand. "I don't want that to happen again... not this time... not with you."

A lump lodged in her throat and it took nearly superhuman effort to swallow it. Cat's eyes stung and she blinked rapidly as what he said hit home. Apparently, he wasn't thinking about their diverse careers or the probability of separation. A sliver of doubt and a glimmer of hope both manifested inside her. Part of her said it was unwise to pursue this any further, while the other part didn't care. In the end her mouth answered without her even thinking about it.

"Okay," she blurted.

"Okay?" He sounded surprised.

Her throat tightened in apprehension but there was no going back now. She nodded and smiled up at him. "Okay. You lead, I'll follow."

He gave her a pensive smile and traced the line of her jaw with one finger. "No," he said in a low voice. "We go together."

Chapter Six

Cat stopped in front of her quarters and looked at Ryan expectantly, but he wasn't looking at her. He was looking around the area, muscles tensed, as if he expected someone to pop out from behind one of the portable buildings.

"Ryan," she began, cupping his chin and forcing him to look at her, "*what* is it? You've been wound tight ever since we got within sight of my house."

He chuckled and shook his head. "It's nothing." His eyes narrowed a bit and he ran a finger over her cheek. "I had a great time tonight, and today, all day."

Cat smiled and her insides turned into a warm puddle of mush. Warning bells started to ring, but the throb of her heartbeat drowned them out. "Me, too."

"You free tomorrow?"

Her pulse jumped. "I am."

"How'd you like to spend another day with me?" he asked softly.

The look in those dark blue eyes made her breathing quicken. "I'd love to," she replied, her voice barely above a whisper.

A wistful smile softened his features. "Outstanding."

He paused, his gaze locked with hers. After a few moments, he leaned toward her and she closed her eyes, anticipating the kiss. When his lips brushed her cheek disappointment rose up in her, but she forced herself to smile.

"I'll see you tomorrow," he said.

"I'll be here." She turned to open her door, but he grasped her arm lightly. Cat looked at him in silent question.

"Before you go in," he began, "promise me something."

"Anything."

Several seconds passed before he spoke. "Promise me you won't get mad."

She frowned and uncertainty wound through her. "Why would I get mad?"

"Just... promise me." He took her hands in his and looked at her fingers. "Please."

Cat blinked. "I promise I won't get mad."

He smiled then, a wide, boyish smile. "Okay. Good night, Cate. I'll see you tomorrow."

A thrill of excited anticipation ran the length of her spine. "You will. Good night, Ryan."

He took a few steps back and waited until she backed into her quarters and closed the door. She heard the crunch of gravel beneath his boots as he walked away. Cat pressed a hand to the wooden panel and listened until she could no longer hear his footsteps. Then she shrugged out of her coat and hung it up. Smiling, she turned and her jaw dropped.

A large, metal tub lined with what looked like parachute material sat in the middle of the room, steam rising from the mounds of bubbles that nearly overflowed the rim. Candles stood on her desk, nightstands, and on her footlocker. At first, she thought they were real until she took a closer look. They were battery-powered, flameless candles, a relief because anything with an open flame was strictly forbidden in base housing. Still, the flickering light looked real enough, giving the room a sensual, romantic air.

She walked toward the tub, pausing when something on her desk caught her eye: a silver wine bucket and it wasn't empty. Cat reached for the bottle and pulled it from the ice, and her brows shot up. Johannesburg Riesling. *What the hell?* She slid the bottle back into the ice and turned toward the tub again.

Cat took two steps toward the bathtub and something in her periphery froze her. Slowly, she moved to the side of her bed and ran a hand over the burgundy nightgown laid out over the rough, wool blanket. It was made of what looked and felt like silk velvet, the material soft and luxuriant to the touch, and she imagined it would feel incredible against her skin. With great reverence, she lifted it up by the slender shoulder straps, the fabric shimmering softly in the dim light, and held it against herself. Simple yet gorgeous, it had a deeply plunging décolleté and a back that would leave her bare to the waist. Slits on either side of the gently flared skirt would expose her legs to the hip. The gown was definitely *not* made to sleep in. Heat flooded her cheeks and she gulped.

"Wow."

Next to the negligee was a small, sealed envelope with "Cate" printed across the front, and she had no doubt who had written it. Cat eased down on the edge of the bed and draped the gown over her pillow. With trembling fingers, she opened the note and pulled a single sheet of paper from within.

Cate, please don't take this the wrong way. I didn't buy this so you could wear it for me. I want you to wear it for you. You are so beautiful, and you should always feel beautiful, even in this wasteland. Enjoy the bubbles and the wine. I only wish I could have done more. Ryan.

The words on the page blurred and Cat blinked rapidly. Ryan had obviously eavesdropped on her conversation with Tripp, and he'd decided, war-zone notwithstanding, to try and make her wish come true. She couldn't remember the last time a man had put so much thought and effort into such a sweet, selfless gift. Closing her eyes, she held the note to her heart for a moment, savoring the warmth that spread through her, and then she jumped up and made for the door. *There's no way I'm letting you leave without, at the very least, a thank you.* She didn't bother with a jacket as she ran outside, her eyes searching for any sign of him. A few blocks down a lone figure walked away. She immediately started running.

"Ryan!" she called. Either he couldn't hear her or it wasn't Ryan. Cat closed the gap and tried again. "Ryan!"

The figure stopped beneath a streetlight, turned, and her heart soared. It *was* Ryan. She ran up to him. He looked at her in surprise, and then his expression shifted to dismay as she stared at him, her voice refusing to function.

"You're mad," was all he said.

Cat didn't reply. Instead, she grabbed the front of his shirt with both hands and pulled.

When their lips met, heat burst inside her sending ripples of warmth over her skin. Ryan seemed startled by her attack at first, but it didn't take him long to catch up. He cupped her head and she leaned into him.

His mouth covered hers, and suddenly she was no longer the aggressor. His hands trailed over her shoulders and down, his fingers fanning across her lower back as he pressed her closer. The male animal in him asserted its dominance and a rumbling started. It reminded her of the roar the mountain had made as it collapsed in on itself. She felt the familiar surge of excitement tinged with a tiny sliver of fear. Never one to shy away from danger, Cat released his shirt, wound her arms around his neck, and gave in to it.

The entrance of his tongue into her mouth was tentative, cautious, but it lit a firestorm of desire that nearly buckled her knees. His arms tightened around her and heat settled between her thighs as her breasts were crushed to his chest. Alternating pulses of hot and cold danced through her. His lips moved with exquisite sensuality over hers. He kissed her deeply, thoroughly, leisurely. When he finally pulled back she could barely catch her breath. *Best... first kiss... ever....*

Cat couldn't open her eyes. "I'm not mad," she whispered at last.

Ryan chuckled, put her feet back on the ground, and pressed his lips to her brow. "Are you sure?"

She tucked in beneath his chin and enjoyed the strength and warmth of his embrace. "How did you...?"

"Know, or get it done?"

"Both."

He rubbed his hands up and down her back. "Well, I heard you and Tripp talking on the helo about what you wanted when you got back to base. Getting it done was considerably more difficult, but thankfully I have connections and a couple of teammates who were all about helping me out."

Something clicked and she thought back to the comment Mack had made: "*Lots of people needing favors recently.*" She smiled and wished she could be there to see Ryan's face when he returned to his quarters and found *his* surprise.

"You didn't have to do that," she said, "but thank you. Tell Mack and Grady I said thank you to them as well." She pulled back and gave him a slanted look. "And I don't even mind that they broke in."

"Does this mean you won't shoot them?"

She put her head on his chest again and inhaled his warm, woodsy scent. "They're safe."

They stood quietly for about a minute, but Cat would have been happy to stay there for much longer. He was warm, strong, and seemed as content as she to enjoy the closeness. *But for how long?* Her heart thumped hard as a flicker of uncertainty danced through her brain, but when he rested his chin on top of her head and tightened his embrace it vanished.

"You'd better get back if you want to enjoy it before it gets cold," he said at last.

"I'm fine right here so I don't want to," she replied, "but I will. After all the trouble you went to it would be a crime to waste the hot water and bubbles."

"Yes, it would." He released her. "Come on, I'll walk you."

He shrugged out of his jacket and draped it around her then looped his arm over her shoulders. Cat couldn't remember a time when she'd felt as safe as she did at that moment. She snuggled into the thick, insulated coat and inhaled the faint scent of his cologne. It was a clean, spicy fragrance that captured his essence so completely she knew she'd never forget it.

When they arrived at her quarters, Cat took the jacket off and handed it back to him. He smiled and put it on.

"Thank you again," she said. "Would you... would you like to come in for a glass of wine?" She stuffed her hands in her pockets. "I can't drink a whole bottle by myself."

He tucked a stray curl behind her ear. "I would, which is why I'm going to say no."

Cat bit her lip and looked down at the ground. "Then I shouldn't even ask if you want to scrub my back, should I?"

"Nope," he replied. He leaned down to look her in the eye. "Because I think you know the answer to that question." He took a step closer to her. "When you're done, don't worry about the tub. Mack said he'd take care of it while we're out tomorrow."

Cat couldn't find her voice, so she nodded. She closed her eyes when he pressed a hand to her cheek and her pulse jumped. She sensed the kiss a split-second before his mouth covered hers, but there was no way she could prepare for her body's response. Liquid heat replaced the blood in her veins and even the cold Afghan night couldn't chill her. He threaded his fingers through her hair and molded them to her head as he deepened the kiss. Desire thrummed along every nerve. Ryan took his time, as if there was no war going on around them and they had all the time in the world simply to taste each other. Cat gripped his forearms, uncertain her legs would continue to hold her, while he gently explored her mouth.

When he finally ended the kiss, it was as if the stars had been extinguished and the cold rushed over her. Ryan pulled her to his chest and wrapped his arms tightly around her. After a few moments, he released her.

"Good night, Cate," he whispered. With a final kiss to her temple, he turned and walked away.

Cat stood there, frozen to the spot until she could no longer hear the crunch of gravel beneath his boots. She took several deep breaths as the silence pressed down on her. When she finally opened her eyes, he was gone. The chill she felt this time went deeper than the frigid mountain air. Wrapping her arms around herself she turned and entered her quarters.

She looked at the bubble filled tub for a moment, then poured herself a glass of wine and took a long, slow drink. The cold, sweet liquid tasted like heaven and she finished the glass, savoring every drop. Cat refilled her glass and put it on the floor next to the tub, pinned up her hair, stripped down, and climbed in. The water was still quite hot, and she wondered vaguely how Mack and Grady had accomplished that. The nearby showers were often lukewarm at best, making a six-minute shower seem much longer. With a contented sigh, she picked up the wine glass and sank down in the bubbles.

"To you, Ryan Heller," she said, lifting her glass in salute. "Here's hoping you like your gift as much as I love mine."

***

Ryan walked into his barracks, ignoring the sly smiles and wry grins from the guard and the rest of the guys he passed on the way. Apparently, his date with Cat had been a major subject of conversation. He shrugged out of his jacket and waved at Grady as he approached his bunk.

"So, how'd it go?" Grady asked. "Did you bat one out of the park?"

Ryan lifted one brow and smiled. "I'm not sure I know what that means, and I'm not sure I want to."

Grady put his Guns and Ammo magazine aside and sat up. "C'mon, old timer," he said. "Did you make it to first base, second, home plate? Enquiring minds want to know."

"Too bad," Ryan said. He tossed his jacket on his bed then turned his attention to the combination lock on his locker. "I know you youngsters don't think twice about jumping in and out of bed with whomever, but us old timers? Well, we tend to take things a little slower. I actually like to know a girl's name before we start rubbing body parts."

"Yeah," Mack agreed as he entered the room with a towel draped around him. "He's a dinosaur, Mouth. Besides, even if he made it around all the bases he'd never tell." He laughed and flopped down on his bunk. "Reaper here is one of those 'honorable' guys. A dying breed, I say. Almost extinct, thank goodness. Makes the rest of us look bad."

Ryan laughed and reached for his jacket as he opened his locker. When he turned to grab a hangar from inside the tall, narrow cubicle he froze. "What the hell?"

"What?" Grady asked. When Ryan didn't reply, Grady hopped off his bed and walked to Ryan's side. He whistled, his eyes widening. "Wow. Where'd you get that, Reap?"

Ryan grasped the Enfield musket and pulled it from inside the locker. He shook his head slowly then glanced at Mack. Mack leaned back against his pillow, fingers laced behind his head, a self-satisfied smile on his face. Ryan's eyes narrowed.

"So, *that's* what you've been grinning about all afternoon," Ryan said. "When did she come by?"

"While you were at the Exchange buying *bubble bath* and *flameless candles,*" Mack replied with a grin and a deliberate, exaggerated lisp. "You almost caught her. I had to sneak her out the back way so you guys didn't bump into each other."

Ryan looked at the musket. "You shouldn't have done this, Mack," he said. "I can't accept this."

"Why the fuck not?" Mack asked, getting to his feet. "You did something nice for her. She's not allowed to return the favor?"

"No, she's not," Ryan replied. "She saved our lives. I wanted to show her how much I appreciated that."

Mack snorted and tossed the wet towel at him. "I think she knows," he said with a scowl. He jerked on a pair of sweat pants then stood toe to toe with Ryan. "She did something nice for us, you did something nice for her, she did something else nice back, now it's your turn. That's how it works, Ryan."

"It's not a competition, Mack," Ryan said flatly.

"Reaper," Grady began.

"You're right," Mack said, interrupting Grady. "So, don't make it one. She wanted you to have that musket, but she didn't think you'd take it from her. Apparently, she has you pegged or you and I wouldn't be having this conversation."

"Just take it," Grady offered.

"Stay out of it, Mouth," Mack and Ryan said in unison. The two men then glared at each other.

"She doesn't have to buy me gifts," Ryan said in a taut voice.

"Of course she doesn't, dumbass," Mack shot back. "She obviously did it because she *wanted* to. Accept it, and the next time you see her, presumably tomorrow some time while Grady and I are removing that tub from her housing unit, say *thank you* and let it go."

Ryan shook his head. "I can't—"

"Why not?"

"Ryan," Grady said.

"Because it wouldn't be right," Ryan shot back, ignoring the younger man.

"And giving it back would be?" Mack asked, incredulous.

Grady tried again. "Reaper."

"It's the principle of the thing, Mack," Ryan shot back.

Mack gave him a bored look. "And what principle would that be exactly?"

"For fuck's sake, take the gun, Reaper!" Grady shouted.

Ryan looked at his teammate, stunned, as did Mack. Grady frowned and ran a hand over his face, clearly frustrated. He took a deep breath and looked Ryan in the eye.

"Do you like her, Ryan?"

Ryan rested the stock of the Enfield on top of his rack. "Yeah."

"And you wanted to do something to show her that, right?" Grady prompted. When Ryan nodded, Grady continued. "Well, she did the same thing so what does that tell you?" Ryan didn't answer and Grady threw his hands in the air. "Come on, dude, I can't believe I'm explaining this to *you*. It means she likes you, too, old man. Seriously?"

"She doesn't have to—"

Grady waved a dismissive hand. "Been there, done that." He pinched the bridge of his nose for several seconds then met Ryan's gaze. "Look, let me spell it out for you. She bought that musket because she wanted you to have it. Giving it back would be like saying it wasn't good enough, so shut the fuck up and take it already." He sighed. "I have three sisters, Reaper, so I know what I'm talking about. Keep the gun, unless you *want* to put the kibosh on this right now."

"I can't believe I'm saying this," Mack began, his eyes wide with disbelief, "but the kid's right."

Anger heated Ryan's chest. "You guys are supposed to back *me* up," he said from between clenched teeth.

"We *are*," Mack said. "We're on your side in this, Ryan." He paused, grinned, and added, "And hers."

"Yeah," Grady agreed. "We're trying to get you laid, bro, because, frankly, you need it. And I have a feeling Red would be one hell of a—"

Grady suddenly doubled over and air whooshed out of him as Mack drove an elbow into the younger man's solar plexus. Gasping, Grady stumbled back to his bed and collapsed on top of the mattress.

"Not to change the subject," Mack began, as if nothing had happened, "but... how'd she like it?"

The look of childlike expectation on Mack's face made Ryan chuckle. "Well," he drawled, "she chased me down and kissed me, so I think we did good."

One red-brown eyebrow shot skyward. "Wait. She *chased* you down and *kissed* you, and you're *here*? What the fuck? Shouldn't you be with her, snug in her little house, scrubbing her back and various other lady parts?" Before Ryan could say anything, Mack looked at him in disbelief. "Oh, hold up. No way. No, no, no. Remember what happened the last time you did this gentlemanly 'I don't want to rush things' shit? You wanted to be all honorable with... what was her name?"

"Heather," Ryan replied.

Mack nodded. "Right, right. Well, remember when you pulled that with her? She dumped you and married that jet jock."

Ryan gave him a bored look. "Yeah, talk about crash and burn. They're divorced now. What does *that* tell you?" He eased down on the bed and laid the musket out beside him.

Mack slapped a hand to his forehead and gaped at him. "Reaper, you're *killing* me. What is *wrong* with you? She's hot and she thinks *you're* hot. In a place like this you take whatever good thing comes along and don't look back, so what's the fucking problem?"

Ryan sighed and ran a hand over the Enfield. "The problem is I like her," he replied. "I've never met anyone like her, Mack, and I *like* her." He picked up the weapon and sighted down the barrel. "I don't want to put it in burners just to flame out."

"Shit purple fuzzies," Mack said softly, easing down on the edge of Ryan's bed. "You're falling for Little Miss Marksman, aren't you?"

Ryan frowned. "It's a little early for that, don't you think?"

"I don't know," Mack replied, narrowing his eyes. "We've been doing this a long time, you and I, and this is the first time I've seen you turn down a sure thing."

Ryan scowled and got to his feet, frustration roiling in his belly. Tossing an annoyed look at Mack he put the Enfield carefully into his locker and peeled off his shirt. "She's not some naïve little airman who thinks making it with America's finest will be the highlight of her career," he said as he grabbed a pair of sweat pants and a t-shirt from the set of drawers inside the locker.

"No," Mack agreed. "She's definitely not some naïve little airman."

"She's different," Ryan added.

Mack scratched his beard. "Yep, you're right there. There are no women on this base, and only a couple of men who could take out bad guys at 1500 meters and more. That definitely makes her different." He crossed his arms over his chest. "There are also no women on this base who have recently chased you down so they could kiss you."

Ryan smiled, sat down, and started to unlace his boots. He replayed their embrace in his head and heat swirled in his middle. "It was a *really* nice kiss," he said softly, more to himself than anyone else. "She even *tastes* good." He pulled his boots off and put them at the end of his bed, still smiling.

"Did you at least get a look inside her quarters?" Mack asked.

"Nope," Ryan replied. "She invited me in, but I said no."

"*Why?*" was Mack's plaintive query.

Ryan looked at him out of the corner of his eye. "Because I'm doing the gentlemanly 'I don't want to rush things' shit."

"Fine." Mack sighed dramatically and went back to his bunk. "You are *so* lucky you have me for a teammate."

Ryan changed into a pair of sweats and a clean t-shirt, then stretched out on his bed and looked at the Enfield standing inside his locker. A moment later a cell phone appeared in his periphery. With the touch of a button a video started to play, and Ryan couldn't help but watch. He smiled as the camera focused on the tub with its mountain of bubbles, and when Grady turned on the flameless candles with a flourish any gay man would envy Ryan laughed. The view turned 90 degrees to the bed where the nightgown was so carefully laid out, and he sobered.

"God, I'd love to see her in that," he said in a low voice.

"Me, too," Grady said.

"Shut up, Mouth," he and Mack said in unison. This time when the two looked at each other they smiled and chuckled.

"Sorry," they said, again in stereo.

Mack shook his head, laughed, and tossed the cell phone on his bed. "I'll bet she looks great in it," he commented. "Maybe, if you play your cards right, she'll model it for you."

"I don't know how you got that so fast," Ryan said. "When I found out what her favorite color was I called you the first chance I got."

Mack shrugged. "Eh, it was nothing," he replied. "I called my little Afghan seamstress and told her I wanted a Jessica Rabbit special. I've bought three for the wife, and let me tell you... when a woman gets that velvet next to her skin it does something to her, bro, something *good*. I told you Maggie's pregnant again, didn't I?"

"You did." Ryan chuckled. "How did you know what size to buy?"

A sly smile curved Mack's mouth. "You should know by now I have an exceptional eye, Reaper." He lifted one bushy eyebrow. "Next time you see Red, ask her. She's 5'10", roughly 160 and size eight slash ten, 38DD, 29, 38, although I could be off on the ass." He grinned and crossed his arms over his chest. "Go ahead, ask."

Ryan shook his head. "No, thank you. I'll take your word for it."

"Aw, man, you're no fun," Mack complained. "I would *love* to see her face if you had the balls."

"Precisely why I'm not asking," Ryan replied. "I want to keep my balls exactly where and how they are." He looked at his friend for a moment then held out a hand. "Thanks again, Mack. I owe you."

"Yes, you do, my friend," Mack agreed. "You most definitely do, and it's going to cost *you* more than a cup of coffee, that's for *damn* sure."

***

Cat slipped into the nightgown and sighed softly. The silk velvet felt fabulous and it fit her perfectly. The thought of Ryan's hands moving where the velvet touched her sent goose bumps fanning over her skin. Cat looked at her reflection for a moment and the mood shifted as she was unexpectedly transported back in time.

"Ready to go, Dad?" she asked, grabbing her clutch purse from the counter. "Brian's bringing the car around, and if we don't get a move on you're going to miss your own retirement party."

"Come here, Catharine," her father said from his recliner. "I want a look at you."

Cat blinked at her father several times then walked over to stand in front of him. Her dad looked her over from the pointed toes of her pumps to the top of her professionally coiffed head as if inspecting his troops. The burgundy evening gown had belonged to her mother originally, but Cat had had to alter it because she stood nearly eight inches taller and weighed forty pounds more. On her mom it had been full length; on Cat the hem fell below the knee. The original design was still evident, however, and Cat thought her mother would have been pleased.

Cat held her arms out and turned in a circle. "So, how do I look?" she asked. "I think Mom would like it, don't you? I tried to stay as close to the original as possible."

Her father pursed his lips and stood in one fluid motion. "I don't question she would like the dress." His steely blue eyes bored holes in her. "What I question is what she would think of the daughter who is wearing it."

That brought her up short and she gulped. "Wh-what do you mean?"

"What do you think your mother would say if she could see you now?" her father asked in a low voice. "What would she say if she knew her only daughter killed people for a living?"

Cat closed her eyes against the memory and the ball of tension it created, and wondered why her brain had spit it out now. The nightgown didn't look like her mother's evening gown, except for the color, and Ryan certainly wasn't her father. Cat met her own eyes in the mirror then ran a hand over the rich velvet. With a dispirited sigh, she started to slide the straps off her shoulders. Her movements were interrupted by a soft knock on her door. Hope sprang to life in her chest.

Rushing to the door, Cat unlocked it and opened it. Her enthusiasm faded when she was greeted by a pair of dark brown eyes instead of the dark blue she'd been hoping to see. The surprise she felt reflected in Mitchell's face as his brows rose and his gaze roved over her. It took her a few seconds to find her voice.

"Peter," she said at last, "what are you doing here?"

The sight of her delicious curves so tantalizingly displayed sent familiar heat burning in his groin, and for several moments he couldn't reply. When he regained his wits he whistled softly then looked past her at the candlelit room and the tub, secretly searching for signs of the SEAL. There weren't any, at least not that he could see from outside, but his hackles went into full bristle at the thought. "Interrupting something, obviously."

She crossed her arms over her chest, as if suddenly aware of how much cleavage the gown exposed. "Only a bath."

His chest went tight but he kept his expression impassive and lifted one brow. "Really, Catharine? *Only a bath?*"

She made an annoyed sound and pushed the door open wide. "I'm quite alone. Now, what do you want?"

Relief that she was alone didn't ease the jealous furor bubbling in his gut, but he couldn't let her see his discomfiture. "After seeing that nightgown I've quite forgotten," he replied with a grin.

Cat rolled her eyes and went back inside, letting the door close in his face. Choking back a growl of anger he jerked the door open and followed her inside. She tossed him an annoyed glance, pulled on her robe, and tied the sash tightly. He was momentarily distracted as a sharp pang of need impaled him. *Damn. It's a crime to cover up such a beautiful body. When I finally have you to myself, you'll never wear clothes again.*

"Remember now?" she asked, hands on hips.

Giving himself a mental shake, he sent her a look designed to communicate that business didn't interest him even as he fought his growing frustration. She ignored him. He ground his teeth together. The lieutenant had to be the reason behind her staunch indifference and a flash of angry heat pulsed through him. The SEAL was turning out to be more trouble than Peter had anticipated.

She let her hair down and grabbed her brush. "Figure out why you came or get out," she said, pulling the brush through the tresses with long, angry strokes. "I'm *not* in the mood."

He decided to put his jealousy aside and try the good-humored route. Cat didn't respond well to aggressive men, but there had been a time his charm had worked on her. "Really?" he drawled. "Wine, bubbles, lingerie... shouldn't all that have *put* you in the mood? And I do believe I smell the faintest hint of that perfume I love. It may not be working for *you*, but it certainly is for *me*." He gave her his patented, soulful, puppy-dog-eyes look, and a barely there smile. In the past, this expression had melted the resolve of any woman he had used it on, including Cat. "You still captivate me, Catharine, like you did when we first met. I've been your prisoner since that day, and I probably always will be."

Her reaction was not what he expected. Without even the slightest hint of softening, Cat tossed the hairbrush down and strode to the door. Using a hip, she knocked it open and stood to the side, arms crossed over her chest. "Leave."

He choked down his rising anger. He took a deep, slow breath, chuckled softly, and slowly walked up to her. "I must admit, the SEAL is giving it the old college try." He grabbed one end of her sash. He wanted to fist his hand in that velour ribbon and jerk her to him, but he forced himself to merely caress the fabric and gave her his best smile. "C'mon, Catharine. You are *so* far out of the lieutenant's league. We both know he doesn't have what it takes to romance a woman like you."

Cat snatched the sash away from him. He resisted the urge to grab her arm and pull her to him. Instead he clasped his hands loosely in front of him. The sultry smile that curved her mouth started a throbbing in his groin.

"Actually, he has *exactly* what it takes to romance a woman like me." She leaned toward him. "He's being a gentleman."

Her scent wrapped around him, testing the limits of his concentration and endurance. She was close enough to touch, and it took all of his will not to. His semi-erect penis, hidden by his clasped hands, twitched. He imagined digging his fingers into her shoulders, pushing her up against the nearest wall, and taking what he wanted. He knew it wouldn't be that easy. He'd had a taste of her during their brief affair, and it had been enough to leave him with a permanent craving. His need almost overwhelmed him but Cat possessed a skill set that would make even the most vicious sociopath hesitant to choose her as his next victim. The thought of the battle that would blaze between them was almost as arousing as imagining the sex itself. He steeled himself, knowing patience would be its own reward. *I'll have you, Catharine, just not yet.* I will catch you off guard, and then I will *have you. Lieutenant Heller will* not *stand in my way.* He pulled tightly on his inner reins and rejoined the conversation.

"A gentleman?" Mitchell repeated, fighting to keep the scorn out of his voice. "How so?"

"Well, I invited him to stay and scrub my back. He declined."

That made him laugh, which, in hindsight, was probably not the right thing to do. However, he couldn't take it back now and decided to go with it. "That just makes him an idiot," he retorted. "What red-blooded male would turn down an invitation like that?" He already knew the answer: *a male I may have to get rid of, if the problem doesn't resolve itself.*

Cat looked askance at him. "Do you *hear* yourself when you speak?" she asked. "Now, tell me why you're here or get out."

Obviously, his attempts to win her over were not working so he tried a different approach and glared at her. Cat gave him a bored look. Finally, he sighed and decided contrition would be more appropriate.

"Fine," he began. "I've started looking into your... allegations, and there may be something there." He looked out the still open door, feigning concern. "I'm sending Parker and Slate to Kabul to meet with a contact." He met her eyes. "I'd like you to tag along."

"When?"

"Sometime next week," he replied. "As soon as I can arrange secure transport."

"Why?" Cat asked, one brow lifted. "Slate is fluent, so what do you need me for?"

He took a step closer, careful to keep his penitent expression firmly in place. "These are dangerous waters, and I trust you, Catharine."

"You don't trust him?"

"Not like I do you," he said softly. *Come on, Cath. Give me this one.* He moved toward her again. "Please, Cath. I need you on this one, before anyone else gets hurt."

Cat backed away, her gut twisting into knots. It wasn't anything Peter had said or done; this behavior was typical for him. Something else was going on. She didn't know what, but she *felt* it.

"Okay, I'll go. Now if you don't mind?" She gestured toward the open door, keeping her face expressionless. "I'll see you Monday." The way he looked at her made her distinctly uneasy, more so than in the past. There was a strange light in his eyes and it sent her inner alarms into a cacophony.

Mitchell stepped outside, then turned and gave her one more head-to-toe look. "Gotta give it to the squid... he has great taste in lingerie... and women."

"Good night, Peter," Cat said abruptly. Grasping the knob, she pulled, but his fingers snaked around her wrist before she could close the door.

"Good night, Catharine." He moved to kiss her hand but she jerked out of his grasp.

"Go call your wife," Cat said, "and *leave me alone.*"

She jerked the door shut and flipped both locks, loudly. Heart pounding, she stood there until she heard him walk away.

Chapter Seven

Unable to silence her inner alarms, Cat moved to one of the windows and watched Mitchell climb into his SUV. He sat there for nearly a minute, the engine idling as he talked on his cell phone. Maybe he was talking to his wife but, somehow, she doubted it. Something was going on, she *knew* it, but she had no clue what it might be other than not good. She needed answers, and at the moment there was only one place she could think to start looking.

Once he drove away Cat dressed quickly and slipped out of her quarters. It took her about fifteen minutes to run to work and she skidded to a stop outside the hangar when she saw Peter's Yukon. Frowning, she crept into the darkness around the side of the building to wait.

Fifteen minutes later, Cat watched as Peter left, got into his Yukon, and turned the engine over. She stayed hidden in the shadows until he drove away, headed in the direction of the Base Officers' Quarters. A glance at her cell phone told her it was shortly after midnight.

"Working late, Peter?" she muttered under her breath. "That's not like you."

Once the SUV disappeared from sight she made her way inside. At this hour, there were only a few personnel on duty, and she knew where all of them were located. Two would be patrolling the hangar and maintenance spaces on the first floor, while the third patrolled the office spaces on the second floor. As a pretense she went to her office and sat down at her desk, flipping through papers until the night watch walked by. Cat pretended not to notice him, until he knocked on the door frame.

"Hey, Miss Beckett," the man said. "What the heck are you doing here? Aren't you on liberty?"

Thompson was an older man, mid-fifties, with soft, pleasant features, salt and pepper hair, and kind blue eyes. Cat knew better than to take the man at face value, however. He wouldn't have been assigned here if he wasn't a formidable force in his own right. They were in the middle of a war zone, after all. She put her papers down and gave him a tired smile.

"Hey, Thompson," she replied. "Yeah, I'm supposed to be. I wanted to double-check that I turned in everything Peter needed from me. I keep thinking I forgot something so I can't sleep."

Thompson nodded and smiled. "I know how that goes," he said, "and soon enough you'll realize you didn't forget a thing." He chuckled and touched the brim of his hat with his flashlight. "Don't stay too late."

"I'll be out of here before you come back around," she said. "Good night, Thompson."

"Good night, Miss Beckett."

Cat went back to her papers, shuffling and pretending to read them until she heard Thompson's feet on the stairs. When the door for the first level opened and then closed, Cat rose and moved to the door of her office.

After checking that the darkened hallway was empty Cat walked quickly and silently to Peter's office. The door was locked, but she expected that. Ears attuned for any sound, she took the small toolkit from the pocket of her jeans, removed two picks from inside, and opened the lock with all of the efficiency of an experienced cat burglar. After checking the hallway again, she slipped into the office and closed and locked the door behind her.

A cursory examination of Peter's desk revealed nothing she hadn't expected to see. When she went through his inbox she was mildly surprised the report from her team wasn't there. Thinking she'd overlooked it, she carefully sorted through the stack of manila folders, but she'd been right the first time. Odd, she thought. Peter wasn't supposed to take work home.

Dismissing the misplaced report, she went through the drawers and found nothing unusual. Cat planted her hands on the desk and looked around the office, perplexed. She wasn't sure what she was doing here or even what she was looking for, but ever since Peter's departure from her quarters her gut had been in a state of upheaval. She had learned to listen to her instincts, she just wished they were telling her more.

Just as she was about to leave, something on the bookshelf caught her eye. One of the books wasn't pushed all the way in, the spine stuck out about a quarter inch. Ordinarily she'd think nothing of it, but this was Peter's office. She'd watched him use a level to place the pictures on the walls and more than once she'd seen him straightening the fringe on the Persian rug that covered the floor. Frowning, Cat walked over to the bookcase and pulled the book out.

A sheaf of papers fell out of the volume and fluttered to the floor. Cat picked them up and looked through them quickly. It was a cell phone bill, or a copy of one downloaded from the carrier's website, an Iranian carrier. The rumble in her gut intensified. Using her cell phone camera, Cat took pictures of the pages, front and back, then refolded them and put them back in the book. She returned the book to the exact position she'd found it.

Just as she reached for the doorknob she heard the sound of the door at the foot of the stairs. Apparently, Thompson was on his way back up. Cat left Peter's office, closed and locked the door behind her, and sprinted back to her office. She turned off the light, then walked into the hallway and pulled the door shut as if just leaving.

"You said you'd be gone before I got back," Thompson said with a chuckle.

Cat pretended to be surprised by the appearance of the guard. "Oh," she said with a nervous laugh. "You startled me."

"Sorry," Thompson said. "You get everything squared away?"

Cat rolled her eyes and locked her office door. "Yes, and you were right, but I had to go through everything *twice* before I convinced myself I didn't forget anything."

"See?" He patted her arm. "By the way, nice job the other day."

She blinked at him.

"I know," he continued, "it's supposed to be hush-hush, but when you save a SEAL team, word gets around."

"Oh," she said, "*that.*" She shrugged and stuffed her hands in her pockets. "It was nothing."

Thompson laughed. "You are a pistol, Miss Becket, no pun intended."

"Good night, Thompson," she said as she turned and walked away. "Keep up the good work."

"You, too, Miss Beckett," Thompson replied. "Sleep well."

Cat gave him a wave and made her way toward the stairs. She cut through the hangar, pausing when she saw the 2½ ton truck parked inside the massive bay doors. Inside the canvas covered vehicle was an entire pallet of ammunition that had arrived by heavy transport the day after their escape from the mountains. What they needed with an entire pallet of bullets she didn't know, but Peter preferred to stockpile supplies rather than order what he needed. Odd that he could requisition tons of ammunition when many platoons and squads were running short. An idea started to form in her head and she wondered briefly how long the truck could be gone before anyone noticed. As long as she didn't take it when Thompson was on duty, she guessed a couple hours, tops. Cat smiled and continued on her way. Maybe now she'd be able to get some sleep.

***

The phone in the barracks chirped as Ryan walked by. Since the rest of his team was either at breakfast or occupied elsewhere, he decided to answer.

"Lieutenant Heller," he said cordially.

"Lieutenant, this is Airman Rodriguez at the back gate. I think you need to get down here, sir."

"What's going on, Airman?"

"Well, sir, there's a redhead here with a truck full of... something. She says you may want to bring some friends, sir, to help offload. And she only has an hour, so she says you need to hurry... sir."

Ryan grinned. "I'll be right there, Airman. Don't let her go anywhere."

"And if she tries to leave?" the airman squeaked.

"Ask her to stay," Ryan replied, "nicely."

"Yes, sir."

Ryan hung the phone up and made his way to the courtyard where Mack and Grady played basketball. Ryan waved them over, and Mack stole the ball when Grady looked at him. With a triumphant shout, Mack dunked the ball.

"I win!" he shouted. He rested the orange orb on one hip and walked over to where Ryan and Grady stood. He grinned and tossed the ball to the younger man. "Never let your superior officer distract you during a game, newbie." Mack nodded to Ryan. "Thanks, Reaper."

"Anytime," Ryan replied wryly. "Now, follow me. It's Christmas, boys, and Santa's at the back gate."

"Christmas?" Grady repeated. "It's February, Reaper."

Mack sighed heavily and smacked Grady lightly on the back of the head. "Seriously?" He pushed Grady aside and fell into step beside Ryan. "Might I inquire who Santa is?"

Ryan looked down at Mack and smiled at the shorter man's knowing expression. "Take a guess, Mack."

"Yee haw!" Suddenly Mack stopped and grabbed his arm. "Wait, you're not going to make us give it back, are you?"

"You don't even know what it is yet," Ryan said with a chuckle.

"Doesn't matter," Mack said. "Do we get to keep it? Don't let me see what it is and then insist we can't take it. You can do that with your own stuff, but don't fuck with mine like that."

Ryan laughed and clapped Mack on the shoulder. "Relax, Mack. I'm not sure what *it* is, but I'm pretty sure we can keep it."

When they rounded the end of another set of modified Conex containers, Ryan could see the back entrance to the SF Compound. Just outside that invisible line Cat leaned against the side of a deuce-and-a-half truck. She wore boots, desert camouflage pants, and a fitted tan t-shirt, her hair hanging loose around her shoulders. He glanced at the airman in the guard shack who was staring at her, and cleared his throat loudly as he walked past. The airman turned, startled. When he saw Ryan looking at him he turned bright red, saluted, and dropped his gaze.

"Nice t-shirt," Grady said. "She sure fills—"

Mack elbowed Grady in the solar plexus again and the younger man doubled over. "Why look!" Mack exclaimed, throwing his arms wide as he approached her. "It's Mrs. Claus!"

Ryan stood a few feet back as Cat laughed and hugged the shorter man. His gaze roved over her, and he had no trouble understanding what stunned the airman. She really *did* fill out that t-shirt. The fact she could look *that* good in arctic camouflage, desert camouflage, and jeans was nearly his undoing. He knew without a doubt she'd *rock* that nightgown.

"Merry Christmas!" she said, walking to the back of the truck and lowering the tailgate. "I know I'm late, but better late than never, right?"

Ryan and Mack followed and Mack let out a low whistle. Ryan looked at her.

"That's a lot of ammunition," he said. "How did you—?"

"Don't ask," she interrupted him. "I have to have this truck back in...." She checked her watch, ". . . forty-three minutes. That gives you roughly half an hour to take what you can." When they didn't move, she waved a hand in front of their faces. "Hello? Tick-tock."

"Are you sure?" Ryan asked.

"Reaper," Mack growled.

"I'm sure," she said. She grabbed a box of 5.56 and a box of .50 caliber rounds and handed them over. "Get a move on, boys, or what's behind curtain number one goes away."

While the Special Forces were some of the best supplied troops in Afghanistan, there were times when even they ran short of ammunition. Ryan put two fingers between his teeth and whistled at the guard. The airman snapped to and trotted over.

"Sir?"

"Call Barracks 34 and tell Lieutenant Pearson to get his team out here ASAP. We have an offload."

"Yes, sir."

Grady had recovered sufficiently to reach the back of the truck, and his eyes widened when he saw the boxes and boxes of bullets. He whistled. "Wow."

"Stop talking and start unloading," Mack said.

"I've got a better idea," Grady said. "Be right back."

Mack looked after the younger man in disbelief as he dashed off. "Where the hell is *he* going?"

As Mack and Airman Rodriguez took armloads of ammunition and stacked them next to the guard shack, Ryan pulled Cat to the side.

"Seriously, Cate," he began in a low voice, "where did you get this?"

"Seriously, Ryan," she replied, looking up at him with those amazing eyes, "don't ask."

"Tell me you're not going to get in trouble," he said, frowning. She smiled, her cheeks dimpling, and the last part of his frostbitten heart finally melted.

"I'm not going to get in trouble," she said.

A moment later there was shouting and eight men crowded around the truck. As they started to grab boxes a honking sound drew the crowd's attention and they collectively turned. Ryan moved to the side of the crowd so he could see as Grady appeared driving a forklift. Cat followed.

"I'll be damned," Ryan and Mack said in unison. The two looked at each other and smiled.

"The kid ain't so dumb," Mack declared.

Cat laughed. She stood between them and put a hand on each man's shoulder. "He learned from the best."

"Yes, he did," Mack agreed. "Now, stand aside, Mrs. Claus, and watch us work." He hopped up into the back of the truck.

"What the *hell* is going on here?"

Silence fell like a guillotine and Ryan groaned inwardly. He glanced at Cat then walked slowly around to the other side of the truck. His fellow SEALs parted like the Red Sea before Moses, leaving a path between him and their Commanding Officer, Commander Doug Ferris.

At fifty, Commander Ferris, call sign Diablo, was a SEAL's SEAL. After spending more than ten years as a SEAL himself, he was promoted and had taken over as their CO two years ago. There was not a more respected officer on base, no matter the branch of service. The Commander had a Bronze Star, Navy Cross, Distinguished Service Medal, four Purple Hearts, and countless letters of commendation to illustrate his level of commitment and bravery. He was also a handsome man with piercing gray eyes, dark hair graying at the temples, and sharp, chiseled features. His mere presence commanded respect, and silence, like now.

Ryan took a deep breath, approached the Commander slowly, and stood at attention. Ferris stood at parade rest, his hands clasped crisply behind his back, his chin lifted, his eyes locked on Ryan.

"Lieutenant."

"Sir."

"Do you want to tell me what is going on here? I don't believe I've heard such a commotion since Carrie Underwood decided to pay us an unannounced visit."

Before Ryan could reply Cat stepped in front of him, putting herself squarely between him and his CO. Ryan ground his teeth together and barely resisted the urge to move her.

"Excuse me, Commander," she began, "but the commotion is my fault." She held out a hand and met the Commander's gaze directly. "Catharine Beckett, at your service, sir. Forgive me for spoiling your otherwise quiet morning."

To Ryan's great relief, and annoyance, the Commander shook her hand firmly, a slight smile on his otherwise stony face.

"So, you're the one causing such a stir around here," Ferris said. "Beckett, eh? It's not the first time I've heard that name. In fact, I've heard it quite a bit in the past few weeks."

"I hope in a good context, sir," she said.

"The best," he replied. He glanced at the truck. "I hope this won't force me to revise my opinion, Miss Beckett."

"As do I," she said.

Ferris walked around both of them to the back of the truck. Ryan glanced down at Cat who looked at him with wide eyes, shrugged helplessly, and mouthed, "Sorry." Ryan turned around and followed his CO, Cat right beside him.

"That's a lot of ammunition, Beckett," Ferris said. He turned a probing gaze on her. "Do I want to know where this came from?"

"Actually... it's yours," she replied. She clasped her hands in front of her and glanced at Mack, then Ryan, then looked at Ferris and lied. "I heard a convoy of weapons and ammunition was stolen a few weeks ago. Well...," she paused and gestured at the stacks of boxes, ". . . here it is. I know it isn't the full shipment, but it should be enough to... tide you over until your next regular shipment arrives."

Ryan lifted his chin when Ferris looked at him.

"You knew about this, Lieutenant?"

"Yes, sir," Ryan replied, "about five minutes before you did, sir."

"And where exactly was this... *found?*" Ferris asked.

Ryan figured Cat had an answer handy, so he merely looked at her and crossed his arms over his chest. She must have recognized the silent reprimand and her brows drew together.

"I'm not sure, sir," she replied in a low, cool voice. "I just know it's yours. I can take it back if you like."

"Aw, man," Mack muttered under his breath. Ferris' head snapped around. When Mack saw he had his CO's attention he dropped his gaze. "Sorry, sir."

Ferris looked from Ryan to Cat and back and a twinkle entered his steely eyes. "Grady!"

"Yes, sir?"

"Can you really drive that thing?"

Ryan glanced at Grady, who stared at his CO as if he wasn't sure he'd heard correctly.

"Sir?"

"Can you drive that thing or not, petty officer?" Ferris stood to the side and gestured for Ryan and Cat to move as well. "Show me what you've got, Mouth."

Grady grinned and started the forklift's engine. "Yes, sir!"

Ryan smiled as Grady maneuvered the forklift, Mack guiding from inside the back of the truck. In less than a minute the pallet was out of the truck and crossing into Special Forces territory.

"Take that to the armory, petty officer," Ferris bellowed at Grady's back.

"You got it, sir!" Grady shouted back.

Mack, standing on the side of the forklift whooped in excitement and saluted. Commander Ferris chuckled and returned the salute.

"All right everyone," Ferris said, "back to what you were doing. The circus is over."

Ryan knew better than to follow his fellow SEALs into the compound. He glanced at Cat, but she was watching the Commander, her expression blank.

"Lieutenant," Ferris said formally, hands behind his back again.

Ryan came to attention and his abdominals tightened. "Sir."

"At ease, Reaper," Ferris said. "I'm not going to chew your ass."

"You're not, sir?" he asked. He allowed himself to relax, but only a hair.

"No, son," the man replied, "at least not here." He glanced at Cat. "Especially not in front of anyone else." He gave Ryan a wry smile. "Of course, in the future I would like to be notified when ammunition shows up on my doorstep, but in this case? In this case, I'll make an exception."

The tightness in his middle released. "Thank you, sir."

"Miss Beckett."

Ryan looked at Cat as she lifted her chin and faced down the commander like he was anyone else. Ryan smiled. Even though he'd been annoyed when she'd stepped in earlier, he had to admire that kind of backbone, especially when it was so nicely packaged.

"Commander?" she said.

"I trust there won't be any more... *recovered* ammunition coming my way?"

"No, sir, there won't," she replied. Then, the dimples appeared. "Unless, of course, you'd like there to be...?"

"No, Miss Beckett," Ferris said, extending a hand. Cat grasped his fingers and shook them firmly, and Ferris grinned. "I'm still not sure how to explain *this.*"

"Well," she began, "the RFID tags were removed when it was stolen, so the chances of anyone looking for it are almost nonexistent." She shrugged and closed the tailgate. "Perhaps one of your SEAL teams came across a terrorist weapons cache. Who's to say otherwise?" She leaned against the truck and gave the commander a wide-eyed, innocent look and a smile.

Ferris narrowed his eyes on her. "Lieutenant."

"Sir?"

"Keep a close eye on this one," the commander recommended, "she's trouble." He gave Ryan a wry smile. "I assume you're going to spend the remainder of your day off extending our most gracious thanks to Miss Beckett?"

Ryan grinned. "Of course, sir." Cat's cheeks went pink and he chuckled.

"Very good then," Ferris said. "Miss Beckett, I trust we will meet again."

"I certainly hope so, Commander," she replied.

"As do I," Ferris said. He turned on his heel and strode onto the compound, Airman Rodriguez snapping to a salute as the commander passed by. "As you were, Airman."

Ryan chuckled, shook his head, and looked at Cat out of the corner of his eye. "He's right, you know. I am going to have to keep a very close eye on you." He faced her and crossed his arms over his chest. "You really shouldn't have stepped in like that."

Cat looked off into the distance and stuffed her hands in her pockets. "Yeah, I have a habit of doing that." She gave him a sidelong glance. "Oh, wait. You should know that. You're alive because I stepped in when I shouldn't have."

"Wow." Ryan looked down his nose at her. "You're going to throw *that* at me?"

Cat looked at him for a moment then she scowled, sighed, and dropped her chin. "No." She scuffed the toe of her boot in the gravel. "I'm sorry, Ryan, really. I know I shouldn't have gotten between you and your CO, but—"

"But what?" Her discomfiture almost made him chuckle, but he kept his expression serious.

She looked at him with wide eyes. "I didn't want you getting in trouble because of *me*."

He gaped at her. "Are you *kidding*? You show up at my compound at 0830 with a truck full of untagged, unmarked ammunition, and you don't want *me* getting in trouble?" Cat gave him a look that reminded him of a petulant child caught with her hand in the cookie jar, and he bit back a laugh.

"Yeah, well, I don't have the UCMJ to worry about," she shot back.

"No, but there *are* these things in the other world called *laws*," Ryan said. "I'm pretty sure they apply, even where *you* live."

"Mm, sometimes," she admitted. "See, I kind of work in a... *gray* area."

"You're telling me they don't frown on *theft* at the CIA?" Ryan said, leaning a shoulder against the tailgate.

"Not always," she said, wiggling her brows at him. "Depends."

"On *what?*" He couldn't *wait* to hear this.

"On what one is stealing and where the stolen goods are going," she replied promptly, her cheeks dimpling as she faced him. "On one hand, if I was taking the ammo and giving it to the Taliban, I'm pretty sure they'd frown on *that.*" She shrugged. "Since I'm giving it to you guys, and we're all *supposed* to be on the same side, it's not really *stealing.* It's more like a... a lateral *transfer.*"

Ryan stared at her for a moment, then threw his head back and laughed. If Airman Rodriguez wasn't watching them with such interest, he would've grabbed her and kissed her soundly. As it was he walked around to the other side of the truck, out of Airman Rodriguez's line of sight, and crooked a finger at her. Cat looked at the airman first then at him, and then approached him, her brows drawn together in a frown.

"What?" she whispered.

Instead of answering Ryan jerked her into his arms and covered her mouth with his. A cry of surprise escaped her before she melted against him. Her lips were soft and tasted like cherries, and Ryan realized, with no small amount of surprise, that he'd never *really* been kissed before... not like this. He'd experienced fewer fireworks in Boston on the Fourth of July.

Her arms wound around his neck and he deepened the kiss, acutely aware of the delicate touch of her tongue to his, her breasts against his chest, the sleek length of her back beneath his fingers, the faint scent of jasmine, like the bubble bath he'd bought for her. He pictured her in that negligee. Parts of him went hot he didn't want to, at least not here behind a truck with some twenty-something airman fifteen feet away. Knowing enough not to test his limits, Ryan pulled back. Eyes still closed, he rested his chin atop her head and took a deep, steadying breath.

"Thank you," he whispered.

"Any – any time," she stammered. She pressed her face into his neck, her breath warm on his skin. "And while I hate to cut this short, I have...." Her voice trailed off then she said, ". . . just over 20 minutes before I need to hightail it back to work."

Back to work? Disappointment filled him, but he knew in their world things changed on a dime. He pulled back and looked down at her. "So... we're not spending the day together?"

"We are," she replied. "We will." She frowned. "Won't we?"

He held back a sigh of relief and cupped her face. "We will." He brushed her lips with his then looked into those emerald eyes. "How long will it take for you to return the truck?"

"Mm? What?" She blinked. "Oh. Fifteen minutes."

He kissed her again and welcomed the surge of heat that ensued. "I'll meet you at your house in thirty. That enough time?"

"Mm." She closed her eyes and stood on tiptoe. "Okay."

"Lieutenant."

"Yes, Airman?"

"I can see your legs, sir." Rodriguez cleared his throat. "And hers."

"That's nice," Ryan replied. "Look the other way, Rodriguez."

"Yes, sir."

Ryan captured her mouth again, unwilling to let her go yet. When he felt his libido start to assert itself he pressed his lips to her brow, released her, and took a step back. "Half an hour, Cate." Never before had 30 minutes seemed like such a long stretch of time.

She gave him a look that would melt the polar icecaps. "Don't be late."

He ran a finger over her cheek, her skin like satin to the touch. "Not a chance." He smiled. "Don't get in trouble."

The dimples were back. "Not a chance," she mimicked. She turned and walked toward the driver's door, but stopped and turned to him. "Wait. I almost forgot."

"What?"

Cat pulled a business card from her pocket and slipped into the one on the front of his uniform. She laid a hand over it briefly then gave him a shy smile.

"It's my numbers, all of them," she said. "My cell is on the back."

"Don't you want mine?" Ryan asked.

Cat lifted one brow then got into the truck and rolled down the window. "I already have your numbers, Ryan." She grinned. "*All* of them." She started the deuce's engine. "See you in half an hour."

Ryan watched as she drove away, then shook his head and started walking back toward the compound. "You've got more than my numbers," he muttered under his breath. When he saw the grin on Rodriguez's face he scowled. "What did you see, Airman?"

Rodriguez's smile vanished and he dropped his eyes. "Nothing, sir."

"Exactly." He stood there until the airman looked at him then he smiled and patted the younger man on the back. "Good man. I like you, Rodriguez. I don't care what anybody says."

Chapter Eight

Cat pulled the truck along the outside of the north wall of the hangar, put it in neutral, and set the brake. She hopped down, peered around the wall into the open hangar, and watched as the daytime security guard, a man named Stewart, finished his inspection of the vast, mostly empty space. The man checked that the exterior doors to the adjoining maintenance spaces were locked, rattling each handle in turn, and then he slowly made his way to the central doors that led to the interior spaces. It wasn't until he entered the hallway that her heart began to pound, because now came the fun part: getting the truck back without Stewart realizing it had been taken at all. If she was quick and quiet all would be well. If she wasn't, or if Stewart's hearing was keener than she expected, she was going to have some *serious* explaining to do.

After the blue painted double-doors closed behind him Cat climbed back in the cab and flipped a quick u-turn, the tires squealing softly when they hit the painted concrete. She parked the deuce where she'd taken it from, against the interior of the north wall of the hangar. The engine chugged a couple times when she turned it off, and then all went quiet. The *thump-thump* of her heartbeat throbbed in her ears, and she took a deep breath.

Cat silently counted to ten before moving. As she grasped the metal handle she heard the click of a dead latch, the sound echoing off the walls of the hangar, and a second later one of the heavy blue painted doors swung inward. *Ah, shit.* She quickly ducked down behind the steering wheel, peering through the narrow gap between the side-view mirror and the truck frame. Her pulse went from jog to run. She held her breath as Stewart stuck his head out, a puzzled look on his face.

His gaze swung back and forth, and he did a double-take when he saw the truck. *Go back inside, Stewart, because there's no way any CIA security guard worth a damn would miss a two-and-a-half-ton truck, now is there?* She knew he couldn't see her because the cab was cast in shadow, but her heart continued to pound. He stepped into the hangar and looked at the deuce, obviously confused. *Nothing is wrong, everything is fine, Stewart, just go back inside.* After a few moments, he scratched his head then shrugged and walked back the way he'd come. Cat didn't breathe until well after the door had closed. Once her heart rate was back in the high-normal range, she pocketed the keys, quietly exited the passenger door of the truck, and slipped outside.

She paused, leaned against the outside of the hangar's north wall, and took a breath. Glancing at her watch she saw 12 minutes had passed since leaving the SF compound. Heat surged into her cheeks as she remembered Ryan's kiss and she couldn't stop the smile. Grinning, she set out for her quarters at a dead run.

It took her ten minutes to reach her little house. If Ryan was punctual, and she guessed he would be, that gave her less than ten minutes. Cat grabbed a towel, a robe, and the Ziploc bag that carried her toiletries. Hopefully, there would be an open shower stall.

When she got back into her quarters she had three minutes left before Ryan's arrival. Cat quickly changed into jeans and a button up shirt with a tank top underneath, and then ran a comb through her wet hair. She'd just hung her towel up and tossed her clothes into her locker when there was a soft rap on her door.

Remembering her disappointment of the previous evening, Cat slowly approached the thin, wooden panel. She closed her eyes briefly and took a deep breath.

"Who is it?" she asked, praying Mitchell didn't answer her.

"It's Ryan," he called back.

Cat grinned and did a little dance, then composed herself and opened the door. "Hey."

"Hey, yourself," he replied.

She stepped back. "Come on in," she said. "It's not much but it's home, temporarily."

He hesitated. "I don't think so, Cate."

Cat gaped at him. "Come on, Ryan. It's broad daylight, for Pete's sake."

"Not in there, it's not," he replied with a wry grin. He pointed at one of the windows. "Light blocking curtains, eh?"

"What's the matter?" she asked, lifting one brow. "Worried I'll kiss you?"

Ryan looked at her, his expression solemn. "No. I'm worried *I'll* kiss *you* and *you* won't stop me." He paused and took a step toward her. "Tell me I'm wrong."

Cat gulped and it took her a moment to find her voice. "Well," she said, "I can't say whether or not you'd kiss me, but... you're right. If you did... I wouldn't stop you."

"Which is why I'll stay right here," he said softly.

Heat suffused her cheeks and she looked at her toes, uncertainty pooling in her belly. "I'm sorry if I'm too... *forward* for you—"

"That's not it, Cate," Ryan interrupted her. "Hell, six months ago...." A rueful grin curved his mouth and he ran a hand over his hair. "Six months ago I would have accepted your invitation without thinking twice."

She glanced at him quickly and crossed her arms over her chest. Her uncertainty now had an edge, and it pressed sharply against her heart. "What happened six months ago, girlfriend stab you in the back or something?"

His expression sobered a bit. "No, Taliban actually." He shrugged. "He tried anyway. He failed, but when you come that close to crossing the line between life and death you tend to reevaluate yourself, and the choices you make."

Apprehension curdled in her belly and her throat tightened. "And now... you're thinking twice... about being with me."

He met her eyes, and the intensity of what she saw in that sapphire gaze made her gulp again. He took another step toward her and continued. "I thought about *that* twice before we even left the caves." He dropped his chin. "But, like I told Mack, I don't want to put it in burners just to flame out."

Cat looked at his bowed head for a moment as her brain processed what he said. Relief spun her and she chuckled softly.

Ryan's head snapped up. "What?"

She shook her head and sat down on the top step. "Nothing," she replied. "It's just I have two brothers who fly F-18's for the Navy." She met his gaze. "So, I know *exactly* what you mean."

He seemed relieved and a small smile curved his mouth. "Jet-jocks, huh? Wow. Your father is a Marine Corps colonel, you have two brothers who are fighter pilots, and here you are. What does the rest of your family do?"

"The oldest two, Charlie and Matt, are Marine officers with Force Recon," she replied. "Matt is in Bahrain, and Charlie is in country... somewhere."

"You don't know where?" Ryan asked.

"If I wanted to I could probably find out," she replied. "But we talk every few days, and if he wanted me to know he'd tell me." She looked up. "Despite whom I work for I try *not* to pry into people's business. We leave *that* to the NSA."

He grinned. "So how did you get my numbers? *All* of them?"

She wrinkled her nose and smiled. "Yeah, well, *Lee* has *no* trouble prying into people's business." Heat climbed up her neck and she looked away from him. "I had your numbers before I even showed up at the hospital that first night."

Ryan chuckled and eased down on the step beside her. "Yet you haven't called me, not even once."

"I... I didn't know if I should," she managed to get out, giving him a quick glance. "I *wanted* to, but I...." Her voice died and she ran a hand over her face. "Let's just say my track record with men isn't stellar." Her cheeks went hot.

He took pity on her. "And what do your other brothers do?" he asked with a chuckle.

Her embarrassment faded and she swallowed hard. "Thank you." She cleared her throat and continued. "The two youngest, Eric and Craig, are fighter pilots and my middle brother, Brian, works for the Department of Defense."

"Holy crap," Ryan said, "your whole family works for the government slash military?" He let out a low whistle. "Talk about gluttons for punishment."

"I know, right?" Cat laughed. "Guess it was in the genes."

"What about your mom?" he asked.

A familiar dull ache made her heart throb once and then it faded. "Mom died when I was twelve," she replied. "Car accident. Dad was never the same after that."

"I'm sorry, Cate," he said softly.

"Yeah, me too." She turned toward him. "What about *your* family?"

"Well, you already know me." He gave her a quick grin and a wink. "I'm the oldest of three children and by *far* the least accomplished."

Cat bumped his shoulder. "Yeah, right."

"No," he replied, "seriously. My dad is an aeronautical engineer who works for Grumman, my mom has a PhD in biology and teaches honors level high school science. My younger brother is a pediatric surgeon and my sister is a lawyer." He shook his head and grinned ruefully. "When people find out I'm in the Navy they always pause, blink, and say 'Isn't that nice?' when they're really thinking, 'what the hell happened?'"

"Aw, to hell with them," she said. "What you do is far more important than anything *they* do."

"Is this where you start telling me what I do *here* enables what they do *there?*"

"Are your parents proud of you?" she countered. When he nodded she bumped his shoulder with hers again. "Then that's all that matters. And yes, what you do here enables what they do there."

"Funny," he began, looking at her out of the corner of his eye, "you don't seem like the cheerleader type."

Cat rolled her eyes. "I'm not."

"Bet you'd look great in a short skirt," he commented, a mischievous twinkle in his eye.

"*Don't* go there," she warned.

"Not to change the subject, but why is your hair wet?"

A flutter of insecurity whisked through her and Cat unconsciously ran a hand over the damp waves. "After I took the truck back I ran here, which meant I needed a shower." She looked at him out of the corner of her eye. "Why? Is something wrong?"

The look he gave her made her heart thud.

"No," he replied softly, "but you didn't have to run." He picked up a wet curl and pressed it to his nose, inhaling deeply. "I would've waited for you."

The tone of his voice made her heart somersault and something moved into her esophagus. It took her several moments to find her voice. "There is only so much time we can spend together, Ryan," she said. "I didn't want to waste any of it."

"You are *something*," he mused, those dark blue eyes searching hers. "You *are* the perfect woman."

Perfect? A shaky laugh escaped her and she shook her head, grateful for the chance to break eye contact. His gaze did strange things to her insides, things she was unfamiliar and quite uncomfortable with. After *that day*, her father had never looked at her the same again, and the things he'd said had colored every relationship since then. The men she'd dated after her first kill had looked at her the way Ryan was looking at her now, with desire and even affection, but they hadn't known about her extracurricular activities. Ryan *knew.* The realization that she was in uncharted waters sent a chill of fear through her. She put on her "CIA Face" and swallowed hard.

"I'm about as far from perfect as anyone can get," she replied, "but this I *have* to hear." She gave him a sidelong glance. "C'mon, give it to me."

"You're beautiful," he began, "even without a drop of makeup on."

That flutter settled in her stomach and twirled there. "Depends on the person looking," she shot back.

"You're smart."

Her cheeks burned and that flutter grew stronger. "That depends on who you ask."

"You're a crack shot." When she opened her mouth to speak he pressed a finger to her lips and continued. "You run like a gazelle, you're constantly putting yourself on the line for others, you're an expert in firearms, and...." He paused and that grin returned, ". . . you can be ready to go in under ten minutes. Ask any guy. That, my dear Cate, is the description of the perfect woman."

His humor tempered her embarrassment and Cat groaned. "Men."

"Can't live with 'em," Ryan said, "can't shoot 'em." He chuckled. "Oh, wait. *You* can."

Inwardly she winced. "Perhaps I shouldn't have been so quick on the trigger the other day."

"But then you wouldn't have me sitting here next to you," he said, "completely captivated." He gave her a quick grin and leaned toward her. "I'm your prisoner, Cate. Go easy on me, please."

The memory of her most recent confrontation with Peter roared into her mind, anger and indignation flaring hotly in her chest. She gasped softly and rose in one fluid motion. She stared down at him, and her heart thudded for an entirely different reason now. It pounded against her sternum like a fist on a door. Each beat grated against the inside of her chest as if the fist was wrapped in sandpaper. "I don't want you to be my *prisoner*," she said at last. "I don't want *any* man to be my prisoner."

Ryan stared at her and his brows drew together. "Whoa, Cate. It was a figure of speech." His expression sobered. "Is that Mitchell's problem? Is he still... *captivated?*"

Her throat tightened and she scowled. "I told you I didn't want to talk about him."

"Which answers my question," Ryan said. His eyes narrowed a fraction. "What does he have over you?"

She crossed her arms over her chest and clenched her jaw. "Seniority."

His brows rose. Silent and unblinking he watched her, and she turned her face away. His gaze was intense and made her decidedly uneasy. As the seconds stretched out the anger in her chest faded and cold shame took its place. Ryan wasn't Peter, yet in that split second the two men had merged in her mind. Cat squeezed her eyes shut.

"There are rules against sexual harassment, you know," he said softly.

"I know, but that 'he said, she said' thing can be a real bitch."

He stood and rested his hands on her shoulders. "Do you want me to talk to him?"

Cat's head snapped around and she gaped at him, horrified. "God, no," she said. "No, you don't... no. People who cross Peter seem to... disappear."

Dark brows shot skyward. "What do you mean... *disappear?*"

"Not like *dead* disappeared," she amended. She looked up into those dark blue eyes, eyes filled with concern, and sighed. Shoulders bowed, she sat back down on the top step and rested her elbows on her knees.

"About six years ago, shortly after Peter took over supervising my unit, this analyst started hassling me." Ryan crouched in front of her, bringing them eye to eye and Cat met his gaze. "He was the type who didn't understand the word *no.*"

"And... Mitchell saved you from him."

She nodded. "One day Peter caught him bothering me in the hall outside our offices. He told the guy to go back to work and then asked me what happened." Cat looked away and that cloak of shame got heavier. "I... spilled it, all of it. He listened, quietly, and then said not to worry. The guy wouldn't bother me again."

"And how long did it last?" Ryan asked.

"About a week," Cat replied. She closed her eyes at the memory. "Peter stepped in again and, last I heard, the guy was working a substation in Greenland outside the Arctic Circle."

"But you simply traded one harasser for another," Ryan said. "And how do I fit into all this? Three is usually a crowd, Cate."

Cat's eyes snapped open and a glimmer of panic brightened at the soft, resolute tone of his voice. It was a tone that said he was willing to walk away. She searched his face briefly and wound her fingers through his. "Peter's the one who doesn't fit, Ryan. And he's not competition, if that's what you're thinking."

He scowled. "Do you *really* think that's what I'm thinking?"

She dropped her chin. "I can handle Peter," she replied with a confidence she didn't truly feel. "He knows better than to force himself on me."

"God I'd hope so," Ryan said, "because if he does... if *you* don't shoot him *I* will."

Cat looked up and was surprised by the ferocity she saw in his face. The warmth she'd felt on the day she'd met him returned and expanded and the cloak of shame evaporated. "Protecting the girl again, eh?"

"I would if she'd let me."

Cat disentangled her fingers from his and pressed a hand to his cheek. "Forget about him," she said softly. "He's not even a blip on my radar right now."

Ryan covered her hand with his, then turned his face and kissed her palm. Cat gulped as heat shot up her arm then burgeoned through the rest of her. She sucked in a breath.

"Who *is* on your radar?" he asked, turning those penetrating eyes on her.

She cleared her throat. "I think we both know who." They stared at each other for a few moments and Cat felt the connections being made as electricity shot through her. This thing between them went much farther than simply physical, or at least it did for her. She hoped and silently prayed the feeling went both ways.

The corners of his mouth lifted and he tucked a curl behind her ear. "Want to go on a picnic with me?"

"A picnic?" Cat repeated. She glanced at her watch. "It's barely ten o'clock in the morning, and you want to go on a *picnic...* in *Afghanistan?*"

"Hey," he began, looking at her in mock reproach, "there are parts of this country that are actually quite beautiful and perfect for picnics."

Cat lifted one brow. "Yeah, but that's not *here*, and we're not allowed to leave base." She looked around. "Where exactly are you planning to have this picnic?"

He tucked another strand of hair behind her ear, his fingers lingering on her neck. "Do you trust me?"

Her reply was immediate and absolutely true. "With my life." A sliver of fear lodged in her heart.

He blinked, then stood and held out his hand. "Then come on. I have just the place."

***

Ryan leaned back against the rock and watched as Cat waved at a departing F-15. The pilot must have seen her because shortly after that he "waved" back with the plane, bobbing the wings from side to side. Then the engines roared and the aircraft went straight vertical, disappearing into the clouds above. Cat watched until the plane vanished, then she leaned against the rock next to him and put her head on his shoulder.

They sat on a blanket roughly fifty meters from the end of the main runway, a veritable buffet of breakfast foods spread out before them. He'd taken several single serving boxes of cereal from the mess hall, a couple cartons of milk and orange juice, apples, oranges, bananas, and grapefruit, two of each, and a carafe of hot chocolate from Green Beans. Oddly enough, they hadn't eaten anything yet.

"You're right; this is the perfect place for a picnic," she said. She shielded her eyes with one hand and stared at the horizon. "Do you forgive me for doubting you?"

She turned her face toward him and he felt himself pulled into that green gaze. "I think I'd forgive you anything." His pulse notched up a bit. "So, consider yourself forgiven."

"That was easy," she said, a mischievous grin twitching about her mouth. "I was hoping for some sort of... penance or something."

Ryan smiled. "Like what?" Her eyes said much her mouth did not, and his heart rate increased a little more.

"I don't know," she said softly. "Surprise me."

His smile faded and he traced the line of her jaw. "You have no idea what you do to me, do you?"

Her expression turned wistful. "Maybe the same thing you do to me?"

He looked at her lips. "This is happening *way* too fast."

"I know."

Ryan moved closer. "So... how do you get off a speeding train?"

"You don't," she replied in a whisper. "You hang on and go with it."

Just as he lowered his head something beeped softly and they both jumped. Cat looked at him in surprise and he growled in frustration.

"It's my pager," he said. "Mack, if this is you or Grady I'm going to kill someone."

Cat giggled and picked up an apple, biting into it as he jerked the pager from his belt. His stomach dropped when he saw the call back number. She must have noticed the change in his expression because she stopped chewing and said:

"What is it? What's wrong?"

He looked at her. "It's my CO," he replied. "I have to go."

Cat swallowed her mouthful and put the apple aside. "Okay."

He stood and looked at their mostly untouched breakfast, disappointment pooling inside him. "Well, let's pack this up and I'll drive you back—"

Cat rose and put a hand on his arm. "Actually, leave it. I'd like to... stay for a while." She glanced around the rock-strewn clay that was typical of the Bagram valley. The landscape was barren, almost completely devoid of plant life, but it had a stark beauty all its own. The Hindu Kush Mountains loomed to the east and north, the jagged peaks adorned with a glistening, snowy blanket that never entirely melted. "I think I may have found a new favorite place...." She paused and glanced at him, ". . . if you don't mind sharing, that is."

"Not at all," he assured her, "but I'm not leaving you here by yourself." She smiled and pulled up the leg of her jeans, revealing the pistol in the ankle holster. Although the presence of the weapon should have made him feel better, at least a little, it didn't.

"You're not the only one who's packing, Ryan. We both know I can use a gun, and a lot has changed since that guy in D.C. put his hands on me."

Ryan grasped her waist and tugged her closer. "I don't feel right just leaving you here."

Cat looked up at him and flattened her hands on his chest. "Duty calls, Lieutenant." She smoothed the fabric of his uniform. "Now, kiss me and get going before you get in trouble."

"Cate—"

She put a finger to his lips. "Kiss me."

Ryan searched her eyes for a moment, then cupped her head in his hands and covered her mouth with his. It was like coming in contact with liquid fire. He tasted the cherry lip balm and then the apple when she met his tongue with hers. He slid one hand down her back and pressed her closer as her fingers fisted in the front of his uniform. Warmth started in the pit of his stomach and roiled through him until even his fingers and toes tingled. He wanted desperately to feel her skin against his, and that was when he pulled back. His heart pounded against his sternum as if it wanted out of his chest, and in that moment he gave it to her without reservation. Ryan pressed his brow to hers and tried to catch his breath.

His gaze wandered over her face, committing each feature to memory. Her breathing was fast and shallow, her cheeks pink and glowing, her lips soft and so, so close. Ryan let out a frustrated growl. "I don't want to go."

"Yes, you do," she whispered. She framed his face and looked deeply into his eyes. "Now get moving, and be safe."

He nodded. "I'll call you as soon as I can."

The dimples appeared. "*You* can call me anytime, sailor." She kissed him quickly. "I'll be waiting."

Cat watched as he walked back to the Humvee, her disappointment growing with each step he took. He paused at the door and waved, then got in, started the engine, and pulled away. She stood there until the vehicle disappeared in a cloud of dust. Her eyes stung and she blinked rapidly. With a dispirited sigh, she sat down by the rock and picked up her apple.

***

Ryan strode into the SF Command Center ten minutes later and was greeted by Mack, Grady, and Lieutenant Pearson, nicknamed Voodoo. He was a few years younger than Ryan, with black hair, brown eyes, and full sleeve tattoos. Ryan grinned and grasped Voodoo's arm.

"Hey, Reaper," Voodoo said.

"Hey, Voodoo," Ryan replied. "You filling in for Digger?"

"Yeah," Voodoo said with a nod. "You assholes are stuck with me until Hollywood is up and running again."

"Aw, shit," Mack said. "Don't we deserve better? I thought the CO *liked* us, Reaper."

Ryan laughed. "As long as they don't send us on any critical missions, we should be all right." They fell into step and made their way toward the main briefing room. "Any idea what's up?"

Voodoo shook his head. "Nope."

"Might be a pickup mission," Grady said. "You know my buddy, Johnston, the Ranger guy? He was telling me they went out night before last but had to abort."

Ryan gave Grady a wry look. "Sounds like Johnston talks too much." He paused and poked a finger in Grady's chest. "*Don't* let me catch you making that same mistake."

Grady held his hands up. "Not on your life, Reaper. I let *them* talk." A sly smile curved his mouth. "I sit and listen."

The four men walked into the main briefing room and Commander Ferris looked up from the map he stood over.

"Glad you could make it, gentlemen," Ferris said. He gave Ryan an apologetic glance. "Sorry to cut your date short, Lieutenant."

Ryan groaned inwardly.

"Date?" Voodoo repeated. "Oh, wait. Were you out with that redhead? Now *that* is a target I'd take out with extreme prejudice." He clapped Ryan on the back. "I'll bet she's one fine—" Voodoo gasped and doubled over when Grady elbowed him in the gut.

"You were saying, sir?" Grady said as if nothing had happened.

"Nice one, kid," Mack said with a chuckle.

"Finished, boys?" Ferris asked with wry twist of his lips. "Let me know so I can begin the briefing."

Ryan scowled at each man in turn. "They're done, sir. What do we have?"

Ferris turned 180 degrees and faced a large screen. He motioned to a petty officer manning a keyboard and a picture appeared.

"Meet Tariq Hassan," Ferris announced. "He's a cousin to the current Afghan President, and he's been an information broker to the US for several years. Somehow, he's managed to keep his affiliation with us secret until about a month ago. Since word got out there have been three attempts on his life, the most recent at a safe house in Kandahar."

A picture of a demolished building that looked as if it had once been apartments popped up. The level of destruction was mind-boggling and Ryan let out a low whistle.

"Eighteen people died in the bombing, but Hasan escaped." Ferris faced them. "The alphabet agencies think he's proven his worth and are determined to keep this guy on the hook. CIA has him in protective custody now and will be sending him stateside ASAP."

Ryan frowned. "If he's already in protective custody what are *we* doing, sir?"

"Going after the man's family."

"Sir?"

Ferris sighed as a picture of a woman and four young girls appeared on the screen. "After the first attempt on Hasan's life he sent his wife and four daughters into hiding." He turned and leaned over the map-covered table. "They were taking refuge in this village here." Pausing, he tapped the map with his index finger. "Since the bombing, Hasan has refused to cooperate unless his wife and daughters are brought into protective custody with him and the US Government *wants* his cooperation." He met Ryan's eyes. "It's our job to get them out."

"Simple extraction?" Voodoo said. "Sounds like a cakewalk to me."

"When is anything *ever* simple in this fucking country?" Mack shot back. He looked at his CO. "Sorry, sir. What's the catch?"

"The catch is we already tried to extract the family once," Ferris replied. "Two nights ago, a squad of Rangers made contact. The packages refused evac, quite adamantly, and the Rangers were forced to abort."

"Fucking Army," Voodoo said with a shake of his head and a good-natured grin. "The dogs couldn't get 'em out so they send in the SEALs. Should've *started* with us."

"Why would they refuse evac, sir?" Grady asked, puzzlement furrowing his brow.

"They're women," Ryan replied, meeting his CO's gaze. "Muslim law forbids women to associate or even talk with men who aren't their husbands or blood relatives."

"That's problem number one," Ferris agreed. "Problem number two? They don't speak English and we don't have a translator to send with you."

Ryan ran a hand over his brow and exhaled slowly. *This* was going to get messy.

"Why not, sir?" Mack asked.

Ferris sighed. "The law of supply and demand, Mack. Many have taken their language skills to more lucrative, less dangerous jobs in the private sector, and the stepped up attacks by AQ and the Taliban on interpreters and their families is proving quite effective on the local front." He shrugged his broad shoulders. "We simply don't have any."

"So," Ryan started, "we're expected to do what, sir? Bind, gag, and kidnap them?"

Ferris leaned his hands on the edge of the table and looked at Voodoo. "Still think it's going to be a cakewalk, Lieutenant Pearson?"

"And they call *me* Mouth," Grady mused under his breath.

"It's easier than most of the missions your team has been assigned," Ferris said, "but it will still present significant challenges." He pointed to a different spot on the map. "After the Rangers aborted Mrs. Hasan fled to a different site with her daughters here, south/southwest of Charikar."

"Do we have confirmation on the new location, sir?" Ryan asked.

Ferris nodded. "Just received word she contacted her husband a few hours ago, and he relayed their coordinates." He gestured for them to come closer and fanned a stack of photos out on the table. "Here are the latest satellite and reconnaissance photos."

Ryan peered at the images. The village was comprised of eight mud and brick huts clustered close together on a hillside.

"Supposedly, the women are holed up here." Ferris pointed to a building on the northern edge of the village. "I don't care how you get them out, gentlemen. Just get them out and get back here."

"Looks like we *will* have to bind, gag, and kidnap them," Mack commented dryly.

Ryan rubbed his beard, his eyes on the photos and his mind working furiously. "Maybe not."

"What are you thinking, Reaper?" Ferris asked.

A slow smile spread over Ryan's face and he met his CO's gaze. "I think I may have the solution to both problems, sir."

Ferris looked at him dubiously. "And what is that?"

"Not what," Ryan said, "but who."

His CO's expression darkened.

"Not interested in guessing games, Lieutenant," Ferris said.

"You met the solution this morning, sir," Ryan said.

Ferris's brows drew together. "Beckett?"

"You want to bring Red in on this?" Mack asked in disbelief. "I know she's good in a fight, Reaper, but I'm not following you on this one."

Ryan looked at his teammates then his CO. "She's a translator, sir, *and* female."

"A translator?" Ferris repeated. His expression was dubious. "Are you certain? I've put in requests at every agency for an interpreter and was told there were none available."

"Technically she's not an interpreter, sir," Ryan replied. "She's a watchdog, a *covert* watchdog. Only a few people know she's fluent, and I'm sure they want to keep it that way."

Ferris was quiet for a few seconds. "I can't send a woman into what could potentially be a combat zone, Reaper."

"Why not? Her own agency did." Ryan saw the uncertainty in his commander's eyes and pressed what little advantage he had. "She's not military and she's not a civilian, so that's kind of a gray area." He glanced at Mack then Grady. "She can handle herself, sir."

"That she can, sir," Mack confirmed. "I haven't seen better marksmanship since... well, *ever*. I'd *really* hate to be on the business end of that .416 when Red sights down the barrel."

"She speaks Dari, Pashtu, and several other dialects," Ryan added. He gave Ferris a meaningful look. "It sure would be a lot easier to get those women to safety with her along. They might actually go willingly."

Ferris focused a sharp, probing gaze on him. He stared at Ryan for several long, tense seconds then asked: "Would she do it?"

"Hell, yes, sir," Ryan responded. "All you have to do is ask. Her supervisor may have a problem with it, sir, but I'm sure a few words from General Mason would pave the way."

Ferris narrowed his eyes. "I know you like this woman, Lieutenant, but you've only known her a few days. Assuming I can get *approval* for this crazy idea, how can you be so sure she'll agree to risk her life on what is basically a glorified search and rescue mission?"

"Sir," Ryan began, choosing his words carefully, "there are people you spend a lifetime getting to know, and there are people you spend a few hours with and feel as if you've known them a lifetime. Cate is the latter. I'd trust her with my life, sir." He didn't know why he felt this deep-rooted conviction, but he did. He hoped the commander sensed how serious he was.

"Me, too, sir," Mack said quietly. "She may be female, but I'd have *no* trouble going into combat with her."

"Me either, sir," Grady affirmed.

When Ferris looked at Voodoo the man shrugged. "I've never met her, sir, but I can name at least half a dozen guys in this compound alone who owe her their lives." He glanced at Ryan. "And if Reaper vouches for her that's good enough for me."

Ferris crossed his arms over his chest and stared at Ryan for nearly a minute. Ryan returned his gaze and waited.

"Very well, Lieutenant," Ferris said at last. "Give her a call."

Elation welled up inside him. "I'll do better than that, sir," Ryan said with a grin. "I'll bring her to you."

Chapter Nine

Cat had just finished a second cup of hot cocoa when she noticed a Humvee headed her direction. With a groan, she put the lid on the thermos, gathered up what was left of the food, and stuffed it in the bag Ryan had brought. *Here it comes*, she thought. She rose, folded the blanket, then sat on a rock and waited for Air Force Security Forces to grill her. Getting in trouble wasn't a concern, but explaining her presence at the end of the main runway would be a hassle nonetheless. Sometimes she thought the AFSF had nothing better to do. Oh, wait. They didn't.

When the Humvee pulled to a stop and Ryan hopped out her jaw dropped and that now familiar squadron of butterflies took off, looping wildly in her stomach. She got to her feet and stared at him as he approached her.

"Miss me?" he asked with a grin.

Hell, yeah. "What are you doing here?" she responded as her heart did a flip. "I figured you'd be headed out on a mission or something."

He nodded. "I will be," he said. "Wanna go with?"

She blinked at him, certain she'd heard incorrectly. "What?"

"We need your help."

She felt her brows shoot up. "I didn't think *SEALs* needed *anybody's* help."

"Hey, sometimes we do, and we have no trouble admitting that." Ryan shrugged. "This time we need an interpreter and they're in short supply apparently." He met her gaze. "It would also help if that interpreter was female."

The light bulb went on and Cat's eyes narrowed. "You're going after Tariq Hasan's family, aren't you?" It was more a statement than a question and she waited for his reaction.

He gaped at her. "How did you...? Wait, never mind." He looked at her expectantly. "So, you in? And so you know, I already told Commander Ferris you'd do it. Please don't make me look bad."

Cat stared at him for a few moments, enjoying his uncertainty. When she'd punished him enough she smiled. "When do we leave?" The look of relief on his face almost made her laugh.

"Right now," he said, gesturing toward the Humvee. "Your chariot awaits, my lady. The Commander would like a word with you."

She laughed. "And I'd like a few words with him." She grabbed the blanket while he took the bag of food. "I don't appreciate having our picnic cut short." They walked back to the Humvee and Ryan opened the door for her.

"He did apologize for that," he said. He closed her door then jogged around the front of the vehicle and slid behind the wheel.

Cat buckled up. "Well, I suppose I'll have to cut him some slack then. Onward, Lieutenant."

They drove onto the SF compound past Airman Rodriguez who looked at her in surprise. Cat waved at him and he waved back, his eyes wide and disbelieving.

"I take it you don't have many women walking the hallowed ground of the Special Forces Compound," she commented.

Ryan laughed. "No, not many."

"Then I am honored," she said with all sincerity. "Thanks for thinking of me."

"Thanks for not making me look bad," Ryan replied, looking at her out of the corner of his eye. "And I find myself thinking about you pretty much all the time."

Warmth pooled in her middle, and then a sliver of fear chilled her. "Don't do that, Ryan. I want you focused on your job, not me."

He gave her a wry smile. "I'm a big boy, Cate. I *can* separate work and... other things."

Heat bathed her cheeks and she dropped her gaze. "Of course you can," she said in a low voice.

Ryan parked the Humvee in front of a two-story, brick building that looked like a leftover from the Soviet occupation. What brought it into the 21st century were the satellite dishes, communication towers, and various antennae bristling from the roof. Cat got out of the Humvee and stared at the drab façade. A sense of awe washed over her and her embarrassment faded. Ryan stood at her side and followed the direction of her gaze.

"What?" he asked after a few silent moments.

"I'm just soaking it in," she said quietly. "Part of the reason there have been no major terrorist attacks on American soil since 9/11 is because of what goes on in this building."

Ryan tipped his head to the side. "Never really thought about it that way," he replied, "but I guess you're right." He bumped her shoulder with his. "C'mon. The boss wants to talk to you."

Cat followed Ryan through the double glass doors that had been covered and reinforced with thick plywood sheets. He led her through the labyrinthine hallways, and for a moment she wondered if this was what a rat in a maze felt like. The few people they passed stopped and stared at her and she merely smiled. Finally, they arrived in the control center.

"Hey, Red," Mack said as he strode forward, hand extended. He pumped her hand twice and clapped her on the shoulder. "So, you joining us?"

Cat looked from him to Grady, and the one man she didn't know. She'd seen him earlier when she'd dropped off the ammunition, but she had no idea who he was. "I hear you *need* me," she replied. She gave Ryan a sidelong glance. "But don't worry, I won't tell anyone."

The familiar stranger walked forward to shake her hand. "Hey. I'm Lieutenant Will Pearson, but everyone calls me Voodoo."

"Pleasure to meet you, Voodoo," she replied. "Everyone but Ryan calls me Cat."

"Let me guess," Voodoo began with a grin and a nod Ryan's direction, "*he* calls you sweetheart."

I wish. Cat glanced at Ryan. "Not even my father calls me that."

Ryan crossed his arms over his chest and looked down his nose at Voodoo. "And *he's* a full bird in the Marine Corps, LT. Let that be a warning."

Voodoo's eyes widened and he nodded. "Got it. No offense, Red."

"None taken."

"I take it introductions are over," Ferris said, entering through a door across the room. "Miss Beckett, it's good to see you again."

"You, too, Commander," she replied.

"Reaper filled you in yet?" Ferris asked.

"Just getting started, sir," Ryan said.

"Continue."

The group gathered around the map table and Ryan pushed the stack of photos toward Cat. There were pictures of the village and Hasan's family, and she studied them and the map as Ryan went over the details of the mission. She listened carefully, and was impressed with Ryan's sense of tactics. It was obvious he knew what he was doing, and while it was a relatively easy mission he treated it as if it was the most important mission he could embark upon.

Ryan pointed to a photo of a rocky outcropping which lay east of the village on the valley floor. "This rise is about halfway between Charikar and the village. We'll stop there and do a scan of the hills above and around the location to make sure it's clear. After that we'll drive to this point north of the village, park, and head south on foot along this ridge. We enter the village, make contact with the packages, and get them out. We want as little interaction with the rest of the inhabitants as possible. Ideally, we get in, secure the packages, and get out, and no one will ever know we were there. We'll evac to the north/northeast, looping around the northern end of Charikar, and then home. Any questions?"

Something niggled at the back of her brain. "Which house are they in?" she asked.

"This one," Ferris said, circling the hut on the photo with a red pen.

Cat examined the photos and frowned. "Are you sure?"

"According to Hasan," Ferris said. He looked at her. "Why? What are you thinking?"

She chewed her lip for a couple seconds, her synapses firing in rapid succession. "I'm thinking if I'm hiding out with my daughters, I want to be able to see anyone coming." She moved the photo to the center of the table. "If she's in this house the only view she has is to the south through the center of the village. She's blind on three sides." She tapped her finger against another house. "*This* house sits higher on the hill than the others and faces east, giving her a clear 180-degree view." Looking up, she met Ryan's gaze then Ferris's. "If it was me, that's where *I'd* be hiding."

Ryan rubbed his beard. "I have to agree, sir." He frowned and looked at his CO. "Is it possible Hasan or his wife lied? And if so, why?"

She knew there could be a hundred reasons, but she focused on the most obvious and reasonable one. "She wants to be ready in case you call again," Cat ventured. "If she's devout, she's not going anywhere with strange men, *especially* Americans. I know we'd like to think honor killings are rare, but they *do* happen. Hasan *does* have a profile to maintain."

"Okay." Ryan flipped through the photos again and she could almost hear his mental gymnastics. "We'll approach the same way. Mack, Cate, and I will make for the upper house. Grady, you and Voodoo take the original target. If the target is clear, you join us up top." He met Grady and Voodoo's eyes. "Clear it fast, and if you make contact let us know. Otherwise, sweep and move out."

"Roger that, Reaper," Voodoo said. "When are we hitting the road?"

"2200 hours," Ferris replied. "It'll take you more than an hour to make the drive to the village, and hopefully by the time you get there all the locals will be asleep. If the stars align, you'll get in, get out, and everyone will be happy." Ferris turned to her. "You up for that?"

A thrum of excited anticipation danced through her. "Of course," she replied.

Ferris nodded. "Good. I'll email your supervisor for his approval. Should only be a formality, especially with General Mason on board."

The commander's comment immediately tempered her enthusiasm. "Um, about that," Cat began, "could I talk to you, sir? Alone?"

Ferris's steely eyes met hers, and then he nodded shortly and gestured toward the door through which he'd entered. She met Ryan's eyes briefly and his brows drew together in a frown before he turned his attention back to the photos. Cat preceded the commander through the door into a narrow hallway. When the door closed behind them she turned to the officer.

"Speak, Miss Beckett."

She pondered him for a moment, trying to think of the best way to word her request. "About contacting my supervisor, sir...." She paused and took a deep breath. "Do you think you could wait to do that, sir, at least until we're on our way back with the packages?"

Ferris crossed his arms over his chest and narrowed his eyes on her. "And why would I do that, Miss Beckett? Mr. Mitchell is your supervisor so he should be apprised of the situation."

Cat knew she would have to tread carefully. No matter how much

Commander Ferris cared about his men, his position with SOCOM involved politics, Mitchell's favorite playground. She tried another tack.

"Given your position here, Commander, I'm sure you've read the after-action reports and are familiar with the last few missions I've been deployed on."

"Since they involved Special Forces, Miss Beckett, yes I am."

The unwavering stare he focused on her was almost as sharp as her father's and made her feel like a naughty child.

"There may be a problem regarding sensitive information in my unit," she said. "And we both know the fewer people who have knowledge of an operation, the better the chance of success. That's why we didn't tell the Pakistanis about the raid on OBL's compound."

"Is there a specific reason you want me to keep this under wraps, Miss Beckett?" Ferris asked. He watched her carefully, and Cat had the distinct impression he could read her mind if he wanted.

"No," she said quickly, shaking her head, "nothing specific, sir. I'm going with my gut. You, of all people should understand that."

"I do," Ferris replied. "However, leaving your supervisor in the dark is a breach of protocol."

Cat's brows drew together. "Well, sir, not... *really*," she said, giving him a beseeching look. When he frowned she ran a hand over her eyes. "Sir, I'm on liberty until 0700 Monday which, technically, means I'm on my own time."

"*Technically*," Ferris repeated, a grim smile hovering on his mouth.

"Yes, sir." Cat pressed her lips into a thin line. "I just think waiting until *after* we've completed the objective to notify Mr. Mitchell would be the best course of action. I would prefer to err on the side of caution, sir, and it's not me I'm worried about. It's the mission. Hasan is an important asset, and the US Government is willing to do just about anything to keep him on the payroll. This may not be as critical as many of the missions you've planned, but I'll bet there are people well above *both* our pay grades who think it is. Correct me if I'm wrong."

Ferris bored holes through her with those sharp, grey eyes, his features as unreadable as granite. After a few tense moments, the corners of his mouth moved upward a fraction.

"E-mails do get lost in cyberspace all the time, Miss Beckett," he said in a low voice, "especially here."

Cat almost heaved a sigh of relief. "Yes, they do, sir."

"And, *technically* speaking," Ferris began, a conspiratorial glint in his eyes, "General Mason is aware of your participation so notifying Mr. Mitchell would only be a courtesy, nothing more."

Cat couldn't stop the grin. "Correct, sir."

"And, since Mr. Mitchell told me he didn't *have* any translators available when I asked for one," Ferris continued, "I think I'm fresh out of courtesy today."

She didn't bother to hide her relief. "Thank you, Commander."

"You're welcome, Miss Beckett," the man replied. "Now, let's finish this briefing. You and my team are going to need to get some rest before 2200 hours."

"Yes, sir."

She and the Commander returned to the briefing room and the table where Ryan and the other SEALs were finalizing the mission details.

"Is everything okay, sir?" Ryan asked when she and Ferris joined them.

"Everything is perfect, Reaper," the commander replied. "Please, continue."

When the briefing concluded Commander Ferris dismissed the team and then left through the same door through which he had entered. Cat sat down in a nearby chair as Grady, Mack and Voodoo made their way toward the opposite exit.

"You coming, Reaper?" Voodoo asked.

"In a minute," Ryan replied, his eyes on her. "I want to go over it one more time with Cate."

Voodoo grinned. "I think she understands —"

"Move, asshole." Mack grabbed the back of Voodoo's uniform and jerked him out the door. "The man said he wants to go over it again."

Cat chuckled and met Ryan's concerned gaze when the heavy industrial double doors shut with an ominous click. He leaned against the map table, arms crossed over his chest.

"Is everything okay?" he asked.

Cat rose and stood in front of him. "Everything is perfect. Didn't you hear the Commander?"

"I want to hear it from you." He jerked his head toward the Commander's private entrance. "What was all that about?"

"Let's say I want to keep the circle of information on this mission... *tight*," she said. "As in, keep it confined to the people in this room and

General Mason."

Ryan stared hard at her. "What about Mitchell? Isn't he in the loop of 'need to know'?"

"Nope," Cat said with a shake of her head, "not this time."

"Why not?"

"Because I don't want this mission going the way of my last three," she said flatly. "The fewer people who know, the better. That's SOP for any mission, you know that."

"But he's your supervisor," he argued.

Cat scowled. "I know." His expression turned speculative, his gaze direct and unwavering. He was doing the math, she could sense it. A worm of apprehension crawled up her spine.

"You think he's dirty."

"I didn't say that," she said softly.

"But you *feel* it."

Cat returned his stare, the strength in those dark blue eyes sending her nerves into overdrive. After a few moments of visually battling with him she sighed and looked away. "Yeah." Her head snapped up and she poked a finger in his chest. "And that stays between *us*, understood?"

Ryan nodded. "Of course." He made the motion of locking his mouth shut and tossing away a key. "To the grave."

"Don't talk like that," Cat said. "It's bad luck."

A faint smile curved his mouth. "I don't believe in luck. I believe in skill and training, which is why I surround myself with highly skilled, highly trained people." He sat down in a chair next to her and picked up one of the satellite photos. "So, what do you really think of the plan?"

"It's solid," she said.

"Any suggestions?" Ryan asked. "I have no trouble with a woman's input."

"I can't think of anything right now, but I reserve the right to revise that at a later time, even right in the middle of the shit if necessary."

"That's cool." He smiled. "I'm not crazy about changing an op midstream, but I'll try to remain open-minded. After all, it's happened before."

"I'll bet." Cat grinned. "Now, since there is the potential for armed confrontation, I assume there won't be a problem with me packing heat?"

"Only if you *don't* bring that bazooka of yours," Ryan replied. "You're a damn fine shot with that necked-down .50, and I'd much rather have targets taken out from a distance than have any CQB going on. Too many locals around that could get hurt."

"Agreed." After a brief silence, she rose. "Well, Lieutenant, I don't know about you but I have a few things that I need to do before we embark on our journey later this evening. Can I beg a ride back to my place, or should I start jogging now?"

Ryan stood and smiled. "I am at your service, my lady. Allow me to escort you back to your chariot."

***

Cat had just finished cleaning her rifle when there was a soft knock on her door. She was pretty sure it wasn't Ryan, so she slowly approached the panel and said, "Who's there?"

"It's Peter, Catharine." There was a brief pause. "I thought we could go get that dinner you promised me."

Cat groaned and ran a hand over her face. "Seriously?" she said under her breath. "Your timing is *impeccable*, for suck-ass timing."

She couldn't really turn Mitchell down without arousing his suspicion, and that was the *last* thing she wanted to do. Cat's mind worked furiously to find a solution to this new problem and came up empty. Finally, she sighed and opened the door.

"It's three o'clock, Peter," she said, interposing herself across the doorway. "A little early for dinner, don't you think?" He gave her a look that at one time would have charmed her. Now all it did was make her angry.

"Well, I figured you'd have plans with the SEAL for later," he began, giving her his most endearing smile, "so I thought if I wanted to see you at all I'd have to make it early."

"Always thinking about me, aren't you?" she asked, with more than a little sarcasm.

His expression sobered. "Pretty much, yes."

"Please. The last time you thought about anyone but you was... well, *never*."

He took a step toward her. "That's not true." He reached for her hand but she pulled away. Mitchell sighed and dropped his chin. "I wish things between us could be different. They *could* be if you'd give me a chance. Losing you, Catharine, is my biggest regret."

"Getting *caught* was your biggest regret," Cat shot back. "Still want to have dinner?"

"I may be a glutton for punishment," he began with a small smile, "but I am hoping we can move past what happened between us. We do have to work together, and it would be nice not to be at odds with you all the time."

Anger simmered in her belly. "The only time we're at odds is when you try to insinuate yourself into my work or my life," she said flatly. "You're my supervisor, you're not my friend, and you're not my lover. You are a co-worker, period."

"It wasn't always like that," he said softly. He gave her a lusty once over. "We were far more to each other once. I remember you always liked it when I—"

"Don't," she interrupted him. She stared at him for a moment and tried to reign in her temper. Finally, she sighed. "Look, I said I'd go with you so I'll go, but I'm up to my elbows in gun oil. Let me wash up then we can get an early dinner."

"Okay."

Apparently, he thought that was an invitation to enter her quarters. He put his foot on the second step and Cat planted a hand in the middle of his chest.

"I don't think so," she said. "You can wait out here."

"Catharine—"

She pushed him back. "Don't *Catharine* me," she said. "And I do have plans for later, so let's make this short and sweet."

Cat closed and locked the door, then left her quarters through the back way and walked quickly to the showers. After washing up she returned to her little house, put on clean clothes, and sat on the edge of her bed. She stared at the door, scowling. The *last* thing she wanted was to sit down at a table across from Mitchell, make small talk, and pretend she had anything other than utter disdain for the man. Finally, she sighed and got to her feet.

When she slowly opened the door Mitchell rose from his seat on the steps and backed up a few paces. He gave her a hopeful look, as if buying her dinner would magically erase their past. Cat pasted a serene expression on her face.

"Lead the way," she said.

Mitchell smiled and they walked to his SUV which was parked around the corner. Cat said nothing as they drove to the chow hall, and Mitchell was also silent. Every few seconds he would glance at her, but she kept her eyes forward.

"Why can't we be friends, Catharine?" he asked at last.

"I try not to be friends with people who lie on a regular basis," she replied in a monotone. "And what would be the point? I have no desire to rekindle anything with you."

"If you'd give me a chance—"

"Stop," she said, turning to him. "Just stop, please." Cat rubbed her eyes and faced forward. "I really don't want to be a bitch to you but I also don't want to be anything else. What happened between us happened, but nothing like that will *ever* happen again. If we have to work together, I can deal with that but *stop* trying to turn it into something it isn't."

"I'm sorry," he said softly.

They rode the rest of the way to the dining hall in silence. Once there they walked in together and Mitchell held the door for her, a penitent expression on his face. After they got their food they sat at a booth near a window facing the flight line. Cat picked up a fork and picked at her meal.

Just when she thought it couldn't get any more uncomfortable, Ryan, Mack, Grady, and Voodoo walked in. Her heart skipped a beat and something in her face must have changed because Mitchell's brows drew together. Cat turned her eyes to her food, but not quick enough. Mitchell glanced over his shoulder and his expression darkened.

"You used to look at me like that," he said in a low, taut voice.

"Key phrase in that sentence was 'used to'," Cat replied. She took a bite of her pasta and watched as the four men got their trays and sat down at a table on the other side of the dining room. Mack was the first to spot her, and he gave her a grin and a wave. Cat smiled and waved back as three more heads turned her direction. She saw the surprise in Ryan's eyes before it was quickly masked. He nodded to her and smiled then bent over his plate.

"The agreement was I give you and your team some time off if you have dinner with *me*," Mitchell said flatly. "Could you at least *try* not to drool over the man while we're together?"

Her gut contracted and she turned incredulous eyes to him. "I am sitting with you, Peter, but we *are not* together. You and I will *never* be together again. Get that through your head... *now*."

That strange light she'd seen the previous evening was back in Mitchell's eyes and a sliver of fear wormed up her spine. She realized she *had* seen that look before and a snapshot of her past vaulted into her mind's eye. It was the same look he'd given her when she'd confronted him about his wife, the look that told her he was mentally scrambling to avoid getting caught in a compromising situation. Her brain pressed a button and the memory started to play.

"Don't tell me you're not married," Cat said. "I *saw* you with her, and it didn't look like either of you wanted to be anywhere but with each other."

Peter looked at her as if she was a recalcitrant child. "Catharine, Gretchen and I merely had dinner to discuss the summer arrangements for the kids. I told you we were still friendly, for the sake of the children."

"I checked your file, Peter." Cat crossed the room, heading for the door. "You don't *have* any children, so save your breath, and I was *in* the restaurant. The two of you couldn't keep your hands, or lips, off each other, so stop with the lies."

His hand snaked around her upper arm with a viselike grip. "You've been checking up on me... *following* me?"

Cat looked at his hand then his face, and for the first time since meeting him she was afraid. "Actually, I was across the street in that tailor shop you love so much, buying you a tie when you and your wife pulled up in front of the restaurant." She tried to shake his hand off but his grip only tightened. "Peter, you're hurting me."

"I love you, Catharine," he said in a low, calm voice. "Don't do this to us."

She jerked away from him. "There *is* no *us*," she shot back. "Go back to your wife. It's obvious she loves you, though I'll never understand why."

Nausea burgeoned sharply and she mentally pushed STOP. She knew why Peter continued to show up every time she turned around. He was stalking her, obsessed, and while she'd understood that she'd never acknowledged what a dangerous problem it was until now. After all, she was *Cat Beckett*, CIA sniper, killer of men, and she could handle *anything*. She closed her eyes and took a deep breath, realizing she had deluded herself. The problem she'd expected to diminish over time wasn't going away, it was getting worse. She clenched her jaw. It was time to try something other than denial and diplomacy. It was time to end this.

"This was a mistake," she said. She put her fork down and pushed her tray away. "I shouldn't have come here." Mitchell grabbed her wrist, hard, and she looked up in surprise. "Peter, you're hurting me." She tried to twist away but his grip only tightened. *"Let go of me."*

"He can't do for you what I can," Mitchell said from between clenched teeth. "You have no idea what I'm capable of. I could give you the world."

She again tried to twist out of his grip, and in the background she heard the sound of a chair being violently pushed back. She knew it was Ryan without even looking.

"I don't want *anything* from you," Cat said, anger burning hotly through her. "And you can rest assured, first thing Monday morning I am putting in a transfer request and telling the Agency my continued employment with them *depends* on you and I *never* working together again." She finally managed to jerk away from him and got to her feet, but Mitchell rose and grabbed her arm, his fingers digging painfully into her flesh.

"You won't get rid of me that easily," Mitchell said under his breath. "No matter where you go, I'll find you. I'll *always* find you."

"Let go of her," she heard Ryan say as if from a great distance.

Cat brought her left fist around and punched Mitchell square in the ear. The man dropped like a stone, hitting his head on the edge of the table on the way down, and she stepped back. She felt Ryan behind her, his hands on her shoulders as she stared at Mitchell's unconscious form, her lungs refusing to function.

"Whoa, nice one, Red," Mack said.

Someone whistled softly. "Damn straight she's good in a fight."

"Shut up, Voodoo," Grady said.

"Cate."

It was Ryan's voice but she couldn't tear her eyes from Mitchell lying prone on the floor. Finally, her body kicked into gear and she sucked in a breath. Ryan turned her to face him and leaned over to look her in the eye.

"Cate, are you all right?"

The sound of his voice and the gentle touch of his hands on her shoulders brought her back to reality. She blinked, gulped, and nodded. Over his shoulder she saw the AFSF headed their way and sighed. "Great."

Ryan turned and looked in the direction of her gaze then faced her again. "Don't worry about them." He took her arm and softly stroked the angry red marks on her wrist and above her elbow. "Once they see these, you won't be the one getting in trouble."

"Maybe not with *them*," she said. She paused and glanced over her shoulder at Mitchell who was starting to stir. "But with *him?*" Cat ran a hand over her eyes. "He'll make *one* phone call, it will all go away, and I'll be right back where I started."

"We all saw what he did," Mack said. "With an entire chow hall full of eyewitnesses, it won't be so easy to make these charges disappear."

"All right," the Air Force sergeant said. The name Anderson was stitched over the front right pocket of his uniform. "Break it up. What's going on?"

Cat was shell-shocked and numb as Ryan explained to Sergeant Anderson what had happened, the rest of the SEAL team backing up his story. She answered the sergeant's questions succinctly, and when the man saw the marks on her arm he scowled and indicated for his compatriots to pick Mitchell up. Mitchell was now conscious but dazed, and the security police had to carry him out of the chow hall because he couldn't walk unassisted. Curious onlookers gaped and whispered, their gazes moving from Mitchell to Cat and back.

"I need you to come down to our station, miss," Anderson said, looking at her with obvious sympathy. "I need photographs of those bruises to submit with my report."

She nodded.

"I'll bring her over in a few minutes," Ryan told the man.

"Okay, Lieutenant. We'll be expecting you."

Mack, Grady, and Voodoo had retreated to their table but they weren't eating. She glanced at them and smiled when Mack winked at her and gave her thumbs up. Ryan shook his head and chuckled.

"Well, Mack certainly approves," he said dryly.

"You don't?" she asked in a wooden voice.

Ryan stood in front of her and frowned. "Hell, yeah, I approve," he replied. "If you hadn't hit him I was going to." He studied her for a moment. "Come on, Tiger. The sergeant is waiting. I'll drive."

"Okay."

Cat walked toward the entrance to the chow hall, Ryan's hand in the small of her back. The lookey-loos were still looking and whispering, but she ignored them. Once outside Ryan led the way to the Humvee, opening her door for her with a small smile. She met his gaze, climbed in, and buckled up.

Ryan was silent as they pulled away from the dining hall, his expression a blank slate. After he made the turn onto Disney Drive, Cat stared out the window and sighed.

"I'm sorry, Ryan."

"For what?" When she didn't look at him he reached over and turned her face to his. His expression was fierce, dark brows drawn together. "Hey. You don't need to apologize for anything. You didn't do anything wrong." He released her and put his hand back on the wheel.

She shook her head and covered her eyes. "I should never have gone there with him."

"I *was* sort of surprised to see you with him," Ryan said in a low voice. "Why were you with him?"

Cat scowled and self-reproach climbed into her throat. "Because I'm an idiot." When she glanced at him Ryan lifted one brow and she dropped her gaze. "I agreed to have dinner with him."

"Why?"

Cat planted a foot on the dashboard and rolled the window down, needing the air. It was several moments before she spoke, and when she did her voice was hushed. "My team and I have been in country for nearly three months, and it's been *nonstop* since we landed. We went straight from one mission to the next without a break." She frowned. "After this last op went south I asked Peter what it would take to get the team the weekend off."

"Let me guess," Ryan began, "having dinner with him is what it took." He turned his gaze to the road. "I know we've spoken about sexual harassment, Cate. Why do you keep giving this guy a pass?"

"Because I thought I could handle it," she said, nearly choking on the guilt and remorse. The emotions clotted in the back of her throat, dark and viscous. "What was an hour of my time if it meant a three-day liberty for my team?"

"I don't know your team very well," Ryan said softly, "but I don't think they'd want you to put yourself in that position, even if it meant a month off."

The understandable observation didn't make her feel better. "I know. Like I said, I'm an idiot."

The conversation died as he pulled into the parking lot of the AFSF main office, which was nothing more than a large tent in the middle of a large field covered with gravel. Cat looked at the tan canvas for a long moment then turned to Ryan. What she'd expected to see in his eyes and what she actually saw was so different her breath caught.

"Are you really okay?" he asked in a whisper, concern etched on those handsome features. He pressed a hand to her cheek, his gaze roving over her face. "Maybe you should sit out the mission tonight. We'll hogtie the women and drag them back."

Cat covered his hand with hers and smiled. "Not on your life, Ryan. I'll be fine."

"It's not only you," he said. "I have to think of the entire team and the op."

"I know," she replied. "You need everyone at 100%. I'll be fine, I promise."

He stared at her for another moment or two then nodded once. "Okay. Let's go get this over with. He's not getting a pass this time."

Chapter Ten

To Cat's surprise, the whole process with the Security Forces was relatively painless. She gave her statement to Sergeant Anderson, pulled up her sleeve so he could photograph the red marks that would undoubtedly turn into bruises, and then signed the bottom of his report. All in all, she was in the bustling tent for just over an hour. During all of this Ryan had given his statement to another officer, then pulled up a nearby chair and sat down. Every time she glanced at him he gave her a smile. His presence alone made the process much easier.

"Where is he?" she asked as the sergeant was putting his own signature on the report.

Anderson looked up briefly. "Mr. Mitchell? He's in the brig, ma'am."

Cat thought about that for a moment, and the mental picture pleased her. "Hmm. That's actually one place in the world he's probably never been and never thought he would ever go. Poetic."

"Justice," Ryan added softly.

Anderson gave a humorless chuckle. "I just got off the phone with the quartermaster before you two walked in." He met her gaze. "Apparently, your friend is none too happy with his new digs and is quite vocal about it. Insists you attacked him."

"Of course, I did. That's what everyone saw, isn't it?"

One corner of Anderson's mouth lifted in a grim smile. "Yes sirree, Bob, it sure is. That's why you're the one with the bruises and he's the one behind bars." He closed the manila folder and extended his hand to her. "Sorry for what happened to you, ma'am. Hopefully this will teach him a lesson and he'll stay away from you."

Cat shook the man's hand and rose. "It won't," she replied, "because he's my supervisor. Monday morning will sure be interesting."

"Can I make a suggestion, ma'am?" Anderson asked. When she

nodded he continued. "If this happens again, punch him in the throat as hard as you can. Sometimes to defend yourself you have to put somebody else down... sometimes permanently." He grinned. "But you didn't hear that from me."

Cat smiled. "Of course not, Sergeant."

"I didn't hear it either," Ryan said, rising to shake the sergeant's hand. "Thanks, Sergeant. I'll make sure she gets home."

"Very good, Lieutenant." He turned to her and handed her a business card. "If he gives you any more trouble you call me, Miss Beckett, any time of the day or night."

"Thank you, Sergeant. I'm sorry for all the trouble."

"Don't be," he said with a dismissive wave of his hand. "I was there for an early dinner, and you livened up an otherwise routine and dull day. I should be thanking you." He smiled. "You take care now."

Cat nodded and preceded Ryan out of the tent.

"Well, that was easier than expected," Ryan commented. "Do you really think he'll bother you again after all this?"

She walked to the passenger side of the Humvee and leaned against it, looking up at Ryan as he moved to stand in front of her. "I don't know," she admitted.

"Has he ever put his hands on you before?" he asked in a low voice.

She nodded slowly. "Once. Peter and I were... romantically involved, a long time ago. About a month in I found out he'd lied about being divorced. I broke it off with him and he grabbed me like that. The difference was he didn't do it in front of dozens of people, and he only touched me once." She frowned and met Ryan's gaze. "Something else is going on with him, Ryan. It's not like him to be so... *obvious*. Peter doesn't *do* things he can't get away with."

Her mind flew back to the hidden cell phone bill she'd found in Mitchell's office. Something in her gut told her there was a connection, but right now she had more important matters to focus on, such as the upcoming mission with Ryan and his team. After they'd rescued Hasan's family she could start digging.

"What is it?" Ryan asked, studying her face carefully.

"Nothing," she replied. She met his dubious gaze and smiled. "Thanks for being here."

"You bet." He reached for the door handle. "Come on. I'll take you home. We have a mission tonight."

Cat moved so he could open the door then climbed in. "Yes, we do."

After closing her door, he ran around to his side and got behind the wheel. "All right. I'll drop you off, head back to the compound to take a nap, and then I'll swing by and pick you up at 2130—"

"No," she interrupted, "that's not a good idea."

Ryan's brows drew together in a scowl. "Why not?"

She closed her eyes as the enormity of her situation hit her fully upside the head. She wouldn't blame Ryan at all if he decided to cut her from the mission; if she was in his shoes she would probably do the same. Under the circumstances, her twisted relationship with Peter had morphed from a personal nuisance into a professional problem.

"Cate?"

She took a deep breath and stared at the toes of her boots. "I think Peter's having me followed." A lump formed in her throat. "You know, maybe I *should* sit out tonight. Right now, it seems I'm more of a liability than an asset."

"I don't believe that," Ryan said, "but if *you* do... maybe you should." He reached for her hand. "I've seen you under pressure and you didn't even blink. You weren't expecting us to crash your party, you weren't expecting to have to bug out of your mountain caves, but you handled those curveballs without skipping a beat." He pressed his lips to her fingers. "You going to let an ass like Mitchell throw you off your game?"

Cat stared into the blue eyes of the man who was very quickly worming his way into her heart, and something in her chest swelled. The sensation both frightened and exhilarated her. "How can you have such faith in me? We've only known each other a few days."

Ryan's expression softened. "In this line of work, you learn to become an expert judge of character in a fraction of the time." He released her hand and brushed his knuckles over her cheek. "Like I told Ferris, there are some people you spend a lifetime getting to know...."

"And others you just meet and feel like you've known them a lifetime," Cat finished in a whisper. She gulped and closed her eyes against the onslaught of emotions that rolled over her. Ryan warmed her and at the same time scared the hell out of her, bringing on an icy wave of apprehension she couldn't direct. She was accustomed to controlling her feelings, but with Ryan it was next to impossible. She turned her face toward the window and took several deep breaths.

When Ryan pulled to a stop in front of her housing area he turned off the Humvee's engine. "What's wrong, Cate?"

"Nothing, other than I'm back on that speeding train, and I'm not sure how I feel about it," she replied. Before he could move or speak she opened the door and hopped out. She started to walk away, but guilt rose like bile. She couldn't leave him like that. Gravel crunched beneath his boots as he slowly approached her and she forced herself to face him. "Thanks again for having my back." Heat crawled up her neck and she dropped her gaze. "You know, I don't think I would've had the nerve to hit him if you hadn't been there."

"Then I'm doubly glad I was," he replied. "And you dropped him like a bad habit."

Cat chuckled and glanced at him. "I did, didn't I?" This time when she looked up she found herself caught in that sapphire gaze, unable to look away. Her pulse pattered against her larynx, a sensation she usually felt only when sighting down the barrel of her rifle.

A pensive smile curved his mouth. "You should get some rest," he suggested. "I'll see you in a few hours." He paused and his brows drew together. "I *will* see you in a few hours, won't I?"

"You certainly will," she said, that pattering speeding up into a steady thrum. "You guys need me."

His brows shot skyward and he looked at her in mock surprise. "We do?"

"Yes," she answered. "See, *you* tend to handle the women with kid gloves. Me?" She shrugged and grinned. "I don't have that problem."

Ryan chuckled. "Roger that, Tiger. 2130."

"2130," she affirmed. "I'll be there."

***

Ryan finished tying the black turban around his head and glanced at the clock. 9:15 p.m. After grabbing a tin of dark grease paint, he closed and locked his locker, then grabbed his weapons and headed for the door.

"Let's go, gentlemen," he said over his shoulder to Mack and Grady. "Briefing room in ten."

"Roger that, Reaper," Mack replied. "We're on your six."

"I'll meet you there," he told them, jerking open the barracks door. "Gotta meet Cate at the gate."

"Aw, cute," Mack said, "you made a rhyme."

"He's a poet and doesn't know it," Grady added with a grin.

Ryan shook his head. "Yeah. Real original, guys."

Their laughter was the last thing he heard before closing the door. He made his way quickly down the stairs and across the compound, passing Voodoo on the way.

"Collecting our translator?" Voodoo asked, turning and walking backwards.

"Affirmative," Ryan replied over his shoulder. "We'll meet you guys in the briefing room."

"Roger that," Voodoo said with a grin. "We'll be waiting on you two."

When Ryan came around the corner of the last barracks and saw her standing at the guard shack talking with the watch he wasn't at all surprised that she was early, and was even less surprised by the jump in his heartbeat. She was attired similarly to him in dark pants, a dark shirt, and boots, her hair hidden beneath a dark turban, and the traditional scarf, also known as a shemagh or keffiyah, tied around her neck. Was there *anything* she didn't look good in? The .416 hung over her shoulder, but as he approached she handed the weapon to the watch, a Ranger named Hobbs. The man whistled softly, admiring the rifle as he would a Playboy centerfold.

"Beautiful," Hobbs breathed.

"Yeah, I never go anywhere without Charlie," she was saying as Ryan walked up. "I named it after my oldest brother. He has a .50 cal and I told him I wanted one, so he got this for me. Said it was like his little sis: packed a .50 cal punch, but in a smaller package."

"And I've heard you can really deliver with that smaller package," Hobbs said. He handed the rifle back to her. "I'd love to take that baby out to the range sometime."

"Smaller package?" Ryan said with a dubious chuckle. "They realize 5'10" isn't small for a woman, don't they?"

Cat looked over her shoulder and grinned at him, her cheeks dimpling. "Well, I'm smaller than *any* of them, so I suppose it's all a matter of perspective."

"I suppose so," Ryan agreed. He looked at Hobbs. "She's with me sergeant." Saying those words startled him as he pondered the double meaning, but then he was overcome with a sense of *rightness*. Their eyes met and he smiled at her. She smiled back.

Hobbs nodded. "Commander Ferris called just before she walked up." His expression turned serious. "Be careful, man," he paused and blushed, "and ma'am. Come back safe, all of you."

"Will do, sergeant," Cat said. "Maybe one day next week we can head out to the range and I'll let you have Charlie for a while."

Hobbs smiled. "That'd be great. You know where to find me."

"Yes, I do," she said with a grin. "Good night, sergeant."

"Good night, ma'am," Hobbs replied. "Reaper."

"Night, Rabbit," Ryan said with a nod. "We still on for b-ball Sunday afternoon?"

"You know it," Hobbs replied. "And this time, LT, we'll kick your asses."

"Keep saying that if it helps," Ryan said with a laugh. He smiled at Cat. "C'mon, Tiger. Briefing's in five." They started walking toward the command center, and Ryan gave her a sidelong glance. "How are you feeling?"

Her cheeks dimpled. "I'm good, Ryan. Took a nap, Skyped with Charlie for about 20 minutes, did my nails...." She held up her hands and showed him her short, unpolished nails. "Ready to go."

"Glad to see you're dressed for *night ops*," he said with a mischievous grin.

Cat lifted one arched brow. "Well, the only other outfit I have that would be suitable for night ops is that negligee you gave me." Her smile turned wicked. "I didn't think that would be appropriate for *this* particular mission."

Ryan did a double-take, and turned his eyes forward as images of her wearing the burgundy velvet flashed in his head. "Yeah, you're probably right about that one." He shook himself and cleared his throat, unwelcome heat blossoming in his belly. "While I don't think anyone on the *team* would have a problem with it, I have a feeling the devout Muslim women would raise an eyebrow or two."

Cat laughed. "Or three...."

"And it wouldn't be practical." He looked at her and wiggled his eyebrows suggestively. "Darn the bad luck."

"Focus, Lieutenant," she said with a chuckle and a shake of her head.

The two of them passed through the plywood reinforced glass portals into the sacred halls of the Command Center. With a mission scheduled there were even more people in the CC at this hour than there had been earlier in the day, and Cat got just as many startled looks as she had before.

"Tell me something, Cate," Ryan said.

"What?"

"Do you ever go anywhere like this and *not* have people stare?"

"Like *this?*" She thought about it for a second. "No. But, I'm not usually in a place like *this*. People outside the military tend not to stare at women in the workforce."

"What are they, blind?" he mused under his breath.

"What?"

"Nothing," he replied quickly. "Absolutely nothing."

They walked into the briefing room at 21:28:43. The rest of the team was there, as well as several additional technicians who would be their support team, monitoring them by satellite, monitoring their communications, ready to call in the cavalry if things went south.

"Glad you could join us, Reaper," Commander Ferris said with a wry smile. "Evening, Miss Beckett. Is there, perhaps, something the two of you would like to share with me?"

Ryan met Cat's gaze, but before he could speak, she did.

"I suppose you're referring to the incident at the chow hall this afternoon," she said. When Ferris nodded, she said, "Since you already know what happened, obviously, what else would you like me to tell you, sir?" Her voice was neutral, but there was a hint of pink high on her cheekbones and a mutinous set to her jaw.

Ferris narrowed his eyes on her. "Should I be concerned about your participation in this evening's mission, Miss Beckett?"

"No, sir," she replied, lifting her chin, her brows drawn together in a scowl. "What happened, happened, sir, and there's no changing it. As to whether it will affect my performance tonight the answer is *no*. I *can* separate my personal and professional lives, sir."

Ferris stared hard at her for a moment then looked at Ryan. "Lieutenant? Do you have anything to add?"

Ryan leaned his hands on the edge of the table. "Only that if I thought for a *second* Cate couldn't handle the op, she wouldn't be here now, sir." He returned his commander's stare directly. "If you have concerns, sir, you can ask her to sit out. But that's your call, Commander, not mine."

Ferris pursed his lips then turned to the rest of the team. "Gentlemen, since you were all witness to what happened at the mess, what are your thoughts? This mission involves all of you, not only Miss Beckett and Lieutenant Heller."

"I have no problems with Red coming along," Mack said flatly. "Personally, seeing the way she dropped that guy makes me even more certain she's the right man... err, *person*, for the job, sir."

"I second that, sir," Grady said with a nod. "Got no problems with Red on this mission."

"I'm with them, sir," Voodoo said. "She's part of the team as far as I'm concerned."

Ferris looked at each man in turn and then fixed his eyes on her. "Very well," he said. "Looks like you're in, Miss Beckett."

"Thank you, sir," she replied with a smile. "I'll do my best not to disappoint."

"I have no doubt." A faint smile softened the commander's stony features. "Welcome aboard, Miss Becket. You ready for this?"

"As ready as anybody can be, sir," she replied.

"I see you brought your own weapon," he commented.

"That's Charlie, sir," Ryan said. When she looked at him in surprise he gave her a wink.

Cat smiled and turned her attention back to the commander. "Yes, sir," she affirmed, patting the barrel of the .416. "I try not to go anywhere without him. He's better than my American Express card."

A chuckle traversed the room and a surge of pride warmed Ryan's chest.

"All right," Ferris said, rubbing his hands together. "Let's go over the mission again and get this bitch underway." He shot her an apologetic glance. "Sorry."

"Don't be," she said with a wave of her hand. "I'm one of the guys, sir. The only word that bothers me is the 'c' word, and unless it's directed *at* me, I can even overlook that."

"Noted," Ferris said with a smile. "Now, let's get to it."

***

"There they are," Ryan said quietly, pointing left into the south/southwest. The pickup truck hit a bump in the sand and rocked, nearly sending Cat into the roof. She planted her hands on the ceiling and looked in the direction he was pointing.

"Yep," she replied, staring at the rocky ridgeline through her night vision goggles. "Looks deserted from here, but we can only see one side."

"True." Ryan grabbed the satellite phone and hit a key. "Reaper to Command, come in."

"Go, Reaper."

"Requesting Predator flyover of hot zone. We don't see anything from here, but the drones have better eyesight than we do. Copy?"

"Copy that, Reaper. Stand by."

Ryan drove toward the tumble of rocks rising from the desert floor and stopped the pickup at the formation's base. The trucks driven by Grady and Voodoo pulled alongside. The Toyota 4X4's lights were blacked out, but otherwise they looked like any other trucks in Afghanistan, dented, scratched, rusting, and purposely so. Humvees didn't blend into the local population's vehicles. The trucks, however, fit perfectly. The one she and Ryan rode in had a mount in the bed for a mini-gun, as did the truck Grady and Mack were in. Voodoo's was stock and would be used to transport Hasan's family unless air-evac was necessary. In the wilds of Afghanistan, emergency extract was always a possibility.

Cat scanned the surrounding countryside but nothing moved except tumbleweeds. It had been like this since they'd rounded the southern end of Charikar and set out across the barren valley floor. While no sign of opposition was a good thing, for some reason it made her nervous.

The sat phone chirped and Cat jumped.

Ryan looked at her strangely and hit the speaker button. "Go ahead, Command."

"Predator flyover of hot zone approved. Sit tight, Reaper. Drone is launching now and will be over you in twenty."

"Roger that, Command. Extend my thanks."

"Willco, Reaper."

Ryan punched the off button and put a hand on her shoulder. "You okay?"

Cat chuckled. "Yeah, I'm just a little jumpy." She met his concerned gaze. "Is it only me, or is it *way* too quiet out here?"

Ryan turned his gaze back out the window and did a horizontal scan. "I was just thinking the same thing." He gave her a grim smile. "But if there is anything out there we *can't* see the drones will pick it up. So, for now, we wait."

Sitting didn't appeal to her. Needing to work off some nervous energy, Cat unbuckled her seatbelt. "Mind if I go up top and take a look? Not that I don't trust the drones...."

"Sure. I'll go with." He keyed his personal microphone. "Mack,

Voodoo, sit tight. Drone will be overhead in twenty. In the meantime, Tiger and I are going up top to take a look."

"Roger that, Reaper," Mack replied.

"Roger, Reaper," Voodoo said. "Be a shame to waste that starry sky."

Cat was already out of the truck and picking her way carefully up the rocky hill. The NVGs turned the desert night into a green day, so she had little trouble seeing where she was going. Ryan was right behind her, his feet moving as quietly as hers over the stones and boulders. When she reached the top, she picked a relatively level outcropping and got into the prone position. After scanning the descending slope before her and seeing nothing, she pushed the NVGs back on her head, slid the rifle off her shoulder, and deployed the bipod. Ryan lay down next to her, scrutinizing the flat expanse with a set of night vision binoculars.

Cat had put a starlight scope on the .416, which came in handy as she put her eye to the reticle and panned slowly left to right, from 90 degrees south of their position to 90 degrees north. The scope turned the ebony Afghan night into a black and white day tinged with faint smudges of green and sepia. It was almost like looking at an old photograph, or a badly colorized black and white movie. As far as she could tell, there was nothing moving except members of their team and a few small, nocturnal animals.

From her vantage point the village was only a couple of miles away, and all seemed quiet. Cat studied the squat, square homes, detecting nothing other than faint light from inside two of the houses. It could have been candles or firelight; from here she couldn't be certain. The remaining windows were dark.

"See anything?" Ryan whispered.

"Negative," she replied. "It seems all is quiet on the western front."

"Seems so. Let's head back down and wait for the drone."

"Roger that," Cat agreed. "I'll follow you."

"Cate."

Cat turned and looked at him and he smiled.

"We've discussed this before," he said. "Ladies first."

"I'm one of the guys, remember?" she asked with a wry twist of her lips.

Ryan shook his head. "Not to me," he shot back. "Not ever."

Cat gaped at him for a moment then chuckled and shook her head. "Fine." She put the cap on the scope, retracted the bipod, and donned her NVGs. "I'll go first so you have something to look at."

"That's more like it," he said with a grin.

When their feet hit the valley floor Ryan walked to Mack and Grady's truck and leaned on the driver's window. Cat stood at Ryan's side and glanced across the hood when she heard a door open. Voodoo approached the passenger side of the truck, striking a pose similar to Ryan.

"All clear?" Grady asked.

"Looks like it," Ryan replied. "We'll head to the rendezvous point north of the village, wait until we have confirmation from the drone, and then we'll go in."

Voodoo glanced at his watch. "Predator should almost be here." As if to prove him a prophet, a dull whine reached their ears and a moment later the drone flew over them at an altitude of roughly 1000 feet. All eyes turned skyward. Voodoo watched the unmanned vehicle as it passed and shook his head. "Sometimes I amaze myself."

"Not hard to do," Ryan said to her under his breath.

Cat chuckled softly.

"All right," Ryan said, rapping his knuckles on the truck's door, "mount up and follow me. Let's get this motherfucker started."

They drove north around the ridge and headed north/northwest toward the point where the hills the village was nestled into dropped, flattened, and melded back into the valley floor. Ryan parked behind another tumble of boulders and killed the engine, Grady and Voodoo following suit. The village was due south from their position about half a klick, blending into the rolling slopes beneath the moonless sky. Cat smiled as Ryan used the rearview mirror to apply dark, thick stripes of grease paint to his face. When he finished he handed the tin to her.

"Your turn," he said. He watched her closely as she moved the mirror and dipped her fingers in the thick cream. When she was done, she turned her face to him and he looked down his nose at her. "Nice job, but don't forget your neck."

"Where?" Cat asked, lifting her chin and studying her reflection.

Instead of replying Ryan took the tin, leaned toward her, and swirled his fingers in the grease paint. With soft, sure strokes he gently applied the dark make-up to her throat. Cat gulped as he moved from the base of her neck above her collarbone to the side beneath, over, and behind her ears. Then he did the same on the other side of her neck. He wasn't looking at her, concentrating on what he was doing, but she felt his breath on her skin. Cat closed her eyes and tried to control her pulse.

"There," he said at last. He capped the tin and put it in a pocket. "It's all good."

"Thank you," she said in a whisper. She opened her eyes and was caught by his gaze.

"Anytime," he replied.

They stared at each other for a moment then Ryan smiled and pulled back. The sat phone rang and just like that, the charged current passing between them died, much to Cat's relief. This was neither the time nor the place to be distracted by raging hormones.

"Evening, Command," Ryan said, one hand on the steering wheel. "What do you have?"

"Have completed Predator sweep of hot zone and you are cleared to proceed. Repeat, you are cleared to proceed."

"Roger that, Command," Ryan replied. "You still have eyes on us?"

"That's affirmative, Reaper. We're popping the corn and waiting for the show to begin. Satellites are lined up to maintain surveillance, copy?"

"Copy that," Ryan said. "Enjoy the popcorn and save some for us."

"Willco, Reaper. There's a fresh bag waiting for you when you and your team get back. Good luck, gentlemen, and ma'am."

"Copy. Reaper out." Ryan took a long, slow breath then turned to her. "Okay, Tiger. It's show time."

Chapter Eleven

The five of them climbed the hills until they reached an elevation that put them above the village. Once there, they moved quickly and quietly south, Ryan in front, Cat behind him, and Mack, Grady, and Voodoo bringing up the rear. Cat occasionally glanced back and Mack was always quick to give her a smile. The only sound other than the faint scrape of their boots over rock was a mournful wind coming out of the mountains to the north behind them. The moaning draft drowned out any noise she or the team might have made, but it also chilled her. Cat pulled her scarf up over her nose and stayed close to Ryan.

They reached a small ridge and Ryan ducked down behind a tumble of rocks. The rest of the team followed suit. Slowly, he eased up and peered over the closest boulder into the village below. Using his night vision binoculars, he scanned back and forth from one end of the rural community to the other. After several minutes of this, he crouched down and turned to them.

"Mack, map."

Mack immediately pulled a topographical chart out of his pocket and flattened it on the ground.

"All right," Ryan began, pointing to a spot on the map, "we're here. The village is roughly a hundred meters to the southeast from where we are now. From this point, Voodoo, you and Mouth head down the hill and recon target one. Mack, Tiger, and I will continue south and come down behind the other house. By the time we reach our destination you two should have had time to sweep the first hut. If you find the packages there, let us know ASAP and we'll break off and rejoin you here." He pinpointed another location on the map. "If the women aren't where they're supposed to be, *you'll* join *us* here," he paused and tapped a different spot, "and we'll recon target two."

"And if the women aren't in either location?" Mack asked. "I really don't want to do a house-to-house in this village, Reaper."

"Me either," Ryan agreed. "For now, we're going on the information we've been given and Tiger's gut." He met each of their eyes. "If we can't locate the packages then we'll decide what to do next. If it's a house-to-house, so be it. Hopefully," he paused and glanced at Cat, "one of our information sources is correct and we won't need to kick in any doors tonight."

"Roger that," Voodoo agreed.

"All right, any questions?" Ryan looked at each man then at her, but no one spoke. He smiled. "Okay then. Head out. Keep it low, swift, and silent."

Cat's adrenaline started to pump and she gave Grady a smile as he and Voodoo broke off and headed toward the location the SEALs had originally been given. When they disappeared from sight, Ryan handed the map back to Mack.

"Okay, it's our turn," Ryan said. "Tiger, you're behind me, Mack, you bring up the rear."

Mack grinned. "Gladly." He gave Cat a wink. "Now I know why you like being last out, Reaper. The view is so much better from back here."

Cat smiled and punched him lightly in the arm. "Focus, Chief."

"Yeah," Ryan agreed with a frown. "What *she* said."

They quickly traversed the distance to the house Cat had picked as a possible secondary location, clambering over what was little more than a goat trail. She caught glimpses of the house as they moved around the rocky outcroppings and curves in the trail. The closer they got, the faster her heart beat. She took slow, deep breaths, calling on the calm she employed when shooting. Now was not the time to lose her cool.

The simple home was a single-story mud and brick house measuring roughly 20'X20', and it was surrounded by a low stone wall that she guessed would barely reach her waist. The wall formed a small courtyard in front of the dwelling, but there was barely a yard of space between the rear of the home and the roughly hewn barrier. The sides of the home she could see each had a single, glassless window covered by simple shutters. The dark wood of the shutters was like a black eye in an ancient face, and her adrenaline output increased as she imagined other hidden eyes watching their approach from those voids. She breathed deeply and evenly and kept moving.

Ryan had picked a checkpoint at the juncture of the north and west walls, and as they reached their rendezvous the radio clicked.

"Reaper, Voodoo."

Ryan pressed his fingers against the mike at his throat. "Go ahead, Voodoo."

"That's a no-go on target one. I repeat, the packages are not in target one. Proceeding to secondary rendezvous point."

"Roger that, Voodoo. See you in five." Ryan gave Cat a wry smile. "Here's hoping you're right, Tiger. If not, I'm going to have to give you a crash course in kicking down doors."

"Let's hope it doesn't come to that." She crept up slowly and peeked over the top of the wall. "I think I'll head in the back way. Doubt anyone's going to be looking out that window, unless they're suspecting attack from a herd of goats."

Ryan grabbed her jacket and jerked her down. "Hold up."

Cat frowned at him. "No one's coming out to greet us and there's only one way to find out if she's in there. Somebody needs to go in and I think it should be me."

"No," he argued, "we wait for Voodoo and Mouth, and then the four of *us* go in. After we clear the house, that's when *you* go in."

"Yeah, and that worked *so* well for the Rangers." Cat scowled, irritation warming her chest. She pulled her braid from inside the turban and draped it over her shoulder. "Mrs. Hasan and her daughters were so frightened they started throwing crockery. Somehow I doubt a lone woman will get the same reaction."

"Not to contradict you, Reaper," Mack began carefully, "but she's got a point."

"And if that house is filled with AQ or Taliban?" Ryan said. "What then?"

Her heart thudded. "Then this is going to be a really short mission," Cat answered, locking eyes with him, "and I'm going to count on you four to get me out."

He stared at her mutinously for a few moments. "I told you I didn't like changing the mission in midstream."

"And I told you I couldn't think of anything I'd change about the mission, but I reserved the right to change my mind," she replied. "Well, I've changed my mind." She glanced at Mack then looked back to Ryan. "We're only revising one, tiny aspect of the mission. Does it really matter who goes in first? This is a war zone, not a playground, and we don't have time to fight over who gets to be first in the lunch line."

"I don't like it," Ryan said flatly.

"You don't have to," she replied, "but you also don't have to protect me. Tonight I'm one of your guys—"

"And I'd care just as much if it was one of them," Ryan shot back.

"It's true," Mack said with a melodramatic sigh and a roll of his eyes, "he would."

Her frustration climbed into anger territory. "I'm sure you would, but like all of you I have a job to do." She touched his arm. "Let me do it, so we can get out of here and go home."

A muscle in his cheek twitched, his jaws clenched. "Fine." He shot an angry glare at Mack then impaled her with his gaze. "But you're not going alone. We'll be on your six, and we'll stay right outside until you give us the all clear. Got it?"

"Roger that, Reaper," she replied with a curt nod. "Thank you."

Before he could reply Grady and Voodoo joined them. Grady looked at Cat then Ryan, and his smile faded.

"Hey, guys," he began, uncertain, "what's happening?"

"Tiger's going in," Ryan said in a taut voice. "We'll wait outside until she gives us a sitrep on the packages."

Voodoo glanced at Grady, then Mack, and then looked at Ryan. "Okay, change of plans, but that's cool." He met Cat's gaze then shifted his eyes to Ryan again. "Isn't it?"

"It's fine," Mack said flatly. "We're right behind you, Tiger. Go on."

Cat looked at Ryan and waited until he gave her a nod. She gave him a quick smile, but he didn't return it.

"Ignore him, Tiger," Mack said. "Reaper's just very 'by the book'." He patted her back as she crawled past him. "He'll realize you're right and quickly get over himself, trust me."

She nodded and made her way down the west wall behind the house, careful not to make a sound and keeping her head down. Behind her she heard Mack whisper:

"Pull your head out, Reaper. We are *not* here to babysit Red; we're here to babysit the *other* women." Ryan only grunted in response. She smiled.

While part of her was offended at Ryan's overprotective attitude, another part of her was warmed by it. No one had tried to protect her since she'd graduated high school and taken that dive off the high board into the real world, and it was sort of nice to know someone cared. She glanced back and Ryan met her eyes, his face expressionless as he trailed a few feet behind her.

Pausing, she carefully lifted her head to orient herself. The window was a few feet to her right, the shutters closed. With practiced ease, she hopped the wall and crouched behind the house, pressing her back against the rear of the home and listening for anything. She smiled when she heard a faint snoring. Cat keyed her mike.

"Well, there's *somebody* here," she whispered. "Going for the shutters."

"Careful," Ryan replied. "Keep your head down."

"Roger that."

Adrenaline pumped through her at double the volume, heightening her senses. Cat slid up the wall until she was standing, then she pulled a knife from her belt and opened it with a flick of her wrist. The wooden shutters were more for propriety than security, as they typically had only a single leather tie to bind them shut. She flattened her left arm across the bottom of the wooden slats to hold them in place then used her right hand to slide her knife through the gap in the center. With one quick, upward swipe, she felt the blade catch briefly on something before the sharp edge cut through. Keeping her left arm in place, she retracted the blade on the knife and slipped it back onto her belt.

Her heart drummed steadily against her sternum as she crouched beneath the window, still holding the shutters closed. She waited a moment, exhaled slowly, and then carefully opened them. The leather hinges squeaked softly, but the low snoring from within continued undisturbed. Cat waited another few moments, but when no one sprang through the window to confront her she slowly lifted her head and peered inside the hut.

The NVGs illuminated the pitch dark interior of the house. The only light came from an ancient cast iron stove in the far corner, dying embers glowing white in the goggle's view. Close to that stove on a pair of worn, dirty mattresses slept four young women between the ages of about six to sixteen. The front of the house had a pair of windows covered with faded blankets, the corners tied back to leave narrow openings. Lying across the only door on a smaller, even more worn mattress a woman of about thirty dozed fitfully. Other than the beds and a rickety table with two chairs, the dwelling contained no other furniture or even cookware. Obviously, the women were only sleeping here. Cat crouched back down.

"I think we hit the jackpot, gentlemen," she whispered. "I've got five women, one adult and four juveniles. It looks like them, but I'm going in now to make sure they're Hasan's family. If I don't contact you in five, come in with guns blazing."

"Roger that, Tiger," Ryan replied. He lifted his head and peered over the wall at her. "Watch yourself."

"Kind of hard to do without a mirror," she responded with a chuckle, "but I'll be careful."

She knew he was watching her every move as she boosted herself up onto the thick sill, but she paid him little mind, her eyes on the house's occupants. Her heart rate jumped another point when one of the girls shifted and Cat waited a moment, then she swung her legs over and around and dropped to the ground in a crouch position. Her pulse quickened again as the woman stirred and mumbled, but it leveled off when mother and daughters remained fast asleep. Cat's eyes moved from the adult to the children and back as she slowly approached the woman. Her boots whispered over the floor, the leather creaking ever so softly. When she reached the woman's side, she took a few slow, deep breaths and pushed the NVGs back on her head. Making sure her braid was visible she put one foot on either side of the woman's waist, careful not to touch her. Once in position she knelt down and straddled the woman, covered her mouth and nose firmly with her left hand while bearing down on her chest with the right. The woman's eyes snapped open, and they immediately widened in fear.

"Asulam Alaykum," Cat said in a hushed voice. She switched into Dari. "I'm not going to hurt you, I'm here to help. Now, I'm going to release you, but please don't scream. You'll only frighten your daughters and my friends. My friends are armed." She paused and waited for some of the woman's alarm to fade, and said, "Do we understand each other?"

The woman nodded. Cat slowly sat back onto her haunches and dropped her hands to her sides. When no scream was forthcoming, she stood and stepped back. The woman sat up.

"Who are you?" she asked in a whisper.

"Caterina," she replied. "I'm with the United States government. Are you Mrs. Hasan?"

"Yes," the woman said with a nod.

Cat turned her face away and keyed her mike. "Reaper."

"Go, Tiger."

"We've got them," she replied.

"Are we clear to enter?" Ryan asked.

"Give me a minute," Cat said. "The girls are asleep, and you might scare them."

"Roger that. Let me know."

"Will do." Cat turned back to Mrs. Hasan. "Ma'am, I need you to wake your daughters and gather whatever belongings you can in five minutes. We're here to get you out, and we need to leave as soon as possible."

Mrs. Hasan's eyes widened. "You are here to take me to my husband." It wasn't a question.

Cat nodded. "Yes, ma'am."

"How did you find me?" she asked.

"Your husband, ma'am," Cat replied, frowning. She saw the fear in Mrs. Hasan's expression and wondered at it. "You called him earlier and he relayed your location to us."

"No!" Mrs. Hasan exclaimed in a harsh whisper. She jumped to her feet and backed away, holding her hands in front of her. "No, no, no!"

A shiver of uneasiness chilled her. "Ma'am, calm down," Cat said. "We're here to help. The terrorists who are after your husband may know where you are, so we need to get you into protective custody now."

"No!" She stopped and started praying, then exclaimed again, "No! If you take me we will all die, I will die, and my daughters will die! No!"

The girls stirred as Mrs. Hasan began to wail. Cat gripped her upper arms firmly and shook her once. The woman went silent and stared at her, stark terror brightening her eyes.

"Ma'am, get a hold of yourself," Cat said in a cool, calm voice. She met the woman's gaze and gently rubbed her arms. "It's all right, ma'am. We'll protect you. The men trying to kill your husband won't touch you or your daughters, I promise."

Mrs. Hasan's eyes filled with tears and her chin trembled. "You do not understand," she whispered. "I am not hiding from the men trying to kill Tariq. I am hiding from Tariq because *he... he* is the terrorist."

Cat was dubious. "Why do you say that?"

A flash of anger shone briefly in her dark eyes. "I may be a woman but I am not *stupid*," she spat, wiping the tears from her cheeks. "Nor am I deaf, nor blind, and yet he seemed to think I was all *three*. I know Tariq was working with your government. He would meet with your people, and only hours later he would meet with Taliban and extremist sympathizers in our home. I listened to him brag how easily duped your CIA was, how well the plan was working." Her eyes welled.

Cat was starting to get that churning sense of doom in her stomach. "All right," she said in a low, soothing voice. "Please, continue."

Mrs. Hasan pressed a trembling hand to her mouth and choked back a sob. "One night, when he did not realize I was listening, he exulted that his wife and daughters would be heroes after they died in the next planned attempt on his life." She glanced at her sleeping children and a wave of misery contorted her face. "He said... he said once that happened his handler would trust him completely and the US would give him asylum." Her gaze was tortured as she lifted her eyes to Cat's. "Then he said the real jihad could begin... on *your* soil." The tears started in earnest now. "I could not let him hurt my daughters. May Allah forgive me, but I could not let him martyr them for his cause."

Cat squeezed her eyes shut and exhaled slowly, hands on hips. It looked like the plan was going to have to change again midstream. She was getting that tingling feeling, the one she always got before things went south.

"I tried to tell the others who came," the woman said in a tearful voice, "but they did not understand me. They did not understand...." She covered her face and began to weep softly.

A growl of frustration escaped Cat and she took a step back. Mrs. Hasan glanced at her and must have misread her expression because in the next moment she dropped to her knees at Cat's feet and grabbed her hands.

"Please, you must help us!" she sobbed. "Please! He will kill us if he finds us!"

Because of course he will. God forbid anything ever go as planned. Cat didn't want Mrs. Hasan to think she was angry at her or her daughters, so she put on a neutral expression and helped the distraught woman to her feet. "Of course, we'll help you," Cat replied. "Of course." She paused and took a deep breath, her mind spinning. After a moment of tense silence, she put a hand on Mrs. Hasan's shoulder. "Listen to me. I have four friends who are going to join us, so I want you to wake your daughters and tell them not to be afraid, all right?" After the woman nodded Cat continued. "All right. After that, gather only what you need. As soon as you're ready we'll get you out of here and to someplace safe."

Mrs. Hasan sniffed, nodded again, and shuffled over to where her daughters were sleeping. As she roused them, Cat keyed her microphone.

"Come on in, guys. Front door is open."

"Roger that."

Cat moved the mattress, opened the door and then walked to the back of the room. Ten seconds later the SEAL team entered the simple hut, their rifles sweeping back and forth. When they saw all was well, the four men relaxed and lowered their weapons. Ryan looked around, and then turned to Grady and Voodoo.

"You two keep watch out front," he instructed them, "and stay low. We still want to get out of here without any other contact."

"Roger that," Grady replied.

Voodoo nodded, and then the two strode back out the door to take up crouched positions on either side of the rickety wooden gate set in the outer wall. Mack, meanwhile, had engaged the youngest of the girls. She was a beautiful child with large, dark eyes and black hair, her piquant face dirty and smudged. Mack crouched in front of her and pulled a piece of candy from a pocket, his face splitting into a grin when the girl smiled and snatched the treat from his fingers. Now all the girls were interested, gathering around him as if he was Santa Claus. It was a heartwarming scene, but it did nothing to lessen the chill in her bones.

Ryan chuckled as he watched the exchange, but when he looked at her his humor vanished and his brows drew together. Leaving Mack where he was, Ryan approached her.

"What is it?" he asked in a low voice.

Cat sighed heavily. "I think we have a problem," she said, "a *big* problem."

"What?"

Cat glanced at Mrs. Hasan, who was helping her daughters gather their meager belongings. "Do you want to know why the Rangers couldn't get her out the other night?" She met Ryan's gaze and scowled. "It wasn't because of her faith, it was because she's hiding from her *husband*, and she says *he's* the terrorist." Cat snatched the turban from her head and cursed softly. "It all makes sense now."

"What do you mean?"

"You saw the photographs of the building bombed in the last attempt on Hasan's life," she said. "From all reports, he walked away with barely a scratch. The three agents guarding him? One died, one lost a leg, and the other is now legally blind and missing his left hand." She sighed softly. "Plus, Mrs. Hasan said she heard her husband planning to sacrifice her and her daughters in the next attempted assassination. Said it would increase his credibility. I'm inclined to believe her. This is *just* the sort of thing AQ and the Taliban would do."

Ryan tipped his head back and stared at the ceiling. "Shit."

"They're prepping for another Khost type attack," Cat said.

"Seven CIA agents killed by a man they *thought* was an asset," Ryan mused.

"Exactly, only this one's going to be at home." She put her hands on her hips, frustration boiling hotly. "AQ wants a mole, so they groom Hasan and give him enough credible intel to feed us so he *looks* legitimate. Then they *try* to kill him so we think they want him dead for switching sides. After that, the US Government decides to give him an all-expense paid, one-way ticket to the States. Asylum for services rendered."

"They played us," Ryan said, lines of anger bracketing his mouth, "and we fell for it, hook, line, and sinker."

Cat ran a hand over her hair. "Son of a bitch. What are we going to do now?"

The sound of an argument cut into their conversation. Cat's head snapped around and she stared as Mrs. Hasan berated her oldest daughter in low, harsh tones, shaking a fist in the girl's face. In Mrs. Hasan's hand was a cell phone. When she finished her tirade, she threw the phone against the wall with impressive force, shattering it into a million pieces. Then the woman slapped the girl soundly. Mack slowly rose, eyes wide, but he remained silent.

"What the hell?" Ryan asked under his breath.

"Her daughter called Hasan," Cat said. "That's how he knew where they were." She met Ryan's gaze. "That means he knows we're probably here as well. We need to get out of here and the faster the better."

At that moment, Grady appeared in the door. "Reaper, I think we're about to have company."

"Fuck. What now?" Ryan growled as he walked outside.

Cat touched Mrs. Hasan's arm lightly. When the woman looked at her she said, "Stay here and finish gathering your things. I'll be right back."

Mrs. Hasan nodded, tears streaming down her cheeks, then she walked over to her oldest child and embraced her tightly. Cat's eyes stung as all five women came together, clinging to each other. She met Mack's eyes and smiled.

"Stay with them?" she asked.

Mack nodded and pulled more sweets from his pockets. Cat looked again at the frightened family then walked quickly outside.

Ryan and Voodoo were crouched on the south side of the gate to her right, Grady on the north to her left, scopes and binoculars trained into the southeast. Cat crouched beside Ryan and followed the direction of his gaze. In the darkness, it was easy to see the six pinpricks of light.

"Vehicles?" she asked.

Ryan nodded and adjusted his binoculars again. "Yep, three of them and they're headed this way fast." He huffed angrily. "That's what I get for even *thinking* we'd get out of here without firing a shot." He gave Cat a wry look. "So much for a simple SAR."

Cat slid the rifle off her shoulder and deployed the bipod, resting it on top of the wall. "How far out are they?" she asked.

"Couple of miles, tops," he replied.

"Okay." Cat pulled the ballistic calculator out of her tac vest. "Do you know how to work one of these?"

Ryan lifted one brow then gave her a small smile. "Yes, ma'am."

"Good. Get me a firing solution."

"Wait a second."

Cat turned to him. "What?"

Ryan waved at Grady. "Let's get the women out of here *before* you start shooting."

"Good idea," Cat agreed.

She leaned the rifle against the wall and quickly walked back into the house, Ryan and Grady on her heels. Grady waited by the door as Ryan approached Mack and spoke in hushed tones. Cat walked up to Mrs. Hasan. The woman sat near the stove on the mattress with her daughters, each with a small pack over their shoulder. When Cat walked up, Mrs. Hasan said something to the child in her lap, handed the girl to one of her sisters, and rose.

"What is happening?" the woman asked, anxious.

"We're getting you out of here," Cat said. Mrs. Hasan opened her mouth to protest but Cat raised a hand. "Don't worry. We will *not* be handing you over to your husband." She knew she shouldn't have made such a promise, because it was a promise she might not have the power to keep. Her stomach twisted at the possible lie, nevertheless she meant it and she planned to do everything she could to keep the family safe.

Mrs. Hasan's eyes filled with tears again and she grabbed Cat's hand, squeezing it tightly. "Thank you. Asulam Alaykum." *Peace be upon you.*

Cat smiled. "Alaykum asulam." *And upon you, peace.* "Now, I want you and your daughters to go with these men, alright? They will protect you."

"Are you not coming also?" Mrs. Hasan asked.

"I will be right behind you," Cat replied. She clapped Mack on the shoulder and gave Mrs. Hasan a pointed look. "They do not speak your language, but as long as you stay close, copy what they do, and move quickly, you and your daughters will be fine." When Mrs. Hasan nodded, Cat smiled and turned to Mack. "They're all yours."

"What if I need them to do something?" Mack asked.

"I told her to stay close, do what you do, and move fast," Cat replied. "Just... don't put your hands on them unless you absolutely have to."

"Got it," Mack said. "Thanks, Tiger." He looked at Ryan. "See you guys at the trucks."

"We'll be on your six," Ryan replied. "Oh, by the way, radio silent until we rendezvous. Don't want anyone picking up any transmission they shouldn't, eh?"

Mack nodded, then smiled and gestured for them to follow him. Mrs. Hasan gave Cat another grateful smile before she herded her daughters out of the house. Cat and Ryan walked outside and watched until they disappeared into the darkness.

"All right," Ryan said, moving back to the wall. "Let's get this party started. Voodoo, you got eyes on our guests?"

"Roger that, Reaper," Voodoo replied, staring through his scope. "We've got three trucks with more than a dozen hostiles, and they are armed. They're about a klick out."

"Roger that," Ryan said, working the handheld computer. "Stay frosty and don't lose sight of what's right in front of us."

"We're still clear close to home," Voodoo replied. He gave them a grim smile. "But once that cannon goes off we won't be."

"I know," Ryan said ruefully, "but we don't have a whole lot of choice. Hopefully, the locals will hunker down when they hear gunfire rather than rushing into the village square."

Voodoo chuckled. "Maybe they'll think it's thunder."

Ryan shook his head. "Doubt it."

Cat positioned the rifle, uncapped the scope, pressed her eye to the reticle, and sighted the crosshairs on the 700-meter mark. Ryan read off the numbers and she made the adjustments. Time slowed to a crawl as she waited for the first truck to enter the kill zone. The vehicle drew close and that familiar tension kicked her pulse up. She inhaled deeply several times then slowly exhaled. Holding her breath, she waited for the pickup to cross the invisible line, took aim at the driver, and squeezed the trigger.

The .416 boomed. Smoke blossomed from beneath the vehicle and the truck veered out of sight. She reloaded.

"Hit," Ryan said a couple seconds later.

He quickly read off a new set of numbers and Cat adjusted the rifle. She fired and nothing happened. The remaining two trucks kept coming. "Damn it," she said under her breath. She reloaded as Ryan recalculated, adjusted the .416, and evened out her breathing. When the truck drove into the crosshairs she squeezed the trigger again. The driver spasmed and the truck jerked sharply to her right. The front tire sank into the soft sand, flipping the vehicle. It rolled several times, the insurgents in back flying out and landing on the valley floor. The third truck had no time or room to avoid a collision, and Cat heard the sharp, violent crunching of metal as the last pickup plowed into the other.

About a second later, midnight turned into high noon as the final truck exploded in a burst of fury and light. Cat jerked upright and stared as the fireball expanded, roiled outward, and ascended skyward, flames and smoke spewing like lava from a volcano. The shockwave raced across the desert floor, through the village, and over them in a flurry of dust and wind.

"Whoa," Cat whispered.

"Holy shit," Ryan said.

"Wow," Voodoo said. "Those guys aren't fucking around, are they?"

"I guess not," Cat replied, awed. The size of the blast told her the bomb had been significant and meant for one purpose only. "Screw simply taking out the wife and kids. Let's be thorough and eliminate the entire village, including the military personnel sent to rescue his family." She peered through the scope and surveyed the scene. "There are still hostiles down there, and if I know anything about terrorists it's that they always have a Plan B."

"Then let's get the hell out of here," Ryan said. "The villagers knew enough to stay down when you were firing, but now they want to see what the hell is going on."

Cat capped the scope and folded the bipod, glancing down the hill as she picked up her shell casings. Sure enough, about a dozen villagers had left their homes and were staring at the blazing inferno still burning on the dark desert sands. Thankfully, that meant the locals weren't looking at *them*.

"Come on," Ryan said, gesturing back the way they'd come. "Voodoo take point." When she turned to follow Voodoo, Ryan put a hand on her arm and she turned to him. Ryan gave her a grim smile. "Nice shooting, Tiger. Glad you were along for the ride."

"I'll second that, Reaper," Voodoo said with a quick grin. "Now follow me, Tiger, we're bugging out."

Chapter Twelve

Mack was playing peek-a-boo with the youngest daughter when Voodoo, Cat, and Ryan made it to the vehicles. The women all sat in the back of Voodoo's truck, and at least they didn't look terrified anymore. Their expressions reflected the uncertainty of their situation, but Ryan also saw determination in Mrs. Hasan's eyes. He had to admire her fortitude, given that her own husband was trying to kill her and their children.

When Mack caught sight of him he patted the youngster on the head and handed her back to her mother. Ryan walked to the front of his truck and waited for his team to join him as Cat saw to the women. He glanced at her as she conversed quietly with the mother then focused on his men.

"What the hell happened?" Mack asked. "We saw the fireball from here."

"You guys okay?" Grady asked.

"We're all good," Ryan replied. "One of those trucks was a bomb, apparently."

"What the hell?" Mack asked. "That was a pretty big boom, Reaper."

Ryan lowered his voice and leaned in closer. "Mrs. Hasan isn't hiding from assassins," Ryan told them. "Her husband is the one trying to kill her and the girls. Apparently, he's an AQ plant and right now, aside from the wife, we're the only ones who know it."

"Fucking great," Grady mumbled.

Mack groaned and ran a hand over his face. "Wonderful." He glanced at the back of the truck and scowled. "So, what do we do with them? We're supposed to deliver them to the flight line for transport to Kabul and a happy, tear-filled reunion with dear old dad. There's a C-130 prepped and waiting on us."

"I know," Ryan said, leaning against the driver's side door. "I'm going to have to call Commander Ferris and give him an updated sitrep."

"He's not going to like this," Mack said with a shake of his head. "He's not going to like this one bit."

"*I* don't like it," Ryan said, "and I'm pretty sure Mrs. Hasan and her children aren't too crazy about it either." Out of the corner of his eye he saw Cat approaching and went silent until she joined the circle. He met her gaze and asked, "How are they?"

"Scared," Cat replied, leaning a hip into the front left quarter-panel of the truck. "She asked me to give them some privacy so she could tell the girls who their father really is."

"This fucking blows," Voodoo commented. "DHS and the CIA are going to be all over this if we don't turn them over."

Cat's eyes widened and she looked at Ryan. "We're not turning these women over to them, are we?" she asked, obviously alarmed. "Hasan will kill them."

Ryan frowned as he pondered the situation. Either way he looked at it, they were going to wind up stuck between a rock and a hard place, and he really didn't like the outcome of either situation. He had his orders, but following those orders might very well result in the death of an innocent woman and her four children. He'd seen it before. Ryan cursed and rubbed his chin.

"Right now, let's concentrate on getting out of here. If there are more assholes with truck bombs out there they're probably heading this direction so we need to evac now and head back to base." Ryan pinched the bridge of his nose and sighed heavily. "Grady, I'll ride with you and put a call into the Commander on the way. Mack, since the girls seem comfortable with you I want you to drive Voodoo's truck. Cat, go with him."

"We need to put the women in front," she said. "If we need to book it out of here they'll get kicked out of the back on this terrain."

"Right," he acknowledged. "Fine, if they have no problem sitting in a car with men they're not related or married to."

Cat gave him a small smile. "I don't think that's a major concern for her right now. I'll ride in the back of Mack's truck and man the mini-gun, just in case."

"No. You drive Voodoo's truck and get the women situated," Ryan said. "Mack, you're back in your ride." He looked at Voodoo. "Hook it up, Voodoo, and be ready to rock and roll."

Voodoo grinned and rubbed his hands together in anticipation. "Fucking awesome!" He chuckled. "I *knew* this op was going to be fun."

"All right, let's get to it," Ryan said. "We're still in enemy territory so keep your eyes open."

He glanced at Cat and she gave him a wink before she turned and walked toward the truck Voodoo had driven. Ryan sighed again and got into the passenger seat of his ride.

As Grady started driving north/northeast toward the outskirts of Charikar Ryan grabbed the satellite phone and dialed.

"Command, Reaper," he said.

"Good to hear from you, Reaper. What the hell happened? We had you on satellite and then we lost you."

"Truck bomb," he replied, "big enough to destroy the entire village."

"Casualties?"

"Negative," Ryan said, "unless you count the guys driving the truck."

"Pursuit?"

"We're clear for now. Do you have us on satellite?"

"Affirmative, just reacquired your signal. You're heading north/northeast toward Charikar, correct?"

"Affirmative," Ryan replied. He checked the map and read off their approximate coordinates. "Shouldn't be hard to see us since we're probably some of the only things moving at...." He paused and checked his watch, ". . . 0150."

"Affirmative, Reaper. We've got you. Sitrep."

Ryan rubbed his eyes. "Is Commander Ferris present?"

There was a brief pause. "I'm right here, Reaper. What do you need?"

"I need to speak with you on a secure line, sir." Ryan waited a few seconds but there was no response. "Sir, it's important."

"You know my number, LT," Ferris replied. "I'll be waiting for your call."

"Roger that. Reaper out." Ryan hung up the phone and ran a hand over his brow.

"What are you going to tell them?" Grady asked.

"The truth," Ryan replied. "If they turn those women over to Hasan they'll be dead before the day is out." He huffed softly then pounded a fist into the dashboard as his insides wound tight. "Fuck! I'm really starting to hate this fucking place."

"Starting?" Grady repeated. "I hated it before we ever got here, so you're *way* behind"

"I guess." He turned, looked out the rear window, and keyed his mike. "Tiger, this is Reaper."

"Go ahead," she replied.

"How you guys doing back there?"

"We're good. The three oldest girls are with me, Mrs. Hasan and the youngest are with Mack. Everything okay?"

"Just getting ready to call Commander Ferris and give him a heads up," Ryan answered. "I'll pass the word once I have word to pass."

"Roger that, Reaper. Tiger out."

Ryan faced forward again and dialed the secure number that would connect him directly with Commander Ferris. The man picked up after the first ring.

"Give it to me, Reaper. What happened?"

Ryan quickly explained the situation and wasn't at all surprised when Commander Ferris cursed fluently. He waited patiently for his CO to finish venting.

"Sorry about that, LT," Ferris said when he was done.

"No worries, sir," Ryan replied. "What do you want us to do?"

"I have to make a few phone calls," Ferris answered. He was silent for a couple seconds then said, "Reaper, do you remember that safe house you guys used a couple missions back?"

Ryan thought about it. "The deserted farm off the main road north of Charikar?"

"That's the one," Ferris replied. "If you don't hear from me by the time you hit the main road I want you guys to hole up there until you do."

"Is it still deserted, sir?" Ryan asked. "That was a couple of months ago."

"The Army was flying strafing runs over that section of the valley a couple of days ago," Ferris replied. "It was cleared vacant before they started their practice flights, and I doubt anyone's moved in since then, but I can't say for certain." He sighed. "I don't want you bringing the family here until I can make some arrangements, and that may take more than an hour."

"Understood, sir," Ryan said. "But what about satellite coverage? We're being watched, and someone's going to ask why we're not headed straight back to base with the packages."

"Let me worry about that, Lieutenant," Ferris said. "I'll get the eyes in the sky turned elsewhere. Just try to stay under the radar until you hear from me."

"Will do, sir," Ryan replied, "and thanks. I really don't want the blood of women and children on my hands."

"Neither do I, son," Ferris agreed. "Command out."

Ryan hung up the phone and massaged his temples. He felt one hell of a headache coming on.

"So, what's the verdict, Reaper?" Grady asked. "It *sounds* like it went well."

"Remember the deserted farm we holed up at a couple months back?" Ryan asked.

"Yeah."

"Well," Ryan began, "if we don't hear from el Diablo by the time we reach the main road he wants us to go there and hang out until we do."

"And if it's occupied?" Grady asked.

Ryan sighed and reached for the first aid kit. "We'll cross that bridge when we get there, Mouth. Let's hope it doesn't get burnt down behind us."

***

Cat leaned against the crumbling remains of a mud wall, her eyes trained on the stars. Her watch beeped, alerting her that a second hour had passed since they'd arrived at the tumbledown clay house. There was no roof, the front door hung haphazardly from one ancient hinge, one of the walls had almost completely collapsed, and the others had large, gaping holes. The hut had obviously been the target of large caliber weapons. Inside, the women slept in a corner under Mack's watchful gaze, covered by three Government Issue gray wool blankets. Home sweet home.

"Hey."

She smiled and tipped her head back farther. Ryan stood on the other side of the wall, leaning over her with a faint smile on his face and his hands stuffed in his pockets.

"May I?" he asked, indicating the vacant spot on the ground next to her.

She patted the earth and gazed once again at Orion, her favorite constellation.

Ryan eased down beside her and stretched his legs out in front of him. "How you holding up?" he asked. His voice was low and velvety, but they'd all spoken in little more than whispers since embarking on this particular mission. In the vast, empty spaces of Afghanistan where the only background noise was often the wind, even a faint murmur traveled like the shout from a bullhorn.

"I'm good," she replied. She turned her head and looked at him, but he was looking at the stars. "How are you?"

"Fine," he said shortly. He bent one knee and rested an arm on it. "I'm just getting really sick of this shit."

"Which shit," Cat asked with a low chuckle, "the mud and dirt, the people always trying to kill us or all the shit in general?"

Ryan scowled and gazed toward the horizon. "The shit where we don't know who the real enemy is." He shook his head and his scowl deepened. "This isn't like World War II or Vietnam, or even the Gulf War. At least then we *knew* who the bad guys were. Now...? They all look alike. Half of the time the people we're sucking up to are the ones who turn and stab us in the back, with a massive nail bomb, and the rest of the time innocents are getting caught in the crossfire." He picked up a rock and threw it. "I can fight soldiers, but how do you fight fanaticism?"

"Honestly?" Cat asked.

Ryan turned his head and met her gaze. "Yeah, honestly."

"We kill them until they quit," she replied flatly. "That's the only way."

His brows rose. "Wow," he said after a brief pause. "You're a black and white kind of girl, aren't you?"

She shrugged. "Maybe." She sighed softly and looked across the desert. "Extremists of any ideology are like germs, Ryan. It doesn't matter what their beliefs are, you have to eliminate enough of them that they lose the desire to infect anyone else." She glanced at him. "Is it harsh? Hell yeah, but what's the alternative?"

"I don't know, Cate," he replied, "and I don't think anyone else does either."

They lapsed into comfortable silence. After a few minutes, Cat leaned her head against his shoulder.

"Hey," she began, "about earlier when I changed the plan—"

"Don't," Ryan interrupted. "Don't apologize, you were right." He leaned his head against hers. "If we'd gone in we would've scared those women to death, which probably would have brought the entire village down on our heads."

"So... you're not mad?"

He chuckled. "Not at all. Mack says I'm very intense when I'm working."

She smiled. "Well, he's right."

The sat phone chirped and they both sat up. Ryan looked at her and pulled the phone from his vest.

"I'll go check on the women," she said, getting to her feet, "get them ready to roll."

He nodded and gave her a smile. Cat turned on her heel and walked toward the ramshackle dwelling, stepping over the rickety door and into the single room. Voodoo sat in a window smoking a cigarette behind his hand to hide the glowing tip, Grady was cleaning his NVGs, and Mack crouched near the youngest girl watching her sleep with a pensive smile. Cat smiled and walked up to him.

"She reminds me of my youngest," Mack said absently, brushing a lock of dark hair from the girl's brow. "God, I miss those rug rats."

"How are they doing?" she asked softly.

Mack rose. "They're sleeping, which I don't understand." He tugged on his beard. "If my spouse was trying to kill me and my children I wouldn't be able to close my eyes."

Cat crossed her arms over her chest and leaned a shoulder into the nearest wall. "She's a tough one. I really hope we can help them, and not use them to further some political agenda."

"Me, too," Mack agreed. "And I hope it happens soon. It's going to be dawn in a couple hours."

Ryan appeared in the doorway. "Everyone up. We're heading out."

Cat walked toward him. "What's happening?"

"We're to take Mrs. Hasan and her daughters to Bagram and straight to the detention facility," Ryan replied, his expression grave. "They're expecting us at the West Gate and we're supposed to drive right through, no stops."

Her stomach dropped. "We're taking them to the *prison?*" Cat gaped at him. "You've *got* to be kidding."

"Wish I was," Ryan answered. "Commander Ferris doesn't like it either, but it's pretty much the only place in the entire country where we can guarantee their safety."

"At least we're not handing them over," Mack said. "That's a plus."

"Yeah, that's something." Cat glanced at the still sleeping women. "And it's not any worse than where we found them."

"Someone from DHS will be waiting for us at the detention facility," Ryan continued. "Once we hand the women over, we're done." He looked at Cat. "He said to tell you that e-mail you two talked about will probably never make it out of cyberspace."

A smile curved her mouth. "Roger that."

He glanced at Mack and Grady then took her arm and led her away a few paces. "Look, I know you're going to want to stay close to them—"

"But I can't," Cat finished for him. "I know." She looked at the sleeping girls. "I can't even visit them, because I'm not supposed to know they're there."

"You can go with me," Ryan said. Cat's head snapped around and he smiled. "I'm going to need a female chaperone if I want to visit them, right?"

A lump formed in her throat and her eyes stung. Cat blinked rapidly and dropped her gaze. "Y'know, if we weren't here I'd kiss you right now."

Ryan leaned a little closer. "If we weren't here," he said, "I'd let you."

"Reaper," Voodoo interrupted.

They looked at him. His eyes were narrowed and focused out the window to the east.

Ryan walked to his side. "What is it?"

"We might have company," Voodoo replied, "again." He hopped out of the window and pointed.

Ryan looked in the direction Voodoo was pointing and scowled. "Let's wait and see if they turn off the main road," he said, picking up his NVBs and training them out the window. "I don't want to pick a fight unless we have to."

Cat moved to the remnants of the east wall and crouched behind the crumbling clay. Mack moved to her side. There were two cars on the main road roughly a klick to the east driving south toward Charikar. She uncapped the scope, raised the rifle, and peered at the speeding vehicles.

"I see two in the first car and three in the second," she said, "but I don't see any – wait. They're armed. Looks like AKs."

"Keep on going," Ryan mumbled under his breath, "just keep on going." He peered through the binoculars.

She watched the moving cars, her heart dropping when they slowed down and then stopped on the main road.

"Tiger," Ryan said, "get the women into the trucks and hide them."

"You got it," Cat said. She capped her scope and slung the rifle over her shoulder. Moving to Mrs. Hasan's side she gently shook her. The woman opened her eyes. "Come on, help me get the girls and grab the blankets. We need to move."

Cat picked up the youngest girl and shook the others, speaking softly. They rubbed their eyes, but obediently followed as Cat walked quickly through a hole in the back wall and approached the pickups. She waited until the older girls climbed into the bed of Voodoo's truck before handing the still sleeping youngster to her oldest sister and climbing up after them.

"Stay down," she told them. Mrs. Hasan lay down and told the girls to do the same then Cat spread the blankets over them. "Whatever you hear stay put and stay quiet, okay?"

"What is happening?" Mrs. Hasan asked.

"Hopefully nothing," Cat replied. "We'll be leaving shortly, all right?"

Mrs. Hasan nodded and pulled the blanket over her head. Cat hopped down, put the tailgate up, and ran back into the hut.

"What's the verdict?" she asked, moving back to her spot by Mack.

"They're still sitting there," Mack replied. "What the fuck are they doing?"

Cat peered through her scope. "It looks like they're arguing."

"Any idea what they're saying?" Ryan asked her.

She shook her head. "I'm pretty good at reading lips, but not from this distance."

"Well, we can't wait here forever," Ryan muttered. "It's going to be daylight soon. I do *not* want to be caught off-base after sunrise."

The group fell into a tense silence as the two cars continued to idle on the side of the road. She slipped her finger onto the trigger of the rifle when one of the doors opened. The dome light shone like a beacon in the darkness, illuminating the faces of the car's occupants. Her heart nearly dropped out of her chest.

"Holy shit," she whispered.

"What?" Mack asked.

Cat blinked and pressed her eye closer to the scope. "The driver," she began, adjusting the focus. "He's a dead ringer for Ahmed Ali."

"And *he* is?"

"One of the FBI's most wanted," Ryan answered.

"He was involved in the bombings of the US embassies in Tanzania, Dar es Salaam, and Nairobi," Cat added. "What the hell is he doing here? He's supposed to be in Karachi."

"As long as he doesn't pay *us* a visit," Mack said, "I don't really give a shit. He's not part of tonight's mission."

Her mind spun in a million different directions and her breathing quickened. The man who resembled Ali got out of the car, went around to the other side and climbed into the backseat as the man in the backseat slid behind the wheel.

"Looks like a Chinese fire drill," Grady commented.

"Now let's hope they drive on," Ryan said.

"Yeah, let's," Cat mumbled. "If that *is* Ali, I can almost guarantee they have more weapons than the AKs I saw."

The team heaved a collective sigh when the beaten up sedans continued on their way.

"First bit of good luck we've had," Voodoo said.

Ryan nodded. "You can say that again." He took a final look then dropped the binoculars. "Now let's get the fuck out of here."

***

Shortly before dawn the small convoy approached Bagram's west gate. To their left the Hindu Kush Mountains were a deep purple topped with a light frosting of pink and peach. The colors were so vibrant they reminded Cat of a scene from a Disney animated movie. Any other time she would have admired the whimsical effect, but it wasn't any other time.

She was riding with Ryan who had taken point, Mack was behind them in the truck with the women, and Grady and Voodoo brought up the rear in the third truck. Lined up across the entrance to the base was a gauntlet of heavily armed soldiers, and two Humvees with mounted .50 caliber machine guns.

"Command, this is Reaper. We're coming in hot."

"Roger that, Reaper. The gate is aware and waiting on you. Signal twice on approach and drive right through."

"Roger that," Ryan replied. "Reaper out."

When they made the left turn from the frontage road toward the base's west entrance, Ryan flipped the emergency lights twice and the line of soldiers parted like a human gate. The convoy drove through, barely slowing, and the ranks closed behind them. Cat sighed and closed her eyes. They'd made it.

"You okay?" he asked.

"Yeah," she replied, leaning her head back. "No offense, but as exciting as this whole thing was, I'm glad it's over."

He chuckled. "I know how you feel," he said. "We spend so much time getting prepped and pumped up for a mission, and as much as I love my job it always feels good when you've completed the objective and are back home."

"Especially without casualties," she added.

"Amen to that."

They fell into a comfortable silence as Ryan drove toward the detention facility. When they approached, Cat's eyes roved over the building. The glass and metal glinted like a freshly minted coin as the sun finally peeked over the top of the Hindu Kush. It was an impressive structure, and no doubt a million times better than the gulag that had originally housed insurgents, but it was still a prison. She shuddered as she thought about Mrs. Hasan and her daughters locked in that cold, utilitarian edifice.

"When we get there, you should probably stay in the truck," he said. "Homeland Security and CIA will be waiting inside the intake station. Voodoo and I will park outside, but Mack's going to drive on in, so unless you want to meet some of your coworkers...."

"What are they going to do with her and the girls?" she asked.

Ryan shook his head. "Above my pay grade, but I imagine there will be some sort of Q&A session or debrief."

"You mean interrogation," she said dryly, looking at him out of the corner of her eye.

"Yeah," he replied, his expression darkening. He went silent for a moment then keyed his mike. "Mack this is Reaper."

"Go ahead, boss man."

"How are they doing back there? Still holding on?"

There was a brief pause. "They're still hunkered down," Mack replied, "but I imagine they'll be glad to get vertical. They're probably freezing their asses off."

"Probably. You know what to do when we get to the detention facility."

"Roger that," Mack responded. "You guys have to park outside but I get to drive on in. Sometimes it pays to be the one delivering the cargo."

"Sometimes," Ryan agreed with a chuckle. "Reaper out."

Cat planted a foot on the dashboard and stared at the toe of her boot.

"What are you thinking, Cate?" Ryan asked softly.

"I'm thinking I don't want them to go in there by themselves," she replied. She looked at him. "You realize they won't want to believe her, don't you? They're going to question everything she says because they *want* Hasan. They *want* to believe he's on our side." Her eyes shifted back to the prison. A sense of dread coiled around her heart. "I know what it's like to try and convince someone what they *think* they know isn't true." She glanced at him. "Nobody likes to be told they're wrong, especially when they think they're smarter than you are."

He rubbed his chin. "Well, I can't tell you what to do," he said at last. "Only you know how much trouble you may or may not get in." He pulled around to the east side of the facility and parked to the side of a large rolled metal door. The reinforced barrier was closed, but as he shut off the engine there was a deep groan and the gate began to ascend. Voodoo parked between him and the door and Mack waited patiently until he could drive through. After the truck disappeared into the building, Ryan turned to her. "Make a decision, Cate. If you want to go with I'll back you up 100%."

"Reaper, come in."

Ryan frowned and keyed his mike. "Go ahead, Mack. What is it?"

"I don't know quite how to say this so I'll just say it. That Mitchell guy is here with the people from Homeland Security, and he ain't wearing prison orange if you know what I mean."

Her lungs contracted. Cat looked quickly toward the entrance and slunk down in her seat. Thankfully, Voodoo's truck was parked between her and the intake station, so Peter hadn't seen her. He stood inside the facility conversing with several fellow agents and three people she didn't recognize. They had to be the team from Homeland Security.

"I guess that answers *that* question," Ryan said quietly.

"Shit." She ran a hand over her face then slammed her fist into the door as a hot burst of anger warmed her throat. "How does he *do* that?"

"What? Always show up where you are?" he asked. "Must be a gift."

"For him," she shot back, scowling. "For me, it's a curse." She stared at her nemesis, and scooted down some more when his gaze swiveled their direction. "Son of a bitch."

"You never know," he began, "he may be getting ready to call you."

"What's he going to call me?" she asked, her voice laced with sarcasm. "Bitch, Red Sonja, destroyer of careers and lives?"

Ryan chuckled. "I was thinking more to request your translating services, but I imagine any number of things may be going through his head." He opened the door and stepped out. "Wait here. I'll be back ASAP."

She nodded and watched as Ryan walked into the intake station. He conversed quickly with Mack and the rest of the team, and she guessed he was telling them to keep mum about her involvement. Her eyes narrowed when the four men approached Peter's group. There was a brief, unanimated conversation, and the haughty look Peter tried to hide as he talked with the SEALs made her blood boil.

"Screw this," she said under her breath.

Setting her jaw, she opened the door of the truck, hopped out, and walked toward the intake station with long, brisk strides. When Peter caught sight of her his eyes widened and he fell silent, causing the rest of the group to turn and follow the direction of his gaze. She glanced at Ryan, and a smile curved her mouth when he shook his head and fought a grin.

"Morning, gentlemen," Cat said, facing them with her feet apart and her hands clasped behind her back. "I have the feeling you're going to need a translator."

Chapter Thirteen

Cat leaned against the wall of the interview room and smiled as the girls devoured the trays of food the guard had brought in. It was obvious they hadn't had a decent meal in a while. The youngest picked up a bunch of grapes and approached, holding them out to her. Cat crouched down and accepted the gift, ruffling the girl's hair. The child giggled and scampered back to the table.

"She's beautiful," Cat said, absently popping grapes into her mouth. She turned and looked at Mrs. Hasan who stood to her right, her eyes locked on her children. "They look a lot like you."

A smile curved the woman's mouth. "They are the best part of my life," Mrs. Hasan said. She glanced at Cat. "Ariahn told me she likes your hair very much and wanted to know what she had to eat to make hers so."

Cat chuckled and rose. "How do you explain that is *not* how it works?" She turned to the young mother. "I'm sorry we had to bring you here, Mrs. Hasan. Unfortunately, it's the only place where we can keep you safe, and I promise it's only temporary."

"Please," the woman said softly, "call me Yasmeen, and at least here we will have food, shelter, and be able to bathe." She ran a hand over her covered hair. "That is far more than we have had since going into hiding."

One of the two doors in the room opened and Peter stood there, his face carefully blank. He motioned for Cat to join him. She looked at Yasmeen.

"I'll be back soon," she said. "You should eat something."

Yasmeen smiled softly and nodded. Speaking in low tones to her daughters, she joined them and laughed when one of the girls climbed onto her lap. Cat smiled then left the room.

As soon as she stepped into the observation room and the door closed behind her the mood polarized. She watched the family through the one-way glass for a moment, then crossed her arms over her chest and turned to Peter.

"Yes?" A muscle in his cheek twitched and she recognized he was angry, angrier than she'd ever seen him.

"I can understand you're upset with me for what happened yesterday," he began in a tightly controlled voice, "but to go over my head like this? I would never have thought you capable of doing something like this to me."

Cat stared at him. "My decision had absolutely *nothing* to do with you, Peter. In fact, when the SEALs asked for my help, *you* weren't even part of the thought process. It's not always about *you.*"

"I should've been notified," he said from between clenched teeth. "I could have you fired for this kind of insubordination."

She looked at him in disbelief for a moment, then stood toe to toe with him and got in his face. Anger heated her to her scalp. "Knock yourself out," she said in a low voice, "but you may want to have a chat with General Mason first. He approved the mission... and me." She gave him a cold smile. "And, given what happened in the chow hall yesterday, who do you think has a better chance of getting *who* fired?"

A sneer twisted his lips. "When I bring up that pallet of stolen ammunition I'd have to say the odds are pretty much even."

"Really?" She laughed. "When you bring up that pallet of stolen ammunition I'm sure your superiors are going to ask you why the RFID tags were removed... per *your* instructions." She arched a brow. "I've already spoken to the crew chief and confirmed that those *were* your orders. Also, he was kind enough to put it in writing so if that's the card you want to play... go right ahead."

He stared at her and she smelled his impotent rage. He was fairly shaking with it. After several tense, pregnant moments, he narrowed his eyes on her and said, "You're going to regret this."

"Peter," she said, "I've regretted meeting you since the day I saw you with your wife in Georgetown and realized how naïve I'd been, so I'm *way* ahead of you on that one."

At that moment, another door opened and the CIA/Homeland

Security team entered the observation area and introduced themselves. The lead agent was a wiry man in his mid-fifties named Michael Heston. He was roughly her height, had brown hair, and intelligent pale blue eyes that almost didn't look natural. He was dressed casually in a button-up shirt and khakis, but there was nothing informal about his manner. Despite his laid-back attire, Cat had a feeling he was not a man to be taken lightly.

"All right," Heston said in a voice tinged with a slight Texas drawl, "we've been brought up to speed. We've read a little about you, Miss Beckett, and we've spoken with the SEAL team. Now, let's have a chat with Mrs. Hasan. Mr. Mitchell, you and your agents are free to go. I think we have it under control here." He gave her a quick glance. "I'm assuming you're still willing to serve as an interpreter, Miss Beckett?"

"Of course, Mr. Heston," Cat replied. She glanced at Peter who scowled at her before turning and leaving the room. Cat turned her gaze back to Mr. Heston.

He gave her a tight smile. "Good, but do me a favor first." When she nodded, he said, "Go wash some of that grease paint off your face, Miss Beckett. I like to see who I'm conversing with, if you don't mind."

Cat chuckled. "Not at all, sir."

"And drop the sir," Heston added quickly. "I *work* for a living."

"Of course. I'll be back in five."

True to her word, five minutes later she re-entered the observation room, freshly scrubbed, damp tendrils of hair curling around her face. Heston looked up from the folder he was perusing and gave her a curt nod. Her fellow CIA agents were nowhere to be seen, leaving only Heston and his two colleagues.

"Much better," he said. He gestured toward the door that opened into the interview room. "Shall we?"

Cat led the way. Yasmeen looked up when she walked in and the woman smiled, her smile wavering when the three serious looking men followed behind.

"It's all right," Cat said quickly. "They want to ask you a few questions, hear your story."

"Very well," Yasmeen replied. She rested her elbows on the edge of the table.

At that moment, a female Army sergeant with the name Williams stitched on her uniform entered the room and gestured for the girls to follow her. Yasmeen half rose out of her chair but Cat put a hand on her shoulder and approached the female sergeant.

"What are you doing?" Cat asked.

Williams looked at her then glanced at Heston. "We have another room for the children," she replied. "It's just for the duration of the interview. There are coloring books, board games, or they can nap if they want."

"I want to see it," Cat said. Williams glanced at Heston again and Cat turned a frosty eye on the man. "I'm not letting you put little girls in a prison cell. They've been through enough."

Heston nodded and Cat followed the now annoyed sergeant down the hall to another interview room. It looked exactly like the one they'd just left, but the sergeant hadn't lied. On the table was a pile of coloring and activity books, crayons, paper, pencils, stickers, and other crafty type items. Cat saw a box of checkers, dominos, playing cards, and along one wall were four cots with blankets and pillows. There was also a box filled with snacks and juice boxes.

Cat turned to the sergeant. "Sorry," she said. "I just don't want to frighten them anymore than they already have been."

Williams seemed to thaw a little. "I get it, ma'am, they're kids. I'll stay with them while you're conducting the interview, and afterward they'll be moved to more comfortable quarters with their mother."

"Thanks," Cat replied. Williams nodded but didn't reply as Cat walked back the way she'd come. She entered the interview room, gestured for the girls to follow her, and Yasmeen nodded when they looked at their mother for permission. The two younger girls grasped Cat's hands tightly as she led them to the other room, the older children no more than a step behind her. Once inside Cat introduced Sergeant Williams.

"This is Sergeant Williams," she said to her captive audience. "While your mother and I speak with those men Sergeant Williams will wait here with you. You can color or play a game or sleep if you want, and when we're all done they'll move you and your mother someplace more comfortable, all right?" The weary, sad-eyed girls nodded. "Okay. I'll be back soon with your mother. Be good."

When she turned to leave, the youngest wrapped her arms around Cat's leg, her eyes tearing up. Cat pried the girl loose then crouched in front of her.

"You'll be all right," Cat said softly, brushing the hair from her brow. "In a little while you'll be back with your mother and everything will be fine. Now, go to your sisters." She looked at the oldest child who gave Cat a small smile when the youngster rushed into her sibling's arms. "Try to sleep, little ones. It will go faster that way."

When she walked out of the room the oldest was tucking blankets around the younger two. Cat glanced at Williams, and the woman gave her a thumbs up. She sighed and returned to the other room.

"Is everything well?" Heston asked.

Cat met his direct gaze. "As well as can be expected, given the circumstances." She paused then said, "Thank you."

Heston nodded. "I have children of my own," he said. "I know if they were in a place like this I'd be up in arms." He narrowed his eyes on her. "Now, let's get this over with."

"All right," Cat said, sitting down next to Yasmeen. "Ask away."

"Just have her tell her story," Heston said. "We'll save the questions for afterwards."

It took more than an hour and nearly an entire box of tissue for Yasmeen to tell her story through Cat. While she tried to maintain her objectivity, in her mind Cat saw the crosshairs of her rifle sighting in on Tariq Hasan, and it was a picture that almost made her smile.

Yasmeen finished her narrative, and then Heston and his two friends asked a few questions. The woman answered quickly and without reservation. After two or three more queries Heston pulled a sheaf of photographs from a folder and laid them on the table. He fanned them out and pushed them toward Yasmeen.

"Ask her if she recognizes any of these men," he said.

Cat was taken aback for a moment because even *she* recognized some of the men in the pictures. She translated Heston's request and Yasmeen picked up the photos. It took her less than 30 seconds to identify four of the six men, and Heston exchanged a significant look with one of his teammates. Cat recognized the expression and hope started to blossom in her chest. They were concerned.

"All right," Heston began, rising from his chair and gathering his papers, "I think we're done here. Thank Mrs. Hasan for her honesty and her cooperation."

Cat did so and Yasmeen nodded slowly then said in halting English, "Thank you."

"Now, we're going to sit down and discuss what to do next," Heston said. "In the meantime, one of the female sleeping quarters has been set up for Mrs. Hasan and her children. They won't be free to wander around, but they should be more than comfortable and they won't be completely locked down." He gave Cat a wry look and a faint smile. "I trust that meets with your approval, Miss Beckett? Unless, of course, you'd like to inspect said quarters?"

Cat smiled. "No, Mr. Heston, but could I go with them and help them settle in?"

His smile widened a bit. "Of course, I expected that." He stepped into the hallway, his comrades a few steps ahead of him. "When you're done you can join us in the conference room down the hall."

"Yes, sir." When he lifted one brow and gave her a stern look she chuckled. "Sorry. Of course, Mr. Heston. I'll join you shortly."

The sleeping quarters for the prison guards were in a small, walled in compound attached to the intake station. The larger of the two buildings housed male guards, the smaller the few women who worked at the detention facility. A cinderblock wall separated the two structures. Inside the women's building were six four-person rooms, each with four twin sized beds, four lockers, four sets of dresser drawers, an attached bathroom, and they were quite spacious given the setting. Compared to the hut where Cat had found Yasmeen and the girls it was positively luxurious.

A fifth bed had been put in the room to accommodate all five women, and waiting on top of one of the dressers were two boxes. One held more snacks, drinks, games, and activities for the children, and the other contained an array of toiletries: soap, toothpaste and brushes, shampoo and the like. There was a stack of towels and washcloths on top of another dresser, and some hospital type scrubs in various sizes to fit them all, and thankfully they weren't orange. Yasmeen examined the gifts with something akin to awe.

"You treat your prisoners better than most of the people in my country *live*," she said in a hushed voice. The girls, meanwhile, were busy deciding who got which bed. Apparently, they were not accustomed to having their own place to sleep.

"You're not a prisoner," Cat said. Yasmeen glanced at the armed female sergeant sitting in the hallway outside and Cat shook her head. "She's there for your protection, not to keep you captive."

"But we cannot leave at our discretion," Yasmeen stated.

"No." Cat sighed softly. "I know it's not ideal, but it is only temporary."

Yasmeen gave her a sidelong glance. "You will come to visit?"

"Of course," Cat replied quickly, walking up to the woman and taking her hands in hers. "As often as I can. You make a list of what you need and want, and I'll make sure you get it."

Yasmeen looked down at their intertwined fingers, then met Cat's eyes and smiled. "Thank you, Caterina. Asulam Alaykum."

"Alaykum Asulam," Cat responded. "And you're welcome. Now, I have to go. I know you're all probably exhausted. You should bathe and change and get some rest. I'll come back this evening."

"We will dine together?" Yasmeen asked with a hopeful smile.

"You bet," Cat said immediately. "Get some rest, and I'll see you later." She waved at the girls, then stepped into the hallway and closed the door behind her. Turning to the sergeant she said, "Take good care of them, please."

This sergeant, whose name was Guitierrez, actually smiled. "I will, ma'am. Don't worry. I come from a large family and I have four sisters myself, so this will almost be like going home."

"Thank you, sergeant."

"You're welcome, ma'am."

Cat smiled when she heard the sound of laughter from inside the room, then she turned and made her way quickly back to the intake station.

". . . shouldn't dismiss Hasan on her word," someone said as she opened the door and slipped into the conference room, taking a seat at the far end of the table. The men hadn't noticed her yet. "He's a valuable asset, and his wife may be making the whole thing up so she can claim asylum and get a free trip stateside."

"She identified four men who are on the FBI's most wanted list of terrorists," Heston shot back. "That's *well* outside of his sanctioned activities. Did any of *you* know he was meeting with such high-profile targets?"

The room went dead silent.

"I thought not," Heston continued. "I, myself, find her to be quite credible, and there is the issue of the truck bomb. Only a few people knew of her location, so how did the terrorists know exactly which remote village to send their weapon of mass destruction to? Hasan has the connections to make that happen, and I've never been a big believer in coincidence."

"But we've been grooming him for years," the other man argued. "We've invested a lot of time and money in this relationship, and I'd hate to see it flushed down the shitter because of an unhappy wife with a grudge."

Up until that moment Cat had been silent, but she could no longer hold her tongue. "Are you serious?" she asked, scowling. "I don't know what interview *you* were in, but what I saw was a woman afraid for her life and the lives of her children, not an unhappy wife with a grudge."

The dissenter tossed her an angry glare. "Hasan's information has always panned out. We've never had a reason to doubt him, until now."

"Hmm." She narrowed her eyes on the man. "I imagine that is exactly what seven other people thought right before al-Balawi blew them to bits in Khost." She lifted one brow. "He's always been a straight up guy, *until now.*"

"That's not fair—"

"The hell it's not," Cat interrupted, planting her hands on the table and rising out of her chair. "Extremists don't *switch sides.* They tell you what you want to hear, right up until they kill you. What part of that do you *not* get?"

The man snorted in derision and looked at Heston. "Who the hell is this woman and why is she involved in this conversation?"

"Because she has firsthand knowledge of this situation, Monroe," Heston replied softly. He looked at her. "And I, for one, welcome her insight." He flipped open a brown folder with the CIA's logo emblazoned on front. "This isn't the first time your file has come across my desk, Miss Beckett."

His expression made her distinctly uneasy and she slowly sat down, leaned back in her chair, and lifted her chin.

"The first time I heard your name was five years ago," Heston continued, perusing the contents of the brown folder. "UN delegation in Baghdad...." He paused and looked up at her. "That *was* your first kill, wasn't it?"

Monroe looked startled, as did the third gentleman who had, wisely, remained silent.

"Wait," Monroe, began, "she's *that* Beckett?"

Cat said nothing, her eyes locked with Heston's as her insides started to churn.

"The delegation came under fire from a sniper," Heston said, "who killed... let's see... eight people, including two Marine guards before you—"

"You don't have to replay it for me," she interrupted, "I was *there.*"

"And after what you did, one of those dead Marines was posthumously awarded the Medal of Honor," Heston continued, "because you used *his* rifle to take out the sniper. Agency thought it best that the world *not* know a CIA agent, and a woman, had fired the fatal shot."

"I didn't want a medal," Cat said sharply.

Heston nodded. "I know. The report said it was your idea to say Gunnery Sergeant Takahashi was the hero so his family could remember him that way and reap any possible benefits that might come because of the award."

The image of that day flashed in her mind, as did the image of the one face she remembered. She swallowed hard and stared at the wall. "And your point would be...?"

"You're more than simply an interpreter," Heston replied. "You have a unique perspective I think we could benefit from in this particular situation."

Her eyelids fluttered and she stared hard at him. The anger that had been simmering burst upward in a surge of red heat. "You want my *perspective?*" He nodded and Cat took a breath, trying to reign in her temper. "Fine. Here it is. You're insane, all of you. The highest honor these extremists can achieve in life is to die for Allah in *jihad,* or are you unfamiliar with that particular tenet of their beliefs? If so... you definitely shouldn't be *here.*"

"Michael," Monroe started to complain.

Heston impaled him with a sharp look. The man went silent and Heston nodded at her. "Continue, Miss Beckett."

"If you think for *one* second you can trust Hasan, you're crazy," she continued, allowing her frustration to run loose as her cheeks warmed. "That truck bomb wasn't a love letter from daddy. Also, let's not forget Hasan gave you their location, most likely in anticipation that you would send in the Special Forces to retrieve them. So, not only did he plan to destroy the village, he was hoping he'd get to take out American military personnel as well."

Monroe rolled his eyes and groaned. "That's pure speculation—"

"Speculation or not," Cat interrupted, "if you give his wife and daughters back to him they will be dead before the door closes in your face." She stood again and leaned on the edge of the table. "Then, gentlemen, not only will you have the blood of an innocent woman and four young girls on your hands, you'll have on your hands the blood of whomever else Hasan kills when his endgame finally reveals itself. Therefore, if nothing else, you may want to think twice before letting him set foot on American soil, but that's just my *perspective*." She pushed her chair back. "Now, if you'll excuse me. I'm done here."

She slammed the door shut with far more force than was necessary and stalked toward the exit. The Army personnel watched her stride by with curious expressions on their faces, but she ignored them. When she reached the heavy industrial door leading outside she pushed the bar and shoved for all she was worth.

"Miss Beckett!"

Cat ignored the call and kept walking. The early morning sun assaulted her and she shielded her eyes.

"Miss Beckett, wait!"

"No."

"Beckett!"

She whirled on Heston, hands fisted. "What?"

"Listen—"

"No, *you* listen!" she raged, reaching the end of her tolerance level. She pointed a finger in his face. "You fucking political types sit in your fucking offices and board rooms and make decisions from thousands of miles away that get *other* people killed! I will *not* be party to that. Not again!"

Heston sighed. "You won't be. This isn't Baghdad where you watched eight people die *and* had to take a life because the higher-ups refused to acknowledge that someone on the ground might have better information than their analysts in the office next door. In this instance, I'm in charge and I plan to listen to what you have to say."

Cat paused and took a deep breath. Heston's calm demeanor in the face of her tirade made her realize she was overreacting. Apparently, the adrenaline was still working its magic. She took another breath and consciously tried to slow her racing heart as Heston's words sunk in. "I'm sorry?"

"The final decision doesn't rest with me," he said, "but more than likely whatever I recommend will be the decision the Director makes." He met her gaze. "I'm going to recommend asylum for Mrs. Hasan and her daughters, and that we cut all ties with Tariq."

"You... are?" Her hands unclenched.

"Yes," he replied with a nod. "Your blunt assessment of the situation was what I wanted to hear, what I wanted my colleagues to hear."

Her eyes narrowed. "What's the catch?"

"No catch," Heston answered. "I'm sick of being played for a fool, too, Miss Beckett."

"So...." She paused, digesting what he'd said, "... you're *not* going to send her back to her husband."

"No, we're not." He gave her a serious look. "They'll stay here until arrangements can be made, which may take a while, but as long as you're in country you can visit them whenever you like. I'll make sure prison personnel are aware."

She eyed him warily, waiting for the other shoe to drop. When no shoe drop was forthcoming, she said, "Thank you. I'm going to hold you to that."

"And I know you can," he said, a smile tipping the corners of his mouth, "from more than a mile away."

Cat looked at the ground. "Also... I'm sorry for biting your head off. You didn't deserve that."

Heston gave her a wry smile. "Adrenaline is a tricky thing. Once it gets pumping it takes hours for the effects to wear off, so think nothing of it." He chuckled. "I'm just glad you didn't pull a weapon on me."

She stared at him for several moments, uncertain whether he was joking or not. His expression didn't change, so she nodded and said, "So am I." Without another word, she turned to walk away.

"One more thing, Miss Beckett."

She paused and faced him again.

"When you decide you want to transfer out from under Mr. Mitchell's supervision," Heston began, giving her a meaningful look, "send *me* the paperwork." He handed her a business card. "I'll make sure it gets approved, for you and your entire team." When Cat's eyes widened, he nodded. "Yes, I know what he did, and he's been doing it for years, hasn't he?"

"How...?"

"Like I said, this isn't the first time I've read up on you," Heston replied. "And, because he's your supervisor I had to do a little reading up on him, too. Guilt by association."

Cat crossed her arms over her chest. "Why would you do that for me?"

"I have a niece about your age." Heston glanced at her arm. "How are the bruises?"

She automatically rubbed her bruised wrist. "I'll be fine."

Heston nodded slowly. "I imagine you will." His gaze slid past her. "Well, it looks like your ride is here. That *is* your ride, isn't it?" He pointed behind her.

Cat looked over her shoulder and when she saw Ryan standing beside the idling Humvee she couldn't stop the smile. He'd obviously showered and changed his uniform. There was no trace of grease paint or desert dust to be seen. He looked delicious.

"I'll take that as a yes," Heston said with a chuckle. "We're done here, Miss Beckett. If I need you I know where to find you."

She faced him, studied him for a moment then extended her hand. "Thank you, Mr. Heston. I don't know how they found the one guy in the entire Agency with some common sense and sent him here, but I'm glad they did."

He grasped her fingers firmly. "I'm DHS, Miss Beckett, not Agency."

"Of course." She lifted one brow. "My mistake."

"It's been a pleasure," Heston said, a sly grin warming his features. "I'll be expecting that paperwork before the week is out."

"You'll have it before *Monday* is out." Cat looked at him solemnly. "Thank you again for not sacrificing them."

"That's *supposed* to be what we do," Heston replied. "Protecting the innocent." He released her and took a step back. "Y'know, your father and I worked together quite a bit during the twilight of his military service. You remind me a lot of him." He smiled. "Tell him to give me a call if he's ever back in D.C. We'll go play a couple rounds of golf."

"I will. Thanks again."

"Get out of here, Miss Beckett," Heston said, a twinkle in his eye. "I'll talk to you soon I'm sure." With that, the man turned on his heel and walked back into the detention facility.

Cat waited until the door closed behind him, then she turned and ran toward Ryan. He opened his arms, closing them around her when she threw herself against his chest.

"Whoa!" he exclaimed as she nearly bowled him over. "Easy, Tiger."

Cat closed her eyes and breathed deeply, absorbing his strength as she inhaled his clean scent. Tears gathered behind her eyelids and a lump formed in her throat, her arms tightening around his neck. The knowledge that Yasmeen and her girls were safe, at least for the time being, filled her with joy. Her cynical self knew Heston's promise might be nothing more than lip service, but it was more than she'd expected, and for now it was enough. The combination of relief, exhilaration, and adrenaline overwhelmed her usually ironclad self-control. Try as she might, she couldn't hold back the wave of emotion that rolled over her and her shoulders shook as she started to cry.

"Cate?" Ryan said, his voice filled with concern. He put her feet on the ground and pulled back to look at her, his brows drawn together. "What's wrong?"

She grinned up at him. "Nothing," she replied, framing his face with her hands. "Nothing is wrong."

He looked confused and gently ran his fingers over her wet cheek. "Then why the tears?"

"Because the Agency *finally* did something right," she said. "For once people were put ahead of politics." She flung her arms around his neck and hugged him again. "Mr. Heston is going to recommend asylum for Yasmeen and the girls, and he's going to recommend the Agency cut all ties with Hasan."

"Outstanding." Ryan chuckled and tightened his embrace. "You did it."

Cat jerked back and looked up at him. "No, *we* did it." She searched his eyes. "Thank you for not being the typical macho American Special Forces soldier. If you hadn't included me in this mission, which broke *several* codes in the Special Forces handbook I'm sure, this little drama would have a very different ending, an ending I don't even want to think about." She traced the strong line of his jaw. "You're an amazing man, Ryan Heller, and meeting you has made coming to Afghanistan well worth the trip."

He stared at her, his expression solemn, those deep blue eyes holding hers. "If we weren't here," he said softly, "I'd kiss you right now."

"No matter where we were," she said, "I'd let you."

A pensive smile curved his mouth and he brushed his knuckles over her cheek. "You are *something*."

The touch of his hand sent a warm tingling over her skin and she gulped. As much as she wanted him to kiss her, she knew better with the prison and its many eyes looming behind them. He was an officer and he was in uniform, but the way he looked at her.... For the second time in as many minutes she felt as if she would drown beneath a wave of emotion. Giving him a small smile she stepped back.

"How about some breakfast, Lieutenant?" she asked, tipping her head to the side. "I don't know about you, but I'm starving."

Instead of replying he gestured toward the Humvee and opened her door. "After you," he said with a smile.

Cat shook her head. "No, Ryan. We go together."

Chapter Fourteen

Ryan parked in front of Cat's quarters and looked at the tiny plywood house. She, too, was looking at the structure, her face expressionless.

"Home sweet home," he said at last. "How are you feeling?"

A small smile curved her mouth but she kept her eyes trained out the window. "I'm good," she replied. "I'm still a little wound up, but that's normal."

"Yep," he said with a low chuckle. "It's the adrenaline. Whenever we complete a mission it always takes me a few hours to relax, no matter how long I've been awake." He paused, wishing she'd look at him. "A shower helps sometimes."

She smiled wistfully. "Wish I had Mack's tub," she commented. "A good, long soak sounds awesome right now."

He rested one hand on the steering wheel and smiled. "I could arrange that for you."

Her head whipped around. "You don't have to do that."

"But I would," he replied, tucking a stray curl behind her ear. "It's a nice picture... you, up to your neck in bubbles, candlelight, and a glass of wine." Ryan trailed his fingers down her neck and focused on the pulse fluttering in her throat.

There were so many things he wanted to say to her that he didn't know where to start, and when she turned those wide, green eyes on him all coherent thought completely vanished. The entire evening played back in his brain in two seconds flat and he relived every emotion he'd felt since they'd embarked on the mission: excitement, annoyance, apprehension, fear, relief, exhilaration, pride. Then something else entirely filled his chest and for a moment he couldn't breathe.

"What is it, Ryan?" Cat asked softly, her brows drawn together in concern.

Instead of answering he put a hand behind her neck and pulled her close. He searched her eyes for a moment then covered her mouth with his. She was startled at first, but then she closed her eyes and melted against him. He pressed her closer, his lips slanting over hers. She flattened her hands on his chest, her mouth soft and pliant. He explored her, savored her. He wanted to touch and taste every inch of her, and the thought of having her naked in his arms sent his pulse skyrocketing. Heat started to build in his belly, spreading slowly outward as she met his tongue with hers.

"*. . . you're right. If you did kiss me... I wouldn't stop you.*"

He fought for control as her softly uttered words echoed in his head. He didn't want to stop but he knew he had to. Taking his time, he counted the heartbeats as he slowly ended the kiss. He didn't look at her, because his body was already urging him to kiss her again. Ryan pressed his lips to her brow and exhaled slowly as she tucked in beneath his chin.

"Wh-what was *that* for?" Cat asked in a breathless voice.

"That was for me," he replied softly. "I've wanted to kiss you since the farmhouse."

"Oh. Okay."

He would have been content to sit there forever with her, her breath warm on his neck, her arms wound loosely around his waist. He closed his eyes and rubbed his hands up and down her back. Wrapping his fingers around her braid he tugged on it gently and looked down into her upturned face. It was almost his undoing. Her eyes mirrored what he was feeling, and her silent invitation nearly snapped his resolve. He steeled himself and pulled back.

"You should probably go," he said at last, "get cleaned up and get some sleep. It was a long night."

A flush stained her cheeks and she dropped her chin. "And you probably have an after-action report to finish," she said in a low voice.

"Nope," he replied. "Did it while you and the alphabet guys were interviewing Mrs. Hasan."

She glanced up at him. "That was fast."

"I had someplace else I wanted to be."

Cat blinked and her flush intensified. Ryan felt the pull in those emerald eyes, so before he kissed her again he exited the Humvee, came around to her side, and opened her door for her.

"Here you are madam, 12001 Disney Drive, Bagram Air Base, Bagram Valley, Afghanistan," he said in a proper British accent. "Would you like me to escort you to your door?"

She laughed and her cheeks dimpled as she exited the vehicle, slinging her rifle over her shoulder. She curtsied deeply and looked up at him through her lashes. "That would be lovely, kind sir."

He laughed and fell into step beside her as they walked the thirty or so feet to her door. When they reached the hut, she stood on the first step and faced him, which made her about an inch taller than him. He stuffed his hands in his pockets and met her gaze.

"Great job last night," he said sincerely. "You should be proud. I am."

She looked away and a shy smile curved her mouth. "Thanks," she replied, "and you have every reason to be proud. We got in, we got out, no casualties, and it looks like there will be a happy ending."

His brows drew together. "You realize that no matter what that Heston guy told you, things could change and the ending might be completely different than what was promised."

Her smile faded and she nodded. "I know, but I'm going to cross my fingers and pray that doesn't happen."

"Just so you're aware," he said. "I'd hate to see you get hurt if they decide to change their minds."

"Thanks, Ryan, but I'm a big girl and I live in the alphabet world. I know how it works."

He watched her face carefully, but all he saw was solemn acceptance. "Okay. You wanna... get some dinner with me later?"

The dimples were back. "I'd love to."

"All right," he said, half turning. "I'll call you later."

"Hey, Ryan."

He turned back and looked at her in silent question. She watched him uncertainly for a moment, then looked away as her cheeks went pink.

"Um, I know it's almost... *lunchtime* and this is probably *really* inappropriate, but...." She paused and met his gaze. "Do you want to come in for a glass of wine?"

His brows shot skyward and he crossed his arms over his chest as his abdominals tightened.

Cat's flush deepened and she stuffed her hands in her pockets. "I mean... it *is* five o'clock somewhere, and we just got off work, so...." She glanced at him quickly then dropped her eyes. "I told you I couldn't drink the whole bottle by myself."

Ryan stared at her for a moment and her discomfiture was oddly reassuring. He smiled and shook his head. "I'd better not. The SPs tend to frown on driving under the influence, especially since US forces aren't supposed to be drinking at all."

"Right," she said, nodding slowly. "Okay then. I'll... umm... I'll see you later."

"Yes," he agreed. "You will."

She watched him walk back to the Humvee, and waved as he drove slowly away. After he disappeared from view, she opened her door and stepped inside with a dispirited sigh.

She closed and locked the door behind her, then propped the rifle up against the wall and slowly undressed. Although she was disappointed Ryan had declined her invitation, she wasn't at all surprised. She smiled as she remembered their conversation over breakfast. Even though they'd only known each other a few days, she felt as if she'd known him for much longer. They had talked nonstop, never running out of things to say. There had been no awkward pauses, no tense silence which, for her, was new. Her last 'relationship' had been with Peter. She'd only dated a few men since then, but she couldn't remember it being so... *easy*. There was no denying the chemistry between them, but there was also something more, something that ran deeper than simply physical. It was as if she'd known him before and they were getting reacquainted.

Cat slipped into a bathrobe and flip-flops, and her heart did a somersault when she thought back to the kiss they'd just shared. Her lips tingled and she pressed her fingers to them. She closed her eyes and her breathing quickened as she imagined making love with him, the chiseled, muscular planes of his body pressed intimately to hers, his hands on her flesh, his mouth.... She groaned in frustration and ran a hand over her face, which was hot and flushed. Frowning, she undid her braid, brushed her hair quickly, then grabbed her toiletries and made her way to the showers.

By the time she had lathered, conditioned, scrubbed, lotioned, and returned to her quarters she had herself somewhat under control. She combed out her hair then cleaned up the room, tossing her dirty clothes into her locker. As she did so she caught sight of the velvet nightgown. She paused and reached for the gown, rubbing the luxurious material between her fingers. On impulse, she pulled it off the hanger, dropped the robe, and slipped the negligee over her head. She closed her eyes and a pleasurable shiver coursed through her as the soft, heavy material slithered deliciously over her skin. Smoothing the fabric, she did a turn in front of the mirror, the skirt flaring out. That was enough to give her an idea.

Cat closed the light-blocking curtains then gathered the flameless candles which she'd stored in the bottom desk drawer. She put one on each nightstand and one on her desk, turning them on as she went, and smiled as a golden glow showered the room with iridescent light. She then took the wine bottle from the mini-fridge, grabbed the goblet from where she'd put it inside her locker, and poured herself a glass. The final touch was music. "Romantic Piano" poured softly from the speakers on her laptop, filling the room with slow, sensual sound. Now, if only Ryan were here.

Cat lay down on her bed and slowly sipped the wine. As the candlelight and music washed over her, she felt the last of the adrenaline wear off. She sighed softly and pictured him: the eyes so blue they were almost violet, the sharp line of his jaw, the lips that made her melt, the tall, athletic body, the smile that was like sunlight to her soul. Desire swirled in her belly, and now it wasn't adrenaline making her edgy. She wanted him so much she ached.

Frustrated, she sat up and put the wine aside. She looked around the room then turned off the candle closest to her. Shaking her head, she rose, and was about to turn off the second candle when there was a soft rap on her door. Her head snapped around.

"Just a minute," she said after a moment of surprised silence. Cat grabbed her robe, slipped it on, and tied the sash. Her bare feet whispered over the floor as she approached the panel and said, "Who is it?"

"It's me, Cate. Can we talk?"

She was so stunned that for a moment she couldn't move.

"Cate?"

She blinked, shook herself, and opened the door. She looked at Ryan with wide eyes and backed up as he walked up the steps and into her quarters. He closed and locked the door behind him then turned to her. Looping an arm around her waist he pulled her against him.

"I changed my mind," he whispered.

His mouth covered hers and, unable to move, she mentally braced herself for the chemical reaction she knew was coming. It didn't take long to realize she would've had better luck standing against a tidal wave. The truck bomb she'd witnessed explode was nothing compared to the heat that flooded through her.

His lips moved with exquisite slowness over hers, gently teasing them apart. Cat clutched the front of his uniform as his arms enfolded her, his heart beating steadily beneath her fist. Just the feel of him made her knees weak. Ryan touched his tongue to hers, his movements cautious and unhurried. With a low moan, she released his shirt and slid her fingers up and over his shoulders. She clasped her hands behind his neck and pressed the length of her body to his.

She gasped when his lips left hers to trail leisurely over her jaw. He nuzzled her ear and then started to nibble. She inhaled sharply.

"I thought you said you didn't want to put it in burners yet," she whispered, breathless.

"What I *said* was I didn't want to put it in burners just to flame out." He lifted his head and looked into her eyes, his expression solemn. "And I still don't." Ryan watched her carefully, his brows drawing together. "You up for that?"

She caught her breath at what she saw in those sapphire depths. The warmth of joy and chilling fear both leapt in her chest, each fighting for dominance, but it wasn't much of a battle. Joy quickly overpowered fear and she smiled. "Absolutely."

It was then Ryan seemed to notice the change in her room's decor. He looked from one candle to the other and then turned wide eyes to her. She glanced over her shoulder at the scene, swallowing hard when she realized what it must look like to him. He released her and stepped back.

"Are you expecting someone?" His expression went neutral. "Should I... leave?"

She flushed to the roots of her hair. "No." With two long strides, she walked over to her laptop, hit a button, and silenced the music. She turned the candle on the desk off and glanced at Ryan. "It's not what you think. I was just...." An amused glint entered his eyes as he lifted one dark brow and she dropped her gaze, her cheeks burning. "Never mind." She walked around the bed to turn off the last candle, plunging the room into darkness. Just like that, the romantic mood was gone.

She ground her teeth together in frustration and crossed her arms over her chest, unable to face him. When the music suddenly started again she turned her head slightly. A faint glow from behind her let her know he had switched the candle back on. In her periphery, she saw him walk to the nightstand on the other side of the bed and turn that candle on, and she had a pretty good idea where he was going next.

He moved up behind her, and she stiffened when he reached around her to flip the switch on the last candle. She licked her lips, her heart rate going from a canter to a steady gallop as he straightened and stood at her back. Her arms fell to her sides and she fought the urge to lean against him. He was so close she could feel the heat from his body.

"You were just... imagining." Ryan brushed her hair to the side, exposing her neck, and goose bumps shivered over her skin. She gulped when his fingers grazed her throat. "So... I'm not the only one." He pressed his lips to a spot behind her ear. "Are you wearing it?"

The husky rasp of his voice sent her heart into palpitations. Cat exhaled and nodded slowly once. He moved closer and she sucked in a breath when he reached around her with both hands. Frozen, Cat tried to control her pulse as he worked the knot on her sash loose and let the velour ties fall. The robe fell open but she stood as still as stone, her heart pounding. With slow, deliberate movements Ryan lifted the robe from her shoulders, slid it down her arms, and tossed it aside.

There was a long pause, and then he whispered, "Damn."

Cat felt him back away, and while part of her wanted to turn to him and reclaim the warmth he radiated she couldn't. She bit her lip and waited for him to say something, anything.

"Cate. Look at me."

Her stomach flipped and she shook her head once. She was used to staring death in the face, but looking into the eyes of someone she was falling in love with was something else entirely. Her heart was clearly in the crosshairs, and if he didn't feel the same it would be a kill shot.

"Please."

She hesitated, her heart pinging off the inside of her chest like a pinball. *Might as well get it over with. Standing here like this is accomplishing nothing.* Finally, she forced herself to move and slowly turned around. Summoning her will, she straightened her spine, lifted her chin, and opened her eyes.

Ryan sat on the edge of her desk, his hands clasped in front of him. His gaze roved over her several times, almost as if he didn't believe what he was seeing. After nearly a minute he exhaled slowly and looked at her, incredulous.

"My God," he breathed. "Why isn't every man on this base beating down your door?"

It took her a moment to find her voice. "There's only one man on this base I *want* beating down my door."

He stood and walked to her, his eyes narrowing a fraction as his gaze wandered over her face. "You have me."

Cat's heart flip-flopped. "Do I?"

He cupped her head in his hands, his expression serious. "You've had me since day one, Cate." He lowered his head and kissed her then pulled back a fraction of an inch. "Since the first shot."

And, just like that, the romantic mood was back.

She closed her eyes and wrapped her arms around his waist as he kissed her again. His mouth moved over hers slowly, languorously, his movements a sharp contrast to the wildfire bursting to life inside her. The touch of his tongue to hers was the equivalent of putting an open flame to the driest tinder, and she clung to him, her legs turning warm and rubbery. She fisted her hands in his uniform, but it wasn't material she wanted to feel. Cat wanted to *feel* him, the warmth of his skin, the ripple of muscles beneath her fingers, his body pressed to hers, *all* of him.

When she pulled back with a frustrated growl he looked at her in silent question. Heat rose in her cheeks, but there were other parts of her much warmer so she ignored her own shyness and undid the buttons on his uniform. The blouse fell open and she slid her hands up and over his shoulders. Without a word, Ryan shrugged out of the garment and let it fall.

Focusing on his chest, she tugged the tan t-shirt from his pants, her heart drumming against her sternum. She pulled the garment halfway up, exposing his ridged abdomen before he took over, peeled the shirt off over his head, and tossed it aside as well. Her gaze wandered over his muscled chest and stomach for a moment then she closed her eyes as pure lust impaled her. Ryan didn't have a six-pack; he had an eight-pack, each muscle well defined and clearly visible. She trailed her fingers lightly over his flat belly, then up over his chest, his skin smooth and warm to the touch. Her insides quivered and when she met his smoky gaze there was no going back. She experienced a moment of pure terror as her heart defected to Ryan, but only a moment. Somehow, Cat knew her heart was safe with him.

She reached for his hand, wound her fingers through his, and led him to the edge of the bed. She looked down at the plain spread for a moment then faced him.

"Cate...."

She pressed her fingers to his mouth and shook her head slightly. Her eyes locked with his, she eased down on the bed and lay back. He stood over her for a moment, his expression unreadable, but when she reached for him he didn't hesitate. Ryan came down on all fours over her, straddling her hips, the muscles in his broad shoulders moving fluidly. He looked at her for a few seconds, then lowered his head and captured her lips.

This kiss, unlike the gentle, exploratory kisses from only a few minutes past, was demanding, ruthless. Cat's head spun as Ryan ravaged her mouth, stealing her breath. Liquid fire spread through her and she grasped his waist, trying to pull him closer, needing to feel his body pressing down on hers, but there was no moving him. Arching her back, she brushed her breasts against his chest and gasped softly as electricity crackled through her. The shock settled with throbbing intensity between her thighs, and it was almost more than she could stand.

Cat unfastened his belt and the buttons on his pants. As she slipped her hand inside the waistband of his trousers, someone banged on the door, hard. Ryan jerked back suddenly, and it was almost like having a bucket of cold water dumped on her.

She groaned, frustrated, her body still humming. "You've *got* to be kidding me."

Whoever it was banged again, harder, and the tiny house fairly shook from the force of it. Both of their heads snapped up, their eyes flying to the thin portal.

Ryan frowned, sat back on his haunches, and looked at her. "Are you expecting guests?"

"No," she growled. She came up onto her elbows. "No, I'm not."

"Do you think it's Mitchell?" Ryan climbed off the bed and scowled. "Maybe I should answer it—"

The fist banged again.

"Cat, it's Tripp. Open this door. We need to talk, *now*."

She met Ryan's surprised gaze, then flopped back on the bed and grasped her forehead with one hand, as if she had a headache. "Ah, hell."

"Let me guess," Ryan drawled, "you didn't talk to him about what happened with Mitchell."

"No, I didn't, Ryan." Cat squeezed her eyes shut. "I didn't really have time."

He chuckled, obviously amused by all this. "Well, you better make time before he huffs and puffs and blows your house down."

She lifted her head to glare at him, but when she saw him standing there, her robe dangling from one finger, she sighed in resignation. "Fine." She rose and snatched the dressing gown from his hand then pointed at him. "But *you* aren't going anywhere."

He crossed his arms over his chest and grinned. "Wasn't planning to."

Cat jerked the robe on, but her resolve melted when she met Ryan's gaze. She hesitated a moment, made a disappointed sound, then put a hand behind his neck and kissed him soundly. His hands grasped her waist as she deepened the kiss, and she completely forgot why she'd gotten up and put her robe back on. At least she had until Tripp knocked again.

"Cat! I know you're in there, and if you don't come out I'm coming in."

Pulling back, she sighed. Ryan fought a grin.

"Go talk to him," he said. "I'll be right here."

She pouted. "You better."

Ryan chuckled, put his hands on her shoulders, and turned her to face the door. Then he gave her a light shove and a smack on her backside. "Move it, Tiger."

Before she could take a step, Tripp pounded again.

"Cat!"

"Okay!" she shouted. "I'm coming!"

Cat strode to the door, opened it, and stepped outside. Bright sun assaulted her and she blinked. Tripp stood back a few paces, his fists on his hips and a scowl on his face. She shielded her eyes and glared at him. "Seriously? Are you *trying* to knock my house down?"

"Maybe you should answer your door faster."

"And maybe *you* should knock like a *normal* person instead of the Incredible Hulk." Cat dropped her hand and squared off with him. "What is so urgent you felt the need to break down my door?"

He stared at her for a few moments, his expression stony. He was angry, but there was something else in his eyes she couldn't quite define, until he spoke.

"How long have we worked together, Cat?" he asked in a low voice. "Five, almost six years?"

The change in tone caught her off guard. He sounded hurt, and she blinked. "Um... yeah, about that."

"And we're pretty close, right?" He searched her eyes. "I mean, I don't think of you as just a coworker. You're like my... *sister*. I consider you one of my best friends, and I thought you felt the same."

Cat's eyes widened. "I *do*, Ben." She approached him and put a hand on his arm. "You *are* one of my closest friends. Why would you think otherwise?"

A muscle in his cheek twitched. "Because I had to hear about what happened with Mitchell from Sergeant Anderson when I should've gotten that information from *you*." His dark brows drew together. "Why wouldn't you tell me about something like that?"

So, she had been correct. She closed her eyes, dropped her chin to her chest, and sighed. "You're right, Ben. I'm sorry." Her hand fell to her side and she glanced at him quickly then looked away, shame heating her cheeks. "For what it's worth, I was *going* to tell you."

"When?"

"This afternoon, actually," she replied.

He crossed his arms over his chest. "Why wait?"

She rubbed her eyes. "Because I have several things I need to talk to you about, you and the team both." She looked at him. "I just wanted to... do it all at once, get it done and over with."

His glare remained. "Why were you with him in the first place? You, of all people, should know better than to poke a snake."

Cat swallowed hard and looked at the ground.

"Oh, I get it," he said softly. "That's how we got our three-day pass." She didn't reply and he looked at her in disbelief. "What the *hell* were you thinking?"

"I was thinking we all needed some down time," she shot back. "I know *I* did, and I figured a couple hours would be a small price to pay."

Tripp leaned over until they were nearly nose to nose. "Don't ever do that again," he said from between clenched teeth. "I don't care if that asshole offers us a month off, it's not worth the price, and *none* of us would *ever* ask you to do that."

"I know," she whispered, her eyes stinging. "I said I was sorry."

"You know he's not stable where you're concerned, don't you?" Tripp studied her for a few moments, then sighed and shook his head. "What if that had happened here instead of in a chow hall full of witnesses? Women get killed every day by their ex-lovers, Cat."

That sparked her temper. Cat's eyes narrowed and her head snapped up. "I think you know I'm not your typical woman, Tripp. Give me a *little* credit."

"Funny," he said softly, taking her hand and pushing the sleeve of her robe up. He gently stroked the dark purple fingerprints on her wrist and above her elbow. "You bruise like one."

Her bravado vaporized and she pulled away, tugging the sleeve of her robe back down. "Trust me. It won't happen again." She looked at him and was touched by the concern in his eyes. She pressed a hand to his cheek. "I promise."

Tripp covered her hand with his. "And how are you going to keep that promise? You two have played hide and seek for years now, and he's always found you. What's different this time?"

"Well, for starters, Monday morning I'm putting in a transfer request," Cat said. "And, if you guys want to go with me I have someone above Peter who will push the paperwork through for our entire team."

Tripp's gaze wandered over her face for a moment. "You're serious."

She nodded. "I'm done, Tripp. I'm tired of having him chase me all over the globe."

He studied her for a bit before a small smile tipped the corners of his mouth. "About fucking time you got out from under that SOB, no pun intended." His brows drew together. "This renewed sense of purpose wouldn't have anything to do with one tall, dark-haired SEAL, now would it?"

Unbidden, color surged up her neck and into her cheeks. She dropped her gaze. "Maybe."

"Hmm. I knew I liked Lieutenant Heller for a reason." He paused and looked at her as if seeing her for the first time. "Hey, why aren't you dressed? It's almost...." He paused and looked at his watch, "... 11:30. Time for lunch, sleepyhead, not breakfast. What gives?"

Her flush intensified to the point she thought her head would burst into flames. She looked up at him and saw the proverbial light bulb go on. A sly smile curved Tripp's mouth and his eyes narrowed.

"You're not alone in there, are you?" Her lack of a response answered his question, and he chuckled. "Out-fucking-standing." Before she could stop him, he walked up to the door, banged once, and said: "You better do her right, Lieutenant, because if I hear your performance is anything less than stellar you and I are going to have to talk."

Cat gaped at him. "Tripp!"

"I'll do my best, Tripp," was the muffled reply from inside her quarters. "Waiting on you guys."

She groaned and covered her face with her hands. Tripp laughed and pulled her against his chest.

"Go get 'em, Tiger," he said, hugging her tightly. "Me 'n the boys will be playing Texas Hold 'em with a bunch of Aussies, so come by when you're ready to chat." He pulled back and chucked her under the chin. "Show that SEAL how it's done, sweetheart. And have fun. You deserve some."

Chapter Fifteen

Ryan had just put his boots and socks neatly at the foot of the bed when he heard the door handle turn. He sat on the edge of the mattress facing the door and rested his elbows on his knees. Something in his chest tightened as Cat walked into the room and shut and locked the door behind her, but he kept his expression neutral.

Her face was flushed, and when she glanced at him the flush intensified. Slowly, she walked up to him, arms crossed, eyes diverted.

"Sorry about that," she said in a low voice.

"Don't be." Ryan reached for her hands and wound his fingers through hers. "He's looking out for you. That's what friends do."

Her brows drew together. "I know. I didn't mean that part." She bit her lip. "I meant the...."

"Ah." Ryan chuckled. "The *performance* part."

Her cheeks were blazing now, and Ryan felt the familiar tug as his gaze wandered over her averted face. She squeezed her eyes shut and nodded shortly. Ryan smiled, stood, and slowly untied the sash of her robe. Cat sucked in a breath when he slid his fingers around her waist and pulled her close. He watched the rapid rise and fall of her breasts as she shrugged out of the robe, and when the velour puddled around her feet his heart began to pound steadily against his sternum. His gaze wandered over the ripe curves so tantalizingly displayed in the burgundy velvet, and his groin tightened. He couldn't *wait* to get her out of that nightgown.

"Forget about it," he whispered, tracing the line of her collarbone. "I already have."

Cat didn't reply, her teeth worrying her lower lip. He trailed his fingers up her neck, tucking a fall of damp hair behind her ear, then leaned over and kissed her cheek.

"Now," he said, "where were we?"

She cried out in surprise when he scooped her up in his arms and deposited her unceremoniously on the bed. Her hair haloed around her head, the red strands glowing copper beneath the candle's golden glow.

His eyes narrowed. "*You* were right about... there." Ryan paused, giving himself time to take in the whole picture. He hardened as his gaze wandered over the lush breasts, the rounded hips, the long, sleek legs, and when he imagined those long legs wrapped firmly around his waist he grew harder still. Ryan ground his teeth together and came over her on all fours again. "And I was right about... here, give or take."

"I don't want you there," she said in a breathless voice.

She ran her fingers over his jaw, those green eyes drawing him in and pulling him under. Ryan leaned a couple of inches closer, not willing to give up any more ground than that, at least not yet. "Where do you want me, Cate?"

The look in her eyes was answer enough. The next moment she knocked her fists lightly into the insides of his elbows, unlocking his braced arms. She gasped softly as his weight came down on top of her. Then she gave him a sinful smile and wrapped her arms around his neck.

"Getting warmer," she said.

"Hmm." He brushed her lips with his. "Let's see if we can't improve on that."

Ryan shifted his weight and stretched out beside her, loving the way she fit against him. He let his gaze wander over her face for a moment, then lowered his head and covered her mouth. His insides clenched as she sighed and pressed herself closer to him, her softness melding with the hard planes and hollows of his body. When his tongue demanded entrance to her mouth she gave it freely and heat pulsed through him. Ryan explored her, taking his time, gauging her reaction. He ran one hand slowly from her velvet clad hip to her neck, his fingers moving leisurely over her bare back. Her skin was even softer than the velvet and she trembled beneath his touch. She tightened her hold on him, her breasts crushed to his chest, the contact of their bodies doing amazing things to his heart rate. He didn't think he could want her more, until Cat wound one leg over his. Ryan was certain he couldn't get any harder, but as she moved her hips toward him he did and a muffled groan escaped him.

Threading his fingers into her hair, Ryan gently pulled her head back to expose the pale skin of her throat. He pressed his lips to the pulse racing there and smiled when she gasped. Nuzzling her neck, he slipped one finger beneath the strap of the nightgown and slid it off her shoulder. As he did so he noticed the bruises on her arm and paused.

The anger that flared in his chest did nothing to diminish his desire for her. In fact, the rush of protectiveness he felt only made him want her more. Ryan lifted his head and looked into those emerald eyes.

"If he ever touches you again I'll kill him."

Cat blinked and ran her fingers over his bare chest. "He won't." A slow smile curved her mouth. "*You*, on the other hand...." She covered his hand with hers and moved it to her breast. She closed her eyes and whimpered softly as he moved his fingers back and forth, the velvet rubbing over the taut peak. Ryan's groin tightened again and he pressed his lips to the rounded swell. Suddenly the velvet was in the way.

Ryan pushed her onto her back and came over her, straddling her thighs. With slow, deliberate movements, he hooked his thumbs in the straps of the gown and pulled them down until she was naked from the waist up. He leaned back on his heels and took a deep breath, exhaling slowly.

"Wow."

A flush crept over her skin but she returned his gaze boldly. Her breathing was rapid and shallow, and when he cupped her breasts in his hands she closed her eyes and bit her lip. He ran his thumbs over her dusky nipples. Cat moaned softly, her fingers clutching the blanket.

Her breasts fascinated him, but they weren't enough. He wanted more. Her eyes flew open when he got off the bed and she looked at him in alarm, until he slipped his fingers inside the nightgown at her waist. Leaning up on her elbows, she watched as he slid his hands over her hips and down the length of her legs, pushing the gown down as he did so. When he reached her ankles, he grabbed the tangle of rich fabric and tossed it aside.

"God Almighty," he breathed, his gaze raking over her. He shook his head. "This is one mission I might need help with."

With all the grace of her namesake, Cat rose and stood in front of him. "Allow me."

Ryan tried to regulate his breathing as she finished what she'd started before Tripp had interrupted them. Once his pants were unbuttoned she trailed her fingers lightly over his stomach and downward, and his abdominals clenched involuntarily. A wicked smile curved her mouth as she slipped her hands inside the waistband of his briefs and slowly pushed them and his pants past his hips. Ryan stood unmoving, his pulse shooting up as she knelt in front of him. He closed his eyes and clenched his jaw when she tugged on his trousers. Cool air and warm fingers whispered over his skin but he hardly noticed, because Cat was busy planting soft kisses on his belly, her hands moving steadily down his legs. When his pants and briefs finally lay around his ankles he stepped out of them, kicked them to the side, and looked down at her. What he saw in her eyes made his heart jump.

She pressed her lips to his thigh and heat seared through him. Her tongue darted out to taste his skin and he tensed. He had a pretty good idea what she was planning to do next, and he wasn't at all sure he could handle it. He was so hard he ached, and the thought of her mouth on him was almost enough to make him lose it. Steeling himself, Ryan reached down and pulled her to her feet.

She seemed startled at first, but then a low, sultry laugh escaped her and Cat stepped closer, her breasts grazing his chest. He exhaled, electricity pulsing along every nerve. He jumped and air hissed out from between his teeth when her hand closed around his shaft. His eyes flew to her face. She watched him carefully then started a slow, sensual massage. He ground his teeth together as the heaviness in his groin increased. Finally, he took hold of her wrists.

"Stop."

Tipping her head to the side, Cat gave him a small smile and released him. Eyes locked with his, she eased down on the edge of the mattress, and he was transfixed by the graceful movements of her body. She gave him a smoldering look, then lay back and stretched out on the bed, arms over her head and back arched. Ryan's breath caught as the golden light shimmered over her skin, illuminating the curves and accentuating the hollows on her long, lithe form. He wanted her so much it hurt. Cat reached out to him and he wound his fingers through hers.

"God, you're beautiful," he whispered.

"So are you," she breathed, tugging on his hand.

He lay down beside her, his gaze wandering over her face and coming to rest on her lips. His mouth descended, crushing hers and demanding entrance, and she gave it to him. He was lost in her, the taste of her kiss, the rapid beat of her heart, the satin of her skin beneath his fingertips.

It was almost too much. The throbbing in his groin sharpened and he slid a hand up her leg, stopping at the juncture of her thighs. She moved her pelvis against his fingers and he growled. She moved her hips again and moaned in protest, but he was going to take his time. He continued to ravage her mouth, his fingers lazily sifting through the crisp curls and going no further. As much as he wanted to touch her he didn't want to rush things. She covered his hand with hers and tried to slide it between her legs, silently urging him onward, but he gently disentangled himself and shook his head.

"Uh uh," he said against her mouth. "Not yet."

A disappointed murmur escaped her and Ryan smiled as he trailed his lips over her jaw, her throat, and lower. She tensed when he pressed his mouth to the swell of her breast, his tongue leaving a hot, wet trail over her skin as he moved closer to his goal.

He circled the dusky peak without touching it, and he felt her coil up like a spring. He teased her mercilessly, her frantic whispers and low moans making him hotter and harder. Her head thrashed back and forth, her fingers clenching the pillow, her body trembling. When he finally took the taut nipple into his mouth a cry of pleasure escaped her and she arched her back, pressing herself more firmly against his tongue. Ryan reveled in her response, first suckling, then nibbling, then suckling again. She grasped his waist as he came over her on all fours, his mouth hot on her breast.

"Ryan...!"

Hearing his name wrenched from her lips made him smile, and gave him the strength to hold back. His body wanted desperately to lose himself inside her, but his heart and his brain weren't quite ready for that yet. After all, a challenge *had* been issued, and he had no desire to have Tripp question his manhood. However, even a US Navy SEAL had his limits. Ryan wanted to be sure he pushed past Cat's limits before he passed his own.

"Ryan, please...!"

He continued to suckle her, then pulled back and looked up. "Please what, Cate?"

"I need you," she said in a fervent whisper. "I want you... inside me."

His penis throbbed and he took a deep breath. "All in good time, Cate. All in good time." He returned to her breast and the hard, dark pink nipples.

Cat groaned and tried to pull him closer but, as strong as she was, she couldn't move him. Ryan lifted his head and met her gaze. Her eyes were ablaze with desire, her breathing ragged. He drew one hand slowly up her inner thigh and was rewarded when he saw the fire burn hotter in those emerald green depths. She stared at him, her eyelids fluttering slightly and her tongue darting out to wet her lips as he slid a finger inside her. He found her clitoris and caressed the swollen nub, his movements slow and methodical, then he lowered his head to suckle her breast again. Cat whimpered and covered her face with her hands. He delved a little deeper and the tautness in his groin expanded outward. She was so tight, her flesh hot and slick, and the thought of burying himself inside her nearly ended his resolve.

He stretched out beside her, the contact of their bodies sending electricity pulsing along every nerve. Her soft cries of pleasure grew louder as he slipped another finger inside her and began to move them slowly in and out of her body. His thumb massaged her clit with deliberate, feather-light strokes, and her legs began to tremble.

Her hips moved in rhythm with his hand, her skin flushed, her hair in wild disarray around her shoulders. Ryan looked up and knew without a doubt he'd never seen anyone so beautiful. Her lashes were a dark arc over her cheekbones, her lips swollen, her breasts heaving with each labored breath. The soft cries turned into low moans as he thrust deeper and applied a bit more pressure. Each passing moment was a test of his will, his body in tune with her increasing arousal. His hips jerked involuntarily as her muscles tightened around his fingers, and he imagined those same muscles contracting around another part of his anatomy. Taking a deep, slow breath, he fought for control and started reciting the UN's Rules of Engagement in his head.

Cat swiveled her hips faster, but he had no intention of ceding control yet. He was having too much fun pleasuring her. His fingers moved in and out of her body with deep, slow, gentle strokes. Focusing again on her breasts, he nibbled each taut nub as if it was something to be gently and carefully devoured. He loved the way her nipples hardened against his tongue, and he took his time, fully enjoying her heated response. Taking one rosy tip into his mouth, he sucked lightly and grinned when her soft cries increased in frequency and volume. It wouldn't be long now.

A few minutes later, eyes tightly closed, Cat went silent and completely still. For several seconds she didn't even breathe and he smiled, knowing full well what was next. Suddenly her body bowed and her internal muscles clamped down on his fingers, her legs shaking, her hands fisted in his hair.

Ryan captured her lips and kissed her deeply, taking her cries of release into his mouth. She shuddered violently and clung to him, her fingers digging into his shoulders. His tongue melded with hers and he continued to caress her clit, his touch delicate but relentless. Tremors pulsed through her, the sleek muscles of her abdomen contracted powerfully as she climaxed. Ryan ended the kiss and pulled back to watch her orgasm crash over her. It was like watching huge waves thunder onto shore. At first it was fierce, but as the moments passed the waves softened to swells, then the swells to gentle ripples. When the last spasm faded, Cat went completely limp and took in a huge gulp of air. Ryan flattened his hand on her belly, a great sense of contentment washing over him.

Propping his head on his hand he looked at her, one finger making slow circles around her bellybutton, and he smiled as color surged into her cheeks. When her breathing returned to somewhat normal, she rolled toward him and pressed her face into the crook of his neck.

Cat's body was still buzzing, warm pulses radiating out from her belly to her fingers and toes. Even her scalp tingled. She couldn't remember the last time a man had paid such keen attention to her pleasure without regard for his own. She took another deep breath and snuggled closer to him.

"Are you... good at *everything* you do?" she asked.

He chuckled. "No." He pressed his lips to her temple, his fingers moving in slow circles over her back. "However, there *are* certain activities I put extra effort into."

"*Really?*" She ran her hands over his chest and kissed the pulse thrumming in his neck. "I would *never* have guessed."

"Hmm." He cupped her bottom and pulled her close. "I suppose I need to work a little harder then."

His erection was hard against her belly and for a moment she lost all train of thought. Her vulva throbbed, her nipples tightened, and Cat bit her lip, desire shooting through her as if her climax had never happened. She wound her leg over his.

"It's not that you didn't work... *hard* enough," she said in a low voice. "You didn't give me what I... *wanted.*"

A hint of a smile curved his mouth and he curled his hand around her hip. "And what was that again?"

She threaded her fingers into his hair and pulled his head down. "You," she replied, less than a hair's breadth separating their lips, "inside me."

"Ah." He grinned. "I think I can arrange that."

She kissed him deeply, then pulled back and smiled. "I certainly hope so."

Ryan slid his hand down her leg, hooked his fingers behind her knee, and pulled her thigh up to his waist. She felt him, hot and hard, pressing against her flesh, but when she moved her hips forward he backed off. Chuckling, he dipped his head and suckled her breast.

"Patience, Cate."

"*That* is a virtue I don't have a lot of," she breathed.

"And yet... you're a sniper, an endeavor that requires *considerable* amounts of that virtue." He flicked her beaded nipple once with his tongue.

She gasped. "Shooting and sex... *vastly* different activities."

"Not really." His breath was hot on her skin. "Both require skill, and precision, and... *staying power.*"

Cat closed her eyes and groaned in frustration, an aching need pulsing between her legs. Knowing he was so close only made it worse. She kneaded his shoulders, pleasure impaling her as he rolled one nipple between his thumb and forefinger, his mouth firmly fixed over the other. Slowly, Ryan pushed her onto her back. He then covered her body with his, settling neatly between her thighs as he returned to suckling her. His lips and tongue wreaked havoc with her senses. It didn't matter where he touched her, each sensation translated from the point of origin to that sensitive spot between her legs, one building upon the other until she was certain her body would short circuit. When his fingers found her clit again she stifled a moan and her hips jerked.

"Look at me, Cate," he whispered.

Cat took a shaky breath and looked into those stormy blue eyes. He leaned up on his elbows, his hands framing her face, his expression serious. Slowly, inch by inch, he sank into her, and she couldn't look away from him. She inhaled sharply as the friction between their bodies sent her into sensory overload. Her breasts crushed to his chest. His pelvis pressed to hers. It was almost like climaxing in slow motion, each movement exaggerated, each sensation amplified. She'd never experienced anything like this, a pleasure so intense it sent her heart into palpitations. Winding her arms around his body she gasped as he gave one final thrust and came into her fully.

"Ryan...!"

"Ah... *fuck.*"

The guttural words sent a bolt of electrified current straight to her core. He clenched his jaw, his fingers moving over her face as if he was a blind man memorizing her features. Cat moaned softly as he pulled back a few inches then pushed forward again, filling her completely. Her breath caught as he began to move in and out of her body, his pace leisurely and sensual, his penis hot and hard inside her. That wonderful, infuriating tension coiled in her belly, and Cat moved her pelvis faster. Ryan froze and grasped her hips.

"Patience, Cate," he said in a harsh whisper.

She nearly cried.

He growled, a sound that rumbled in his chest and sent lust racing through her. He started to move again, slowly and deliberately, and with each passing second he seemed to grow thicker and harder. She whimpered and wrapped her legs around his waist, trying to draw him deeper. He buried his face in the crook of her neck and groaned.

His hips melded with hers in an unhurried tempo. Cat turned her face, seeking his lips, and when his tongue touched hers a rush of heat seared through her. His fingers moved to her breast and plucked gently at the taut nipple. The spring in her belly wound tighter and she moaned against his mouth, her hands molding to his head. Ryan kissed her deeply, the thrust of his tongue matching the thrust of his body, and she didn't know how much more she could stand. Pleasure sizzled along every nerve, and as the minutes ticked by the tension built to an almost intolerable level.

"Ryan... please! I don't know how much more of this I can take...!"

She looked up at him and he clenched his jaw, the cords in his neck standing out. She closed her eyes as his hardness slowly left her body, then returned, filling the void inside her. It was heaven and it was torture, and with each push of his hips he drove her closer and closer to the edge. She'd never experienced anything so powerful, her heart pounding like horse's hooves against her breastbone as he tested the limits of her endurance. The pleasure was beyond intense, the tension building and winding tightly inside her.

"Ryan! Please...!"

He kissed her. "Should I stop?" he asked against her mouth.

"God, no...." She shook her head and dug her fingers into his shoulders. "Don't ever stop...."

Cupping her breast Ryan lifted the rounded swell to his mouth, and Cat felt the spring start to give. He suckled her lightly then a little harder, and when he nipped at the taut peak her body could take no more. The scrape of his teeth against her nipples, the thickness and hardness of him as he moved smoothly in and out of her body, the ripple of his muscles beneath her hands sent her reeling. A ragged moan escaped her as ecstasy started to roil outward from where his body joined hers to the rest of her.

"That's it, Cate," Ryan said in a low, gravelly voice. "Come with me, baby."

"Ryan...!"

"I want you to come with me...."

Cat hid her face against his chest and choked back a cry as ecstasy slowly rippled outward from the deepest part of her. The ripples grew in intensity and speed, shockwaves radiating outward until she was engulfed by them. He was hot and hard inside her, and the coil finally snapped. Vibrant colors flashed behind her eyes and she cried out in wonder. Her breath caught as her body convulsed, her muscles contracting tightly around him. She heard him groan deep in his throat. The pulses exploded outward, peaked, and gradually softened. She tried to catch her breath as she floated back to earth.

He continued to move inside her, his hips maintaining the slow, sensual rhythm, and she wrapped her arms tightly around his neck. His breathing was short and shallow, and another, deeper groan vibrated through him. He searched for her hands, laced his fingers through hers, and moved faster. With every hard, measured thrust of his pelvis he growled. The sound of his pleasure reverberated through her and just when she thought it was over a second, stronger swell hit. The pleasure rushed, pinnacled, and seemed to hang there, suspended, her body rocked by surging, furious pulses. Cat locked her thighs around his middle as wave after wave of hot, tingling sensation crashed over and through her. His hands slid beneath her to cup her bottom and she moaned against his shoulder as he shuddered. With a feral cry, Ryan gave a final, powerful thrust, seating himself to the hilt. He froze for a split second then his entire body shook, his hips jerking with the force of his climax. He pressed his face into her neck, his breath rushing over her skin in heated waves.

She clung to him taking long, slow breaths, trying to get her heart beat under control as the last tingles danced through her and slowly faded. Her fingers dug into his muscled shoulders, her ankles locked together in the small of his back. He took a deep breath, shuddered, and exhaled slowly, his lips near her ear. When he turned his face to nibble her earlobe Cat sighed, content.

She would have been happy to stay right there beneath him, the feel of his body on hers a welcome pressure. When he leaned up on his elbows to look at her she almost pulled him back, but his expression made her heart flutter.

"What?" she asked.

His eyes narrowed on her face and he brushed her hair back. "You are something, you know that?"

Cat flushed. "So are you."

He smiled. "Like I said, there are some activities I put extra effort into."

"I'll say." She squeezed her eyes shut. "That's the first time I've... ever... experienced...." Her voice trailed off as embarrassment seared her cheeks.

"Multiple orgasms?"

She gulped and it took her a moment to find her voice. "Yeah."

"Good." He pressed his lips to her cheek. "At least now I know you won't forget me."

The note of sadness in his voice touched something deep inside of her and her eyes snapped open. She stared at him and framed his face with her hands, her fingers stroking lightly over his beard.

"Forget you? I could *never* forget you. Why would you say that?"

A pensive smiled curved his mouth and he traced her lips with one finger. "Because eventually you'll move on. The military will send me to some other shithole third-world country to 'spread democracy' and our paths may never cross again." He kissed her softly. "In the years to come when you think of me... I want to know those memories make you smile."

The blush of release vanished and a cold wave washed over her.

Cat gaped at him for a moment then pushed him off her and sat up, wrapping the blanket around herself. "Don't," she said in a low, fierce voice. "*Don't* talk like that."

"Cate...."

"*No.*" She stared hard at him. "I don't want to think about that right now. Right now, I'm here, you're here, and we can be together. I don't know what the future holds for us, Ryan, but I intend to enjoy *every* minute I have with you because we may not have a tomorrow."

His expression sobered. "Ignoring the facts won't change them, Cate."

"Yeah," she said, angrily, "well, we'll cross that bridge when we come to it." She glared at him. "We're not there yet." She blinked and drew back from him as a stab of pain skewered her. "Or... are we?"

He smiled and sat up. "Easy, Tiger." Ryan threaded his fingers through hers and pressed his lips to the back of her hand. After a lingering kiss, he met her eyes. "God, I'm glad I changed my mind."

She pulled away and scowled, still stinging from his blunt assessment. "Why *did* you change your mind?"

Ryan's expression turned wistful and he grabbed a long curl, rubbing it slowly between his fingers. He leaned forward and kissed her bare shoulder. "I got all the way back to the compound before I remembered I was a United States Navy SEAL. SEALs don't run away from things that scare us, we run *toward* them." He looked at her. "So, I came back."

Cat blinked. "I... I... scare you?"

He frowned and put a hand behind her neck. "No." Ryan searched her face and his expression softened. "No, *you* don't scare me. The way you make me *feel* scares me." He paused, released her, and swung his legs off the side of the bed, presenting her with his back. "I'm falling for you, Cate, fast and hard." He glanced at her. "That doesn't happen to me."

She stared at him and it took her several moments to find her voice. "Wh-what?"

"I know," he said with a chuckle. He turned away. "Crazy, right?"

She looked at his broad shoulders for a minute, then got off the bed, came around to his side, and knelt in front of him. His expression was carefully neutral, and Cat rested her hands on his thighs. "Yeah," she agreed, "but I'm all about crazy." She closed her eyes. "What's really crazy is you *know*... about *me*, and you're not running the other direction."

"*You* are the most beautiful thing I've ever seen." He cupped his hands around her neck and nudged her chin up with his thumbs. "Why the hell would I run away from *you?*"

She swallowed the lump in her throat and looked into his eyes. She knew she could make something up and Ryan would believe her, but after his confession she didn't want to lie, not to him. She licked her lips and forced herself to speak. "After my... my first kill, my dad... he told me if I ever cared about a man I'd better be prepared to lie about what I did... what I'd... *done.*"

Ryan frowned. "Why?"

Her eyes stung and she blinked rapidly. "Because, um... because no *decent* man would ever get involved with a woman who... who *killed* people." The pain of her father's words returned like a fist to her gut and Cat took a deep slow breath. "He said any man who knew... who knew about me would be too... too *scared* of me to ever love me." She forced a smile. "So, tell me again what's crazy?"

"Your father is," he replied, his voice reverberating with restrained anger. "He should *never* have said that to you." His fingers stroked her jaw. "Is it wrong that I want to kick the shit out of him right now, and I haven't even met him?"

She smiled, leaned forward, and laid her head on his chest. "Always protecting the girl."

Ryan kissed her brow and wrapped his arms around her, his hands moving up and down her back. "Not always." He pulled back and looked down his nose at her. "She doesn't always need my protection."

Cat yawned and settled against him. "Hmm... maybe not, but she still likes having you around."

"Yeah, but I think she's using me for my body."

Lifting one brow, she gave him a bored look and rose. "You have a problem with that?" A startled cry escaped her when Ryan jerked the blanket from her, grabbed her around the waist, and tossed her onto the bed. Then he stretched out beside her, his hand flattening on her belly. Her heart leapt and the familiar warmth spread through her.

"Not at all," he replied with a wicked grin. "As long as she doesn't forget there's more to me than my physique."

Cat looked at him, solemn. "Oh, she knows there's more to you, and she wants to tell you... you're not falling alone."

He studied her for a moment then kissed her. The touch of his mouth to hers was gentle, but she felt the tightly restrained passion behind it and the embers in her ignited. When he ended the kiss and moved away, the tenderness in his eyes made her breath catch.

"Good." He slid one hand around her waist and pulled her toward him. "Then we fall together."

***

Mitchell sat inside his SUV, jaws clenched, hands wrapped tightly around the steering wheel as he watched Catharine and Lieutenant Heller. His chest heaved with tightly controlled rage. The two-inch screen on the receiver didn't have the best picture given the low frequency of the video transmitter he'd hidden in Catharine's quarters, but it was good enough. When the Lieutenant covered her body with his Mitchell ground his teeth together then turned off the monitor. He stared out the window at her little plywood house a mere thirty feet away, and then pounded his fist into the dashboard, once, then twice, then again. When he'd vented some of his anger he took a deep, cleansing breath.

"You shouldn't have done this to me, Catharine," he whispered. "You really shouldn't have."

Chapter Sixteen

Ryan propped his head in his hand and watched Cat sleep. A small smile curved her mouth and in slumber she had no worries. She looked young and pretty, and something in his chest expanded to the point breathing became difficult.

"You're in trouble, Ryan," he told himself. He ran a finger over the silken cheek. "*Big* trouble."

He glanced at the clock and saw it was nearly 3:00 p.m. As much as he wanted to stay next to her he couldn't. He feathered his lips over hers then carefully rolled away from her, folded the covers back, and rose.

Ryan quickly dressed then sat on the edge of the mattress and reached for his shoes. He felt the bed move a split second before she pressed herself against his back, and he turned his face toward her as she wound her arms around his neck. He smiled as she nuzzled his ear.

"Leaving without saying goodbye?" she asked softly.

He curled his fingers over her forearms and shook his head. "Never. You looked so peaceful I didn't want to wake you yet."

Cat kissed his neck. "I'd rather have you wake me than wake up to an empty bed."

Warmth started to swirl in him. He was intensely aware of her breasts pressed into his back, and the fact that if he did a simple 180 degree turn he'd have her wrapped around him again. Ryan closed his eyes and took a deep breath. "I wouldn't do that."

"Good."

She released him and he glanced over his shoulder as she wrapped the sheet around herself and got to her feet. He watched her, an amused smile on his face. Cat walked around to his side of the bed and knelt between his thighs then lifted her emerald eyes to him.

"About dinner."

His gaze wandered over her face. "What about it?"

She looked at him uncertainly. "Well, I know I said I'd have dinner with you, but I sort of promised Yasmeen I'd visit her and the girls and have dinner with them."

Disappointment welled. "Oh," he said. "Okay."

Cat rested her hands on his thighs. "Come with me."

Ryan's brows drew together. "Would she be okay with that?"

"I don't see why not." She smiled and ran her fingers over his jaw. "Since I'll be there, too. Then, after dinner...." She leaned forward and brushed his lips with hers, "... we can work on dessert, if you're free."

Ryan molded his hands to her head and deepened the kiss. Knowing that nothing but a thin sheet separated him from the body that had given him such pleasure sent heat rippling through him. She leaned into him and sighed, her arms sneaking around his waist as he plundered her mouth. He remembered the explosive climax he'd experienced mere hours earlier, and simply the thought of making love to her again made him hard. The melding of their bodies had created a chemical reaction unlike any he'd ever felt before. It had taken sex from a purely physical encounter to something far more wonderful, treacherous, and complicated. He ended the kiss and pulled back, his pulse racing.

"You're dangerous," he whispered against her brow. "If I didn't have a meeting with Commander Ferris in an hour I'd toss you on this bed and we'd do dessert right now."

"And if I didn't need to talk to Tripp and the rest of the team I'd let you."

Ryan chuckled and rubbed his hands over her back as she tucked in beneath his chin. "So, dinner with Mrs. Hasan and the girls then back here for dessert?"

"Sounds like a plan."

He pulled back and looked at her. "Hey, I have a friend who works in the chow hall, and he makes the best qabili palau I've ever tasted. Why don't I call him and see if he'd be willing to rustle some up? That, along with some naan and tea, would be perfect."

"No," she said softly, "*you're* perfect."

"No, I'm not." He ran his fingers through her hair. "But, if you want to think that, who am I to say otherwise?" He kissed the tip of her nose. "I'll call Ahmad and find out about the food. If he can't do it, what else would they like to eat, do you think?"

"I don't think they'll care, as long as there's no pork involved. A couple of veggie pizzas should work just fine." Cat wound her arms around his neck. "Now, you better get going. You don't want to keep Commander Ferris waiting, do you?"

He framed her face with his hands and stared at her for several seconds that weren't nearly long enough. "If I wouldn't get in trouble...."

She smiled, kissed him, then rose and extended her hand. "Come on, sailor."

She looked like a Grecian goddess in that sheet, her hair tumbled around her shoulders in riotous waves. Ryan took her hand and let her lead him across the room, grabbing his uniform blouse on the way. He shrugged into it at the door, and stood patiently while she buttoned it, his arms looped loosely around her waist. When she was done, she smoothed her hands over the shirt, her expression pensive.

"What is it, Cate?"

Cat shook her head and smiled. "Nothing." She looked up at him through her lashes. "I'll see you around sixish?"

"Here, or at Tripp's?"

"Probably Tripp's." She wrinkled her nose. "I have a feeling this is going to be a much longer conversation than I want to have."

Ryan chuckled. "Well, get it over with and text me your location. I'll pick you up then, and we'll head out to the prison." He leaned over and kissed her quickly, because he knew if he lingered he would probably keep Commander Ferris waiting. "See you in a few hours."

"That you will."

He left her quarters, but didn't look back until he was at the driver's door of his Humvee. She gave him a wave then closed the door. Ryan grinned and slid behind the wheel.

Ten minutes later Ryan pulled into the SF compound, parked, and made a beeline for his barracks. Thankfully, it was empty. Mack and Grady were obviously occupied elsewhere which was fine with him. He had roughly forty minutes before he had to meet with Commander Ferris, and getting into a Q&A session with his teammates about where and how he'd spent the last few hours was not on his agenda. Grabbing his toiletry bag and a towel, he rushed to the showers.

He returned to his quarters after showering and trimming his beard, and had just finished dressing when he heard the door open. He glanced over his shoulder as Mack walked in. His teammate was sweat-covered and carrying a basketball under one arm. When Mack saw him, he grinned and flopped down on his rack.

"Hey, Reap. Where you been?"

Ryan looked in the mirror and turned his attention to his collar insignia. "Nowhere."

He should've known better.

Mack put the basketball aside and sat up, his eyes narrowing on Ryan's back. "Really?" He glanced at his watch. "You've been gone for nearly six hours, Ryan." He met Ryan's gaze in the mirror. "Nowhere... are you serious? You gonna stick with that?"

Ryan put his things away, closed up his locker then turned to face his friend. "It's not important, Mack." He saw understanding dawn in Mack's sharp brown eyes and groaned inwardly.

"You've been with Red, haven't you?"

"I can neither confirm, nor deny."

"And that is the same as a confirmation, because if you hadn't been with Red you'd have simply said no."

"Mack, you know me. What do you think I'm going to say?"

"You just said everything you needed to." Mack studied his face. "You do seem... *content*, a little softer around the edges if you will. Love looks good on you, Reap."

"Love?" Ryan looked at Mack, incredulous. "I've only known her a few days, Mack. Don't you think that's a little premature?"

"I don't know." Mack tugged on his beard. "Is it?"

Ryan glared at him. "Will you stop?"

Mack laughed softly. "Fine, fine, but I have to know one thing." He crossed his arms over his chest and grinned. "How'd she look?"

Ryan stared at his friend for a moment, then sighed and came around the end of the bed. Easing down on the edge of the mattress, he planted his elbows on his knees and gazed at the floor. "Fucking *awesome*." Ryan shook his head and exhaled slowly. "I think I'm in trouble with this one, Mack. She's got my head spinning so fast I can hardly think sometimes." He looked up and met Mack's curious gaze. "You ever feel like that?"

Mack moved to sit across from him. "Sure have, when I met Maggie, and we'll be married 11 years this July. I've never wanted another woman since meeting her."

Ryan ran a hand over his hair. "I don't know what I'm doing here, Mack. It sounds cliché, but I've never met anyone like Cate. Kissing her is like...." He paused, searching for the words. "It's like coming in contact with a... a live wire. I can't... *think*, I can't... *breathe*, and it goes *way* deeper than just sex. The thought of not being with her... it kills me."

"Yeah, well, there's so much chemistry between the two of you I'm surprised a meth lab doesn't spontaneously appear every time you and Red are within 20 feet of each other." Mack gave him a serious look. "That's not something you find every day, Ryan."

Ryan sobered. "I know." He met Mack's gaze. "I *really* don't want to fuck it up."

"Then don't," Mack said simply. "You're one of the finest, most intelligent men I've ever known, Ryan, honorable to the core, open the dictionary to the word 'integrity' and there's your picture." He stood and clapped Ryan on the shoulder. "You may never meet another Cate, brother. Grab her with both hands and don't look back."

That said, Mack grabbed his shower bag, a towel, and left the barracks. Ryan stared after him, and a smile slowly spread over his face. He finished dressing then left the barracks, whistling as he went.

***

Cat made her way to the common area in the center of the section of barracks where her team was housed. As he'd said he would be, Tripp was sitting at a table playing cards with six other men, three of whom she didn't know. She walked up behind him and peered at his cards, careful to keep her expression neutral. Bam-Bam and Burgess were also playing, while Tonto, Doc, Lee, and Techno sat nearby. Tonto was texting, Doc was reading a magazine, Techno was playing a handheld video game, and Lee was watching Tripp. Tripp held two pairs, sevens and aces, but he was betting much bigger.

"I'll see your case, and raise you two more," Tripp said. Bam-Bam scowled and tossed his cards down, as did one of the strangers. The other players seemed game, and the betting continued.

Cat smiled and took up a vacant seat next to Lee. "Who's winning?" she asked under her breath.

"Who do you think?" Lee responded. "Ever met anyone who can out-bluff Tripp?"

"No."

"Exactly." He paused and gave her a sidelong glance, his brows drawn together. "What's going on, Tiger?"

She continued to watch the game. "I told Tripp I needed to meet with everyone. Didn't he tell you?"

"That's not what I'm talking about." He narrowed his eyes on her. "You look... *happy*, and you're... *glowing*."

Cat turned to him and lifted one brow. "I am not."

A sly smile split Lee's face. "Are, too."

"There's no glow. Drop it, Lee."

He chuckled. "Dropping it, boss." He bumped her shoulder with his. "Looks good on you, though. Next time you see Lieutenant Heller, tell him I said hello, and well done."

Cat couldn't stop the smile or the heat that crept into her cheeks and she cursed silently. Lee grinned and gave her a knowing look but, wisely, remained silent. Thankfully, he seemed to be the only one who had noticed.

When Tripp won the hand, he raked in his winnings and said, "Okay, gents. The boys and I need to take a break and converse with Mom. Let's meet back here in... half an hour?"

"Fine, mate," one of the Aussies said with a smile. The name Kingman was stitched over his pocket. "But I plan to win back everything you've stolen from me."

"Stolen?" Tripp looked at the man with wide eyes. "I don't know what you mean."

"Yeah, yeah," Kingman said. He rose from his chair and grinned. "Just consider yourself warned." He glanced at Cat and his brows rose. "This mom?"

Cat rose and extended a hand. "Guilty as charged. Cat Beckett."

Kingman shook her hand firmly, did a vertical scan, and whistled softly. "Wish my mum looked like you. Then again, no I don't." He gave her a wink. "Be a mite strange to find myself attracted to my own mum."

"Back off," Tripp said. "She's taken."

Kingman gave her another once over, and sighed. "The good ones always are. Pleasure to meet you, Miss Beckett."

Cat chuckled. "The pleasure was all mine and please call me Cat."

"Will do," Kingman replied. "You can call me Russ." He released her and turned to his fellow Aussies who had been watching this exchange with amused interest. "C'mon, mates. Let's give Mom and the boys some privacy."

Cat waited until the Australians walked away, then she turned to

Tripp and smiled. "They seem like a good bunch."

Tripp flipped his chair around and straddled it. "They are. Now let's get this over with. We only have half an hour before I have to finish robbing them blind."

Cat chuckled and sat on the edge of the table, the men gathering in a semi-circle around her. She looked at each face, and realized with no small amount of surprise how important each of these men had become to her. They were like her brothers, as if she needed more. Her eyes stung and she blinked rapidly. Lee seemed to sense her hesitation and spoke up.

"Okay, boss, we're here. What's up?"

Cat gave him a grateful smile. "Well, there are things we need to discuss." She glanced at Tripp, but his face was expressionless as the block of granite it had been carved from. Cat gulped and continued. "First, I need to tell you about something that happened yesterday. Tripp already knows, but I wanted the rest of you to hear it from me." She gave Tripp an apologetic glance and he smiled.

"Go ahead, Tiger," he said softly "I didn't say anything."

She took a breath and nodded. "Okay." She looked down at her lap for a moment then lifted her eyes to them. "Mitchell assaulted me yesterday in the chow hall."

Tonto, Techno, and Lee rose out of their seats.

"What?" Lee asked.

"I heard about some sort of scuffle at the mess hall," Tonto said with a scowl, "but I had no idea it was you. What happened?"

Cat decided simple was better. If they wanted to ask questions then she'd elaborate. "I was having dinner with him, and when I decided I wanted to leave he tried to stop me."

Techno growled, his eyes sparkling angrily. "What do you mean, 'he tried to stop you'?"

Dropping her chin, Cat shrugged out of the cardigan she wore and held her arm straight out in front of her. Peter's handprints were clearly visible around her wrist and above her elbow, the reddish-purple marks a stark contrast against her pale skin. Doc sucked in a breath and moved to her side.

"What the hell?" He took her wrist and ran his fingers softly over the bruises then met her gaze. "Why?"

"You'd have to ask *him* that," Cat replied.

The silence stretched out for a couple of moments then Techno asked the million-dollar question. "Why were you having dinner with him?"

Cat looked away, shamefaced, but before she could answer Tripp did.

"How do you think we got a three-day pass, gentlemen?"

His voice was low and angry, and Cat wished she could crawl beneath a rock. She crossed her arms over her chest.

"You shouldn't have done that," Burgess said, his voice vibrating with anger. "We all know he's a little cuckoo when it comes to you, and none of us would *ever* ask you to put yourself in that position."

"I know, but hey," she began, "it wasn't *entirely* self-sacrificing. I wanted some time off, too, and I figured I could handle him for an hour or so."

"And what do you think now?" Bam-Bam asked, hands clenched at his sides.

"I think that brings me to the second item we need to discuss." She looked at each man, and was both ashamed and warmed by the anger she saw in their eyes. "Come Monday morning I am putting in a transfer request. My continued employment with the Agency hinges on *never* working with Peter Mitchell again."

Tonto frowned. "You've tried that before, Cat, and your request was denied. What makes you think it will be any different now? Mitchell has a lot of friends at the top."

Cat nodded. "Yes, he does, but I have someone above him who is willing to push my transfer through, and...." Her voice died off, because now came the really hairy part. She was relatively certain they'd want to come with her, but not one hundred percent. They'd been a team for nearly five years now and she loved each of them more than she'd realized until that very moment. Her eyes stung again. Taking a breath, Cat squared her shoulders. "This person also said he'd be willing to push through your transfers as well... if you want to come with me, that is."

The silence was deafening and her throat tightened with anxiety. After several taut seconds, Bam-Bam stood and stepped forward.

"I'm with you, boss. Where do I sign?"

"Me, too," Burgess said.

"You know who I'm with," Lee said, "and it's not Mitchell."

Techno nodded. "Damn straight."

Tripp rose and stood in front of her. "I think you know I'm with you," the large man said. "We've been together too long to break up the band now."

"We're a team," Tonto said, his arms crossed over his chest and an angry scowl on his sharply sculpted features. "Take more than Mitchell to end that."

Cat looked at Doc, the only one who hadn't spoken yet. "It's okay if you don't want to go with me, Doc. You have to do what's best for you."

Doc met her gaze, his expression fierce. "There's no fucking way I'm leaving you guys," he said from between clenched teeth, "but don't ever do that again."

Cat nodded and blinked back tears. "You got it," she whispered. "I promise."

Doc hugged her tightly, then released her and stepped aside. One by one each member of the team embraced her, and when Tripp finally pulled her against his chest it was all she could do not to burst into great sobs of relief.

"Nicely done, Tiger," he whispered against her hair. "You didn't really think we'd let you get away from us that easily, did you?"

Cat shook her head, her vocal chords refusing to function. It took her almost a minute to regain her composure. When she had herself under control she stepped away from Tripp and faced the group again.

"Well, that went a lot better than I thought it would," she admitted with a sheepish smile.

"Really?" Lee asked. "You didn't seriously think we'd want to stay with Mitchell, did you?"

"No," Cat replied. "I was about 99% sure you guys would stick with me, but that 1% was killing me."

Tripp looped an arm around her neck and ruffled her hair. "We're with you, Tiger, 100%."

"Hey," Burgess said suddenly, "what did you mean when you said she was taken? *Is* she taken, and by whom?" The rest of the group looked at him as if he was nuts then burst out laughing. Burgess frowned, perplexed. "What?"

"Never mind, Burgie," Lee said. "I'll tell you later."

"All right, guys," Tripp said. "We have twenty more minutes before the Aussies get back. Food run anyone?"

"Hey," Cat said, putting a hand on his arm, "I need to talk to you and Lee, alone."

Tripp nodded. "Okay." He looked at Doc. "Food run, Doc?"

"Sure," Doc replied with a smile. "BK good?"

"Works for me," Tripp said. "Double Whopper, go large with onion rings and Dr. Pepper."

"Lee?" Doc asked.

"Chicken sandwich," Lee said. "Medium with fries and root beer."

"Got it. What about you guys?"

As Doc turned to the rest of the team to get their order, Tripp walked toward the quarters he shared with Lee and Techno. Once the three of them were inside, he closed the door and faced her.

"Go, Tiger."

Instead of answering, Cat took out her cell phone and pulled up the picture she'd taken of the cell phone bill from Peter's office.

She handed the phone to Lee first. "What does that look like to you?"

Lee frowned and studied the image. "Looks like a cell phone bill from a...." His eyes widened and he looked at her as he handed the phone to Tripp, "... an Iranian carrier. Where did you find this?"

"You don't want to know," Cat replied.

Tripp stared at the picture, his brows drawn together. "Lee, pull up the data sheets from our last after action report."

Cat studied his face, his expression starting alarms in her head. "Why? What is it?"

"One of those numbers looks familiar," Tripp replied. He followed Lee as the other man walked to the one desk in the room and sat down in front of the laptop. He leaned over Lee's shoulder as Lee started typing. After several minutes, Lee frowned.

"What?" Cat asked, moving to their side.

"The report," Lee said. He hit a few more keys. "It's not on the server, at least the data reports aren't."

"What?" Tripp said. He turned the laptop and started typing then huffed. "He's right. The after-action report is there minus the data attachments."

"Peter should have submitted those reports," Cat said.

"I know," Tripp agreed. "I gave him everything Friday, and he said they'd be uploaded to Langley before he left that evening."

Lee smiled, got to his feet, and walked over to his locker. "Lucky for you guys," he began, opening the locker, "I keep copies of *everything*."

A wave of relief hit her. "You're not supposed to do that," Cat said with a small smile.

Lee emerged from inside the locker, a flash drive in one hand. "I know, but if I hadn't, we wouldn't have *this*." He walked over to the laptop, plugged in the flash drive, and after a few strokes of the keyboard a spreadsheet appeared. Tripp pointed.

"Right there," Tripp said. "I *knew* I recognized that number."

Cat leaned over Lee's shoulder and looked at the data sets, an icy hand taking hold of her heart. She looked at the timeline, and that hand started to squeeze.

"Pull up the reports from the first two missions," she said in a hushed voice.

"Why?" Lee asked, even as he started typing.

Another spreadsheet appeared and he paused, allowing her time to study it. The invisible hand squeezed again and she took a ragged breath.

"Right there," she said. She glanced at Tripp. "It's the same number."

Tripp's expression darkened. "And look at the timeline."

Lee looked at the image, then switched screens and examined the first one. His eyes widened and he turned to her. "Less than an hour before each Special Forces team was ambushed a call was placed to the terrorist cell from that number." His gaze swiveled back to the screen. "And, looking at the directional data, the calls were placed from...." He paled visibly, ". . . *here*."

"What?" Cat trailed a finger down the screen and what she saw made her blink. "How do you...?"

Lee gave her a sheepish look. "Remember before the first mission I told you I thought I could increase the sensitivity and reception range of the equipment?" When she nodded, he continued. "Well, I... I did it."

Cat gaped at him. "I specifically told you not to mess with the equipment, Rick."

"I know." He shrugged. "I couldn't help it, Cat. The engineers who built the stuff really didn't utilize the full potential of their own design."

She shook her head. "So, the calls came from here, but where exactly?"

"Well, the equipment originally had a 180-degree field of vision." Lee looked at her. "I got it up to 260, but the directional data gets fuzzy at the outer edges." He tapped a few more keys, pulled up a map of the local area, and sighed. "The closest I can get is roughly a six-klick radius of this cell tower here... inside the fence on the western border of the base."

Cat chewed her lip. "Okay. Pull up the last set of reports." She was hoping against hope she was wrong, but a glance at the last spreadsheet was like having ice water dumped over her head. She grabbed her forehead with one hand and walked away from the desk.

"Holy shit," Lee said. "Three strikes and we're out." He turned and looked between her and Tripp. "What the hell is going on?"

Tripp stared hard at her. "Where did you find that number, Cat? Because whoever owns that cell phone is a traitor and has almost gotten us killed on three separate occasions."

For a couple of seconds she couldn't breathe. A wave of nausea rolled over her and she thought she was going to be sick.

"Where, Cat?" Tripp asked again.

"Peter's office," she whispered. "I found it in Peter's office."

Tripp's eyes widened and he took a step back. He stared at her in disbelief then eased down on the edge of the nearest bed.

Lee gaped at her. "How... why...?" He paused and took a breath. "What were you doing in...?" He closed his eyes. "Wait. Never mind, I don't want to know."

"Why, Cat?" Tripp asked. "Why'd you go looking?"

She sat on the bed across from him and rested her elbows on her knees. "I don't know, Tripp. Something felt... *wrong*." She met his eyes. "When we got back from the mountains Peter was waiting for me *inside* my quarters. I told him we had a leak he needed to look into, and at first he accused one of you guys."

"What did you do?" Tripp asked.

"I hit him." She laced her fingers together and stared at them. "Thursday night he shows up on my doorstep, late, and says there might be something to my allegations." She glanced first at Lee then Tripp. "He told me he was sending Slate and Parker to a meet in Kabul and he wanted me to go along."

A muscle worked in Tripp's cheek then he rose in one fluid motion. "No fucking way. You're not going."

"Tripp...."

His hand sliced through the air, cutting her off. "No. Fucking. Way." He shook his head. "You *know* how many convoys get ambushed at that choke point in the pass. Taliban stream over those hills like roaches, overwhelm the vehicles, kidnap or kill everybody, and then disappear. It's a set-up. He's going to send you out, then make a phone call and give you up, you realize that, right?" He pointed a finger in her face. "You're *not* going to Kabul."

Tripp walked over to his locker, stared at it for a moment then punched it as hard as he could. Cat jumped up, startled, and stared at the crumpled metal.

"Fuck!" Tripp raged. "Motherfucker set the Rangers up, set the Para-rescue guys up, the SEALs, and *us*. I *knew* I hated that son of a bitch for a reason." He punched the locker again and Cat rushed to him, grabbing his arm.

"Stop!" She held tightly to his elbow, but she knew if he really wanted to hit the locker again she wouldn't be able to stop him. Rage radiated out from him in waves, and for some reason that had an oddly calming effect on her. She raised her voice a notch. "Benjamin David Trippler, get it together, do you hear me? I need you. I need you calm, focused, and thinking, because we have to figure out what we're going to do *now*."

"We kill him," Tripp said in a deadly voice. He fisted his now bloody hand. "We fucking *end* him."

He tensed up and she knew what was coming. She released him and interposed herself between Tripp and the hapless locker. "Stop," she said, her voice low but tinged with steel. She rested her hands on his chest and met his angry gaze. "Don't you think killing him is too easy? Think orange jumpsuit, life in Leavenworth, or better yet... Guantanamo. Isn't that a prettier picture?" Cat watched as the rage literally drained from his face. After a moment, he nodded then returned to his seat on the bed.

"Okay, Cat, you win," Tripp said. "What now?"

"Yeah," Lee said, "what do you want us to do?"

She chewed her thumbnail for a moment and sat down beside Tripp. She looked at Lee. "You're our computer geek, and you have the degree in forensic accounting. Use it. Peter's not giving up classified information out of the goodness of his heart. He's getting paid, so find out where the money is and where it's coming from."

A grim smile curved Lee's mouth and he nodded. "I can do that."

"What about me?" Tripp asked, his voice low.

"Well, after you see Doc and get that hand checked out, I want you to start looking into Peter's background." Cat pressed a hand to his cheek and turned his face to hers. "I don't believe he's been a traitor the entire time. What happened at the chow hall was totally out of character and totally against *all* of our training. Something triggered this. Check out his marriage, his friends, and his family, whatever you have to do to find out why."

Tripp gave her a curt nod. "You got it."

"And," she added, "keep this between *us*, got that? I shouldn't have to tell you information like this gets people killed, and I don't want anyone of us in any more danger than we already are. Tread carefully, gentlemen, and keep everything on the down-low because if he gets wind we're onto him...." She dropped her chin. "I hate to load you guys down with this, but...." Her voice died and she met each man's gaze. "I couldn't do it alone."

"You were right to tell us, Cat," Lee said, his expression somber.

"Yeah," Tripp agreed. "Besides, we're your go-to guys. You couldn't pull this off without me and Lee."

For the second time that day Cat nearly cried. Her eyes welled with tears and she reached out to each of them. When they wound their fingers through hers, she smiled. "Thank you."

"Anytime," Lee said, squeezing her hand.

"We're with you, Tiger," Tripp said, "but what are *you* going to do? Mitchell watches you like a hawk."

Cat released them and thought about it for a moment. Then she rose and rested a hand on Tripp's muscled shoulder. "Me?" She looked first at Tripp then Lee. "I'm going to stay off his radar and start connecting the dots." Pressing her lips into a thin line, she scowled. "It's time to nail the bastard."

Chapter Seventeen

Ryan loaded the box of food into the Humvee, his mouth watering as the aroma of fresh-baked *naan*, Afghan flatbread, and *qabili palau*, a popular lamb and rice dish, filled his nostrils. He glanced at his watch and saw it was 5:40 p.m. and frowned. He had yet to hear from Cat. Pulling his cell phone out of his pocket, he dialed her number and waited. She picked up after the fourth ring.

"Hello?"

"Hi, beautiful," he said. "You ready for dinner?"

She paused and sniffed. "Um, yeah, I am. Do I need to order pizza?"

"No," Ryan said slowly, frowning. She didn't sound right, and his gut was telling him something was up. "Ahmad came through. I just finished loading a traditional Afghan dinner into the Humvee, and I'm ready to come get you. Where you at?"

"Our picnic spot," she replied. "I'll see you when you get here."

Before he could reply the phone clicked off and Ryan stared at it for a moment before slipping it into his pocket. "Okay. I'll see you in a few."

He pulled up near their picnic spot about ten minutes later. She was sitting on the ground and leaning against the same rock they had leaned on the other day. Twilight softened the landscape, the final rays of sunset lending faint hints of violet and orange to the otherwise bland backdrop that was the Bagram Valley. Cat's eyes focused on the F-15s taking off, the plane's afterburners glowing gold and pink in the twilight. Ryan approached slowly, hands in his pockets.

As soon as she looked at him he knew something was wrong. Her expression was completely neutral, and the smile she gave him barely lifted the corners of her mouth. Ryan sat down beside her and stared down the runway.

"Wanna talk about it?" he asked after a brief silence.

Cat leaned against him. "Yeah, but I can't." She took a shaky breath. "Just... sit here with me for a minute, okay?"

Ryan wrapped an arm around her shoulders and pulled her closer. "You got it, babe." He pressed his lips to her temple. "We'll sit here for a few and enjoy the quiet, all right?"

She nodded in reply, then climbed onto his lap and pressed her face into his neck. He felt the warmth of her tears on his skin.

"Did the talk with the guys go that bad?" he asked softly.

"No." She sniffled again. "That went great. What sucks is the part I can't talk about."

"Okay." Ryan laid his cheek against her hair and closed his eyes. "I'm here... if you need me."

"Thanks, Ryan," she whispered. Her voice caught. "That means a lot to me."

"You're welcome."

They sat like this for nearly ten minutes, until Cat sat up and swiped a hand over her cheeks. She took his wrist and looked at his watch.

"Six-oh-three," she said. "We'd better get going."

She tried to climb off his lap, but Ryan stopped her. When she looked at him he cupped her chin.

"Are you sure you're all right?"

Cat smiled wistfully and ran her fingers over his beard. "Yes."

"Is there anything I can do?"

"You already have." Her eyes drifted to his mouth briefly. "When I'm with you, Ryan, everything is right with the world and I can forget about the madness...." She paused and looked toward the mountains, ". . . out there. *That* is the greatest gift anyone has ever given me."

Cat turned her eyes on him and Ryan's throat closed up, and when she pressed her lips to his that familiar electricity sizzled through him. He threaded his fingers into her hair and cupped her head, deepening the kiss. She tasted like cherries, and he knew from that moment on cherries would forever remind him of her. Heat started to build in him, so before he embarrassed himself he ended the kiss and pressed his lips to her brow.

"C'mon, Cate," he said after a few perfect, silent moments. "Let's go."

Cat got to her feet and then helped him to his. A brief smile glimmered on her lips as she threaded her fingers through his and walked with him back to the Humvee.

They pulled up in front of the detention facility at 6:15, but it was another ten minutes before they were reunited with Yasmeen and her girls. Both he and Cat had been patted down, much to Cat's obvious annoyance, and the food had also been thoroughly inspected. As they waited for approval, he noticed Cat seemed jumpy, distracted, almost apprehensive. He chalked it up to whatever was going on at work and turned his attention back to the Army personnel. Finally, satisfied neither he nor Cat were planning a breakout or a riot, a male sergeant walked them to the female quarters, then did an about face and returned to the intake station. The female sergeant assigned to the women gave them a cursory glance and returned to her magazine.

Ryan stood back as Cat knocked on the door, and smiled when the door opened and she was nearly bowled over by the two youngest girls. Cat laughed as she crouched down, hugged them tightly, and then ruffled their hair. Yasmeen said something and the girls released her, scampering back the way they'd come.

"Wow," she said, rising as Yasmeen approached her, smiling. "That was quite a welcome."

"They have been looking forward to seeing you again, Caterina," Yasmeen replied. "Asulam Alaykum."

"Alaykum Asulam," Cat responded. Her eyes widened when Yasmeen embraced her, and she looked at Ryan in surprise. He smiled, his smile fading when Yasmeen turned her dark eyes on him.

"Who is this?" Yasmeen asked, eyes narrowed.

Cat looped an arm through his and smiled. "He's a friend," she said. "Yasmeen, this is Lieutenant Ryan Heller, United States Navy."

"Asulam Alaykum, Mrs. Hasan," Ryan said, giving her a small bow. "It's a pleasure to meet you."

Cat translated and the woman smiled.

"Alaykum Asulam, Lieutenant," Yasmeen replied, inclining her head, "and please, call me Yasmeen. Any friend of Caterina's is a friend of mine as well."

Ryan listened as Cat interpreted. "Thank you, Yasmeen," he said, returning her nod. "Please, call me Ryan."

"I hope you don't mind, but I invited him and *he* brought dinner."

Cat hefted the box from Ryan's arms. "Ryan thought you might like some qabili palau, naan, and sweet tea. I hope you're hungry, because there's lots of it."

Yasmeen's brows rose and she looked at Ryan with wide eyes. "Qabili palau is the girls' favorite. It has been a long while since we have enjoyed such food, and they will be thrilled." A smile curved the woman's mouth. "Thank you for your kindness. Please, join us?"

Again, Cat served as interpreter. Ryan smiled at Yasmeen and nodded.

Cat watched this exchange and smiled. Yasmeen's invitation was not only a request for him to eat with them, but also an offer of friendship and respect. During her time in Afghanistan Cat had realized the average citizens were a warm, hospitable people caught in the middle between the Taliban and Al Qaeda and the US-led coalition. It was a bad place to be, trapped between heavily armed forces engaged in fierce battle, but the Afghan people had an inner strength that carried them through, and she admired that quality more with each passing day. She met Ryan's eyes briefly and knew he, too, realized the deeper meaning behind the invitation. She turned to the female sergeant.

"Sergeant... Mello," she said, reading the woman's name tag.

Mello put aside her magazine and rose. "Ma'am?"

"Is there a... common area or a rec room, some place we can all eat?" Cat asked.

"Of course, ma'am," Mello said with a nod. "Right this way."

Mello walked crisply down the hall, then did an about face and gestured through an open doorway. Cat walked into the large room and placed the box of food on the nearest table, smiling as the rest of the group filed in. She immediately removed the food containers from the box, and smiled when she found a large tablecloth, serving utensils, and paper plates and napkins underneath the aluminum trays. There were also three large thermoses and paper cups.

"Outstanding," she said. She looked at Ryan. "Looks like your friend, Ahmad, thought of everything. Thank him for me."

"What do you mean?" Ryan asked.

Instead of replying, Cat started moving chairs, coffee tables, and end tables out of the way, clearing an open spot in the center of the room.

"What are you doing?" Ryan asked as he helped her move the furniture.

"In Afghanistan meals are typically taken while seated on the ground." Once a space was cleared, Cat took the tablecloth and flicked it out with a snap of her wrists. After settling the cloth on the floor, she grabbed several thick, foam cushions off a nearby couch, and tossed one to him with a grin. "Grab some floor, Ryan."

The girls had been watching this exchange with interest, and clapped excitedly when they realized what was going on. Sergeant Mello chuckled and sat in a chair near the door. As Yasmeen and the girls took their cushions and sat in a circle on the ground, Cat and Ryan grabbed the trays of qabili palau and flatbread, placing them in the center of the tablecloth. Then they, too, joined the circle.

Yasmeen immediately started serving, passing the plates around. Cat glanced at the sergeant.

"Sergeant Mello."

"Ma'am?"

Cat waved her over. "Join us."

Mello's mouth opened in surprise. "Oh... I don't think I should, ma'am."

"You have to be here anyway, right?" When the woman nodded, Cat smiled and pointed at a cushion. "So, grab a seat. If you've never had qabili palau, trust me, you'll *love* it." When the sergeant hesitated, Cat lifted one brow. "You won't get in trouble, if that's what worries you."

Yasmeen looked at the young woman and gave Cat a meaningful glance. "Please," she said, indicating for her daughter to move over one spot. Yasmeen patted the cushion to her right. "Dine with us. You have to eat, yes?" Cat translated and smiled.

Mello hesitated. "I'm... I'm on duty, ma'am."

Cat looked at Ryan who was seated directly across from her and gave him a pointed look. Ryan grinned.

"That's an order, sergeant," he said. "Get over here and eat."

Mello looked surprised then a smile slowly blossomed. "Yes, sir."

And, with a kind gesture and shared tea, the group went from virtual strangers thrown together over food, to what looked like close friends and family. Tea and conversation flowed freely, and the room was quickly filled with talk and laughter. Even Sergeant Mello seemed at ease and ate her fair share of the popular dish.

"You were right, ma'am," Mello said, scooping a third helping of the lamb and rice onto her plate. "This is amazing."

At Yasmeen's curious glance, Cat translated.

"It is delicious," Yasmeen agreed. She looked at Ryan. "This is some of the best qabili I've ever tasted, Ryan. Please, give my sincerest compliments to the one who made it."

After Cat told him what Yasmeen had said, Ryan nodded. "Thank you. I will."

He looked at her and grinned, and Cat's heart flip-flopped inside her chest. Unbidden, heat crept into her cheeks and she dropped her gaze as Ryan's grin widened. A glance at Yasmeen revealed the woman had noticed the exchange, a smile twitched about her mouth. Cat focused on her flatbread as she felt her flush deepen.

"Well, I've had all I can eat," Sgt. Mello said a few minutes later. She inclined her head toward Yasmeen. "Thank you for including me, ma'am. This was... well, this was *awesome*." Cat translated and Yasmeen smiled.

"You are most welcome, sergeant," Yasmeen replied, smiling. "Thank you for joining us."

Mello nodded, smiled, and returned to her seat by the door.

Cat turned when she heard Yasmeen tell the girls to start cleaning up. She watched as the youngsters obeyed, and smiled when Yasmeen moved to sit beside her.

"So, was it really good, or were you just being polite?" Cat asked.

Yasmeen smiled. "Truly, that was the best qabili I've ever had, even better than my mother's." She grinned and laughed softly. "But you cannot tell anyone I said that."

Cat chuckled and sipped her tea. "My lips are sealed." When Yasmeen looked at her strangely she grinned. "That means I won't say a thing."

"Ah." Yasmeen chuckled. "Perhaps one day I will understand your language and the many odd sayings you Americans have. And they say *Dari* is difficult to learn."

A squeal made both of their heads snap around, and Cat laughed when she saw Ryan beneath all four girls. They were laughing and tickling him, but when he growled and reared up they shrieked and scattered. He started crawling after them on all fours, and before a minute was up the two younger girls were riding him like he was a horse. A lump formed in Cat's throat as she watched him frolic with the girls, his smile even wider than the children's. After letting the children ride him for a few minutes, he crawled over to the ping-pong table situated against the far wall and gently set them aside. Picking up a ball and paddle, he handed a second paddle to one of the girls and gestured toward the table.

"He wishes to show you how to play," Yasmeen said when the girl looked at her quizzically. The child's expression brightened and she scampered back to the ping-pong table.

Cat watched as Ryan instructed the girls in the fine art of ping-pong, fascinated. He couldn't speak their language, yet somehow he managed to demonstrate the basics of the game so they understood, and in minutes they were slapping the ball back and forth. Yasmeen turned and gave her a knowing look.

"He is very good with them," Yasmeen said softly.

"Yes, he is."

"A man who enjoys children makes an excellent father," Yasmeen said. She glanced at Ryan then returned her dark eyes to Cat. "Ryan will make an excellent father someday."

Cat nodded and her chest tightened. "Yes, he will."

"Is he your husband?"

Cat looked at her in surprise then dropped her chin. "No, no he's not my husband."

"And, yet, you wish he was." When Cat looked at her Yasmeen smiled. "I see the way you look at him. That is not the sort of look one friend bestows upon another. You gaze upon him the way a lover would."

Cat hadn't realized she was so transparent, and yet Lee had noticed something was different about her immediately. Like it or not, she was going to have to be very careful about that. She looked at Ryan, who laughed as a ping-pong ball whizzed past his head, and a great sadness dropped over her shoulders like a cape.

"We're from two different worlds, Yasmeen," Cat said in a hushed voice.

"No." Yasmeen leaned over to look Cat in the face. "You and I, Caterina, are from two different worlds. You and he...?" She gave Ryan a sidelong glance. "The two of you are from the same place."

"Geographically speaking," Cat began, "yes, but otherwise? Otherwise we're from very different places."

Ryan glanced at her and grinned, missing a point as another ball flew past him. His opponent laughed and sent another ball his direction but he seemed not to notice, his eyes locked with hers still. Cat smiled and chuckled when a ball pinged off the side of his head. He looked at the girl in mock outrage and immediately gave chase, eliciting peals of delighted laughter.

"You may be from different places, yet he looks on you as you do on him." Yasmeen searched her face. "Does it involve the work you do?"

"Yes," Cat replied with a nod.

"You do not work for the same people?"

Cat shook her head. "No."

"And yet, he was there last night, was he not?" When Cat turned to her Yasmeen looked at Ryan out of the corner of her eye. "He was the leader. I remember thinking he was very tall and very broad." She smiled softly. "He is much more handsome without all that paint on his face."

There was no denying that. Cat sighed. "Yes... he certainly is."

Yasmeen turned to her and took Cat's hands in hers. "Caterina," she said, her expression serious, "if you love him, do not let what you do stand in the way." Her brows drew together. "You are fortunate to live in a country where the man you spend the rest of your life with is not a stranger until the day you marry. Love is a luxury many women here will never experience. *You* have been given a gift. Do not set it aside so easily."

Before Cat could reply, Ryan's voice cut into her thoughts.

"Cate."

She looked at him and he nodded toward the door. Cat turned and her guard immediately went up when she saw Mr. Heston standing there. She glanced at Yasmeen.

"Excuse me a moment."

Cat rose, walked through the doorway, and into the hall. Crossing her arms over her chest she faced the older man.

"Mr. Heston."

"Miss Beckett." The man glanced into the room when one of the girls laughed. "They told me the Hasans had visitors and I suspected it would be you."

One brow shot skyward. "Who else would be visiting them?"

"Outside of me, my two associates, and you," he said, "no one." He looked through the doorway again. "I see you brought Lieutenant Heller with you." He met her gaze. "Impressive resume on that one. He's a genuine American hero."

"As are all of our men and women in uniform," Cat added. She scowled. "Why are you checking up on my friends?"

"I make it a point to know everyone involved," Heston replied. "Since I'm involved with you and you're involved with *him....*"

"Guilt by association," Cat finished for him.

"Yep, but don't worry. The Lieutenant doesn't have so much as a parking ticket."

Cat frowned. "I'm so glad you approve."

Heston gave her an annoyed look. "Why the hostility, Miss Beckett?"

"Why are you here?" she asked flatly.

"I wanted to talk with you."

"You know where I work," Cat said, "you probably know where I live, and if you don't it would take you what, *one* phone call to find out?" She took a step toward him. "Why here? I came to visit Yasmeen and the girls, not to be interrogated or translate while *she's* interrogated. Haven't they been through enough?"

He grasped her arm lightly and led her a few paces down the hall. "I came here," he began with great patience, "to speak with *you* because I knew this was the one place on base I could be relatively certain we wouldn't be watched or listened to."

Cat's brows drew together. "Who would be watch...?" Her voice died and she blinked slowly as realization hit her like a fist between the eyes. She exhaled sharply and dropped her chin.

"When was the last time you swept your hooch for bugs, Miss Beckett?"

Cat took a deep breath and ran a hand over her face, her heart dropping. "Before we left for the mountains."

"Not since returning?"

"No," Cat whispered, shaking her head. She thought of what had gone on in her quarters since returning from her last mission and squeezed her eyes shut, mortified. If someone was listening they'd heard her and Ryan... and if they'd been *watching*...? Her stomach roiled dangerously. "Oh, my God."

"Here, take this," Heston said softly, his expression sympathetic. He pressed something into her hand. It was smaller and thinner than a typical flash drive but otherwise looked the same, and it was a glossy black plastic.

"What is it?" Cat asked, careful to keep it hidden.

"State of the art technology," Heston replied with a small smile.

"You're used to dealing with that sort of stuff, aren't you?"

"It looks like a flash drive," she commented.

"And when inserted into a computer it will even function like one," Heston said, "complete with 'encrypted' files and programs. However, what it appears to be, and what it *is* are two different things. Turn it on here." He pointed to a small, circular button on the back of the housing. "Then, put it in your pocket, walk through your quarters, and go somewhere you won't be observed. Red light means audio, green light means video, and both means...."

"Audio *and* video," Cat said in a hushed voice.

"Exactly. If you get a positive indication, turn everything electronic in your quarters *off*, lamps, cell phones, anything and everything you don't want destroyed." Heston flipped a piece of plastic back to reveal a small knob on the side of the device. "On this setting you have a three-meter spherical radius. For every click to the left you move the knob you double the radius. Select your radius," he paused and pointed to a larger, square button, "then press this and anything powered up within that radius, electrically or otherwise, will fry. On the highest setting, you'll knock out every electronic device in an area bigger than a football field, so be careful."

"A mini EMP?"

Heston smiled. "Not quite, but something like that."

Cat met his eyes, surprised at the concern she saw reflected there. "I knew you weren't from Homeland Security."

His expression didn't change at all. "Why do you say that?"

"Someone from Homeland Security wouldn't have something like *this* on them." Cat slipped the detector in her pocket. "Also, someone from DHS would have neither the interest nor the authority to push through a transfer for a CIA agent. Such a person might be able to *influence* a decision regarding a transfer, but that person wouldn't ask me to submit the paperwork directly to them."

His smile remained firmly fixed. "Maybe I have friends at the Agency."

Cat lifted one brow. "Really?"

Heston chuckled. "Glad to see you are as sharp without a rifle as you are with one."

She stared at him for a moment. "Why do I feel like I'm up to my neck in quicksand and sinking fast without even knowing it?"

"Because you are," he said. "But don't worry. You're about as deep as you can get."

"This has to do with Peter, doesn't it?" When he remained mute Cat leaned toward him. "What are you *not* telling me?"

"Things I *can't* tell you... *yet*," Heston replied in a low, even voice. "Just keep doing what you're doing and... watch your back. In time this will all play out."

"And, in the meantime, my team and I are what?" She put her hands on her hips. "Along for the ride, collateral damage, cannon fodder?"

"Unfortunately, *you*, Miss Beckett, are an integral part of what is going on because of certain relationships you have." Heston clasped his hands in front of him and lowered his voice. "Your team, on the other hand, shouldn't even know what is going on until someone has been given enough rope with which to hang themselves."

Cat thought of Tripp and Lee and wondered briefly if that assessment included them. "Why don't you simply arrest this person?"

"Because it's not what you *know*, it's what you can *prove*." He gave her a pointed look. "And in a case like this you'd better be damn sure you can prove your allegations 100%, or things will turn into a circus real quick and this person will walk." Heston's expression hardened. "I *know* you don't want that."

Cat stared at the floor for a moment. After taking several deep breaths, she lifted her eyes to Heston's. "This person walks that means I have one final kill to make."

Heston's brows rose and he gave her a long, assessing look. "I understand now how you earned your moniker, Miss Beckett. Guess what they say about redheads, and tigers, is true."

"And what is that, Mr. Heston?"

"Don't piss one off unless you *want* to die," Heston replied with a chuckle, "especially when that redhead, or *tiger*, has *your* particular set of skills."

Cat ignored the remark. "So," she said, "how does this work? Do I report to you now?"

"No." He shook his head. "Just keep doing what you're doing, and when the time is right I'll contact you."

"And if this person suspects I'm onto him?"

Heston's expression darkened. "Don't do anything to put yourself in any more danger than you're already in." He gestured at her pocket.

"On the highest setting, that device sends out an electrical burst our tracking satellites are tuned to pick up, but don't use it unless you absolutely have to."

"In other words, I'm on my own until you decide I have what you need," she said, her voice laced with sarcasm. "Or, until I'm in imminent danger."

"Isn't that the way it usually works?" Heston asked. "You were initiating your own investigation, weren't you?" Cat scowled at him for a moment and then gave him a terse nod, and a smile lifted the corners of his mouth, barely. "Then continue. I can't point you in the direction you need to go but from what I've read and observed of you, I don't need to. Your gut seems to serve you quite well in that regard."

Cat leaned against the wall and gazed up at the ceiling. "Fine, I'll keep doing what I've already been doing." She looked at him out of the corner of her eye. "What about Yasmeen and the girls?"

"It'll take a few weeks," he began, "but they should be stateside by the end of next month at the latest."

"Do I have your word on that?"

Heston sobered. "These days a man's word doesn't mean a whole lot to most people, Miss Beckett, and for good reason. Apparently, you and I are old school." He extended his hand to her. "You have my word Mrs. Hasan and her daughters will be naturalized US citizens before the year is out, even if I personally have to take her and her daughters to all the classes, meetings, and whatever else is involved."

Cat looked at his hand for a moment, then wrapped her fingers around his and shook firmly. "And you have my word this ends one of two ways."

"What ways are those, Miss Beckett?"

"Option A, life in Guantanamo, Leavenworth, or a comparable facility. Option B, dead center in my crosshairs."

Heston released her hand, his eyes narrowed on her face. "You're a serious woman."

"This is serious business," Cat shot back. "There are a lot of people who could get hurt here, Mr. Heston, people I care about."

"Then they should sleep well." Heston smiled. "If there's one thing you are exceptionally gifted at, Miss Beckett, it's protecting the people you care about." He paused and tipped his head to the side. After a few moments, he looked at her and said, "Listen to that."

Cat listened. She heard the girls laughing, and it was a sound like pure joy. Ryan growled and they shrieked then burst out into more laughter. Even Yasmeen was laughing as she urged the girls to run from the monster. Ryan did what resembled a Tarzan yell, and she heard the patter of feet as the girls tried to escape.

"Children's laughter is one of the most beautiful sounds on earth." Heston gave her a pointed look. "They're laughing because you are good at your job."

"I wasn't alone, Mr. Heston," Cat said.

"Yes, well we know SEALs are good at their job. They wouldn't be SEALs otherwise." He rested a hand on her shoulder. "Stop looking so serious. Take it from me. You're much prettier when you smile." He patted her arm and stepped back. "Now, I've taken up enough of your time. Go back in there and enjoy yourself because the guards will kick you out at nine."

Cat looked at him, feeling every bit of the frown. "Forgive me if I reserve my thanks until *after* you've held up your end of the bargain."

Heston shook his head. "No forgiveness necessary. Given what you've experienced, you are wise to doubt me. I, on the other hand, have no doubts you'll hold up your end." He smiled. "When this is all over, why don't we get together and we can thank each other over a cup of tea." When her brows shot up his smile widened. "I'm not much for coffee, either."

"Well, when this is over, I'll either be sharing a cup of tea with you, or I'll have a new target in my sights."

Heston chuckled, his eyes alight with amusement. "I'd expect nothing less. Have a nice evening, Miss Beckett. We'll be in contact soon enough."

Cat exhaled slowly and crossed her arms over her chest as he walked down the hall and disappeared through the door. Focusing on a spot on the opposite wall, she tried to reign in the thoughts spinning inside her head.

"Cate?" When she didn't reply and didn't look at him, Ryan stood in front of her and leaned over to meet her gaze. "Cate, you okay? I saw him leave and when you didn't...." His voice trailed off and his brows drew together. "What's wrong? What did he say?"

She looked at him and gave him a small smile. Reaching out a hand, she traced the line of his jaw. "It's not important." She pushed away from the wall and took his hand. "Come on, I'll challenge you to a game of ping-pong."

He tugged on her hand to stop her as she walked toward the door. Cat turned and looked at him questioningly.

"Okay, but what do I get if I win?" he asked softly.

Cat faced him. "What do you want, Ryan?"

His expression sobered. "I'm looking at what I want."

"You have me," she said in a hushed voice.

He trailed a finger from her temple to her throat. "Do I?"

She blinked and stepped closer to him. "Since day one."

Ryan studied her face for a moment then he grinned. "Good. It's a bet then." He took her hand and pressed his lips to her fingers. "C'mon, Cate. I've got a game of ping-pong to win."

Chapter Eighteen

Cat paused, her hand on the door handle of the Humvee, and looked over her shoulder at the prison. Never in a million years had she expected to have good memories of a place such as this, but she knew she'd never forget the time she'd spent with Yasmeen, the girls, and Ryan. They had eaten and played and laughed and talked, and Cat's face still hurt from smiling so much. Even Sergeant Mello had joined in a time or two.

"What is it, Cate?" Ryan asked, turning to follow the direction of her gaze. "What are you thinking?"

She insinuated herself beneath his arm and snuggled close in the chill night air. "I'm surprised that some of the best memories I'll take away from my time in Afghanistan were made here, in a prison." She smiled up at him. "Strange, don't you think?"

"Yeah," he said with a nod. He faced her and pulled her close. "Just tell me you've made other memories outside of this prison you'll remember with equal fondness."

Her throat tightened. "Don't," she said softly.

"Don't what, Cate?"

"Don't start talking about the future and our paths not crossing again and all that." She focused on the buttons of his uniform, unable to meet his gaze.

Ryan put a finger under her chin and tipped her face up. "That wasn't what I was talking about." His eyes searched hers. "Do you want to know what I'm going to take away from my time here?"

"What?"

He stared into the darkness. "I'm going to remember how I *hated* most of it. How most of the time I was dirty, cold, hot, tired, generally uncomfortable in one way or another, and being shot at. I'm going to remember almost being killed more times than I can count, and ...."

He paused and his expression sobered. "I'm going to remember the comrades who fell and never got up again." Ryan looked at her. "Then I'm going to remember tonight, and how a woman and her children made this Godforsaken place disappear for a few hours, and in that time, I was home again, playing with my nieces and nephews." His brows drew together. "But do you want to know what I'll remember most about being here?"

Cat swallowed the lump in her throat. "What?" she whispered.

He cupped her face and his thumbs stroked her cheeks. "You."

Her breath caught. "Ryan...."

"Every time I see an Irish hillside, or an emerald, I'll see your eyes, and remember the way you look at me." His gaze wandered to her mouth. "And every time I taste cherries... I'm going to remember what it was like to kiss you." He traced the outline of her lips. "You've left an impression on me I won't ever be able to shake, Cate, and I don't know if that's good or bad." He lifted his eyes to hers. "I just know it *is*."

Cat thought her heart was going to beat its way out of her chest. She couldn't look away from those azure eyes, and as he stared at her she felt like she was being stripped bare and the secrets of her heart exposed. It was an odd sensation, terrifying, yet liberating at the same time. She framed his face with her hands and stood on tiptoe.

"Ryan."

"Yes, Cate?"

She moved until only a hair's breadth separated their lips. "Take me to bed... or lose me forever."

A slow smile curved his mouth. "Show me the way home, Cate."

"You already know the way," she said in a low voice. She kissed him hard and fast then shoved him away from her. "Get in and drive, sailor, and *don't* get pulled over."

Ryan laughed and walked around to the driver's side of the Humvee. "Yes, ma'am."

When he got within two blocks of her quarters Cat put a hand on his arm.

"Park here," she said. "Don't get any closer."

He pulled over and parked. "Why?"

Instead of answering, she turned to him. "I need you to do something for me."

"Anything."

She stared at him for several moments then took a deep breath. "When we get in there I want you to follow my lead, play along no matter how ridiculous it sounds. And if I ask you to do something, just do it, no questions asked. Okay?"

Ryan looked at her strangely. "Okay, as long as you don't start pulling out whips, chains, and studded collars."

She chuckled and rolled her eyes. "It's a little early in the relationship to bring *those* out." When his eyes widened, she laughed. "I'm *kidding*, Ryan. Sheesh."

Relief swept his features. "Good. BUD/S training was enough domination, submission, and bondage to last me the rest of my life." He gave her a sidelong glance. "You had me going for a minute there."

She smiled and leaned toward him. "I'll have you going for more than a minute pretty soon."

"I have *no* doubts about that," he said with a shake of his head. "None whatsoever."

"So," she began, turning his face to hers, "do we have a deal?"

He studied her for a moment then nodded. "I will follow your lead, play along, and do what you want me to, no questions asked."

"Good." Her gaze moved to his mouth for a moment then she looked at him, her expression serious. "First order of business: turn off every electronic device on you."

Ryan's brows drew together. "What?"

She frowned. "No questions asked, remember?" She reached into his pocket and pulled out his iPhone. "If it has lights, buttons, a battery, or is in any way powered by electricity, turn it off. That includes your pager."

"Cate, I'm on call," Ryan argued. "I have to keep my cell and pager on, you know that."

"Ten minutes tops, I promise." She met his dubious gaze. "And I promise I'll explain why." When he didn't move, Cat pulled out her cell phone and turned it all the way off. "Ten minutes, Ryan. That's it."

He sighed then turned his pager off. "Okay, done. Now what?"

A grin twitched about her mouth. "Now, step into my parlor."

"Said the spider to the fly," he finished for her with a wry twist of his lips. "Are you a black widow?"

She chuckled and leaned toward him. "No, but if I was...." She kissed him, and when his tongue met hers she almost forgot what she was doing. He explored her mouth and that wonderful, familiar tension coiled low in her belly. Before she completely lost her mind, Cat ended the kiss and pulled back, her heart thumping against her breastbone. She exhaled slowly. "If I was you'd die smiling."

She opened her eyes to look at him, and her breath caught. His gaze was hot on her face, desire burning clearly in those sapphire depths. His expression was fierce and primal, and the animal in her responded.

"Take me to bed or lose me forever, Cate," he whispered.

"Let me show you the way."

They got out of the Humvee and walked hand-in-hand to her quarters. When she turned her back to him and searched for her keys he brushed her hair to the side and pressed his lips to the curve of her neck. She faltered as heat knifed through her. He nibbled on her earlobe as she tried to put the key into the lock, and it took her three tries to successfully complete the task. Before she could open the door, Ryan spun her around and pressed her against it, his mouth crashing down on hers.

Cat was unprepared for the wave of sensation that cascaded over her. His kiss was more than a kiss; it was an assault on her senses, a blatant claim on her heart and soul. She was at once hot and cold, terrified and fearless, and when his arms wrapped around her to pull her close her knees turned to rubber. Her breasts tightened, his heart beating beneath her palm. His masculinity overwhelmed her and she was helpless to fight it.

His lips left hers to trail down her neck, giving her the opportunity, however difficult, to speak. "You're cutting into that ten minutes, Ryan," she whispered. A low moan escaped her as his tongue flicked teasingly against the pulse in her throat. "Ryan... please...."

Ryan's mouth covered hers again. Cat clung to the front of his uniform, and when he finally pulled away it took all her strength not to pull him back. His lips feathered over her cheeks and then her brow.

"Well," he said softly, his breath warm on her temple, "since you asked so nicely...." He stepped back and gestured toward the door. "After you."

Cat looked at him and tried to catch her breath. Steeling herself, she faced the door, turned the handle, and pulled. As she stepped into her quarters she slipped a hand into her pocket and wrapped her fingers around the detector. She felt for the small, circular "on" button and pressed it.

The lights were already off, and when Ryan moved to turn them on she took his hand and shook her head. He opened his mouth to speak, but she pressed a finger to his lips.

"No talking," she said. "Not yet." She waited a moment, and when her eyes had adjusted to the darkness she pulled him into the center of the room and kissed him quickly. "Stay here."

A smile and a raised eyebrow was his only response.

Cat walked slowly to the back door and double-checked the locks, then walked to the front door and did the same. He reached for her as she passed him again on the way to her locker, and a low laugh escaped her.

"Nice try."

"I'll be quicker next time," he replied.

She opened her locker and looked at him over her shoulder. "I certainly hope so." Now came the fun part.

Using her body as a shield on one side and the door as a shield on the other, Cat slipped the detector out of her pocket and glanced quickly at the display. Green light. So, someone was *watching*, but not *listening*. She wasn't sure if that was better or worse. Setting the dial on the lowest setting she slipped it back in her pocket. Then she removed her boots and socks, pulled her shirt off, and closed the closet door. Giving Ryan a sultry look, she sauntered toward him.

He stood at parade rest, legs apart, hands clasped behind his back, his eyes locked on her. Pausing at her desk, she depressed and held the power button on her laptop until the computer's indicator light flickered off. Then she reached for the digital clock, picked it up, and jerked the cord out of the wall.

"Ooh," Ryan said with a low chuckle. "Someone's in a mood."

"No." Cat walked up to him and ran her hands over her chest. "Someone doesn't want to know what time it is." She glanced quickly around the room but everything else was already off. "So, everything turned off, Ryan?" He gave her a look that sent butterflies bouncing off her insides.

"Everything but me," he replied in a voice like warm velvet.

She gulped. The heat from his body radiated toward her and she leaned into him. "Then it's show time." Taking his hand, she led him toward the bed, and the thought of what they would shortly be doing made breathing difficult. Then again, the thought of what she had to do before getting naked also made breathing difficult, but for an entirely different reason. Anger blossomed inside her and she pushed Ryan down on the bed.

"Whoa! Easy, Tiger." When she didn't move, he leaned up on his elbows and looked at her expectantly. "So, what now?"

Cat thought about it for a moment. She could press the button and be done with it, but that option didn't really appeal to her. Peter had had her dancing on the end of his string more times than not, so it was only fair that she turn the tables. Torturing him a little would be small reward for all the shit he'd put her through. She only wished she could see his face.

Straddling Ryan's thighs, Cat put a hand on his shoulder and pulled him to a sitting position. Ryan looped his arms around her waist and searched her face as she slowly unbuttoned his uniform blouse. When the last button gave way, she pushed the garment off his shoulders. A small smile curved his mouth and he held his arms up as she peeled his t-shirt off him. The sight of his sculpted chest did strange things to her heartbeat and she took a deep breath, trying to stay focused. Then again, with what she planned Ryan would be the one unable to focus, not her.

Ryan searched her eyes and she wondered if he could see the wheels in her head spinning. She gave him a wicked smile and his eyes narrowed.

"What are you up to?" he asked softly as she moved closer.

She was very aware that the only thing preventing him from making love to her was the fact they both still had pants on. He was already hard, and the thought of having him inside her made her ache. Cat bit her lip and settled herself more closely against him. His eyes smoldered and she felt the heat of him through their clothing. More than anything she wanted to be naked in his arms, her legs wrapped around him, his body joined with hers in the most intimate way. More than anything, she wanted *him*.

Ryan jumped when she unfastened his belt and unbuttoned his pants. Then she pushed him onto his back. He reached for her but she grabbed his wrists and pinned them to the bed, her breasts brushing his chest as she moved closer.

"Don't move," she whispered. She released him, reached into her pocket, palmed the detector, and then leaned over and kissed him.

She'd told him not to move, but he didn't listen. His hands grasped her waist as they explored each other's mouths, and Cat had to keep reminding herself to concentrate. As she did so, her brain kicked into gear and spit out a thought that stopped her cold.

Cat pulled back sharply and looked down into those azure eyes, and the realization of what she was doing sent a wave of guilt crashing over her. She was using Ryan to get back at Peter. She was using a man she was quickly falling in love with to hurt a man she loathed. The self-reproach almost made her choke.

"Cate?"

Suddenly torturing Peter was not so important. Cat blinked, took a breath, and said, "I need you to do something for me."

His fingers fanned out over her lower back. "Name it."

"Find a spot on the ceiling and focus on it, and tell me if you see anything strange in your periphery."

His brows drew together but he did as she asked. "Okay."

Cat leaned down, kissed his neck, and pressed the button. She heard a hiss and a sharp *snap* then the sound of breaking glass from outside. Cat groaned inwardly. She'd forgotten about the light pole outside her quarters. Oh well. That would lend further credence to the idea there had been a power surge. With the well-known unreliability of power continuity on base, Peter shouldn't suspect a thing.

Ryan tensed. "What was that?" He gently moved her to the side and rose.

"What did you see?"

He pointed to a corner of the room. "I saw a flash there, right where the wall meets the ceiling to the left of the door, in the corner."

Her heart dropped.

Cat moved to her desk, retrieved a flashlight from a drawer, then grabbed the chair and pulled it to the corner of the room. After stepping up onto the chair she clicked the light on and trained the beam where Ryan indicated. A tiny glass eye, smaller than a pencil eraser, looked back at her, the wiring behind the lens blackened, curled, and smoking slightly. Had she been looking for the camera it would have been easy enough to find, because Peter had picked an ideal location: close to the rafters, in line with the cottage's electrical wiring, obscured by shadow, and in a spot that wouldn't normally be focused on. But she hadn't been looking, and Cat mentally kicked herself for the lapse.

"Is that a... *camera*?" Ryan asked.

For a moment, she couldn't speak, and her chest filled with boiling anger and cold, penetrating sorrow. Clenching her jaw, she stared at the mechanical eye. She wanted to rip it out of its perch and throw it in Peter's face, but she couldn't. It was really an unremarkable piece of technology, readily available at any cut-rate store that sold "spy" equipment. From the size of the transmitter on the other end of the inch-long wire, Cat guessed the camera would have a range of 10-15 meters, tops. In other words, Peter had to be close by if he was watching. The thought made her stomach roll and she stepped down off the chair.

"Yes," she replied. "That's *exactly* what it is."

Ryan stared at her, incredulous. "How did you know?" Before she could speak she saw the light go on and Ryan set his jaw. "Heston."

She nodded.

"What did you do to it?"

Cat sat down on the edge of the desk and held up the detector. Ryan walked up to her and she dropped it onto his outstretched palm.

"What is it?" he asked, examining the hard plastic. He handed it back.

"A new-fangled bug detector/killer," she replied. "It works like an EMP... sends out some sort of electromagnetic burst that fries everything electronic within a certain radius."

Ryan's eyes widened and he reached into his pocket. "My phone?"

Cat shook her head. "It only affects working electronics," she said softly. "That's why I had you turn your phone and pager off." She crossed her arms over her chest. "Go ahead and check them. They should be fine."

As Ryan checked his electronic gear Cat moved to the bed and sat down on the edge, resting her elbows on her knees. She'd been hoping Heston was wrong, that her quarters would be clean. Now she felt violated, as she had after Peter had assaulted her, only this was worse. Her eyes stung and she squeezed them shut, trying not to think about him watching her in her most intimate moments, moments with Ryan. Rage and sadness boiled inside her, a thick, swirling mix of red and black emotion, and she wanted to confront Peter but she couldn't. Not yet.

She stared at the floor, her mind recycling Peter's betrayal until the toes of Ryan's boots came into view. Cat lifted her head as he crouched in front of her.

"Who would do this, Cate? Who would be spying on you?"

Again, she didn't have to say anything. A second after he asked the question realization dawned and a muscle in his cheek started to twitch. He stood and looked down at her.

"How long?"

Cat tried to swallow the knot in her throat. "Long enough," was her hushed response.

She jumped when Ryan cursed and snatched his t-shirt from the bed. After donning it he buttoned his pants and grabbed his uniform blouse, shrugging into it as he strode toward the door.

"Ryan, what are you doing?"

He paused, one hand on the knob, and looked at her over his shoulder. His eyes were blazing, his brows drawn together in a fierce scowl. "I'm going to look that motherfucker in the eye and ask him why before I beat the living shit out of him."

Cat flew at him and grabbed his arm. "Ryan, stop." When he turned incredulous eyes to her she dropped her gaze but kept a firm grip on his elbow. "You can't."

He looked at her as if she was crazy and shook her off. "The hell I can't." He released the door and faced her. "That son of a bitch was *watching* us, Cate, like we were... *porn stars* in his own personal... *skin flick.*" He backed away from her and the hurt she saw in his eyes was like a knife to the heart. "What happened *between us* was between us. It was *private*, Cate, and it was... *amazing*... and that *bastard* just ruined it."

Cat closed her eyes and pressed a shaking hand to her mouth. Her lungs refused to draw air, and no matter how she tried she couldn't stop the image of Peter sitting outside her quarters and watching them from replaying in her mind. What had been a beautiful, incredible experience was now permanently tainted with Mitchell's shadow. Once again, he had intruded on her life, taken something dear to her, and destroyed it. The fact that it was what she'd shared with Ryan was almost more than she could bear. "I know," she choked out, tears squeezing out from beneath tightly closed lids. She rested a hand on his chest. "I *know*...."

When Ryan put a hand behind her neck and pulled her to him the sob she'd been holding back finally escaped. She pressed her face into his shoulder and wrapped her arms tightly around his middle. His body was taut with anger but as he held her he started to ease up. Cat clung to him as the tears continued to flow and he whispered soft, soothing words, his hands rubbing up and down her back.

"I'm so sorry, Ryan," she whispered. "This is all my fault."

Ryan grabbed her upper arms and pushed her away from him. The scowl was back and Cat's chin trembled as she waited for him to vent his anger on her. She deserved it.

"This is *not* your fault, do you hear me?" he said from between clenched teeth. "This is *his* fault."

"I — I should have... *known*... I should have swept my quarters...." She shook her head. "I should *never* have put you in the middle of this."

He looked at her in disbelief. "You didn't *put* me anywhere, Cate. I *wanted* to be here." He searched her eyes. "I *still* want to be here."

Cat sniffled. "Why? If I was you I would be running for the hills."

He stared at her for a moment then he chuckled and shrugged. "Wouldn't do any good." A wry smile curved his mouth. "That's where I met you."

A short laugh escaped her, and then the tears started again. Ryan wrapped his arms around her and sighed as she tucked in beneath his chin.

"We can get past this," he said softly.

"How?" Cat took a deep, hitching breath. "I can't get th-the... the p-picture of him... *w-watching* us... out of my h-head."

He pulled back and looked down at her. His expression was sad, wistful, but she recognized the steely determination in his eyes. He dragged his knuckles over her cheek. "He's not watching us now." His eyes narrowed slightly. "We can't recapture that memory, but we *can* make new ones."

"Ryan...."

He focused on her mouth, his finger tracing the outline of her lips. "I'm willing to fight for what I want. Are you?" He cupped her head. "Don't let him win, Cate."

The shock she felt when his mouth covered hers traveled from her head to her toes and back in less time than it took to blink. Cat gripped his waist as his fingers threaded into her hair, his lips slanting over hers with both abandon and resolve. He was a man on a mission, and she couldn't have said *no* if she'd wanted to.

He wrapped his arms around her and lifted her off the floor, his mouth never leaving hers. Her breasts tingled as they were crushed to Ryan's chest, and the desire that had been extinguished only minutes past ignited with an even hotter flame. His tongue touched hers, gently at first and then not so gently, and suddenly she couldn't even remember who had been watching them. At this moment, nothing outside the two of them existed.

Cat was vaguely aware Ryan was moving toward the bed, and when he reached it he backed up to the mattress and gently put her feet back on the floor. He released her long enough to shrug out of his blouse and pull off his t-shirt, then he unfastened his belt and pants while Cat knelt to untie his boots. Once he stood before her clad in nothing but his briefs she couldn't help but rise, step back, and admire God's handiwork. She flattened her hand on his chest, his skin warm and smooth beneath her fingers.

"God was *definitely* paying attention the day He made you," she said softly, her pulse jumping. Ryan covered her hand with his, then lifted it to his mouth and kissed her palm. Electricity shot up her arm.

"Nope," he disagreed, his whiskers tickling her palm, "God just threw me together. But you...?" He met her gaze and drew her arm over his shoulder. "You, on the other hand... are a *masterpiece.*"

Cat clasped her hands behind his neck and pressed close to him. "You have *never* had trouble picking up women, have you?"

Ryan shrugged. "Never really tried."

"Exactly," Cat said with a smile. "You're a natural. Beautiful compliments roll off your tongue like honey."

His eyes darkened. "I'd rather have *you* rolling off my tongue like honey."

Her entire body flushed and it took her several moments to find her voice. "Oh... my."

Ryan slowly sat on the edge of the bed and looked up at her, his expression speaking volumes. Cat tried to regulate her breathing and closed her eyes as her imagination ran wild. The ache between her legs started to pulse and expand outward with each beat of her heart until even her breasts throbbed. She inhaled sharply when she felt his lips on her belly, her stomach muscles contracting involuntarily as his tongue made lazy circles around her navel.

"This is a good start," he said softly, "but these pants are in my way."

Goosebumps fanned over her skin and she bit her lip as he loosened her belt and then unbuttoned her trousers. When she started to slide her pants down over her hips Ryan grabbed her hands. Cat looked at him in surprise but he just smiled and shook his head. A shiver shot down her spine and settled between her thighs when he worked his fingers inside the waistband of her panties, adding to the curling, infuriating tension inside her. Closing her eyes, Cat took a deep, steadying breath.

Ryan's hands skimmed over her curves and down the length of her legs with a gossamer touch, until her panties and jeans were nothing but a tangle of material around her ankles. Lifting first one foot then the other, Cat stepped out of her pants and Ryan kicked them out of the way. Then he reached behind her, unhooked her bra, and pulled the undergarment from her. Leaning back on his hands, he let his gaze wander over her from the top of her head to her toes and back several times.

"Cate...." His voice died and he shook his head slowly. "I cannot think of an adjective that adequately describes you. I don't know what to say, because beautiful...." He gave her another lengthy once-over. "*Beautiful* just *doesn't* cut it."

Cat took a step toward him. Ryan sat up. His eyes locked with hers and he slid his hands around her waist. She brushed a lock of hair from his brow, trailing her fingers over his cheek and along his jaw. Taking his head in her hands, she brushed his lips with hers, and then kissed him deeply. Heat traveled through her like lightning, her nipples tightening and the ache in her belly sharpening. His fingers splayed over her back and she gasped as her breasts brushed his chest. Pulling back, she took a ragged breath and whispered, "Don't say anything. *Show* me."

Chapter Nineteen

Cat stirred as something feathered over her cheek once, and then again. She stretched and yawned, and rolled toward Ryan when she felt his fingertips graze her brow. Smiling, her eyes fluttered open and widened when she saw him sitting on the edge of the bed fully dressed. She rubbed her eyes and sat up.

"What's going on?" she asked.

Ryan tucked a strand of hair behind her ear. "Nothing," he replied softly. "I just have to get back."

"What, do they get upset if you miss bed-check?" she teased.

He grinned. "Nope, but if I miss my watch they will. I have the midnight to 0600 shift in the Command Center."

She glanced at the clock. 11:20 p.m. She frowned. "Why didn't you tell me? You should be in your rack sleeping, not here with me."

"Precisely why I didn't tell you." He traced the line of her collarbone. "I can sleep when I'm—"

She put a hand over his mouth. "Don't."

He smiled, kissed her palm, and held her hand to his chest. "I was going to say when I'm off-duty, Cate."

"Oh." She nodded. "Good."

Ryan put a hand behind her neck, his thumb rubbing slowly over her cheek. "I wish I could stay."

"Me, too." She glanced at his mouth and heat flooded her cheeks as she recalled the amazing things he'd done to her with that mouth. He hadn't been kidding about making new memories. Cat closed her eyes and bit her lip as warmth started to grow inside her. "Some other time."

"Tomorrow night?"

"Uh huh," she replied in a hushed voice, still distracted by her erotic thoughts. "Tomorrow night."

"And the night after that?" he asked. Cat looked at him and he brushed her hair back over her shoulder. "Is that one available?"

She nodded slowly and gulped when he leaned closer. He brushed her lips with his then looked into her eyes.

"And the one after that?"

Cat ran her fingers over his beard. "You can have as many of my nights as you want, Ryan."

His expression sobered and he traced the outline of her mouth. "And if I want them all?"

"Then they're yours."

He kissed her again, more thoroughly this time, and she leaned into him. His lips were soft yet firm, and when he ended the kiss she couldn't open her eyes.

"I have to go."

She nodded.

"We're barbecuing at the compound tomorrow afternoon and challenging the Rangers to a b-ball tourney," he said. "Why don't you join us around two?"

"I don't think so." She forced herself to meet his gaze. "I don't want to cut into your time with the guys."

"Screw that." A smile curved his mouth. "They're cutting into my Cate-time. Besides, they want to meet you."

She blinked at him. "Why?"

"You saved some of their asses, too," he replied. "They want to say thanks."

She pulled back and shook her head. "No, Ryan. I... I try to keep as low a profile as possible when it comes to... *that.* The more people who... *know*... the harder that is to do."

"We're Special Forces, Cate," he said. "We understand top secret." He took her hands in his. "Look, nobody from the Navy Times or the Stars and Stripes or CNN is going to be there. It's just us guys and we know how to keep our mouths shut." He squeezed her fingers. "Please."

She frowned. "Ryan, I don't know."

"Hey, I understand you don't want to talk about your sharpshooting skills," he said, "and I get why." He paused and pressed a hand to her cheek. "They're not interested in your work history, Cate. They want to say thanks and talk to a pretty girl for a while. That's all."

Cat looked into those dark blue eyes and realized, with no small amount of surprise, she could deny him nothing. Finally, she rolled her eyes and sighed. "Fine, but the moment someone starts quizzing me I'm outta there."

Ryan grinned. "The moment someone starts quizzing you is the moment I kick someone's ass." He kissed her quickly and stood. "Now get some rest. I'll see you tomorrow afternoon."

"Okay," she said with a smile. "Should I bring anything?"

"Other than yourself?" He grinned and shook his head. "Nope." He walked to the door and paused with his hand on the knob. "Two o'clock."

"I'll be there," she replied. "Now get going before you're late."

Cat watched until the door closed behind him then she got up, locked the door, and returned to bed. As she drifted off to sleep Ryan's face was the last thing she saw.

***

"So, how are things with you and the SEAL?" Tripp asked, his arms pumping in rhythm as they ran alongside the runway.

Cat glanced at him and smiled, a flush creeping into her cheeks.

"That good, huh?" Tripp asked.

"Yeah, well we're less than a week in, Ben," Cat replied. "Relationships are always great at this stage."

"When the sex is hot and there's nothing to fight about," Tripp said with a chuckle. "Funny, I rarely make it past that stage."

Cat laughed. "You rarely make it to the *relationship* stage period. For you it's all about the sex." She looked at him out of the corner of her eye. "When was the last time you *had* a relationship?"

"Ah, relationships are highly overrated," Tripp said, grinning. "Some of us aren't made for them." He gave her a knowing look. "You, on the other hand, are, and I think Lieutenant Heller is an exceptional choice."

"You only like him because he's a SEAL."

"There's that," Tripp admitted, "but he seems like a genuinely nice guy. Sergeant Anderson said he took good care of you when the whole Mitchell thing went down."

"Yes, he did and he *is* a nice guy." They reached the end of the runway and stopped, Cat pressing two fingers into her neck and looking at her watch. "Makes me wonder what he's doing with me."

Tripp scowled. "What the fuck is *that* supposed to mean?"

Cat swiped an arm over her brow. "I don't know, Tripp. I mean, do you realize I haven't been on more than half a dozen dates with the same guy since I broke it off with Peter?" She pulled her water bottle out of her belt, took a swig, and started to stretch. "I've tried to figure out why, and I can't."

"Explain."

"Well," Cat began, "I'd meet a guy, we'd go out and have a good time, or so I thought, and then we'd see each other a few more times and then he'd stop calling."

"You ask them about having a June wedding or something?" Tripp asked.

She frowned at him. "No. It was like they'd dropped off the face of the earth. Then, when I'd call *them* to find out what happened I'd get 'I got back with my ex,' 'I'm moving out of state,' and even 'I decided I wasn't that into you.'" She looked up at him. "*Every* guy, Tripp. I guess I'm waiting for Ryan to say something like that." Cat dropped her gaze. "He already set it up."

Tripp sat next to her on the ground. "What do you mean?"

She reached for her toes and leaned over into the stretch. "He said something about me looking back on the time I spent with him and smiling because I'd be transferred, the military would send him to some other third-world country, and we'd never see each other again."

"He's probably right," Tripp replied, his expression solemn.

"I know," Cat said with a sigh, "but right after we'd made love for the first time? Seriously? Get some mileage out of the girl before you start clueing her in to the fact you're not going to stick around much longer."

"So," Tripp began, "did you sleep with all these other guys, too?"

Cat gaped at him. "God, no." Her heart stutter-stepped as she realized the contradiction she'd made. "Shit. I don't know what I'm doing here, Tripp. Even with Peter, he and I had known each other for months before we slept together. You know me. I'm not the type to bed-hop."

"I know," Tripp said. "That's why I asked." A small smile curved his mouth. "Maybe it's love at first sight."

"Really." She lifted one brow. "You're going with that?"

"Hey, it doesn't happen often, but it *does* happen."

Cat gave him a bored look. "And you know this how?"

His expression sobered. "My mom met my dad at a USO mixer a week before he deployed, and three days later they were married. She said she knew by the end of the first dance she was in love. Dad told me it didn't take him that long." He paused and stared toward the mountains, resting his elbows on his knees. "Once he finished his tour they never spent a night apart. They'd been married 47 years when my dad passed." He gave her a wry smile. "Maybe that's why I haven't had a relationship in forever. I'm waiting for the same thing you've found with Ryan, that special spark you don't feel for anyone else, like my mom and dad had."

"Wow." She took a deep breath. "You never told me that before. You really believe that?"

He nodded. "Yep. Have to. Saw it with my own two eyes."

"I have to admit," Cat said, leaning back on her hands, "when those other guys stopped calling, it stung. But if *Ryan* stopped calling...?" She paused and looked at him, "It would do *way* more than sting."

"You're falling in love with him."

"What's not to love?" Cat closed her eyes. "He's a patriot, he's dedicated, and he's smart, funny, and gorgeous...."

"And if your cheeks are any indication he's good in the sack." Heat flooded her face and Tripp chuckled. "That answers *that* question. Guess he and I don't need to chat after all."

"Stop." She smacked his arm. "You're not helping."

"Sorry, Tiger," he said with a laugh, "but I'm kind of hoping you *do* fall for the guy. You said if you ever got married I would be your maid of honor. I'm getting a little long in the tooth for a bridesmaid's dress so you need to move this shit along."

Cat rolled her eyes. She gave him a small shove, but when his smile faded and his eyes narrowed she immediately went on alert. She'd seen that look before, usually just before she pulled a trigger. He stared past her, and she turned to follow the direction of his gaze.

A vehicle sped toward them, dust curling like rooster tails behind it. Cat slowly rose and Tripp did likewise.

"SPs?" he asked.

"I don't think so." As the SUV got closer her heart dropped. "It looks like Peter's Yukon."

"You're *fucking kidding* me." He walked toward the vehicle about ten paces and looked at her over his shoulder. "Stay there."

"Tripp—"

His glare silenced her. "*Stay there.*" He faced the oncoming SUV again, his hands clenching and unclenching at his sides, a muscle twitching in his cheek.

The SUV pulled to a stop about ten feet in front of him and Cat shielded her eyes as the dust plumes rocketed past the car and over them. Tripp didn't even flinch. She planted her hands on her hips and waited. After about half a minute the door opened and Peter stepped out.

"That's far enough," Tripp said. He didn't yell, but his voice had a cold edge to it that made it carry.

Peter faltered and took his sunglasses off, setting them on the hood. "Afternoon, Ben, Catharine." He looked from Tripp to her and back, and sighed. "I need to talk to her, Tripp."

"The hell you do," Tripp shot back. "Whatever you have to say you can say from right there."

"Trippler," Peter began, giving the large man a tolerant look, "Catharine's your team leader and I'm her supervisor. There are things she and I need to discuss that don't involve you."

"Fuck you, Mitchell." Tripp crossed his arms over his chest. "If you want to talk, you talk from where you are, because if you take one step toward her I'll lay you out on this tarmac. And, unlike when Cat dropped you, you won't need assistance you'll need a fucking *medic.*"

Peter looked at her. "Catharine?"

Cat walked up to Tripp's side. "Whatever you have to say you can say in front of Ben. He is my second in command after all."

"It's about the mission you went on the other night."

She shrugged. "What about it?" She felt Tripp tense up, but his eyes remained fixed forward. Again, she would have some explaining to do. "I'm sure Commander Ferris forwarded the after-action reports to you. Is there some detail you're unclear about?"

Peter stared at her for a moment and she saw that now familiar light in his eyes, the light that said his mind was working furiously. After several tense moments, he shook his head. "It can wait until Monday."

"Don't think you'll be getting her alone then either," Tripp announced. "From now on where she goes, I go, you got that?"

Mitchell pressed his lips into a thin line, gave them a terse nod, then picked up his sunglasses up and put them on. Without another word or even a backwards glance, he got into his SUV and flipped a U-turn.

"Mission?" Tripp asked under his breath when the vehicle disappeared in a cloud of dust. He dropped his hands to his sides and faced her. "What else haven't you told me, Cat?"

"I *couldn't* tell you." She looked up at him. His face was taut with anger and she sighed, dropping her chin to her chest. "I went out with Ryan and his team Friday night."

He gaped at her. "You went on a mission with the *SEAL* team?"

Cat planted her hands on her hips. "Yeah. They needed a female interpreter." She glanced at him. "It was a simple SAR, Tripp, no big deal."

Tripp's brows drew together. "Why did they need a female inter—" His voice died and his eyes widened. "Yasmeen Hasan."

Cat said nothing.

"Did you get her out?" Tripp asked.

"Yeah."

Tripp studied her for a moment. "Okay, then. Good enough."

"That's it?"

"Yep," he said with a nod, "though I wasn't kidding about the where you go I go part."

"Are you serious? You gonna babysit me 24/7?"

"Nope." He grinned at her and took a swig from his water bottle. "Figured I'd alternate shifts with Ryan."

Cat looked askance at him. "Tripp."

"Don't even bother arguing with me." Tripp poured some of the water over his head. "What if I hadn't come running with you today?" He looked around the empty runway. "There's *no one* out here, Cat. He could've run you over, shot you, knocked your ass out and stuffed you in the back of his SUV then driven off base into the wilds of Afghanistan. No one would know you were missing until Ryan or I went looking."

"He still could've done that with you here," she pointed out. "You'd just be an extra body for him to dispose of."

"He's got a hard-on for you, not me." A grim smile curved his mouth. "No pun intended. Besides, he couldn't lift me if he had help." He turned his gaze in the direction of the retreating SUV. "Like you said, the chow hall was an anomaly. He's not likely to make the same mistake twice. He's had a taste of being locked up. I don't think he'll do anything overt to risk that again, do you?"

Cat thought about it and chewed her lip. "I don't know."

"Yeah, me either." Tripp shrugged. "Regardless of what Peter will or won't do, we need to bust him, and soon."

"You're right." She put her fists on her hips. "The sooner, the better."

"About that," Tripp began, "I made a couple of calls to my contacts in New York. They should be getting back to me before the end of the day."

"Okay." She took another drink. "Call me if you find anything out. How's Lee doing?"

"I don't know," Tripp replied. "He spends most of his time with his nose buried in a computer screen, but I'm sure if he'd found something we'd know it." He punched her arm lightly. "Now, shouldn't we head back? If I remember correctly, you said something about spending the afternoon with some Special Forces guys."

The thought of seeing Ryan again made her smile. "Yep. Race you back to the barracks."

"Go ahead, Tiger," Tripp said. "I'll give you a head start."

"What... can't keep up?" she teased.

"That's not it at all," he said, grinning, "but I have to side with Ryan on this. The view is much better from back here."

***

Cat looked at the faces gathered around the picnic table and realized that all in all it had been a great afternoon. She had cheered as the SEALs were victorious in a best-of-five basketball game series, and the smell of roasting meat had made her mouth water. After the game, everyone had grabbed a plate of food and a seat at one of the many tables in the center courtyard, and despite her misgivings, she had thoroughly enjoyed herself. Now the sun had gone down, the food was still being eaten, and the palpable camaraderie made her smile. She was surprised because the terse interactions she'd had with some SF operators prior to this had made her standoffish with men in this MOS. However, the Special Forces guys she'd met that day were funny, good-humored, and personable, completely opposite those previous encounters. And, the endless ribbing Ryan had endured because of her presence had definitely made the trip to the compound worthwhile.

"You sure you don't want anything else?" Sergeant Hobbs asked, handing her a can of soda.

Cat smiled and took the Coke. "No, thank you, Sergeant. I've eaten all I can, but it was a magnificent feast." She looked up as Ryan sat down next to her and plopped a full plate of barbecued chicken in front of him.

"It was a great meal, but she's a girl, Sergeant. They rarely eat like we do."

"She gave her hell though, LT," Hobbs said. "My mama would

love her. Mom always complains that the girls I bring home never eat anything. She says real women eat more than lettuce leaves with lemon juice."

Cat laughed. "Well, that's an endorsement if ever I've heard one." She lifted her Coke. "To your mother, Sergeant. Here's hoping you bring home a girl who eats to her specifications."

"Too bad you're taken," Hobbs said with a quick grin. "Any chance you'd like to defect to the Army?"

Ryan put his chicken leg down. "Hey!"

Hobbs stood and picked up his trash. "Sorry, LT. Had to ask."

"I think you can count the beating you and your guys took on the court as my answer," Ryan shot back, giving Cat a wink. "To the victor go the spoils, Sergeant."

Hobbs laughed and wandered over to the barbecue grill where Grady was diligently tending a large amount of hot dogs and hamburger patties. Cat looked at Ryan, who was inhaling his drumstick, and lifted one brow.

"So, I'm *spoils* now?"

He finished chewing and wiped his mouth and hands on a paper towel. "Well, the word *spoils* has many definitions. I think *bounty* and *great reward* apply in this case." He laced his fingers through hers. "I buy you a cup of tea for saving my ass and I *still* wind up with the better end of the deal. I got you."

Cat stared at him for a moment and her heart rate jumped. "You should write a book."

"About what?"

"Well, *How to Win Friends and Influence People* is already taken," she replied. "How about, *Surefire Pick-Up Lines and How to Charm a Nun out of Her Panties?*"

Ryan laughed heartily. "Catchy. I like it."

Cat shook her head and took a sip of her Coke. "Only you could utter a sentence with the word *coffee* in it and make me want to rip your clothes off."

A chicken thigh froze in mid-air. "Really?" A mischievous twinkle entered his eyes, he leaned closer to her, and lowered his voice. "You can't rip my clothes off me here, but I know a place where you can."

She met his gaze and gulped as she felt a twinge in her belly. "You are trouble."

Ryan's expression immediately sobered. "Speaking of trouble, I got a call from Tripp earlier today."

"You did?" When he nodded, she scowled. "How did he...? Never mind. Lee." She leaned her elbows on the wooden table. "What did Tripp have to say?"

"He said that as of now he and I are on Cat-watch." He lowered his voice a notch, even though no one was paying particular attention to them. "He also said Mitchell tried to approach you today. Is that true?"

Cat sighed heavily. "Yeah."

Ryan frowned. "Is the guy fucking nuts or something? He's arrested for assault and battery against you not two days ago, and he doesn't have the sense to steer clear?"

She propped her chin on her hand and looked at him out of the corner of her eye, both annoyed and pleased. "You know, I have five brothers. Twelve, actually, if you count Tripp and the guys. I neither need nor want any more."

"Well, your real brothers aren't here to protect you, and you won't let your team do it."

"I don't need protecting. I'm a big girl."

"I *want* to protect you." He stared at her for a moment then the mischievous gleam came back into his eyes. "Besides, Tripp and I already agreed. He gets the dayshift, and I get the nightshift, because the nightshift has *so* many more benefits."

She wasn't about to relent so easily. "You're assuming I *want* you to take the nightshift."

He grabbed her hand and pressed his lips to her fingers. "Aren't you the woman who said her nights were mine if I wanted them?" He leaned over to look her in the face. "Well, I want them. I don't plan to sit in a chair at your bedside, unless we're both naked and you're wrapped around me while I'm sitting in that chair."

Heat flooded her face and she closed her eyes as that erotic image flashed in her mind, and she wondered vaguely if the chair in her quarters would support both of them. Ryan brushed his knuckles over her cheek.

"I love it when you blush," he whispered. "You wouldn't think someone with your experience and résumé would be so easily embarrassed."

Cat fought to find her voice. "My résumé doesn't include a lot of experience with overt sexual innuendo," she bit out. "Despite my other worldly *endeavors*, there *are* areas where I'm relatively conservative."

"Define *conservative.*"

She looked at him. "I'm a one-man-woman," she said flatly. "And despite what happened with *us*, I don't usually... hop into bed with some guy I just met." Her cheeks grew warmer when a knowing smile curved Ryan's mouth. She rose and picked up her paper plate. "Besides, we could be married forty years and you'd probably still be able to make me blush. As you can see it doesn't take much."

Ryan stood and moved in front of her, blocking her path. "I'd like to test that theory."

The warmth in his gaze set her back a step and for a moment she couldn't breathe.

"I don't want to fight with you, Cate," he said softly.

"We're... we're not fighting."

He grinned. "Does that mean no make-up sex?"

She rolled her eyes and groaned. "Seriously? Who's using who for whose body now?"

His smile vanished. "That's *not* what I meant." His eyes narrowed on her face. "I love being with you, Cate, and I'd spend every second of every day with you if I could. Since I can't, I'll do like you said. I'm going to enjoy every minute I have with you, whether that's sharing a milkshake at BK, or sharing a bed. It doesn't matter." He backed up a step. "My feelings for you go way beyond sexual, Cate. I thought you knew that."

Cat dropped her chin, shame rasping hotly against the inside of her chest. "I *do* know that, and mine do, too." She bit her lip and shook her head. "I'm sorry, Ryan. I didn't mean it like that." She glanced at him. "Forgive me?"

"Always." He turned her face to his. "Now why don't we get out of here? If you're still in the mood to rip my clothes from me, I'm still in the mood to let you." A pensive smile played about his mouth. "And if you're not in the mood then I will be content to sleep beside you until Tripp takes over in the morning."

"I have a better title for your book." She sighed. "*How to Make a Girl Fall for You in Seven Days or Less*, although I *really* think I nailed it with the 'talk a nun out of her panties' thing."

He laughed, but before he could say a word Mack walked by, a full plate balanced carefully on one hand, a can of soda in the other.

"Like I said," Mack announced, "spontaneous meth lab."

He grinned at Cat, gave her a wink, and kept right on walking. She stared after him then looked at Ryan in silent question.

"Chemistry," Mack called over his shoulder. "You two have it."

Cat smiled and shook her head, her cheeks warming again. Ryan chuckled and took her empty plate from her. After dropping their trash in a nearby trash container he turned to her and gave her a look that made her toes curl.

"Come on, beautiful," he said softly, holding out a hand. "Let's get out of here. It's time for my Cat-watch."

She looked at his fingers for a moment then laced hers through them. "You sure you won't get in trouble for not sleeping in your designated quarters, sailor?"

He kissed the back of her hand. "I have my pager and my cell, and Commander Ferris knows where I'll be." A wry grin curved his mouth. "He said to tell you 'hi' by the way. He was going to join us this afternoon but he had a meeting with General Mason he couldn't get out of."

"Does *everybody* know...?" she asked.

Ryan glanced around the compound and nodded. "Pretty much, but I didn't say a word, I promise." He leaned toward her as they started walking toward the gate. "It's kind of obvious, I guess. Sorry if I'm not good at hiding my feelings."

Cat tugged on his hand and stopped him. "I'm glad you don't hide it, although I wish *I* wasn't so obvious." When his brows drew together she smiled and placed her hands on his chest. "I don't want to hide my feelings from you, Ryan. It's just...." She paused, searching for the right words. "There are certain people I need to keep a poker face with."

He put a hand on her neck. For a moment, she thought he was going to kiss her in front of God and everybody, but a flash glared in the darkness, startling them both. He scowled and turned toward the unwelcome intruder, his posture relaxing when he saw Mack with a digital camera. Mack snapped another picture.

"Those are going straight into the photo album," Mack said with a grin. "Don't worry, Red. I'll get you copies ASAP."

Ryan growled. "Mack."

"Don't mind me." Mack wiggled his eyebrows. "Now, you two lovebirds get out of here before fate decides to send a mission our way." He gave Ryan a pointed look. "Both hands, brother, and don't look back." With that he turned and walked away.

Chapter Twenty

Cat had just finished dressing when there was a knock on her door. The clock read 6:15 a.m., so she had a pretty good idea who was outside. She opened the door and smiled at Tripp.

"Good morning, Tiger," he said, a white bag in one hand and a drink holder with three coffee cups in the other. "You're looking well. I take it you had a good evening?"

Heat suffused her face, but she rolled her eyes and stepped back so Tripp could enter. "Yes, I had a nice evening. You?"

Tripp put the drink holder and bag on the desk and then looked at her over his shoulder. "Well, I doubt I had as much fun as *Ryan....*"

The back door opened and Ryan strode in, freshly scrubbed and dressed. "What about me?" he asked.

She crossed her arms over her chest and gave Tripp a pointed look. "Tripp was saying he didn't have as much fun last night as you did, weren't you, Tripp?"

Tripp looked at her in mock reproach. "Now why you gotta do me like that?" He grinned and handed her a cup. "It's Earl Grey, two sugars." He handed a second cup to Ryan. "Don't know what you drink, Ryan, so it's straight coffee for the two of us."

Ryan grabbed the cup and took a careful sip. "Straight coffee is perfect. Thanks, Tripp." He walked over to Cat and looped an arm around her neck, pressing a kiss to her temple. "And I can pretty much guarantee you didn't have as much fun as I did."

She gasped and punched him lightly in the stomach. "Ryan James Heller!"

"Ooh, the full name." Tripp chuckled. "You're in trouble, buddy. I've been working with her for more than five years and we were two years in before I heard her utter *my* middle name. You've known her what, not even a week yet? That *has* to be some sort of record."

Ryan chuckled and pulled her to his chest. He looked down at her and her heart positively melted when she saw the warmth in his gaze.

"We're setting all sorts of records," he said softly. "Aren't we, Cate?"

She flushed to the roots of her hair, but she couldn't look away. Her nipples tingled and she felt the familiar twinge between her legs as she remembered the previous evening. The chair actually *had* been able to support them both.

"Enough said." Tripp's mouth widened into a Cheshire cat smile. "Her face almost matches her hair."

"Yeah." Ryan ran a finger over her cheek. "I love it when that happens."

Cat humphed and tried to wriggle out of his grasp, but even with only one arm he was able to keep her close.

"Yeah, well the odds of a repeat performance are steadily declining this morning," she said flatly, giving up the fight. "In fact, if you two keep ganging up on me, your chances of getting lucky during your next 'nightshift' are pretty much non-existent, Lieutenant."

Air hissed out from between Ryan's teeth. "Yikes. She reverted to rank again, so that's my cue." He took her cup of tea and looked at Tripp. "Hold these, will you?"

He held both cups out and Tripp obligingly relieved him of the beverages. Cat glared at him, but when he spun her around and bent her backwards over his arm, she couldn't stop the surprised gasp. Ryan's eyes moved slowly over her face, and then he covered her mouth with his. As his lips played slowly over hers her body betrayed her, and despite her silent command not to respond her arms wound around his neck. His embrace tightened around her and the familiar heat started to build, her breasts aching as they were pressed into his chest. When he finally pulled away, she had neither the strength nor the inclination to open her eyes. In fact, even breathing didn't seem all that important at that particular moment.

Ryan slowly stood up, released her, and brushed a kiss over her brow. "I'll see you later, Cate. Have a good day."

When he moved away from her she wanted to pull him back. She wanted to strip him naked and ride him until they were both completely sated and utterly exhausted. She wanted to tell him she loved him.

"Nicely done," Tripp said in a low voice. "I'm beginning to understand what she sees in you."

"I'm not," Ryan replied. "But I'm not going to complain."

"Wise man. Here's your coffee."

Cat forced herself to open her eyes and walk Ryan to the door. When he paused on the landing she thought for a split second he was going to kiss her again, but he just smiled, gave her a jaunty salute, and walked toward his Humvee. She watched him until he drove away, a melancholy sigh escaping her.

"Come on, Tiger," Tripp said from behind her. Her cup of tea appeared in her periphery. "Time to get to work. You'll see the Lieutenant soon enough."

***

Cat stared at the transfer request displayed on her laptop, her finger hovering over the "return" button. Once she pressed that key, the transfer requests for her and her team would be sent to Heston's inbox. She'd checked and double-checked the forms to ensure they were properly filled out, but for some reason she was hesitating. Before she could move, her inbox dinged, alerting her to new e-mail.

She left the forms intact and opened her inbox, a smile blossoming when she saw it was an e-mail with attachments from Mack. Moving the pointer over the attachment, she clicked and waited. A moment later a picture of her and Ryan filled the screen.

"What are you working on, Catharine?" a familiar voice asked from the doorway.

Cat looked at Ryan's face for another moment then lifted her eyes to Peter's. He stood in the doorway to her office but he hadn't entered. "Looking for the data reports from last week because they don't seem to be attached to the after-action report." She tapped a key and the photo disappeared. "Do you need something?"

His expression was somber. "Can we talk?"

"As long as you stay right where you are," she replied.

Peter exhaled a heavy sigh and his shoulders slumped. "Catharine... I have no excuse for my behavior the other day, but I want you to know I am truly sorry." He looked at her with sad, puppy dog eyes. "The last thing in the world I want to do is hurt you."

She crossed her arms on her desk. "Do you want me to show you the bruises?"

He dropped his chin to his chest. "No." He rubbed his eyes. "The Deputy Director has already notified me I am under administrative review, and there will be disciplinary action forthcoming once I return to the States."

Cat thought about that, keeping her expression neutral. If Peter were anybody else, he'd be on the first plane back to the States. Then again, if he was anybody else he'd still be at the detention facility.

"And until then?" she asked.

"Until then I am to stay away from you," Peter replied, "unless we have to interact for work purposes." He stuffed his hands in his pockets. "I really am sorry, Catharine. What do I have to do to earn your forgiveness?"

"You *need* to leave her the fuck alone," Tripp growled from behind him.

Peter actually jumped and spun around to face the much larger man. "Benjamin. You startled me."

Tripp looked over Peter's head to her. "He bothering you, Cat?"

"No," she said in a low voice. "He was just leaving, weren't you, Peter?"

"Yes, yes, I was." Peter stepped into the hallway, keeping as much distance between Tripp and himself as possible. Before he walked away, he looked at her again and said, "I hope you can forgive me someday."

"I have forgiven you," she said, "but that doesn't mean I'll forget what you did. And forgiveness doesn't mean you can bypass consequences. What happened the other day will *never* happen again; do we understand each other?"

"Of course." He gave her an apologetic smile. "Thank you."

Tripp stood in the doorway until Peter's footsteps faded away. Then he walked into her office, closed the door, and sat down. "You okay?"

"I'm fine, Tripp. I was fine before you got here, but thanks." She narrowed her eyes on his face. "But, you didn't come up here to check on me, did you?"

"No." He laced his fingers together and flattened them over his abdomen. "I got a call back from one of my contacts in New York."

Cat held up a hand. "Not here." She looked at the clock. "It's almost lunch time. You averse to having Burger King again?"

He shook his head and rose. "Not at all, Tiger." He opened the door and stood to the side. "After you."

"Wait a minute," she said. "I have to do something first."

"What?" he asked.

She pulled up the picture of Ryan and looked at it for a moment then opened the transfer requests. "I need to cut the cord, Tripp." She pressed enter, then smiled and met his eyes. "Cut it for good."

He grinned. "Outstanding, Tiger. Come on, I'm buying."

Fifteen minutes later they were sitting at a table in Burger King, sandwiches and fries in front of them. Cat took a drink of her soda, then glanced around carefully and lowered her voice. "What did you find out?"

Tripp put his elbows on the table and leaned toward her. "Mitchell's wife filed for divorce about three months ago."

She was stunned. "Really?"

He nodded. "My friend sent me a copy of the divorce papers *and* the pre-nup."

"Hmm," she mused. "Unless she's a complete idiot she has to have known about his numerous affairs, so why now?"

"Maybe she reached the breaking point," he replied with a shrug. "Every person has their limit, Cat. And, according to the papers, she cited infidelity as the reason for the split. According to the pre-nup Mitchell signed, if he and Gretchen divorce because of infidelity he gets nothing."

She gaped at him. It took her a moment to find her voice. "Nothing?"

"Nada, zip, zilch."

She whistled softly. "Well, if that's true, we just found our motive."

"And he has the opportunity every day," Tripp added. "Let's hope Lee can track down the money."

Cat popped a fry into her mouth, still reeling from Tripp's discovery. Peter and his wife had been married almost ten years, and for all appearances it seemed she hadn't minded his philandering as long as he was discreet. She knew she was neither the first nor the last to fall prey to Peter's charm. She shook her head and tried to digest the news.

Her cell phone rang and she jumped. When she glanced at the display her eyes widened and she looked at Tripp.

"What is it?" he asked.

"It's Lee." Cat answered the call. "Yeah, Rick, what's up?"

"I got it, Cat. I found a link." He paused and she heard tapping in the background. "Can't believe it took me this long, but someone was *very* careful. Where are you guys?"

"Lunch," she replied. "Whatever you found, save it, encrypt it, copy it, and hide it. After work tonight we'll meet at your guys" place and take a look."

"Roger that, Tiger." He laughed. "I can't wait to see the look on your face."

"Be careful, Rick," Cat warned him, looking around again. "I don't want anyone getting wind we're closing in."

"Do you know a more careful guy than me?" Lee asked. "Hell, when I have sex I double-wrap my junk."

She squeezed her eyes shut. "Okay, too much information."

"Sorry, but I took every precaution known to man, and then made up some more precautions and followed them, too. Nobody will know anything until we want them to."

"Good. Now try to make it look like you're actually doing something work related, please. Oh, and you'd better sweep the offices and your quarters for any sort of bugs."

"I do that daily, Cat," he said reproachfully. "Don't you?"

She rolled her eyes. "Not as often as you apparently. Just... do what you need to do and we'll talk about this tonight."

"You got it, boss. See you later."

After hanging up the phone she groaned softly and ran a hand over her face.

"Did Lee find something out?"

Cat met his eyes. "So he says."

"This may be coming to a head real fast, Tiger," he advised her. "You need to watch yourself around Mitchell. Don't be looking at anymore pictures of Ryan where he can see your face."

Her brows rose and she stared at him.

Tripp smiled knowingly. "You get this... *dreamy* look in your eyes when you look at the Lieutenant."

She bristled. "I do not."

"Do, too."

Cat frowned. "Tripp!"

He shrugged. "Sorry, Cat, but I'm not the only one to notice your... softer edges. This morning Burgess asked me if I thought you looked different. When I asked him what he meant, he shrugged and said, 'I don't know, she just seems different.'"

She gripped her forehead with one hand and exhaled sharply.

"Don't worry," he continued. "With what happened the other day

Mitchell has been a little preoccupied, but if you don't watch yourself...? Mitchell is downright territorial when it comes to you, Cat. I think part of the reason I'm not on his radar is because he knows our relationship is more familial than sexual." Tripp's expression sobered. "Speaking of relationships, I've been thinking about something you said."

She frowned. "What?"

He took a sip of his drink. "You told me you haven't been on more than half a dozen dates with the same guy in almost five years, that three or four dates in they drop off the map." When she nodded, he reached across the table and took her hand. "Did you ever stop to think perhaps Peter had something to do with that?"

She blinked at him. "Do you know something you're not telling me?"

"No," he replied with a shake of his head. "It's just something to consider." He watched her carefully. "If Peter *is* the reason those other guys ducked out, it's probably a good thing Mitchell isn't wise to you and Ryan yet."

Cat felt the blood drain from her face and she stared at Tripp, dread pooling in her stomach and clogging her veins with ice. Her eyelids fluttered and her jaw worked soundlessly as the full implications of what Tripp was saying hit her like a 500-pound bomb.

"Cat?" Tripp's brows drew together. "What is it?"

"Oh, God," she breathed, closing her eyes. "I just painted Ryan a target."

He chuckled and squeezed her fingers. "Only if you give yourself away, Tiger. Take it from me; you have one hell of a poker face when you decide to put one on."

"You don't understand," Cat said under her breath, "he knows, Tripp. Peter knows."

A shadow of concern flitted over his sharply carved features. "What do you mean he knows? How?"

Tears stung behind her eyelids and her lungs were frozen. It took her more than a few moments to find her voice, and when she did it was barely more than a whisper. "I found... I found a camera in my... in my quarters." She looked at Tripp and saw the shock on his face. "My house was clean when we left for the mountains, Ben."

He leaned back in his seat and looked toward the ceiling. "Ah, hell."

Pain blossomed in her chest and she fisted her hands. "I've got to... I've got to break it off with him—"

"No." Tripp covered her hands with his. While his touch was gentle his voice was tinged with steel. "No, Cat. If Mitchell knows you and Ryan are more than friends, and you suddenly break it off for no apparent reason? That will make him suspicious."

Cat closed her eyes and took several deep breaths. In her mind's eye she imagined herself taking aim at Mitchell, once again calling on the reservoir of calm she accessed when shooting. Only moments ago she'd been near panic, but now she felt the control returning. Flattening her hands on the table, she opened her eyes and looked at Tripp.

"Then we need to nail him, and do it fast," she said, "before I get Ryan killed."

"You really think he'd go after a SEAL?"

"No," Cat replied. "But if Peter can't intimidate Ryan, and if he can't get Ryan transferred, what *can* he do?" Tripp's brows drew together and he looked at her in silent question. She continued. "How did Ryan and I meet, Tripp?"

Tripp's brows rose and he straightened in his seat. "Shit. Feed SOCOM bogus intel and get the SEALs sent on a phony mission."

She nodded. "Exactly. Then all Peter has to do is sit back and let the terrorists do his dirty work for him." She gave Tripp a pointed look. "And we both know what *they'd* do to a SEAL team, don't we?"

Tripp exhaled slowly. "Fuck me." He ran a hand over his face. "We can't let that happen."

Cat set her jaw. "We won't. I'll kill Peter myself first."

***

"What do you have?" Cat asked, grabbing a chair and pulling it up beside Lee. Tripp eased down on the edge of the nearest bed, his elbows on his knees.

"I have the Holy Grail," Lee replied, grinning. His dark eyes danced with excitement. "Took me a while to find it, but the angels are singing now."

"You swept this place for bugs?" Tripp asked.

"Absolutely," Lee said. He pointed to what looked like a desktop pencil sharpener. "And, I have this." He pulled the shavings tray partway out and Cat heard a brief, high, soft whine. "Jamming device. It's my own design. Want one?"

"I'd like ten," Cat replied. "Now get on with it."

"Yeah," Tripp urged, giving her a grin. "She's got a date."

She scowled at him then turned her attention back to Lee. "Go on, Rick. Dazzle me."

"Very well." He laced his fingers together and bent them backwards, cracking his knuckles loudly. Then he started tapping on the keyboard. "The first day I got nowhere. I checked Mitchell's credit cards, bank accounts, investment portfolios, which are nearly bankrupt by the way. I looked at everything and came up dry. Then I tried something else." He pulled up what looked like a roster. "I compiled a list of relatives' names, from both his and his wife's side of the family, all the way to their step-neighbor-in-law-twice-removed, and I got a hit." Lee pointed to a name near the bottom of the list.

"Gladys Emmerson," Cat read. "Okay, I'll bite. Who is she?"

"Ms. Emmerson is Gretchen Mitchell's great aunt on her mother's side," Lee answered. He punched another button. "And, according to this, she has two accounts at the Grand Cayman National Bank, each with more than three million in assets."

"Gretchen's family *is* rich," Cat pointed out. "It wouldn't be unheard of for someone with a lot of money to invest in an offshore bank."

"True, but since Gladys Emmerson has been dead since 1987...?" Lee gave her a pointed look. "I also cross-checked for any other Gladys Emmersons. There aren't any. Not to mention the accounts were only opened three months ago via wire transfer."

Cat's feline senses were starting to tingle. "Could you tell from where?"

"Yep." Lee started typing then gestured toward the screen when the page he was looking for appeared. "Swiss-Arab Financial via Qatar Worldwide Bank. The Feds have been investigating the latter with Interpol ever since 9/11 for their alleged terrorist ties and money-laundering activities." He looked at her. "Interestingly enough, Afghanistan's current president has an account at this very bank, as do many of his relatives, including one Tariq Hasan." Lee lifted one brow and smiled. "I think someone's been a very naughty boy."

She chewed her lip for a moment. "It's not enough. We can't tie Peter to the money. This is all circumstantial. It won't even get us an appointment with the Director, much less an arrest and conviction."

"Then we'll keep digging until we have enough," Tripp said. "If these are Peter's accounts, he opened them around the same time his wife served him with divorce papers, which means one of two things.

One, the timing of Mitchell's treason and his wife divorcing him are simply unfortunate coincidences."

"And two?" Cat asked.

"Something or someone tipped him that she was going to file, so he immediately went on the offensive. We all know Peter likes the status and comfort that come with his wife's wealth. He's not the type to let that sort of lifestyle go so easily."

She nodded absently, her mind working furiously. "Okay, then. We keep digging."

There was a brief silence.

"What are you thinking, Cat?" Tripp asked, his eyes narrowed on her face.

She turned to him. "What? Oh, nothing, Ben."

Tripp scowled. "Don't lie to me. I can hear the wheels spinning from here."

"Me, too," Lee agreed. "What gives, Cat?"

She stared at the floor for a moment then fixed her eyes on Lee. "I found that bill in Peter's office." She looked at Tripp. "Ten to one if I look in the right place, I can find what we need to link him to that money."

He rose from the edge of the bed. "Don't even fucking think about it."

"Already thought it," Cat replied, rising also. "He has to have something, somewhere that links him to those accounts. Wherever it is, we need to find it, and quick."

"He goes to Kabul twice a week and Kandahar twice a month," Tripp pointed out. "What you want to go looking for could be anywhere in either of those locations."

"His tablet," Lee said suddenly. His eyes darted between her and Tripp. "He never goes anywhere without that thing."

"He's not allowed to use that at work," Cat said.

"No," Lee agreed, "he leaves it in his quarters during work hours, but whenever he goes off-base, that tablet goes with him." A smile started to form on Lee's mouth. "The last time we went to Kabul we had to make a special trip by his quarters to pick it up because he refused to go without it." He gave her a pointed look. "According to Airman Avery, he pays more attention to his tablet than he does to her."

"Since when did you and Airman Avery become confidantes?" she asked, incredulous.

Lee grinned. "She was moping in front of the vending machine one afternoon, and when I asked her what was wrong, she spilled." He smiled and shrugged. "I bought her a candy bar, and ever since then she acts like I'm her BFF."

Cat glanced at Tripp. "She could be a handy ally to have."

Tripp frowned. "What do you mean?"

"I think Peter asked her to follow me the night Ryan and I first went out," she replied.

"Seriously?" both men said in unison.

"She's not a field op," Tripp added.

"And she definitely isn't field op material," Lee said. "She's *way* too naïve for that. Plus, she and Mitchell are sleeping together. How does that make her an ally?"

"She has access," Cat replied. "She's his assistant, so she has access to his files, his computer, and his correspondence, all of it." She gave each man a pointed look. "If she's unhappy with Peter, feels she's being neglected or marginalized, or as if she's doing his dirty work...?"

"She'll be easy to turn," Tripp finished for her.

"And, take it from someone who's been *exactly* where she is...." She smiled. "The airman probably knows *far* more than he realizes and far more than she should."

Tripp gave her a wry smile. "So, in other words, when he gets a hard-on his brain checks out?"

Cat didn't bother to reply.

"How does that help us with our current dilemma?" Lee asked.

"It doesn't," she said flatly. "I'm looking down the road though, and she could be useful so *be nice*."

Lee looked at her in mock reproach. "I'm always nice."

"As to getting access to his tablet," she began, "my idea involves good ol' breaking and entering. Any other ideas?"

"Yeah," Lee replied with a mischievous grin, "but it will still involve B&E." He reached into a drawer and pulled out what resembled a flash drive. It was thinner than a typical USB device and had a different type of plug.

"Let me guess," Cat ventured, "not a flash drive?"

Lee looked at her quickly. "How'd you know?"

She waved a hand at the device. "Never mind. What does it do?"

"If you can plug this into his tablet, this will allow me to create a backdoor into his computer that I can access whenever I want." He held it out to her. "I'll need five minutes once you insert it into the power port, but after that...." He paused and snapped his fingers. "I'm in easier than Santa down a chimney on Christmas Eve. He'll never know I was there."

"His computer is encrypted," she said.

Lee shrugged. "Won't matter. Whatever encryption he has, it shouldn't take me more than a couple minutes, tops, to crack once this is plugged in. After that, I'll upload a shadow program, effectively making me a fly on the wall of everything he does on that tablet."

"Everything?" Tripp asked.

Lee nodded. "And I'll be able to keep an eye on it from right here," he said, gesturing to his desk. "I can program my computer to monitor his, and record everything he does, every website he visits, every e-mail he sends or receives, passwords and log-ins, the whole nine yards. In effect, his computer will be my computer."

Cat looked at him and shook her head. "I think I love you."

"Don't let Ryan hear you say that," Tripp said with a chuckle. "I think he'd take exception." She thought about Ryan for a moment, and Tripp immediately burst into laughter, pointing at her. "There it is, Tiger. There's that dreamy look I was telling you about that you swear you don't have."

"Glad I'm not a mind-reader," Lee said, grinning. "Pretty sure whatever thought just went through your head would carry an NC-17 rating."

She scowled at them and rose. "Zip it, both of you." She looked at the flash drive. "So, all I have to do is plug this into his tablet and give you five minutes?"

"We should use comms," Lee suggested. "I'll need to start working as soon as you plug it in."

Tripp reached for the device. "You should let me, Cat. If you get caught, it'll be far more dangerous for you than me. He'd never try to take me on by himself, not even with backup."

Cat pocketed the drive and gave him a long, assessing look. "When was the last time you picked a lock, Tripp?"

He thought about it for a moment then frowned. "It's been a while."

"Yeah," she agreed. "I practice almost daily. Not to mention the fact that, if I get caught, I can always make up some convincing lie as to why I'm in his quarters. 'We need to talk about what happened the other day,' 'I really want to be friends with you, Peter,' whatever. I mean, he broke into *my* place, so what's good for the goose.... Therefore, unless you're planning to come out of the closet to him and confess your undying love?"

His frown darkened. "Point taken, but I don't like it. You're not doing this alone."

"I won't *be* alone," she replied with a jaunty grin. "The two of you will be on comms listening to everything. If something goes wrong, you come to the rescue. It's only a five-minute drive from the hangar to the BOQ."

"A lot can happen in five minutes," Tripp said, his brows drawn together ominously. "It only takes a second to shoot someone."

"We don't have much choice, Tripp." Cat crossed her arms over her chest. "We've got to get him before he gets someone killed, possibly Ryan's team or one of *us*."

They went quiet. She felt the gravity of the situation pressing down on her as if she'd been thrust into Atlas's position with the world balancing precariously on her shoulders. A glance at Tripp and Lee told her they thought along the same lines. Their expressions were solemn.

"So, when do we do this?" Lee asked, breaking the tense silence.

She thought about it for a moment. "We should do it during working hours." She looked at Tripp. "I'll take off for lunch, and we can use the comms from the equipment. If anyone asks, you're running diagnostics."

"He's headed to Kandahar on Wednesday," Lee said. "I saw the transpo request on the roster. We have to do it before then because he'll take the tablet with him when he goes."

"Then we do it tomorrow," she replied. "Hopefully, we can find what we need and wrap this case up with a pretty pink bow for the Director."

"Hopefully *before* the weekend," Tripp said, obviously trying to lighten the mood. "The Aussies want a chance to win their shit back, and I was of a mind to let them try." The attempt at humor fell flat and the three friends looked at each other silently for a few moments. Finally, Tripp sighed. "Okay. Tomorrow it is."

Cat looked at Lee. "Rick?"

He nodded. "Works for me."

"Very well." She paused and took a deep breath. "Tomorrow we commence Operation Downfall, and if we do this right, he'll never see it coming."

Chapter Twenty-One

"What's wrong, babe?" Ryan asked softly, his fingers making lazy circles on her arm. "You're awfully quiet."

Cat snuggled closer to his side, her face in the crook of his neck, and smiled. "I wasn't a few minutes ago."

He chuckled and kissed her brow. "No, no you weren't. But since then you haven't said a word."

"Maybe you rendered me speechless," she suggested, her cheeks warming, "and I haven't fully recovered yet."

"You're having no trouble speaking right now," he pointed out.

She ran her fingers over his bare chest and pouted. "Can't I just enjoy lying next to you?"

"Of course." He pulled her closer and clasped his hands together, enclosing her in his embrace. "You just seem... distracted."

While they'd been making love it had been easy to push thoughts of tomorrow aside and concentrate on him. In fact, she hadn't been capable of coherent thought while Ryan had played her body like it was a fine instrument and he a master musician. Now, despite the fact she was lying in his arms, their naked bodies pressed together, she couldn't stop thinking about tomorrow and what it might bring. Cat sighed.

"I'm sorry, Ryan." She pulled back so she could look at him. "It's something at work, and I can't talk about it."

"Cate," he began, his expression serious, "you know if you did tell me anything I would never repeat it, right?"

She smiled and traced the line of his jaw. "I know, but I have no right to put you in that position. Also, it would be breaking my nondisclosure agreement." She pressed her forehead to his. "Don't worry, it will work itself out soon enough."

He looked at her wistfully. "Okay, but I'm here if you need me."

Cat's heart swelled until it felt like it was climbing into her throat. "Thank you," she managed to whisper. "That means a lot to me."

"Well, you mean a lot to me." His eyes searched hers. "Not to change the subject... but something has been bothering me."

"What?"

He studied her for a moment, obviously reluctant.

She smiled. "Spill it, sailor."

He was silent for several more seconds then said, "How did your dad know about your first kill? It had to be classified top secret or the entire world would have been buzzing about the first 'female sniper' with a confirmed combat kill. So, if the CIA managed to keep the rest of the world in the dark, how did your dad find out?"

Cat blinked, took a breath, and settled back into his side, her head resting in the curve of his neck. "I don't know," she replied after a brief silence, winding one of her legs over his. "*I* certainly didn't tell him." She closed her eyes, counting his heartbeats as his pulse pattered against her cheek. "Then again, he did spend the last eight years of his career at the Pentagon, so anything is possible. He knows everybody in D.C., including the guy who lives in a cardboard box under the Potomac River Bridge."

Ryan went quiet. His fingers sifted through her hair and she closed her eyes. The warmth of his body leached into hers, the feel of his arms around her a comfort she hadn't experienced in years. For the first time in what seemed like forever, she felt completely relaxed, secure, and safe, an odd state of affairs given what she was smack in the middle of.

"I'm sorry you had to do what you did, Cate," he said in a low voice. "No one should be put in the position where they have to kill or die, but... I'm also glad it happened."

Cat's eyes opened and she pondered that for a moment. Easing out of his embrace, she leaned up on an elbow and looked at him in silent question. He shook his head and stared at the wall.

"I'm not glad you had to kill someone, that's not what I meant." He glanced at her. "But if you hadn't...?" Sitting up slowly, he faced her. "If you hadn't, you might never have been sent here, and we might never have met."

Her heart started to thump uncomfortably against her breastbone.

"Since I met you, I try to think about my life without you in it," he continued, his voice hushed, "and I can't do it, Cate. I don't want to."

Cat dropped her chin. "Ryan, I...."

He pressed a finger to her lips. "Let me finish, please."

She nodded slowly and he gave her a faint, pensive smile.

"I know what I said the other day, about me wanting you to have fond memories of me when we eventually part ways." His brows drew together and he focused on her mouth. "That's *not* what I want." He wound his fingers through hers, pressed his lips to the back of her hand, then held it to his chest and closed his eyes. "I'm falling in love with you, Cate, and no matter how hard I try to... I can't stop this train."

It felt like someone was beating a war drum in her chest, and she wondered if he could hear it. Her eyes stung and she blinked rapidly as she sat up. Cat brushed a lock of hair from his brow then kissed his forehead. Ryan gathered her in his arms and pressed his face into the crook of her neck as her arms wound around his shoulders.

Her throat clogged with emotion. "You don't have to stop this train," she whispered. "We're on it together, Ryan."

He pulled back to look at her, his face taut with anxiety. "My tour here is up in a couple months. I don't know where they'll send me after that."

"They could transfer me next week," Cat said softly, "and I don't know where they'd send me either."

His expression sobered. "How are you at long distance relationships?"

"I don't know. Never been in one."

"How'd you like to give it a try... with me?"

For a moment, she couldn't breathe. She'd been alone for so long it was hard to believe the warmth she saw in his eyes was for her. Her heart was saying, "Yes!" but her brain was less enthusiastic. Her vocal chords knotted in her throat. She stared at him, waiting for him to retract his offer, and when it didn't happen she inhaled sharply. That familiar hot/cold combo of joy and fear leapt inside of her. "You're serious."

Ryan cupped her head in his hands and looked deep into her eyes. "I have never been more serious about anything in my life." His gaze wandered over her face for several long, tender moments, and then he gave her a pensive smile. "I love you, Cate, and I don't know what tomorrow holds for either of us, but whatever it is... I want to face it with you. You game?"

She bit her lip, the stinging in her eyes intensifying. "I don't know." When he pulled back she grabbed his hands and wound her fingers through his. "It's not that I don't want what you want, I *do*. And as much as I would love to wander down the happily-ever-after road with you, we both know we may not be able to do that."

"So," he began, his voice cool as he looked away, "what do we do then?"

Her heart twisted painfully. She wanted to give herself completely to him, but logic dictated she couldn't, not yet. "We take it one day at a time," Cat replied softly. She moved around to look him in the eye. "For however long we have together, Ryan, I'm yours and only yours, whether that's a week, a month, or the rest of our lives." His expression was neutral and her throat tightened. She released him and sat back. "I understand if that's not enough for you and you want to get off the train."

He moved so quickly she had no chance to react. The next thing she knew she was on her back, her body covered by his. He leaned up on his elbows, and the tenderness she saw in his eyes made her insides quiver.

"Not on your life," he whispered. He covered her mouth with his and Cat sighed as heat slowly pulsed through her. Ryan kissed her deeply and thoroughly then pulled back to look at her. "Whatever time we have together, whether it's a day, a week, or the rest of our lives, I'll take it." He brushed the hair from her face. "One day at a time."

Cat's eyes welled with tears and she smiled. "Then I have one more thing to say to you."

Ryan lifted one brow. "And what is that?"

She wound her arms around his neck. "All aboard, Lieutenant. This train is leaving the station."

***

The BOQ, Base Officer's Quarters, was a grouping of double-stacked CONEX containers set up pretty much like the containers on the SF Compound. In this area, there were three rows of ten, two-story containers modified into surprisingly comfortable living quarters. Like most of the base's "barracks," there was a community bathroom in the center of the complex, as well as a common area with BBQ pits and picnic tables.

The previous night, with Ryan sleeping soundly at her side, Cat had lain awake for more than an hour, planning. Slipping into the BOQ after dark would be relatively easy, but getting past the guard shack in the middle of the day was another matter entirely. She glanced at her watch. 11:45 a.m. Well, it was now or never. Cat got out of the SUV, closed the door, and walked around to the passenger side. Picking up the large box sitting on the seat, she bumped the door closed with her backside and walked toward the watch.

She'd dressed for the occasion in tight jeans and a t-shirt she hadn't put on since it had shrunk in the wash. While she wasn't planning to flirt with the watch, because it *could* be a woman, hedging her bets wouldn't hurt. Pulling her cell phone from her pocket as she walked, she hit the speed dial for Tripp.

"Go, Tiger."

"Walking toward the watch now. Be ready."

"Born ready."

Cat hung up the phone and slid it back into her pocket. The watch, a 2nd lieutenant with the name MacKenzie stitched over his pocket, sat a little straighter in his seat as she stopped in front of him and rested the large box on the ledge of the open window. He was a handsome man in his mid to late twenties, with brown hair, brown eyes, and the longest eyelashes she'd ever seen. She leaned toward him and his eyes widened slightly when her breasts popped up onto the ledge next to the box.

"Greetings, lieutenant," Cat said, pasting a slightly annoyed look on her face. "Peter Mitchell should've called to let you know I was coming."

The lieutenant grabbed a clipboard. "Your name, ma'am?"

"Catharine Beckett." She smiled. "But you can call me Cat."

He fumbled with the papers, dropped the clipboard, and gave her a sheepish smile as he had to stand to retrieve it from the floor of the cramped 4'X4' cubicle. "Sorry." His eyes scanned the list as he sat back on his stool. "I'm afraid I don't see your name here, Miss Beckett."

She scowled. "Really? Check again, please." He did as she asked and shook his head. She rolled her eyes and cursed under her breath. "Seriously? He asks me to take *my* lunch hour to straighten up *his* quarters because his wife is flying in on a C-130 this evening, and he forgets to call *you*? As if I don't have better things to do with my time than clean up his crap and put silk sheets on his bed?" She pulled her cell phone from her pocket. "Hold on, lieutenant. We're going to straighten this out now."

"Oh, that's all right," the lieutenant said. He picked up the phone hanging on the wall of the hut. "I have Mr. Mitchell's number right here."

Before Cat could say or do anything he'd dialed, and she slipped her phone back into her pocket as the lieutenant waited for a response. She held her breath and her pulse sped up, but she kept her face carefully neutral. Tripp could do a dead-on impression of Peter, so they had planned for Tripp to sneak into Peter's office and answer the phone if the watch decided to call. She had no way of knowing if the plan had worked, but she'd know in less than a minute.

"Yes, Mr. Mitchell, this is Lieutenant MacKenzie at the BOQ. I have a Cat Beckett here who says you gave her permission to enter your quarters, sir."

She could barely hear the voice coming through the line and she gulped, her pulse jumping another couple of points. She couldn't tell if it was Tripp or Peter, but when the lieutenant looked at her, nodded, and smiled she nearly heaved a sigh of relief.

"Yes, she is very pretty, sir." MacKenzie chuckled softly and listened as the voice continued. "I understand, sir. I'll pretend she was never here. I wouldn't want to cause a misunderstanding between you and the missus." He paused again, listening, and glanced at her. "I can certainly see why your wife might not understand, sir." The voice spoke again. "Very good and thank you, sir. You have a nice rest of your day." MacKenzie hung up the phone and turned to her. "Go on in, Miss Beckett. I assume you have a key?"

Cat smiled and pulled her key ring from her pocket. "Right here, lieutenant." She took a couple of steps then turned back to him. "You wouldn't want to help me, would you?"

MacKenzie laughed. "As fun as that sounds, I have to pass. Don't work too hard."

She rolled her eyes and grumbled. "Fat chance of that happening. This is the last time I *ever* volunteer to do someone a favor."

The watch's laughter echoed through the lines of metal containers as she walked leisurely toward Peter's quarters. Once she was out of the lieutenant's line of sight, she pulled out her phone and dialed Tripp's number.

"Yeah," Tripp said.

"Tell me we're good."

"We're perfect, Tiger. I'm headed back downstairs to help Lee with the 'diagnostics' and Peter just passed me on his way back to his office, his nose buried in a file. I think he's *purposely* avoiding me for some reason."

Cat chuckled. "I can't imagine *why*. You check for bugs first?"

"Yep, but the watch called Peter's secure line so it shouldn't be an issue. Plus, I used one of Lee's little jammers to be safe, and I wore latex gloves if that sets your mind at ease."

Cat took a deep breath and exhaled slowly. "Okay. I'll activate comms as soon as I'm inside. Be ready."

"Ready and waiting on you. Talk to you in a bit."

Cat's eyes darted to and fro as she approached Peter's quarters, but at this time of day any officers who were here were probably sleeping after working the graveyard shift. Putting the box on the ground, she retrieved her picks and quickly worked the tumblers of the lock free. Taking another glance around, she opened the door, picked up the box, and slipped into his room.

After locking the door behind her she activated Heston's device and walked the length of the container. The display didn't light up, and she allowed herself to relax *just* a hair.

The room was dark, but there was enough light filtering through the thin curtains for her to see Mitchell's tablet lying on the desk. A glance around the room revealed nothing of note, everything neatly arranged, the bed crisply made, not an errant sock or shoe to be seen. Peter's quarters were Spartan and obsessively neat, but she'd expected that.

Cat snapped on a pair of latex gloves as she sat down at the desk. Pressing a finger against her ear, she activated her earpiece.

"Ok, Rick, I'm in."

"Roger that, Tiger. All you have to do is power the tablet up and insert the device into the charging port. And don't worry if a password log-in comes up. Once you plug me in, it'll take me two shakes to bypass that."

Cat was careful not to move or disturb anything as she powered up the notebook. The log-in screen popped up, and she took the drive from her pocket.

"Okay, I'm plugging it in now." She slipped the device into the port. "It's done."

Lee laughed softly. "Roger that. Now, sit back, relax, and let me dazzle you... *again.*"

The drive started to hum and the screen started to flash.

"Hey, Rick, is the screen supposed to look like it's going to explode?"

"Yes, ma'am."

"So, I just sit here, now?"

"Unless you want to do something else, yes. I'll be done in five."

She waited a moment then walked over to the cardboard box, took out a set of sheets from the bottom, and shook them out. Then, she rumpled them up and stuffed them back in the box to make it look as if she'd changed the bedding. When that was done, she sat back down at Peter's desk and stared at the rapidly changing screen, fascinated. Shaking herself, she decided that, since she was there, a look in his desk might not be such a bad idea.

She went immediately for the locked drawer, and this lock was even easier than the door. Cat glanced through the hanging files, seeing nothing of interest, and was about to close the drawer when something registered. Her brows drew together as she looked down into the drawer and then looked at the face of the drawer. Her gaze went back and forth several times, until she inserted her hand vertically into the drawer, measuring the depth with her arm. Noting the measurement, she placed her arm against the face of the drawer and her brows rose.

Cat carefully pulled the frame for the hanging files from the drawer, files and all, and sat it on the floor. After a brief, cautious search of the other drawers she found a small flashlight and flicked it on.

"You okay, Cat?" Lee asked.

"Fine. Waiting on you."

She ran the light along the edge where the bottom and side of the drawer met up and her eyes narrowed. She pressed a hand on the bottom of the drawer, then slid her hand forward and back. When her fingers reached the back of the drawer, the metal plate gave way and the front end of the bottom panel popped up about an inch. She smiled and lifted the sheet metal from the drawer.

There was about three inches of space between the drawer's false and real bottoms, and in that space was a thick, brown manila folder. There were no logos or printing of any kind on the folder, so it wasn't an official file. Cat checked for any sort of trip wires or tampering indicators, and then lifted the folder from its hiding place.

Beneath the file folder was a plain, leather bound journal. Pursing her lips, Cat picked it up and placed it on the desk.

She moved to sit on the floor and opened the folder, laying it flat on the drab, gray, indoor/outdoor carpet. The first thing she saw was her name and photograph on the right-hand side top sheet. Cat frowned and started flipping through the following pages. Her entire service record was there, including her initial Agency application, resume, and background checks. It seemed to be an exact duplicate of her employment record, until she saw the photographs. She flipped through the 8"X10" pictures of her, obviously taken when she was unaware.

There was a snapshot taken through the window of her apartment in which she was sitting on her couch with a bowl of ice cream. Another showed her as she ran in the park by the Potomac, and yet another showed her getting her regular cup of tea at a coffee shop roughly a block from her office in D.C. There were nearly two dozen shots of her, all at different times and locations, but she could tell by what she was wearing that some were recent. Cat blinked and took a shaky breath.

The top sheet on the left-hand side was heavy stock and blank. She lifted that first page, and what she saw beneath it made her heart stop cold. Ryan's face looked back at her from that next page. It was another 8X10, and it was an official photograph. He wore his dress whites, his face clean shaven, and an American flag hung in the background. Alarm blossomed coldly in her belly. She had known Peter was a little off-kilter, but the file confirmed he was more than a little off. Keeping such incriminating evidence in such an easy to find spot went against everything the Agency had taught them. Now she was even more concerned than she had been before.

"What's going on, Cat?" Lee asked. "You're way too quiet over there."

Cat swallowed hard and forced herself to speak, hoping her voice sounded normal. "N-nothing is going on. You guys still clear on your end?"

"Of course. We're supposed to be running *diagnostics* after all." He chuckled. "Two minutes, and you can get the hell out of there."

She lifted the photograph and her heart dropped to the floor. "Anyone got eyes on Mitchell?"

"He's in his office," Tripp said. "I can see him through that window that overlooks the hangar."

"Good. Let me know as soon as you're done."

"Roger that."

Cat flipped quickly through the following pages, her eyes skimming the background and service record check Peter had done on Ryan. When she got to the end she was faced with another blank sheet of heavy paper. Her fingers trembled as she lifted it up. When a handsome green eyed, blonde haired man looked back at her, she sucked in a breath.

Lance Collins was a Senator's aide, and the last man she had dated. The 'relationship' had ended six months ago after only four dates, like all the others. Cat's lungs labored for every shallow breath as she slid her thumb beneath the entire stack of papers, lifted them, and let the individual sheets fall, flipping through them slowly from back to front. As each face was revealed, that icy hand she'd become acquainted with a couple of days ago reached back inside her chest cavity and clawed with frozen fingers.

The papers furthest back referenced Ted Carson, stockbroker, the first man she'd dated after Peter. Then was Blake Stanton, bar owner, the man she'd dated after Ted. They were *all* there, every man: Dylan Wells, Jake Morgan, Michael Jacobi, Lance Collins, and, last, Ryan.

Her stomach clenched and her mind spun. Anger burned a hole in the center of the ice gathered in her midsection as she closed the file folder, then reached for the journal and opened it.

The first entry was dated nearly five years earlier, several months after she'd broken it off with Peter. She started to read, blinking rapidly as the tears formed.

June 9th. Followed Ted to his gym today. What does Catharine see in him? I am ten times the man this asshole will ever be. Thought about confronting him during his workout, but there are too many people around. Will wait for a better time....

Cat closed her eyes and tried to breathe, but her throat had closed up. Her lungs burned, and it wasn't until survival instinct kicked in that her airway cleared enough for her to suck in a gulp of air. She turned her gaze back to the journal and skipped forward several pages.

September 26th. Stopped by Stanton's bar this afternoon and started chatting the guy up. Will work him for a week or so before I confront him. Won't he be surprised when I tell him he's been dating my "wife"...?

She gulped.

"We're almost done here, Cat. You ready to go?"

"Yeah," she replied, her voice barely above a whisper. "Just let me know."

She closed the journal and made a decision she knew would have consequences. After replacing the false bottom of the drawer and the rack with its hanging files, she slipped the journal and file into the box beneath the rumpled sheets. The next time Peter accessed the drawer he would realize she'd been snooping. He, in turn, would react and possibly give her what she needed to bring him down. Although it was never wise to provoke a bear, it was better to anticipate an attack than it was to be taken completely by surprise.

"And, we're done," Lee said in her ear. "Remove the drive, power the tablet down, and get the hell out of there."

"Mitchell still in his office?" she asked, removing the drive.

"Yep," Tripp said. "Looks like he's on the phone."

"Cell or hard line?" Cat asked absently as she powered the computer down.

"Hard line," was Tripp's reply.

She stopped what she was doing. "Rick, you have that cell number handy?"

"I do," Lee answered. "Why?"

She made sure the desk was arranged exactly as Peter had left it, then turned and faced the room. "Spoof the caller ID to make it look like it's coming from one of the terrorist's phones and call it."

"Why, Cat?" Tripp asked.

"If it's here, I want it."

"And if it's in his pocket?"

"Hang up," she replied.

"It might be in his car," Lee pointed out.

"And it might be here." She frowned. "Humor me." She heard typing in the background.

"Okay," Lee said. "Dialing now."

Cat waited and her heart jumped when she heard a faint buzzing. Closing her eyes, she listened carefully then followed the sound. To her surprise, the nondescript looking phone was in the nightstand drawer. She'd expected to have to work a little harder to find the cell phone, and she stared at it for a long, tense moment. "It's here."

"Cat."

It was Tripp's voice, and she jumped. "Yeah, what?"

"You take that phone he's going to know we're onto him."

"Hold on a sec," Lee said.

She waited, the typing in the background sounding like muted machine gun fire.

"There. Done."

She frowned. "What did you do, Rick?"

"I used this high-tech equipment for its designated purpose." There was some more typing. "I sent a signal to the phone, pinpointing its location down to the exact longitude and latitude. Now we have evidence connecting him to that phone, Cat, so you can leave it where it is."

"Are Peter's quarters within the radius of that cell tower you pinpointed before?"

More typing, and then Lee chuckled. "Why, yes, Cat, yes they are."

"Bingo." She took a breath and closed the drawer.

"Get out of there, Tiger," Tripp said. "He's still in his office, but there's no point in pushing our luck."

"Roger that," she replied. "I'm heading out now."

She took another careful look around the room to make sure it looked exactly as it had when she entered. Snapping off her gloves, she stuffed them beneath the rumpled sheets, then picked the box up and exited the container. After re-locking the door, she walked toward the entrance, the box held under one arm.

"That didn't take long," Lieutenant MacKenzie commented as she walked up to his cubicle.

Cat rolled her eyes and scowled. "Yeah, well five minutes in Peter called me and said 'never mind, she's not coming,' then hung up. I'd *just* finished changing the sheets."

"Bummer," MacKenzie commented. "I wonder what happened."

"Don't know." She shrugged. "Mrs. Mitchell is... how do I put this?" She pursed her lips and pretended to think about it for a moment. "I think 'high-maintenance' is the nicest way to describe her. She's a wealthy New York City socialite who's never lifted anything heavier than a credit card, so Afghanistan is probably a little outside of her comfort zone."

MacKenzie chuckled. "Probably so. It's a little out of *my* comfort zone, so I can't imagine how a pampered princess would feel about it."

She rolled her eyes. "The dust alone would be enough to send her scurrying back to the airport for a flight home. See you later, LT. Don't work too hard." She turned to walk away, then stopped and faced him again. "Oh, Peter sounded pretty upset, so if you see him...?"

"I won't say a word," MacKenzie said with a smile. "You were never here and none of this ever happened."

Cat smiled back at him. "Thanks. When Peter gets in a mood he can be a real bear, and he has a tendency to take peoples' heads off."

"I know," MacKenzie agreed. "He's been pretty surly the past couple of days. After the first time he snapped at me I figured it was best to keep my mouth shut and nod when he goes by."

"Smart man." She chuckled and gave him a wave. "Enjoy the rest of your watch, Lieutenant."

"Thank you, ma'am. You have a good afternoon."

She walked on. The closer she got to the SUV the easier breathing became, and the slower her heart beat. When she finally slid behind the wheel of the Yukon and closed the door, she took a deep breath and exhaled slowly.

"All right." She ran a hand over her face, then started the engine and put the vehicle in drive. "Here we go."

Chapter Twenty-Two

Cat looked to the sky and watched the planes take off, the roar of the F-15's engines washing over her, the bright cone of light from the afterburners a stark contrast against the dusky mountain backdrop.

"What's wrong, Cate?" Ryan asked softly, his eyes searching hers, "or can't you talk about it?"

She laced her fingers through his and pressed her lips to the back of his hand. "I'm sorry, Ryan. I know I've been a bummer the past couple of days." She held his hand to her breast. "But, hey, there is a bright side."

One dark brow shot skyward. "A bright side?"

She sat up and faced him. "When Peter leaves tomorrow you and Tripp won't be on 'Cat-watch' anymore. Your nights will be your own again."

His expression turned pensive. "Are you trying to tell me you'd rather sleep alone?"

"No," she said with a shake of her head and a quick grin, "but we are sort of cramped in my double bed. I'm sure you'd enjoy the chance to sprawl out for a change."

"Oh, I don't know. I rather enjoy waking up with you wrapped around me."

Cat chuckled. "You are a glutton for punishment, aren't you?"

"All SEALs are. We wouldn't make it through training if we weren't." A small smile curved his mouth and he traced the line of her jaw. "And I'd hardly consider sharing a bed with you punishment."

"Is it time for me to break out the whips and chains?" she teased.

Ryan grinned. "That's okay, Mistress Catharine. I'll pass. Besides, I left my ass-less chaps stateside."

She laughed and leaned her head against his shoulder. "Darn. I'd like to see *those*." A thought struck her and she reached into a pocket of her cargo pants. "Speaking of seeing... did you see this?"

She handed him the photo Mack had taken of them at the compound. After returning to her office she'd printed several copies of the snapshot. One copy had gone in the pocket of her jacket and another even now sat framed on her nightstand.

"Mack," he said with a grin, shaking his head. "He looks as rough-and-tumble as they come, but that man is a romantic at heart. He doesn't take a bad picture either." He held it out to her.

"That's okay," Cat said, snuggling into his side. "Keep it. I have two of my own."

"Two?" He looked askance at her. "Why would you want *two* pictures of my ugly mug around?"

Cat pressed a hand to his cheek and turned his face to hers. She let her gaze wander over his sharply hewn features for a few long, delicious moments, her fingers moving slowly over his beard. In those few moments, she came to a realization that both terrified and thrilled her, so before her brain could kick in to stop them she let the words come. "Because I love your mug, Ryan Heller, along with the rest of you."

His eyes widened slightly and his expression sobered. "You... you do?"

She smiled, finally able to forget about work. Her heart seemed to increase in size until she thought it would push through her ribs. Her pulse vibrated in a brisk staccato against the inside of her chest. She knew, without a doubt, this was the man she wanted to spend the rest of her life with, and she hoped he felt the same.

"It's been a week now, Ryan, but it didn't even take that long." Cat kissed him then pulled back. "You really *should* write a book."

"Only if you help me write it," he said.

She kissed him again. "We'll write it together," she said, their lips nearly touching.

Ryan cupped her head. "That's not all we'll do together."

He covered her mouth with his and Cat thought her entire body would melt. Despite the chill of the deepening night she wasn't the least bit cold. Heat fanned across every inch of skin from the top of her head to the tips of her toes. Ryan pulled her onto his lap, his fingers splayed over her back as he pressed her closer. Cat wound her arms around his neck as he deepened the kiss, and a dizzying euphoria washed over her. Her limbs were warm and rubbery, almost as if she'd been given a narcotic. Never in her life had she fallen so quickly or completely. She was elated, giddy, and *full*, as if a piece of her had been missing until that very moment. When he finally ended the kiss, it was all she could do to draw breath.

"Ryan?"

"Yes, Cate?"

"Take me home," she whispered, eyes still closed.

He chuckled and hugged her tightly. "Yes, ma'am."

***

Ryan walked quietly into his barracks, his watch reading 6:30 a.m. To his surprise, the room was empty, each bed neatly made. Frowning, he glanced at his pager and then his cell phone, but he'd received no calls or messages. Mildly puzzled, he walked over to his rack, dropped his duffle bag on the bed, and opened his locker.

Because of Mitchell's sunrise departure, Tripp had picked Cat up for work early at 5:45 a.m. Ryan smiled, reached into his pocket, and retrieved the key to Cat's quarters she'd given him. Even Tripp had been surprised by the gift. After slipping the key onto his key ring Ryan zipped open his bag and started removing his dirty clothes. When he pulled out the last of the rumpled garments something in the bottom of his duffle caught his eye and he froze. Dropping the laundry on the bed, he picked up the thick, orange manila envelope. A post-it note was stuck to the front of the otherwise unmarked package, and he recognized Cat's flowing script immediately.

Ryan, please hold onto this for me. I need you to put it somewhere safe, and please don't open it or ask me about it. When the time is right, give this envelope to Tripp. I'm not sure when that moment will come, but you'll know. I love you. Cate.

Ryan turned the package over in his hands, noting the abundance of packing tape she'd sealed it with. With a soft 'humph' he opened one of the drawers in his locker, slid the envelope beneath a stack of boxers, and pushed the drawer closed. He stared at the small dresser for a moment then finished putting away his things.

"Hey, Reaper," Mack's voice said from behind him. "You're back early."

Ryan glanced at him. "Doesn't look like it. Where is everybody?"

"We just got a mission," Mack replied. "You should be getting the page right about... now."

Once the words were out of Mack's mouth Ryan's pager started beeping. He glanced at the device, then shook his head and looked at his friend, incredulous.

"How do you *do* that?"

Mack grinned. "It's a gift. Come on. El Diablo is expecting us."

"Let me lock up and I'll be right behind you."

"Oh," Mack said, reaching for the lock on his foot locker, "before I forget I have something for you." He quickly spun the dial, popped the lock open, and lifted the lid.

Ryan closed and locked his locker, turning to face Mack as the shorter man held out an 8"X10" glossy photograph. Ryan took it from him, his eyes widening. It was a close-up picture of Cat, obviously taken when she was unaware at the BBQ the previous Sunday. She looked radiant, her eyes sparkling, her lips parted in a laugh. Ryan exhaled slowly.

"Wow. Thanks, buddy."

Mack stuffed his hands in pockets and beamed. "Thought you'd like that. I have more if you're interested."

Ryan laid the photo on his pillow. "Definitely, but you'll have to show them to me later. Right now, we have a mission briefing."

"Right." Mack grinned. "After you, Reaper."

***

Cat got the text from Ryan as she was sitting down at her desk with a cup of tea and a banana nut muffin. She texted back, "Okay. Let me know if you're heading out." Ryan replied, "I will" followed by a smiley face emoticon with hearts for eyes. Cat chuckled and slipped her phone back into her pocket.

"You look happy," Tripp observed from the doorway. "I guess the combination of Mitchell being gone and Ryan being close by is what it takes to tame the Tiger."

"You think I'm tamed?" she asked.

Tripp walked to one of the chairs facing her desk, sat down, and chuckled. "Not even fucking close." He studied her for a moment. "I guess I never realized how unhappy you were until I saw you happy. It's a good look, Cat. Keep it."

"I wasn't *unhappy*, Tripp." She frowned. "At least I don't *think* I was." She leaned back in her chair. "I guess I was so busy with work I never really thought about it."

"Trust me," he said. "If I could show you a picture of what you looked like before Ryan, and what you look like now, you'd agree you were one unhappy camper. Or maybe *lonely* would be a better word." He folded his hands over his abdomen and grinned. "You certainly didn't *smile* as much."

Heat surged into her cheeks. "Yes... well...."

Tripp chuckled. "Being sexually satisfied tends to bring a smile to one's face."

"Did you have a reason for visiting my office?" she asked crossly. "Or did you trudge all the way upstairs just to give me a hard time?"

"Giving you a hard time is Ryan's job," he said, rising to his feet. When she scowled he held up his hands and laughed. "I'm just saying...."

"Get out," she said. She threw a container of paper clips at him, which he neatly caught and tossed back to her.

"Sorry, Cat." He shrugged. "I've never seen this side of you. The Cat I know has always been razor-sharp, focused to the point of obsessive, and all about business."

"And I'm not any of those things anymore?"

"You are, it's just...." He paused, searching for the words. "Now you seem more... *human.* I know you maintain a strict separation of your work and personal life, more for survival than any deliberate reason, but that makes you appear emotionless and... cold." He leaned his hands on the back of the chair. "You're not a cold person, Cat, and now the guys know that."

She thought about that for a few seconds. "Is that good... or bad?"

"It's good, Tiger." He smiled and walked toward the door. "It's very good."

Cat watched him until he disappeared, then she spun around in her chair and stared through the window out onto the hangar below. Lee and the rest of the team were running actual diagnostics on the equipment this time, and she smiled as Lee said something and the other guys burst out laughing. As if sensing her gaze, Lee looked up and gave her a smile and a wave. She smiled and waved back.

Just then her phone rang and she recognized Ryan's number immediately. "I guess this means you're going out," she said.

"Yeah, sorry. You'll have to sleep with Tripp tonight."

She laughed. "*Not* going to happen. With Peter gone I think I'll be sleeping alone."

Ryan chuckled. "You sure that's wise?"

"Wiser than sleeping with *Tripp*," she said wryly. "But don't worry about me. You and the guys be careful and stay safe, all right? I'm not going to be there to snipe anybody should you get ambushed again."

"We'll be safe. Not sure how long we'll be gone." There was a brief pause. "You'll be here when I get back, won't you?"

Cat was silent for a moment as the implications of being involved with a SEAL loomed again. They'd talked about the inevitability of one of them being sent away, and it seemed that moment was here. Now that it was, she wasn't at all sure how she felt about it. "I should be," she replied at last, "but I can't guarantee anything. I won't be going anywhere before Peter returns to base, but if you're gone for longer than that...."

"I get it." He sighed. "Well, one day at a time it is. You still game?"

"Absolutely," she said with a smile. "Now go get ready, and remember... I love you." She took a shaky breath and realized she was doing a gut-check, like she did before plunging headlong into a dangerous situation. She didn't like this feeling, not even a little bit. It had teeth, like a chainsaw, and even on idle it left her raw and bloody. Cat closed her eyes and whispered, "Come back to me, Ryan."

"Not even the Taliban could keep me from you," he replied. "And I love you, too, Cate. You be careful while I'm gone, and don't let your guard down."

"I won't."

There was a brief silence, and she wondered if Ryan was feeling what she was: cold, all-encompassing fear. Unlike the fear she felt at times while on a mission, she couldn't channel and use this emotion. It floated in her chest like a ghost. She knew it was there but she couldn't touch it, couldn't use it. To make matters worse, there was no accompanying adrenaline to help her harness her fear in this situation. In this situation, she had absolutely no control and no involvement whatsoever. Whatever the outcome of Ryan's mission she would have to live with it, perhaps without him. *That*, more than anything else, scared her to death.

"I'll call you as soon as we get back," Ryan said softly, "but don't wait up. It may be a couple of days."

"I'll be fine," she said, swiping at her traitorous eyes. "You take care of yourself and come back in one piece."

"Yes, ma'am. I love you."

"I love you, too."

When he hung up she clutched the phone and held it to her chest, taking long, slow breaths. Once she had herself under control, she slipped the phone into her pocket, rose, and left her office. While part of her wanted to return to her quarters and curl up on her bed with one of Ryan's t-shirts, she knew the only way she'd maintain her sanity was to concentrate on something else. The sound of her team's laughter was actually a comfort, and by the time she joined them she was smiling.

"All right, guys. Where are we?"

***

Two days came and went with no word from Ryan or Peter. According to Mitchell's transportation request, he had flown to Kandahar to meet with an "asset," but no other details had been given. Airman Avery had said Peter had called daily to check-in, which was normal, and Cat hadn't pressed the issue. Lee was still monitoring everything Peter did on his tablet, so she decided to do her job and wait it out unless Peter did something overt. Thus far, Mitchell was either on a legitimate mission for the Agency, or he was covering his tracks exceedingly well.

"Hey, Tiger," Lee said from the doorway of her office. "It's five o'clock, and it's Friday. With Mitchell still in the field you're in charge, so what do you want us to do?"

She stared at the laptop screen for a moment then closed the lid. "The equipment's up to speed, correct?"

Lee nodded. "Been calibrated to exact specifications, checked, and double-checked. Diagnostic tests are done, alpha testing is finished, and the equipment is ready to either be redeployed for another beta test, or boxed and sent home. Waiting on the Agency for that decision. Any word?"

"Not a peep," Cat said, frowning. "It's almost like they're... waiting for something else to happen first."

Lee sat across from her and his brows drew together. "Waiting for what?"

"I don't know, but I hate sitting here. It makes me nervous." She stood and came around her desk, sitting on the edge in front of him. "Anything new on the Mitchell front?" Lee's expression shifted, sending her into immediate alert mode. "What?"

He stared at her for a moment then sighed. "Mitchell got an e-mail from the Director today instructing him to report to Langley for reassignment as soon as he finishes in Kandahar."

Cat's eyes widened. "Wait... they're transferring *him?*"

He nodded. "The e-mail specifically stated we would be staying together but that he was needed *elsewhere*. The Director hadn't come right out and said it, but the implication was clear enough that even Tripp understood."

She looked heavenward and exhaled slowly. "That can't have made him happy." She rubbed a hand over her eyes. "Did Peter respond?"

"Just to say he'd received the e-mail and would await further orders." He gave her a pointed look. "Totally generic, and really unlike Mitchell."

Lee was right. Peter wasn't the type to roll over and humbly obey in a situation such as this. Every time Peter had come close to getting in trouble, for whatever reason, he'd always put up a fight, emerging victorious and unscathed.

"Well," she began, her mind whirling, "this may be the pebble that starts a landslide, so keep a close eye on what he does over the next couple of days." She stood and walked over to the window. "You guys take the weekend off. Most likely Peter won't be back before Monday, and if he is I'm sure I'll get a call for us to come in."

"If he does come back and you hear from him," Lee began, moving to stand at her side, "you need to call me or Tripp *immediately*." He bumped her shoulder with his and gave her a small smile. "If Mitchell does show up, can I have the nightshift until Ryan returns?"

Cat looked askance at him and chuckled when he winked at her. "You're terrible."

"No," Lee argued with a sheepish smile, "I'm a guy, and you're a hot chick." He shrugged. "I had to try, Cat. No self-respecting, red-blooded American male knows and works closely with a beautiful woman for almost five years without making a play for her at least *once*."

Cat stared at him, incredulous, then laughed and smacked him on the arm. "You had me going there for a second, Rick. You really did."

"I know." He grinned. "You almost took me seriously."

She rolled her eyes, grabbed his shoulders and turned him toward her office door, and pushed. "Get out of here. And try to have a nice weekend, while still monitoring our fearless leader, of course."

Lee chuckled and paused in the doorway. "Will do, boss." His expression softened. "You sure you don't want me to walk you back to your quarters? Everyone else is already gone, and while I'm not a muscle-head like Tripp I do know Tae Kwan Do, and several other Asian phrases."

Cat laughed and waved a hand at him. "I'm fine. Now go, before I change my mind." He hesitated and she groaned. "What, Rick?"

"Any word from the Lieutenant?"

She felt the pang of worry pierce her heart like it had been shot from a high-powered bow, but she kept her face neutral. "No, but I didn't expect any. He's on a mission, and he said he'd be gone a few days."

"But you're still worried about him."

"Of course I am, but I can't curl up into a ball and suck my thumb until he returns, now can I?"

"No," he agreed with a shake of his head. "I suppose not."

"I have a job to do, and I'm going to do it regardless of what's happening elsewhere," she said. "Now if you don't get your ass out of here I'm going to kick it all the way to your barracks."

Lee held his hands up in mock surrender. "I'm going, boss. Hey, if you want to have dinner later stop by the barracks about seven. Tripp and I are going to raid Pizza Hut before he gets into his card game with the Aussies."

Cat thought about it, and while she didn't really feel sociable, she knew it would be better for her not to be alone with her wandering thoughts. However, before she joined her friends for pizza, there was someone she had to talk to.

"I'll do that, Rick," she said with a nod. "Just make sure you have one of those all meat pizzas for me."

"You got it. See you around seven."

She nodded. "See you then."

***

Cat sat in her SUV outside the small chow hall close to the Special Forces Compound. Ryan had told her Commander Ferris usually had dinner there at 6:00 p.m. like clockwork, unless there was a mission prepping to go out or he had a meeting with General Mason. She glanced at her watch and saw it was 5:57 p.m. Another minute ticked by, and then she saw the Commander walking briskly toward the dining hall. Taking a deep breath, she exited her vehicle and approached him as he mounted the stairs.

His brows rose when he saw her and he paused with his hand on the door. She walked up to the bottom of the steps, trying to quell the butterflies bouncing off her insides as he let go of the door and faced her.

"Evening, Miss Beckett."

"Commander. I was wondering if you'd allow me to buy you dinner."

Those sharp, steely eyes narrowed on her, and she felt his gaze as if she'd just been skewered with it.

"As much as I would like to think otherwise," the older man began, "I doubt you're here to buy me dinner and engage in pleasant conversation." He strode down the steps and stood toe to toe with her. "Why don't you save us both some time and spit it out, Miss Beckett. We've always been frank with each other."

Cat couldn't stop the flush that warmed her cheeks. She looked down at the ground for a moment then forced her gaze upward. "I need to talk to you."

"About?"

"The mission Ryan is on."

His brows drew together. Ferris took her arm and walked her away from the entrance of the dining hall. His touch was light, but she felt the strength behind the Commander's grip. When they were away from the proximity of any prying ears, he let go of her.

"You know I can't discuss an active mission, Miss Beckett. I'm surprised you even asked."

"It's not the mission I want to know about."

"Then what?" His expression softened a bit. "If it's Ryan you're concerned about, you can rest easy. I spoke with him a few hours ago, and he and the team are fine. They're hip-deep in Taliban territory but they're all healthy."

Cat ground her teeth together. "Thank you, sir, but that's not what I want to ask you." He remained silent, his eyes sharply focused on her, and she forced herself to speak before her courage deserted her entirely. "I need to know if the intelligence used for Ryan's current mission came from my office, and all I need from you is a yes or no."

He crossed his arms over his chest and stared down his nose at her for a moment. "No."

Relief washed over her so completely it almost made her dizzy. "Okay," she breathed, rubbing a hand across her brow. "Good. Thank you, Commander. That's all I wanted to know."

When she turned to walk back to her SUV the Commander took hold of her arm again. "Wait a minute. I think you owe me more than a thank you." He stared hard at her. "You're relieved, Miss Beckett, and I want to know why. If it concerns my men I *need* to know."

Cat looked into his ruggedly planed face for a moment then sighed. "We've spoken before of a possible problem regarding sensitive intel from my office."

He released her. "We have."

She glanced around and shifted her feet. "All I can say is I've uncovered evidence, *circumstantial* evidence, someone in my office may be communicating with and passing sensitive information to the enemy." She gave him a pointed look. "However, you didn't hear that from me."

Ferris's expression sobered. He stared hard at her for about half a minute then nodded crisply. "Good enough, Miss Beckett. I'm glad we can still be frank with each other."

"Me, too, sir. Enjoy your dinner." She turned to walk away, but his voice stopped her.

"Miss Beckett."

She looked at him over her shoulder. "Sir?"

"Be careful." A slight smile lifted the corners of his mouth. "Lieutenant Heller has fallen pretty hard for you, and I know he'll be anxious to see you when he gets home."

Cat nodded slowly. "Thank you, sir. I'll be careful."

"Have a nice evening, Miss Beckett."

She smiled. "You, too, sir."

***

The sun was almost gone when Cat parked near her quarters. A glance at her watch told her she had about twenty minutes before the guys expected her to show up for pizza. A smile curved her mouth as she walked toward her little cabin, and she realized she was actually looking forward to spending some time with her friends. Once she showered and changed, she would stop by the Coalition Forces barracks and hit her Polish sergeant up for a couple more six packs. The guys would *really* appreciate that.

Her mind drifted to Ryan, and she hoped he was still okay. Commander Ferris may have spoken with Ryan only hours before, but things could change in the blink of an eye when one was behind enemy lines. She said a silent prayer for his and his team's safety, then unlocked her door and stepped inside.

Almost as soon as the door closed behind her she sensed another presence in the room and the tingling of impending doom slithered up her spine. Before she could move an arm snaked around her throat. She felt a sharp pain in the side of her neck and knew immediately what it was. A needle. Then, as suddenly as she had been grabbed she was released.

Cat spun around to face the intruder and the room swayed dangerously. Peter's face wavered in front of her, like it was being reflected in a moving fun house mirror, and a wave of nausea hit her. Cat turned and staggered toward the bed, the floor undulating beneath her feet. She felt like she was standing on the pitching deck of a ship, and swung her arms wide to balance herself, knocking the bedside lamp to the floor. The sound of the breaking bulb was muted and distorted, and seemed to go on and on, like a skipping record. The crunching, tinkling noise continued for several long, grating seconds, and then the room fell ominously silent. She blinked and shook her head to clear it, but that small action only made things worse. The edges of her vision started to go gray and she collapsed on the bed.

Despite the drug, Cat's mind worked furiously. She clawed at the mattress, pulling herself over to the other side, knocking the other nightstand over as she dragged the bedding behind her. Falling into a heap beside the bed, she forced herself onto all fours and crawled toward her desk. She summoned every ounce of strength she had and stood. *So, you want to play? Let's play.* She swayed for a moment then swept an arm across the desk's surface, sending the computer, the desk lamp, and the cup full of pens crashing to the floor. The computer broke in two, keys popping off and flying in every direction. Pens scattered everywhere and the desk lamp shattered into tiny, glittering shards of glass. She smiled inwardly. *Good luck sanitizing* this *crime scene, asshole.*

Peter grabbed her from behind and spun her to face him, sending the merry-go-round inside her head into overdrive. She tried to focus on him and swung. Her fist connected with his nose and had she been able to smile, the sight of blood gushing from his nostrils would have made her grin. She slapped him, splattering the warm, coppery-smelling liquid. He cursed fluently and tossed her onto the bed. Cat dragged her hand across the now bare mattress, leaving a dark smear behind. One of her self-defense instructors had said, "If someone is trying to kill you, fight back as hard as you can. Leave enough forensic evidence behind to make sure that, if they succeed in taking your life, they can still be brought to justice."

The familiar smell of cotton batting filled her nostrils as she lay face down on the bed. Her limbs were heavy and she fought to stay conscious. She managed to roll onto her back, and took a labored breath when Peter straddled her legs and leaned over her. *What now, Peter? You gonna rape me while I'm unconscious? No matter what, you better kill me when you're done, because if you don't you will wish you had.*

She inhaled deeply and tried to focus on him. "What are you doing, Peter?" Her voice was hardly more than a raspy whisper and sounded odd, as if she was talking with a mouth full of cotton balls.

Peter's nose continued to bleed and his face looked warped. He ran an arm over his upper lip. Then, he did something that frightened her more than anything else. He smiled. It was a ghoulish sight, blood contrasting sharply with his white teeth. "Stop fighting it, Catharine. You'll only prolong the inevitable. Just go to sleep, and when you wake up we'll be far away from here."

Away? Her blood chilled. She swung on him again, but it was like trying to hit someone while submerged in mud. Her arm weighed a ton and he easily moved out of her way, his smile widening. Her arm flopped down on the mattress and her vision began to tunnel.

"That's it," he breathed, his voice echoing oddly in her ears. He tenderly smoothed the hair from her face. "Go to sleep. Close your eyes and go to sleep."

Cat's brain screamed for her to stay conscious, to fight it with everything she had, but her body wouldn't cooperate. She realized he wasn't going to kill her, *yet*, but she had a sinking feeling that death would be preferable to what he had planned. Her stomach cramped violently. The dizziness stormed over her like a tornado and her eyelids drooped despite her best efforts. The last thing she saw before she lost consciousness was Peter's maniacal grin. She said another silent prayer, and then slipped into the blackness.

Chapter Twenty-Three

"I'll see that case, and raise you two," Tripp said, his face expressionless as he and Kingman went head to head. The other players had folded and were watching as the two heavyweights of this particular game faced off. Looking down at a full house, aces over queens, Tripp felt relatively confident the Aussie titan would be going down.

Kingman rubbed his chin and silently debated his options. The sound of running feet from behind hardly registered with Tripp. He stared at his opponent, and waited.

"Tripp, I need you to come look at this."

"Hold on, Rick," Tripp replied, watching Kingman carefully. "We're almost done here."

"This is important," Lee insisted.

"So is this," Tripp replied. "Two minutes."

Lee growled. "He's holding a full house, aces over queens, so unless you can beat that, Kingman, you'd better fold."

Groans went up and cards went flying. Tripp stood and spun to face Lee, ready to bloody his friend's nose until he saw the look on Lee's face. "What is it?"

Lee grabbed his arm and started walking back to their quarters. "Come on, big man. You need to take a look at this."

Tripp followed as Lee strode briskly into their CONEX container and sat down in front of the computer. Tripp stood at his side and leaned over, looking at the screen.

"What am I looking at?"

Lee pointed. "See that, right there?" When Tripp nodded, Lee continued. "I've been monitoring Gladys Emmerson's accounts, and the only activity since the accounts opened were deposits made 24 hours in advance of each beta-test."

Tripp rubbed his chin. "So, Gladys was paid in advance for the information she provided."

Lee nodded. "That would be my guess. Like I said, no other activity until a few minutes ago." He punched a couple of keys. "Then, as of 1900 Kabul time, or 0930 Costa Rica time, a transfer of $745,000 was made from Gladys's account to a holding company in San Juan. The remaining money in the account and half of the second account was also transferred...." He paused and gave Tripp a pointed look. "... to Banco de San Juan."

"Meaning what?"

"It looks like Gladys is planning to set up housekeeping in Costa Rica, my friend, a non-extradition country. I did a check for any large purchases of between $500,000 and $750,000 and came up with one, a large estate in the mountains that once housed the country's former president. It was pulled off the market when the banks opened in San Juan this morning."

Tripp exhaled slowly and straightened. "He's getting ready to rabbit." He met Lee's concerned gaze. "You call Cat with this?"

"Tried to. She's not answering. I even spoofed it to make it look like Ryan's number." Lee rose. "She said she'd come by for pizza at seven. I thought she was being fashionably late."

Tripp glanced at his watch. "Well, it's only 7:40, but it's not like her not to answer her phone." He stared at the floor for a moment, then lifted his eyes to Lee and frowned. "I've got a bad feeling about this. Get the guys together, get back to the hangar, and get that fucking equipment up and running. Call Kandahar and see if you can get an update on Mitchell, and then start searching for that phone and Cat's, or any of the other numbers we pulled that day in the mountains. If the Kandahar substation doesn't know where he is, those will be our best bet on a lead to Mitchell's whereabouts."

"What are you going to do?"

"I'm going to find Cat." He took a deep breath. "Hopefully, Ryan is back and the two of them are wrapped around each other, which would be a good reason for her not to answer her phone." He turned to walk away, then stopped and faced Lee again. "And call in Airman Avery. Tell her we need some help with an alpha test."

"Why do you want Airman Avery there?" Lee asked, his expression uncertain.

Tripp gave him a grim smile. "Because if I can't find Cat I'm going to find Peter, even if I have to tear that little girl apart to do it."

***

A painful jolt brought Cat awake, and her head thumped into something hard that sounded like metal. Pain thrummed across her forehead and behind her eyes, a side-effect from whatever Peter had injected her with no doubt. Nausea roiled in her belly and she took several deep breaths of stale, musty air. The first emotion to wash over her was fear but, as always, her training kicked in and that fear very quickly turned to anger. She took several more deep breaths and tried to focus. If she wanted to get out of this alive, she had to remain calm and think.

Cat kept her eyes closed and listened, trying to orient herself. She opened her eyes a fraction. Darkness. She opened her eyes fully, but she already had a good idea where she was: curled up in the trunk of a car. The vehicle sped over another bump, throwing her into the trunk lid again and confirming her suspicion. Once the pain from the impact subsided, she started doing a personal inventory.

Given the size of the space she had to be in a small sedan or a compact car, and the incessant squeaking of the springs and the chugging engine told her it was not one of Peter's typical top of the line rides. On the up side, she was not bound. Cat immediately reached into the small pocket inside the waistband of her pants and nearly cried in relief when her fingers found the detector Heston had given her. Apparently, Peter had been in too big a hurry to search her thoroughly. Her cell phone was gone, as were her knife and pistol, and she had no doubt that when they reached their destination a more exhaustive personal search would be in order. The first thing she had to do was hide the detector. If she couldn't get herself out of this mess, it would be handy to have an EMP that would alert the cavalry.

Reaching down between her legs she unlaced one of her boots and pulled it from her foot. After removing the insole, she searched for something, anything that she could use. Other than some dirty rags, the spare tire, and some trash, the trunk seemed empty. She was going to have to improvise.

Something else she'd learned, although not at Langley, was if trapped in the trunk of a car one should smash out one of the taillights and stick a hand through the opening. The driver wouldn't be able to see, but the cars to the rear would, and more than likely someone would call for help. Unless, of course, you were locked in a car trunk in Afghanistan where the car behind you, if there *was* a car behind you, was probably filled with terrorists. Not that it mattered. Once she broke the taillight, she had no intention of sticking her hand out and waving.

She kicked at the bulb housing until it sheared off, and then she smashed the toe of her boot against the red and orange lens until she heard it crack. Twisting her body around she pried at the hardened plastic, but it wouldn't budge. It took her three hits with her fist to break the outer lens, and her knuckles were bleeding by the time she was done but she hardly noticed. Pulling one of the sharp fragments from its metal frame, she started digging into the thick rubber inside of her boot. She tried to work quickly because she had no way of knowing how long they'd been on the road or when they'd stop. Once she had enough space hollowed out to hide the detector, she put the device into her shoe, replaced the insole, then put the boot back on and quickly laced it. The rubber chunks and extra pieces of broken lens she could find got pushed out the now broken taillight. The shard of lens she'd used to carve her boot she palmed. If Peter got close enough, he was going to find out exactly how her boot had felt. Until then, all she could do was wait.

***

Tripp exhaled slowly, fists on his hips as he surveyed the mess that had once been Cat's quarters. The floor was littered with broken glass and it looked like a tornado had ripped through the small house. He walked over to the bed and immediately noticed the dark, red-brown smear on the mattress. Blood. A sense of foreboding draped over him like an icy cloak. Hopefully, the blood wasn't Cat's.

Tripp pulled out his phone and dialed. Lee picked up after the second ring.

"Find her?" he asked.

"Nope," Tripp replied, "but I did find something else."

"What?"

"Blood. Her place has been torn apart."

There was a brief silence. "Do you think it's Cat's blood?"

"Don't know. Is the equipment up yet?"

"Going down the final checklist as we speak, we'll be up in five."

Tripp surveyed the damage again. "Good. I'll be there as soon as I can."

"We'll start a search as soon as you get here."

"Don't wait for me."

"Roger that. We're on it."

Tripp hung up the phone, looked around the room for another minute then walked toward Cat's locker. Reaching into the rafters above the locker, he pulled out the palm-sized digital video camera he'd hidden. It was still recording. Tripp hit the off button. He didn't have to watch the video to know what was on it and white hot anger began to pulse through him.

"Well, you motherfucker," he said under his breath, "now we've got you. You won't be able to spin your way out of this one." He slid the camera into a pocket and dialed his cell phone. "Hey, Mike, it's Ben. You on duty?"

"Of course," Sergeant Anderson replied. "When am I ever not?"

Tripp chuckled, but it was mirthless. "All right then. I need you to get your guys and a forensic team to unit 12 at the north transient housing area."

"Why? What's going on?"

"I think Cat Beckett has been kidnapped."

There was a brief, taut silence. "We're on our way."

Tripp hung up his phone and walked toward the door when something caught his eye. On the floor underneath the desk was a cell phone, Cat's cell phone. Tripp picked it up, turned it over in his hand, then slipped it into his pocket and left Cat's quarters. After putting the camera in his SUV, he returned to Cat's hut and sat on the steps. The sound of distant sirens reached him. It wouldn't be long now.

***

Cat dozed fitfully, the bumps and jolts of the unpaved Afghan roads waking her every few minutes. She had no way to tell how long they'd been driving, but it was pitch dark outside and a cold draft whistled through the broken taillight. Wrapping her arms around herself, she shivered and curled into a tighter ball to conserve body heat.

When the car finally stopped, it took her a moment to realize they were no longer moving. Her heart started to thud as she listened carefully. The engine chugged a few times then went silent, and then she heard another sound that sent her heart into a fast gallop. Voices. Numerous voices, and none of them were speaking English. Her breathing quickened and she uncurled as much as she could in the cramped space. She flexed her fingers and toes, trying to get the blood back into them. A grating sound made her head snap around, and a moment later the trunk lid popped open.

Before she could move nearly half a dozen rifle muzzles were thrust at her. Cat remained motionless, unable to see past the barrels to the hands holding the weapons. The darkness was all-consuming. Suddenly a beam of light slashed through the inky night, blinding her as it was aimed at her face. Cat shielded her eyes, her pulse at an official sprint. Squinting against the brightness, she waited.

"Get out."

The voice was an unfamiliar one, the accent thick and local. The fact the words had been uttered in English surprised her. She blinked and slowly sat up, the rifles following her moves closely. Her arms and legs hadn't regained full sensation yet, but she had a feeling moving slowly was not in her best interest. Pins and needles peppered her extremities as she climbed out of the trunk. She tried to stand and her legs buckled, dropping her butt-first onto the bumper. A familiar laugh shattered the otherwise quiet night. Anger sputtered to life inside her and her eyes narrowed as a figure strode toward her.

With the flashlight still glaring in her face all she could see were silhouettes. The riflemen moved as a taller man walked through their line. She knew who it was. She'd recognize Peter anywhere.

"You look a mite piqued, Catharine. Were you not comfortable in the trunk of my fine automobile?"

Cat forced herself to stand and took a step toward him. Her eyes narrowed more when the riflemen leaned in, but Peter raised a hand and they relaxed. Their muzzles, however, remained trained on her.

"Where the hell are we?" she asked in a low, dangerous voice.

"Not important," he replied smoothly. "All you need to know is that you will be enjoying the hospitality of my friends here for the next few days. I would like to tell you it will be a pleasant stay, but I can't. I can tell you the level of unpleasantness you experience... is entirely up to you."

Cat turned the shard of taillight over in her hand. "And after that?" Her eyes had adjusted a bit and she could make out his face. When he gave her an indulgent smile, as if she was a disobedient child, that coil of anger in her chest expanded exponentially.

"We'll have to see, won't we?"

She scowled. "I don't think so."

She slid the pointed end of the shard between her index and middle finger, closing her fist around the sharp plastic. An attack on Peter would probably cost her life, but at this point she didn't care. Well aware of what terrorists did to American agents, she took a breath and decided on her final course of action.

Peter must have seen the murderous intent in her eyes because when she lunged, aiming for his throat, he pulled back. The point of the tempered plastic dug into his chin, slicing down and to her right as he tried to scramble away from her, cutting him open along the jaw from his chin to just below his ear. For the second time that day she felt the warmth of his blood on her fingers and smiled. She moved to strike again as chaos erupted around them.

"Don't shoot!" Peter shouted as he moved backwards. "Don't shoot!"

His voice sounded odd and drawn out, like he was a recording being played in slow motion. A myriad of other voices chimed in, speaking in Dari, her brain translating even as she focused on her target. Apparently, the riflemen weren't sure if they should shoot her or not. Time slowed and she tunneled her vision on Peter, pinpointing his jugular. As her arm thrust forward she felt a sharp pain in her head. She froze for a moment, poised to kill. Then she collapsed, dust filling her nostrils as she landed face first in the dirt. Dazed, she blinked, disjointed feet and legs dancing before her as the mob closed in. Peter shouted again for them to lower their weapons and she struggled to get to her knees, intent on ending him. She crawled toward his voice. As she honed in on him she felt another blow to the back of her head. She crumbled, the cacophony echoing in her ears. The sound of a gunshot split the air, and then everything went black.

***

Tripp strode into the hangar and walked into the maintenance space. The team had the equipment up and running, and was monitoring the screens carefully. Tripp walked past all of them and approached Lee, the camera in one hand. Lee had his eyes focused on the computer screen in front of him, oblivious to everything else until Tripp grabbed a chair and slammed it on the ground next to him. Lee looked up, startled.

"Sitrep," Tripp said.

"The Kandahar substation says Peter left this morning for Bagram, hitched a ride back with a civilian contractor's convoy. The convoy hasn't checked in yet, so they have no idea where he is at the present."

"The phone numbers?"

Lee frowned. "The terrorist cell we were monitoring has probably replaced all their old burn phones with new ones, so we're not getting any pings there. We did get a hit on one number, but it's in transit." He pulled up a map of the Bagram valley and pointed. "There. The phone is on and moving north toward the Tajikistan border. Peter's phone hasn't hit, which means it's either turned off or he's using a new cell." He looked at Tripp solemnly. "It's not much to go on."

"Keep an eye on that one phone. It may be the only lead we get."

Lee nodded. "I will. Any news?"

"Anderson and his crime scene unit are going over Cat's quarters with a fine-tooth comb, but I already know Mitchell took her."

Lee's eyes widened. "Are you sure?"

"Yep. There's blood at the scene, and it's not Cat's. The military's forensic experts will analyze it and give us an official report, but that's simply the cake." Tripp held up the small, digital camera. "This, my friend, is the icing."

"What's that?"

"Video of our illustrious leader," Tripp replied. He looked at Lee, anger burning in his chest. "Now that we have him nailed, we can concentrate on finding Cat."

Lee gaped at him. "How did you get video?"

"Cat told me she'd found a camera hidden in her quarters, and that Mitchell had put it there." Tripp looked at the digital camcorder. "I figured if he did it once he might do it again, so I installed one of my own to keep an eye out."

"Did Cat know?" Lee asked, his eyes wide.

"No."

"How long?"

Tripp met Lee's gaze. "Since Monday night. I hid it while she and Ryan were picnicking at the end of the runway."

"So, there's video of them...?"

"Yeah," Tripp said. "I already went through and deleted all the... steamy stuff."

"You didn't watch it, did you?" Lee asked, horrified.

Tripp scowled. "No. Focus, Rick." He held out the camera. "Plug it in and take a look. See if you notice anything I didn't."

Lee plugged the camcorder in and started typing. As a display screen popped up he turned to Tripp. "You sure you deleted all the...?"

"Yes." Tripp rubbed his temples. "Get on with it."

Lee looked at him uncertainly for a moment, glanced over his shoulder to ensure he wasn't being watched by any of the guys, and then hit play. Tripp stared at the floor, elbows on his knees. He'd already seen it, and he was pissed enough. Seeing it again would only further enrage him and impair his judgment. If he was going to get Cat back alive, he needed to have his wits about him. When the recording ended, he heard Lee exhale slowly.

"Shit, Ben. Even drugged she did what she had to do."

"Yep."

"We need to take this to somebody, but to whom?"

Tripp sat back in his chair. "I'd think whoever she sent our transfer requests to would be high on the list. If they're above Mitchell, that's who I'd go to."

Lee's head snapped around. "Do you know who it is?"

Tripp shook his head. "No, but she sent the requests from here. It shouldn't take you long to find out who she sent them to."

"Okay." Lee took a deep breath and nodded. "Okay."

"Go on," Tripp said, recognizing the concern in his friend's face. "And while you do that, I'll tell the rest of the team what's up. We're going to need all hands on deck for this."

Lee stood and took two steps, then stopped and faced him again. "Do you... do you think she's still alive?"

"If he'd wanted her dead, he would've simply killed her." Tripp swallowed the lump in his throat, hoping his voice sounded more confident than he felt. "He went to the trouble of drugging and kidnapping her for a reason, so yes, I think she's still alive."

***

The blackness began to swirl with lighter colors: navy, purple, dark gray. As seconds passed the palette continued to lighten, and as the muted shades became brighter so did the aching in her head. Squeezing her eyes shut, Cat choked back a groan as pain stampeded across her skull with the sharpness of zebra hooves over the Serengeti.

Taking deep, slow breaths, she fought the accompanying nausea and strained to hear anything other than the pounding of blood in her ears. She became aware of whispers, and while they weren't immediately threatening the hairs on the back of her neck prickled nonetheless. She was sitting upright in a chair, a chair with arms, but when she tried to move she couldn't. Moving her feet was also fruitless. As unobtrusively as possible, Cat tested her extremities, trying to discern how she was bound. It wasn't rope or wire because there was nothing cutting into her skin. She twisted her wrist, and as the hairs on her arm started to pull her brain kicked into gear and she nearly groaned. Duct tape. Shit.

Keeping her head bowed Cat opened her eyes a fraction and looked around. Yep, it was duct tape. She had it around her wrists and her chest, and probably around her ankles as well. Scowling, she examined as much of her surroundings as she could without moving her head. The light was dim, probably a single, stereotypical overhead bulb. The perimeter of the room remained cloaked in shadow. All she could see was a roughly ten-foot circle of hard-packed dirt floor, the dull gray of the metal chair she was taped to, the legs of a metal desk on the edge of that illuminated area, and two pairs of feet. From their position, Cat guessed the men were sitting on the edge of the desk and facing each other. She rolled her eyes. Leave it to Peter to turn real life into a scene from a spy movie. All that was missing was the egg-shaped chair and the bald villain stroking a white cat.

"She should be awake by now," Peter said, his voice muffled and coming from behind her. A door scraped open, the hinges squealing in protest. "How hard did you hit her?"

"Not as hard as I should have," a thickly accented voice replied with obvious contempt. "You should let me kill her. She will be less trouble that way."

Peter laughed as if the man were joking. From the sound of the stranger's voice he wasn't, and anger solidified in her belly.

"In a few days, *she* will no longer trouble you," Peter replied. He stood at her side and placed a hand on her head, his fingers sifting lightly through her hair. "I've waited nearly five years for this, and *you* have been paid handsomely for your assistance."

Cat remained motionless.

"Speaking of my payment, when should I expect the rest of my money?"

Peter's hand drifted down the side of her face. "When we are away from here," he said in a hushed voice.

He put his forefinger beneath her chin to tip her face up, and Cat attacked the only way she could. Peter howled as she bit down on his thumb. Her incisors easily cut through the skin to the bone, but before she could apply any more pressure light exploded behind her eyes. Her head snapped around, her jaw relaxing as the stranger backhanded her. He hit her with such force the chair tipped, and she hung there for a moment, dazed. In her periphery, she saw Peter holding his bleeding finger, and then her world tilted as the chair, and she, crashed to the floor. She blinked, dust stinging her eyes, but before she could take a breath the air was forcefully expelled from her lungs as she was kicked in the stomach.

"Stop!" Peter shouted.

A choked gasp escaped her as the foot connected with her midsection again and tears filled her eyes, pain radiating outward from her core. Struggling to breathe, she watched as Peter pushed the man back and put himself between them.

"I said stop!"

"She *bit* you!"

"Yes, she did."

Cat's lungs screamed for air and the moments drew out, each longer than the next, until Peter did something that chilled her more than his previous ghoulish, bloody smile. He laughed.

"Yes, she bit me." He sounded amused, even pleased by her actions and alarm bells rang in her head.

She looked at him out of the corner of her eye as he spun to face her, then crouched in front of her and smiled. Cat gasped, fighting to open and fill her traumatized airways. Despite her lack of oxygen, she noted the neat stitches running along Peter's jaw and the tape on his nose. Apparently, there was a doctor nearby, but Peter would still have a nasty scar. Had she not been struggling to expand her diaphragm, she would have laughed out loud.

"I'd expect nothing less from her." He rose in one fluid motion and faced the nameless man. "Let this be a lesson. Be *very* careful with her, and tell your men to steer clear." He glanced down at her, and the chill burrowed deeper when his expression turned wistful, tender, almost loving. "She *will* kill any of you if she gets the chance." Peter faced his accomplice and continued in a deadly voice, "So don't give her the chance."

The two men who had been sitting on the desk were standing now at either end of the dilapidated, utilitarian piece of furniture, gaping at her. As Peter moved to her back and righted her and the chair she finally got a look at his partner. Her aching jaw nearly went slack, and Tariq Hasan smiled.

"You know who I am, do you not?" he asked. "I see it in your eyes."

"She knows who you are," Peter answered for her. "Everyone with clearance higher than Level 2 knows who you are."

Hasan sat on the edge of the desk and crossed his arms over his chest. "I still think you should let me kill her."

Cat frowned. "Let me loose and we'll see who wins *that* altercation."

Hasan looked surprised for a moment then chuckled. The thing that worried her was even while laughing, the humor never reached his eyes. Hasan had large, dark eyes, much like those of his youngest daughter, Ariahn. Unlike Ariahn, whose eyes were bright and full of life, his eyes were flat, lackluster, like those of a shark, unblinking and unfathomable. This time, the anger she felt wasn't nearly enough to completely quash the seed of fear germinating in her chest.

"Perhaps you are right, Mitchell." Hasan studied her face carefully. "I may find her amusing after all."

Peter stood behind her and Cat resisted the urge to look up at him. He chuckled. "I'm sure you will, but I want you to remember that if you want to get paid, you must follow the rules." He moved to Hasan's side. "See that face and that body? I want them to look exactly the same as they do now, at least, after a relatively normal healing period."

Cat blinked. *Seriously?* Hasan's smile widened.

Peter lifted one perfectly arched brow. "If you want the remaining half million, you cannot scar, maim, disfigure, dismember, grievously injure, or kill her." He looked at Hasan. "Understood?"

"Then what am I to do with her?" Hasan raked his eyes over her. "Play cards?"

"No." Peter shook his head and took a step toward her. "Make her... *uncomfortable*." He gave her a long, assessing look. "She took something from me, and I want it back. I also need to know whom she's told about what she found. Therefore," he paused and looked at Hasan over his shoulder, "do what you must... *within those guidelines*."

Hasan rolled his eyes. "And people wonder why you Americans cannot win this war." He stood and motioned for the two men to leave. "You cannot win because you do not have the stomach to do what is necessary."

"Which is why I'm paying *you* to do it," Peter said sharply. "Now, if you *don't* mind... I would like a few minutes alone with her."

"Very well." Hasan chuckled. "Just stay at arm's length, my friend, unless you *want* to feed her your fingers."

Peter waited several moments after the door closed. He watched her, his expression speculative. Then he pulled a first aid kit from a drawer and started to bandage his finger.

"You can make this easy on yourself, Catharine," he began, wrapping gauze around the still-bleeding digit, "or you can make it difficult."

She said nothing, focused on his movements. Peter applied a piece of tape to the gauze, carefully lined up the items in the kit, and put it back in the drawer.

He gave her a tolerant smile. "All you have to do is return what you took from me, and you'll spend the next few days bound to that chair... unharmed."

She met his gaze. "Somehow I doubt that."

Peter laughed softly. "I can see how you would think that but trust me, I keep Hasan on a short leash. As much as he would like to spend some... *quality* time with you, he wants his money more." He rose and stepped to within a few paces of her, but stayed well out of her reach. "I know you took the file, the journal, and the ledger from the hidden drawer in my quarters. The file and the journal aren't so important, but the ledger... the ledger I need. It contains rather... *sensitive* information. You understand. It's nothing personal, it's just business."

Her pulse leapt a notch but she kept her expression neutral. "And you think I took these things because...?"

"Because I didn't know they'd been taken until I accessed the hidden drawer." He tipped his head to the side. "While your team is quite skilled, that Tripp especially, you're the only one I know who is *that* good."

She lifted one brow. "Maybe you're just getting sloppy."

Anger flamed in his eyes and he slapped her, hard. She was more surprised that he had struck her than by the sharp pain. The stinging fanned over her cheek, followed by heat and throbbing. Cat shook her head a couple times then looked at him.

"Nice. Have you been working out?"

He hit her again, this time with his fist. His knuckles impacted her cheekbone, sending sharper fragments of pain through the bones of her face as her head snapped around. Cat gasped and she could already feel the outer corner of her left eye swelling. For a few seconds, she couldn't see. Bright spots of light obscured her vision. When the flashbulbs finally cleared, she lifted her head a few inches and met his glare.

"Well, then," she said, working her jaw, "I can tell you the journal and the file are in good hands." She gave him a small smile. "As for the ledger... I can't tell you where that is."

His expression darkened. "Can't, or won't?"

"Really?" Her smile widened. "It comes down to syntax for you?"

She expected him to hit her again. His hands clenched and unclenched at his sides, his face black with impotent rage. She braced for the blow but it never came.

"You should thank me," he informed her.

"I should?" She tipped her head to the side. "For *what* exactly?"

He studied her for a moment and the level of anger in his face subsided a little. "I haven't told him who you are and what you *really* do for us." His eyes narrowed on her. "I imagine if he knew you were personally responsible for the deaths of more than a dozen of his fellow... *freedom fighters*, he'd be less inclined to follow my guidelines."

"Oh." She scowled. "Thank you."

"I also didn't tell him you speak the language."

Cat's brows drew together. "And why would you leave out *that* little tidbit?"

"Because I want him and his men to speak freely around you."

She gaped at him for a few seconds then chuckled. "Oh, I get it." She shook her head in disbelief. "You want me to listen in on whatever conversations I hear and tell you what they said." He gave her a stiff nod and she stared at him. Finally, she laughed and said, "Fuck you, Peter."

The rage was back, that strange light blazing in his eyes so brightly she could almost feel the heat from it. After several tense moments, he walked past her and out of her field of vision toward the door.

"Have it your way, Catharine. I hope you enjoy your days with Hasan."

"What happens after that?" she asked.

"Then we're leaving this Godforsaken country," he replied flatly. "We'll have to lay low for a few days until you're sufficiently recovered to travel, but after that...."

Cat threw her head back and laughed. "You really have lost it, Peter. You may as well end it now, because if you think I'm going *anywhere* with you then you don't know me at all." She heard a rustling and jumped when she felt his lips at the curve of her neck.

"Oh, Catharine," he whispered, "*long* before Hasan is done with you, I have a feeling you will be *begging* me to take you away from here."

Chapter Twenty-Four

Ryan's watch alarm went off at 6:30 a.m., but he was already awake. Mack and Grady were still sleeping. After three days in the field, they'd returned to base after two in the morning dirty, exhausted, and relieved. They'd had several close calls during their mission, but they'd all returned with little more than scrapes, bruises, and a new appreciation for that hair's breadth separating life from death.

Mack mumbled and rolled over in his rack as Ryan got out of bed. Ryan paused, and continued to dress when his friend returned to snoring softly. Chuckling, he slipped into his uniform blouse, made his bed, closed his locker, and slipped out of their barracks.

As he drove towards Cat's quarters he felt as if he was back in high school and on his way to pick up his prom date, the one who was *way* out of his league. Once the mission was done, his brain had immediately switched out of professional mode and she was all he'd been able to think about. He'd briefly considered showing up at her door at three in the morning, but after a shower he'd decided against it. Once the sun had breached the horizon however, going back to sleep had not been an option.

The anticipation he felt as he rounded the last corner faded a little at the sight of the security police vehicle. He slowed the Humvee to a crawl, and when police vehicles two and three came into view a shiver of concern brushed up the length of his spine. He drove past them, parked, and looked in his rearview mirror. In all, five police vehicles were lined up in front of the transient housing area, a significant number for a base their size. Ryan climbed out of the Humvee and uneasiness made his muscles tense. He took a deep breath, shook it off, and walked toward Cat's quarters. *Relax, dude, it's probably nothing.*

As soon as her cabin was in sight his gut clenched into a fist-sized knot and he stutter-stepped. Cat's quarters had been isolated from the rest of the housing units by yellow crime scene tape guarded by a soldier with an M16. Trying to mask his anxiety, he squared his shoulders, walked past the guard, and quickly pulled his cell phone out of his pocket. After the third ring, someone picked up and his heart sank when he realized it wasn't her.

"Lieutenant?"

It took Ryan a couple of seconds to swallow the lump in his throat. "What the fuck's going on, Tripp?"

"Where are you?"

Tripp's tone was clipped, emotionless, and Ryan frowned. "Where the fuck do you think I am?" he growled. He glanced over his shoulder at the police moving in and out of Cat's quarters. "I'm at Cate's place, along with half the security police on this base. What happened?"

"Stay there. I'll be right over."

"Tripp—"

"Just stay put, Ryan. I'll be there in five."

Before he could say another word, Tripp hung up on him. Ryan looked at his phone for a few seconds then slipped it back into his pocket and stalked to his Humvee.

Almost to the second Tripp pulled up next to Ryan's vehicle and rolled down the passenger window. "Get in, Ryan. We need to talk."

Something inside him recoiled. *Ah, shit, that's never good.* The set of Tripp's jaw and the carefully blank expression told Ryan he wasn't going to like what came next. He stared at Tripp mutinously for a moment, then jerked open the door and climbed into the SUV. Once he was inside Tripp rolled up the window and pulled away.

"Where are we going?" Ryan asked.

"It doesn't matter," Tripp replied.

"Okay." Ryan looked at Tripp's strong profile, more apprehensive than not. A cold tinge of fear wormed through him and his abdominals contracted. Tripp's continued silence only made his anxiety grow and the temperature inside the Yukon seemed to plummet. "What's going on, Tripp? What's with the SPs?"

Tripp flexed his fingers on the wheel. "Cat's missing."

Ryan blinked. "What? What do you mean *missing?* *He has to be kidding. He* has *to.*

Tripp's granite expression cracked a little and Ryan decided he preferred the previously blank look. Even though he didn't want to believe it, he realized Tripp would never joke about something like this.

He waited for several long, taut seconds, and when Tripp didn't answer a hot spark of anger flashed in his chest. He leaned toward Tripp and asked again, *"What do you mean missing?"* Quiet reigned for several more moments before Tripp let out a long, heavy sigh.

"She's been kidnapped."

Ryan's brows shot up and disbelief engulfed him. "Kidnapped?" He tried to wrap his brain around that. "How? How does a CIA agent get *kidnapped* from one of the most secure military installations in the world?" He watched as Tripp clasped and unclasped the steering wheel, hinting at much stronger emotions bubbling beneath the surface of his relatively cool exterior. When he finally spoke, he did it from between clenched teeth, his voice hushed.

"Mitchell."

That revelation hit Ryan square between the eyes and for a few moments he couldn't breathe. When his lungs started to burn, he sucked in a gulp of air.

"How...? Why...?"

A muscle in Tripp's jaw started to twitch. "Well, I know how he subdued her. How he got her off base and why he did it...? That I don't know."

"Any *theories?*"

"Several, but theories aren't going to help us find her."

"So, humor me."

Tripp gave him a long glance then returned his eyes to the road. "Mitchell's personal life just exploded. His wealthy wife has filed for divorce, and because of the pre-nuptial agreement Mitchell could wind up with nothing but the lint in his pockets. He's been told to report to Langley for reassignment, which probably means he's going to lose his job thanks to his brilliant performance in the mess hall the other day." Tripp paused and took a deep breath. "He also realizes he's losing Cat... to you."

Ryan turned to Tripp, incredulous. *"Losing* her? She was never *his* to lose."

"You and I know that." Tripp gave him a pointed look. "But as far as Mitchell is concerned, she's *always* been his."

Ryan digested this bit of news and then something clicked. "We need to go to my barracks."

"Why?"

"There's something I need to give you."

"What?"

"I don't know, but Cate left a note with it instructing me to give it to you when the time was right." He met Tripp's surprised gaze. "I can't be sure, but I have a feeling this is the moment she wrote about."

"And you have no idea what it is?"

Ryan shook his head. "None, other than it's in a manila envelope and she used almost an entire roll of packing tape to seal it."

"Okay." Tripp nodded then quickly flipped a U-turn. "I hope whatever she gave you gives us something to work with, because right now we have next to nothing."

Ryan took a deep breath, but it did nothing to stop the expansion of dread beneath his sternum. It was cold, thick, and heavy. He swallowed hard. "Me, too, Tripp. Me, too."

***

Cat came awake with a jolt and a startled cry as pain radiated through her left hand. Disoriented, she blinked and looked around. She was still taped to the chair, the room was still cast in darkness, but she was no longer alone.

"Good morning."

Just as she recognized the voice as Hasan's she felt him grasp her ring finger and jerk upward. The bone popped out of joint and she choked down a scream. Tears filled her eyes and trickled down her cheeks as she ground her teeth together. When her middle finger dislocated with a sharp snap she bit her lip to keep from crying out, drawing blood. Cat braced herself, nearly biting through her lip when Hasan took hold of her index finger and pulled.

He paused and backed up a step. Cat focused on the ceiling, her hand on fire. She tried to breathe deeply and evenly, but she could hear her own ragged, hitching breaths. When he moved to her right side, Cat closed her eyes and waited for the inevitable.

By the time he'd gotten to the middle finger on her right hand she could no longer keep back the scream. What made it worse was the fact Hasan said nothing. He didn't gloat, he didn't ask her any questions, he simply moved from finger to finger with frightening ease and amazing precision. He knew exactly where to grip and how much force to exert in order to cleanly dislocate the joint, and he did it as easily as Cat's mother would have snapped pea pods from their summer garden. To her secret surprise, he left her thumbs untouched and stepped back several paces. She was thankful for the reprieve, however brief it might be. Cat dropped her head to her knees and wept softly.

"Peter is anxious to have his things back, and I am anxious to leave Afghanistan." He started walking in circles around her. "We can do neither until you tell him where his ledger is."

"I can't... tell you what I don't... know."

"That is what they all say." He fisted his hand in her hair and jerked her upright, leaning over until their noses nearly touched. "However, they always remember in the end." His gaze moved over her face slowly. "I have had hardened soldiers beg me to end their lives before I finished with them. You should think about that."

Cat winced as his grip on her hair tightened, her scalp stinging. She forced herself to smile through her tears. "Thanks... for the... tip."

Hasan's eyes narrowed. "Peter said you would be difficult." He released her and walked toward the desk.

"Well, I'd hate to... make him a liar," Cat bit out, "any more than... he already is."

Hasan faced her, a pair of pliers in one hand. "You know there are those who believe one should start with the fingernails, and *then* move on to the fingers." He turned the pliers over in his hand, looking at them the way Bam-Bam looked at his explosive devices. "*I* believe that prying off the fingernails *after* one has dislocated the fingers is far more effective. *Much* more painful that way."

Her brain was screaming for her to lie and make something up, to do or say *anything* to make him stop, but it wouldn't matter. When he found out she'd lied, it would be that much worse for her. She'd been trained to withstand torture, but training for this kind of thing was more to satisfy an academic criterion than to prepare an agent to withstand the real thing. No method of training could adequately prepare any person for what another human being was capable of doing to them. More tears formed behind her eyes as she imagined what was to come, but this time she didn't care if he saw them. Cat took a deep breath and was proud when her voice didn't waver.

"Dislocate the bones first, pry fingernails second." She paused and swallowed the lump forming in her throat. "Good to know."

Hasan gave her a tolerant smile and walked toward her. "Shall we begin?"

***

Tripp turned the manila envelope over in his hands then pulled the knife from his belt, flipped open the blade, and sliced through the thick packing tape. Ryan sat on Mack's bunk. His breathing quickened and his pulse throbbed against his windpipe up as Tripp pulled the items from inside.

"What is it?" Ryan asked, anxious.

Tripp looked at the thick file folder then flipped it open. As he started to scroll through the pages Ryan watched his expression get darker and darker, until it was making *him* nervous.

"Son of a bitch."

Ryan rose. "What?"

Tripp handed him the file folder without a word then started flipping through the journal. Ryan looked at his own picture and exhaled slowly as he continued on. "Who are these guys?"

"Every man Cat has dated since Mitchell," Tripp replied. "And this...." He held up the journal, "details every step he made in getting rid of them, including how he planned to get rid of you." He tossed the journal on the bed and sat down, resting his elbows on his knees.

"Wow." Ryan picked up the leather-bound book and thumbed through it. "He was doing *way* more than simply videotaping us."

Tripp's head snapped up. "Wait. You know Mitchell planted a camera in her quarters?"

"Yeah," Ryan replied, sitting across from him. "I was there when she found it." He had Tripp's full attention now.

"How did she find it?"

"She had some sort of bug-detector-killer that Heston gave her."

"Heston? Who's Heston?"

Ryan paused. "I can't really talk about it, Tripp."

"If it's about the mission to rescue Yasmeen Hasan, I already know." Tripp fixed him with a laser-pointed gaze. "Who is Heston?"

Ryan thought about it briefly then decided finding Cate was more important. "He said he was from DHS." Ryan briefly explained the situation. "She didn't go into detail, but he must've suspected something if he gave her a piece of equipment like that."

"Ryan, this is really important. Tell me exactly what this detector looked like and exactly what the two of you did when she found the camera."

The expression on Tripp's face sent his inner alarms screaming, but Ryan calmly explained what had happened. He could tell Tripp's mind was working furiously.

"And that's it," Ryan finished. "Why?"

Tripp's brows drew together. "Did she check her quarters every night after that?"

Ryan nodded. "Like clockwork, same drill every time."

"And she never found another camera?"

"Not that I know of." Ryan frowned. "Why? What's going on, Tripp?"

Tripp rubbed his chin. "After Cat told me about Mitchell putting a camera in her quarters, I installed one of my own to try and catch him in the act of doing... *something*."

That rocked Ryan backwards. "Shit. Cate and I should have made love on the flight line and sold tickets."

"Relax, Ryan. I didn't *watch* it, at least not *those* parts." His brow furrowed. "If she checked for audio and video every night, how did she miss my camcorder?" Suddenly his face dropped and he ran a hand over his eyes. "Oh, shit."

"What?"

"Cat knew if she blew another camera it would look suspicious." Tripp rose. "She would've looked for it instead of frying it." He groaned and stared at the ceiling. "And when she found it, she would've recognized it as mine. Motherfucking shit."

Anxiety stormed over him with sharp, cutting hooves. "What are you saying, Tripp?"

"She knew. She fucking *knew*." He ran his hands over his hair. "*Damn* it, Cat."

The hooves pounded harder. "Okay, you're starting to freak me out. What are you talking about?"

Tripp briefly explained Cat's foray into Peter's quarters, then picked up the file folder and thrust it at him. "She must have taken these from his quarters, knowing it would trigger a reaction. She did it on *purpose*."

Ryan gaped at him. "You think she set this up?"

"Yeah." Tripp nodded and tossed the file back on the bed. "I do." He ran a hand over his brow. "I don't think she knew he'd react *this* way, but she was trying to goad him. She pokes the snake, he strikes, and I get it all on video. Aw, hell."

Ryan rose and walked over to the window. He felt deflated, and scared. Resting his elbows on the sill he looked out over the compound.

"Why, Tripp? Why would she do that?"

Tripp clasped his hands behind his neck. "She was protecting you."

"I don't need protection!" Ryan roared, spinning to face Tripp. "I'm a fucking US Navy SEAL for God's sake! People usually need protection from *me*!"

Tripp took his outburst in stride, leveling a cool stare on him. "We uncovered evidence that Mitchell was directly responsible for the ambush last week. It wasn't an accident. The terrorists didn't happen to be in the right place at the right time, they were *pointed* toward you." He sighed and looked at the floor. "She was afraid he'd do it again, and get you killed."

Ryan shook his head. "She shouldn't have done that."

Tripp looked up. "Tell me you wouldn't do the same for her."

His heart twisted. "In a fucking heartbeat."

"Then deal with it," Tripp said, crossing his arms over his chest. "It's what she does, it's part of who she is, so if you love her at all you're going to have to love that part of her, too. Trust me...." He paused, took a deep breath, and said, ". . . it comes with the package."

There was a sharp rap on the door and Mack stuck his head in.

"I said I needed a few minutes, Mack," Ryan said.

"I know, Reap." Mack opened the door fully and stepped into the room. "Commander Ferris sent me to get you. There's someone here who wants to speak with you, and Trippler."

"Heston?" Tripp asked.

Ryan nodded. "Gotta be."

"Let's go then." Tripp's expression turned menacing as he walked toward the door and Mack quickly moved out of his way. "Let's find out exactly what this asshole got Cat into that I'm going to make him get her out of."

***

Cat whimpered softly and curled into a tighter ball. She'd been released from her chair and tossed into this small, empty, windowless room, where the only door was guarded by two angry-looking men. Apparently, they weren't happy being assigned to watch a mere woman.

Taking several deep, hitching breaths she slowly eased up into a sitting position, careful not to jar her hands. The pain radiated all the way to her elbows in throbbing, pulsating waves that flowed with the beat of her heart. She closed her eyes and fought the tears. Crying would only increase her heart rate and, thereby, her level of discomfort.

Once Hasan had finished pulling off eight of her fingernails he had tossed the pliers aside and returned to using his fists. Her right eye was nearly swollen shut, he'd broken her nose, split her lip wide open, and her jaw was stiff, sore, and probably fractured. During the beating he hadn't said a word, like before. He'd used the brief pauses in between the series of blows to speak and encourage her to give up the ledger. Unfortunately, she had no idea what he was talking about. Perhaps telling them she'd found the file and journal, but no ledger would get him to ease up, but somehow she doubted it. He enjoyed what he did too much.

Cat looked at her dislocated fingers, gathering the nerve for what she had to do next. Sitting cross-legged on the earthen floor, she flattened her left hand on the ground, biting back a cry of pain as she did so. If her jaw wasn't injured she'd be gritting her teeth, so instead she bit down on her already bleeding lip. She took a deep breath and using her right thumb pressed down and popped her pinky back into joint. This was probably a fruitless endeavor, but still she did it. When Hasan returned, he would more than likely dislocate them again, or break them to spite her. She forced her ring and middle fingers back into place. Tears started afresh, and by the time she'd finished with her left hand she was crying in earnest. Thankfully, her guards paid little heed.

Once all her digits had been carefully and excruciatingly relocated, she covered her face with her hands and sobbed. Now the pain was pounding up into her shoulders. With the blows to the head, the sharp ache in her jaw, and the throbbing in her temples she was reaching her breaking point. She prayed Hasan wouldn't return for a while.

Leaning her head back she closed her eyes and tried to rest. She was so utterly exhausted, and in such pain, that when the door opened she didn't bother to look.

"Well... I don't imagine when your father asked me to look after you *this* was what he had in mind."

It took a moment for the remark to register. Cat blinked slowly and looked up into Peter's gloating face. "Wh-what did you say?"

He clucked his tongue. "Come now, Catharine. How do you think I managed to stay out of trouble and by your side all this time?" He smiled. "Your father has powerful, influential friends. I shall miss that perk in our relationship."

"*Relationship?*" She stared at him. "How do you even *know* my father?"

He looked at her silently for a moment then crouched in front of her, resting his elbows on his knees. "I briefed him after your first kill." His expression turned speculative. "I wasn't supposed to, but technically his clearance level *was* high enough, and I *had* to share it with *someone.* I was so thrilled by your triumph, and I thought he would be pleased to know his only daughter was as formidable a warrior as he or any of his sons." He sighed. "Imagine my surprise when he was more... *shocked* than proud. That was when he asked me to stay close to you, keep you safe, and because I was in love with you I happily agreed."

Cat said nothing. The sense of betrayal hurt almost as much as having her fingers dislocated, and suddenly she couldn't breathe. Her relationship with her father had been strained ever since the situation in Baghdad, and now she knew why. Her lungs started to burn and she sucked in a breath, hot rage and cold sorrow swirling like a tornado inside her.

"You can end this, Catharine," Peter said softly. "Tell me where the ledger is."

She fought the storm in her chest and wiped the tears from her cheeks, grimacing as sharp stabs of pain shot through her fingers and up into her wrists. She took a hitching breath then met his gaze. "Even if I knew, you would be the last one I would tell."

He returned her mutinous stare for a few moments then rose and left the room, the door slamming shut behind him. She stared at the ceiling, fighting the tears gathering behind her eyes. Blinking them back, she tried to focus on something, *anything* that would distract her from thoughts of her father.

Cat reached gingerly into her pocket, sucking in a breath when her raw nail beds rubbed against the material. After pulling out the picture Mack had taken of her with Ryan, she ran one finger over his face and the floodgates opened. She pressed her lips to the image, leaving a bloody splotch behind. Then she slipped the photo into her sports bra, curled into a ball, and wept.

"I love you, Ryan," she whispered to the otherwise empty room. Her words bounced eerily around the windowless room, coming back to her in a ghostly echo. Laying a hand over the picture she closed her eyes, but the tears still found a way out. "I love you."

***

Ryan strode through the Command Center and into the briefing area, walked around the center table to the opposite side of the room, and went straight for Heston. Before anyone could say anything or even react he had the shorter man up against the far wall, his hands around the agent's throat.

"What the *hell* did you get her involved in?" he demanded. He felt hands pulling at him and released Heston only long enough to swing at the unwanted intruders. Then he immediately returned to strangling the older man.

"Lieutenant!"

Commander Ferris's voice cut through the cacophony with its characteristic steel and the room went deathly quiet. Ryan released his grip enough to let Heston breathe, but he refused to give up his prize.

"Tell me, you son of a bitch." Ryan leaned forward until their noses were touching. "What did you get her into?" A strong hand clamped down on his shoulder.

"Let him go, Ryan," Ferris said softly. "I know you're upset, I would be, too, but he's here to help."

Ryan looked at his CO, incredulous. "*Help?* He's the one who got her *into* this shit!"

Ferris returned his gaze, his expression one of stoic resolve. "Let him go. This isn't going to help us find her."

With a frustrated growl, Ryan released Heston and stalked to the opposite side of the room. Mack, Grady, and Voodoo filed in and lined up against the wall next to him, their expressions blank.

There was a brief, taut silence.

"You want a go, Mr. Trippler?" Heston asked.

Ryan glanced at Tripp as he stepped through the door. The taller man crossed his arms over his chest.

"Nope, because if I get my hands around your neck I'll snap it." His brows drew together and he scowled. "Answer the man's question. What did you get Cat into?"

Heston squared his shoulders, apparently unruffled. "I didn't get her into anything she wasn't already in."

Tripp took a menacing step forward. "I'm changing my mind about my hands around your neck...."

Heston walked around the table and stood toe to toe with the much larger man. "Don't threaten me, young man."

"Answer the fucking question."

"Enough posturing, gentlemen," Ferris said coldly. "I don't know which one of you is the biggest bad-ass on the block and I don't care. We have a missing CIA agent, and if we don't do something soon this will go from a rescue mission to a recovery mission, and I know none of us want that."

"Yeah, guys," Mack said angrily. "Have your pissing match *after* we get Red back."

"Amen," Ryan said softly.

Tripp's gaze never wavered from Heston's face. "You're up, big man. What do you have?"

Heston stared at Tripp for another moment then moved around the table and stood beside the Commander. Ryan reluctantly joined them as the rest of his team gathered around the table. Heston gestured to a young man seated at a computer and a picture of Mitchell appeared on the large main screen.

"I've been looking into Peter Mitchell and his extracurricular activities for more than four months," Heston began. "However, Miss Beckett was able to gather more information in the last few days than I've been able to uncover since starting the investigation." He looked at Tripp. "I'm guessing she had assistance."

Tripp gave him a bored look.

Heston was silent for a couple seconds, then sighed and looked down at the table. "I got off the phone with our Kandahar substation a few minutes ago." He glanced at Tripp. "I know you called yesterday and they gave you what information they had on Mitchell, but the situation has changed."

"What do you mean *changed?*" Ryan asked, leaning his hands on the edge of the table. Heston took a deep breath, and when Ryan saw the shadow of concern on the older man's face his stomach dropped.

"Mitchell was escorting Tariq Hasan from a safe house in Kandahar to one of our substations in Kabul for questioning before Hasan's transfer to Gitmo." Heston's expression darkened. "They were driving up with a private contractor's convoy: six vehicles, 16 private contractors, seven agents including Mitchell, and Hasan." He ran a hand over his brow. "Because of a washed out bridge the convoy had to take a detour. What was left of the convoy was found early this morning by a search party:

five vehicles and 22 bodies."

"Mitchell and Hasan and one vehicle missing," Tripp finished for him. "Christ, Heston. Why did it take you guys so long to figure out he'd gone off the grid? Weren't you watching him?"

Heston sighed heavily. "Two of the agents killed were specifically assigned that task. The convoy left Kandahar late, so scheduled check-in was just before sunset." The older man shook his head. "As much as we wanted to, sending out a search party after dark is suicide in this country so the search started at dawn. The convoy was found less than an hour later."

"I have a question for you," Ryan said. Heston looked at him and nodded, so Ryan continued. "How did Mitchell get *on* base without going through one of the gates, and after that how did he get Cate *off* base?"

"He had to have help," Heston replied. "We don't know who."

"Is there anything you *do* know?" Ryan ran his hands over his hair and dropped his chin to his chest. He heard footsteps walking away from the table and looked up. It was Tripp. He'd done an about face and was headed toward the door with long purposeful strides. "Tripp. Where are you going?"

Tripp paused with his hand on the door and looked over his shoulder first at Ryan and then Heston. "*You* may not know who helped him, but *I* do." He pushed. "Are you coming?" Tripp strode through the door and kept walking.

Ryan glanced at Commander Ferris, who nodded. Ryan ducked through the door and caught up with Tripp and, side by side, they blazed a path through the mazelike hallways of the Command Center. A glance over his shoulder revealed Heston hot on their heels.

"Where are we going?" Ryan asked.

"Back to work," Tripp said, his expression grim. "I've got a few questions for Airman Avery."

Chapter Twenty-Five

Tripp stalked into the hangar, Ryan and Heston on his heels. On the ride over, he had said nothing and Ryan felt the anger coming off him in waves. Tripp walked up to a blue-painted door, turned the handle, and jerked the heavy metal panel open. Ryan let Heston go through next then followed the shorter man, letting the door slam shut behind him.

Inside the windowless space, Cat's team was busy. Computers hummed, screens flashed, and Lee was moving around the space on his rolling chair, going from one monitor to the next. Techno, Tonto, Burgess, and Bam-Bam each sat in front of a different machine wearing what looked like high-end headphones. At a desk against the far wall Doc sat with a woman in an Air Force uniform. Ryan didn't recognize her, but he figured it was Airman Avery. Tripp walked up to her, and when she looked at him he gestured toward the door.

"Come with me, Airman," he said brusquely. "We need to talk."

Ryan saw the flash of trepidation in her eyes as she rose.

"Oh... okay. Sure."

She preceded them out the door and walked in the direction Tripp pointed, looking back at him over her shoulder every few seconds. They reached an intersection in the hall and she paused. "Um, I think I need to use the ladies room, if you'll excuse me for a minute?"

Tripp took hold of her arm. "I don't think so." He steered her to the right and kept walking.

At any other time, the look on Tripp's face would have given Ryan pause, but he was too worried about Cat to be concerned with what Tripp had planned for Airman Avery. Ryan glanced at her. She was a petite, pretty girl with dark blonde hair, blue eyes, and a slender build. She almost had to run to keep up with Tripp's much longer strides, and when he pushed through a door into another room and released her, her forward momentum nearly propelled her into the nearest wall. Ryan and

Heston followed, Heston closing the door and locking it behind them.

"What the hell?" she exclaimed, fighting to maintain her balance.

Tripp grabbed a chair and pushed it toward her. "Have a seat."

The airman gathered herself, ran a hand over her hair, and looked at him, confused. "Tripp, what's going on?"

"*Sit.*"

Avery appeared taken aback, but she slowly sat down, her eyes never leaving Tripp's face. "What's all this about? And who are these men?"

"That's above your pay grade, Airman," Heston said in a low, cool voice. "And from here on, I'd suggest you don't speak unless you're answering a question. Are we clear?"

Ryan almost felt sorry for the young woman as her eyes widened and she nodded mutely. He was glad *he* wasn't sitting in that chair facing down the angry giant. Tripp took a step toward her and crossed his arms over his chest. Ryan eased down on top of a nearby desk, his heartbeat picking up a bit. Heston stood to the girl's side, his expression completely neutral.

"Where's Mitchell?" Tripp asked.

Avery blinked. "He's... he's in Kandahar... isn't he?"

Tripp's expression turned downright menacing. "I will ask you one more time," he warned her. "Where is Mitchell? And we both know he's not in Kandahar."

Avery went white as a sheet and when she spoke her voice was barely more than a whisper. "I don't... I don't know."

"Don't lie to me, little girl." He leaned toward her. "I will peel you like a grape and take you apart *piece* by *piece* if I have to."

"I don't know!" she exclaimed. Her eyes filled with tears. "I swear to you, I don't know where he is!"

"But he *was* here yesterday," Tripp coaxed, "wasn't he?"

She stared at him for a moment, then Avery's face crumbled and she nodded, tears trickling down her cheeks.

Tripp looked at Ryan then Heston, and then focused on her again. "Spill it."

Avery looked up at him, casting a furtive glance at Heston. When the older man's expression remained stony she looked at Ryan, as if searching for an ally. Ryan returned her gaze with an angry glare and he saw her convulsive swallow. Airman Avery dropped her chin to her chest and cleared her throat.

"He... he called me just before... 1800 hours and asked me to... to pick him up in front of the contractor's hangar on the... the eastern side of the runway." She was quiet for a moment and Heston frowned.

"Go on, Airman."

"He... had me drive him to his quarters. He said he needed to get something and then go back to the office." Her chin started to tremble. "He told me to wait in the car, but when he came back... when he came back he was angry, *really* angry."

"Why?" Tripp asked.

"I don't know," she replied, sniffling, "he wouldn't say." She wiped her eyes. "He told me to drive him back here, and then go to my quarters and wait for his call."

"What did he promise you?" Ryan asked suddenly, getting to his feet.

Three pairs of eyes turned his way.

"Wh-what?" Avery squeaked.

Ryan approached her, anger swirling in his chest. "You had to know he was up to something, so what did he promise you? I find it hard to believe you're willing to risk your career and your freedom because he's good in the sack."

Airman Avery blushed, her jaw working soundlessly.

Tripp turned a frosty gaze on her. "Answer the man."

"I... I...." Her voice died and she took a deep hitching breath as the tears started to flow. "I thought I would like the military, but I don't. It... it wasn't supposed to be like this. I hate it here!"

"Join the club, sweetheart," Ryan shot back.

"He... he told me he had a few things he had to take care of, and then he'd take me away from here." Avery covered her face with her hands. "Peter said it would only be a few more days, and then we'd go somewhere we could be together, get married.... He said it would be just the two of us, and I'd never have to worry about anything ever again." The girl's face was a mask of misery as she started to weep softly.

"He's already married, Airman," Heston said flatly.

Avery's head snapped up. "Wh-what?"

Heston gave her an indulgent smile. "His wife is a socialite worth more than 30 million dollars, not to mention the fact he's been chasing Miss Beckett like a hound on the scent for five years now." He hooked his thumbs in his belt loops. "Where exactly in that equation do *you* and *marriage* fit?"

Her flush deepened. "I don't believe you! He promised me. He *loves* me!"

Tripp pulled the camcorder from his pocket. "You might want to take a look at this."

After flipping open the small display screen, Tripp hit on and held the camera in front of her face. Ryan moved to her side so he could watch, too, and he felt the blood climbing into his face as the seconds ticked by.

"Look at the time stamp," Tripp said. "What time did you drop him off here?"

The airman's breathing turned rapid and shallow. "Just before... before 1900," Avery whispered, her eyes wide and disbelieving as the recording played. When Peter threw Cat onto the bed Avery jumped and gasped, tears leaving silver tracks on her cheeks.

"Still think he's going to take you away from all this?" Ryan asked in a harsh whisper, his lips near her ear. Avery started, as if she'd just realized he was there. As she looked at him, Ryan saw the light of recognition in her eyes.

"You're the... the SEAL Cat was dating," Avery exclaimed.

"*Is* dating," he corrected, leaning on the chair's armrest. "Yeah, that's me, and I'm willing to do anything, to *anyone*, to get her back. So, if you know *anything* about where he's taken her—"

Avery jumped to her feet. The chair skidded across the floor and she backed away from them as if she'd just realized why she was in the hot seat. "Oh, God, no! No!" She held her hands in front of her. "I would *never*... I had no idea...! I swear to you, if I had known he was going to...." Her voice trailed off and she pressed a hand to her brow. "I *like* Cat. I thought I could make Peter forget her, but I would *never*...!" The girl's face fell and she started crying again. "Oh, God. What have I done?"

Tripp sighed and put the camera away. "You spent a lot of time in his quarters, Airman. Did you see or... or hear anything that could help us find her?"

Her expression suddenly shifted and all three men said in unison, "What?"

"I don't... know how to help you find her but... I *have* something that might help you."

"What?" Ryan asked.

Avery's shoulders slumped, her chin dropped, and once again, Ryan *almost* felt sorry for her.

"It's in my bag, in the other room."

Tripp stepped aside and gestured toward the door. "After you, Airman." She started to walk past him and his arm shot across her chest, stopping her. She looked up at him and he leaned toward her. "*Don't* do anything stupid, or I *will* make you regret it."

Avery nodded, her expression solemn, and then she walked quickly back to the other room. Reaching into a laptop bag sitting on one of the desks she pulled out a plain, hardbound book. She ran her fingers over the front then handed it to Tripp. Tripp started flipping through the pages, Heston peering around his bulging biceps to get a look.

"Two nights before he left for Kandahar I saw him writing in it when he thought I was asleep." Avery wrapped her arms around herself and sat on the edge of the desk. "I thought it was a diary of some sort. He's been so distant lately... distracted. I thought if I read it I'd know why, and I could help. While he went to take a shower, I took it from the hidden drawer in his desk."

Tripp fixed her with a hard look. "And when you realized it wasn't a diary, why didn't you put it back?"

Airman Avery looked miserable. Tears filled her eyes again and she covered her face with her hands. "I saw the file with all the pictures of Cat," she said. "And *him*." She glanced at Ryan. "I saw the journal, too, but I left them there." She shook her head. "I don't know why I didn't put it back. I wish I would have."

"I know why." Heston chuckled darkly. "You wanted an insurance policy."

Avery stared at Heston as he approached her.

"Isn't that right, Airman?" Heston narrowed his eyes on her. "You wanted something to hold over his head so he'd *have* to come back to you."

"But Mitchell thinks *Cate* took it," Ryan said, a cold numbness growing inside him. Running a hand through his hair, he turned his back on the distraught girl and tried not to imagine what Cat was going through.

"What *is* this?" Tripp asked, a puzzled frown on his brow as he turned the pages. "It looks like some sort of code. Hey, Rick."

Lee rolled over to him and took the ledger. "Looks like a substitution cipher."

"Can you break it?" Tripp asked.

Lee lifted one brow and gave Tripp a bored look. "Really? Have we met? Hi, I'm Rick Lee, graduate of MIT, forensic accountant, computer genius, all around genius actually. Um, yeah, I can break it." That said, he took the ledger, rolled back to his desk, and bent over the volume.

"So, what do we do now?" Ryan asked, hoping for something to distract himself from thoughts of what Cat was probably enduring.

"Hey, guys," Lee said, "I found something."

Ryan rushed to Lee's side. "What?"

"Not sure." Lee pointed to a set of numbers written haphazardly inside the back cover of the ledger. "Does that look familiar to you?"

Ryan exhaled sharply and a glimmer of hope sparked to life in his chest. "Yeah. Looks like a set of coordinates, lat and long."

Tripp was beside him in an instant. "Burgess, get a map up on that screen and pull up these coordinates." He read off the numbers. Less than 30 seconds later a map of northern Afghanistan appeared with the coordinates highlighted. Heston approached the screen, his brow furrowed.

"Mr. Lee."

"Sir?"

"Check the archives for any satellite or aerial photos of that area."

"Roger that, sir." Lee started typing fiercely.

Ryan walked closer to the screen and scrutinized the display. "That's only about ten miles from the Tajik border."

"Um, Mr. Heston?" Lee said.

Heston turned and looked at him. "Yes?"

Lee faced him. "There is some archived material relating to those coordinates, sir, but I can't access it. Above my pay grade."

Heston walked over to him. "Give me a second?" Lee rolled his chair back a few feet and Heston started typing. About a minute in he paused and looked at Tripp. "Mr. Trippler, escort Airman Avery to a holding cell. I'll decide what to do with her when we have Miss Beckett back."

Ryan's brows rose and he looked at Avery. She paled, but remained silent as Tripp approached her. Head bowed, she preceded him out the door and once the door closed behind them, Heston continued typing. After about another minute, he straightened and stepped back.

"There, Mr. Lee." Heston smiled. "You've just been promoted."

Lee grinned. "Outstanding." He started typing, and a moment later an aerial photograph appeared on the screen. "Here you go. According to the records it's an old Soviet border outpost abandoned after the occupation during the 1980s. It covers roughly an acre and there are three buildings." He turned on a laser pointer. "The largest is a two-story cinderblock building used as the outpost HQ. This smaller building housed a garage and maintenance spaces, and the smallest structure... here...." He paused and stood, "was originally classified as storage, *until* it was physically surveyed by the Army in 2007. Ground penetrating radar revealed subterranean tunnels."

Ryan looked at Lee over his shoulder. "A cave complex?"

"Exactly."

"How big?"

Lee shook his head. "Unknown. Shortly after the entrance was discovered fighting broke out in the area and further exploration was called off." He glanced at his monitor. "It's been used off and on by local terror cells ever since then, and every few months the military goes through and bombs the surrounding hills to encourage the roaches to leave. However, given the isolated location in the mountains, the lack of water or reliable power supplies, and the fact there's only one way in or out, it's not practical for any long-term operation, terrorist or otherwise. Because of that and the proximity to the Tajik border the US Military has deemed it strategically unimportant, and the only current information is satellite photos taken of the general area three months ago."

"I want a satellite over that area now, son," Heston said.

"Sir?"

"I gave you the clearance, Mr. Lee. Make it happen."

"You got it, sir."

"Lieutenant."

Ryan turned and faced him. "Sir?"

"How soon can you and your team be ready?"

Ryan smiled. "Before you can get a bird fueled and ready for takeoff."

The door opened and Tripp strode in. Heston looked at him. "We may have a location on Miss Beckett, Mr. Trippler. I'm assuming you want to be part of the rescue mission."

"Abso-*fucking*-lutely," Tripp replied.

"Good." Heston looked at Ryan. "Let's head back to the SF Compound and get Commander Ferris involved. This will be a three-team mission, Lieutenant, two SEAL teams plus Mr. Trippler's men. And *if* Miss Beckett is there, I don't want a single cinderblock, or tunnel, of that outpost left intact. Do we understand each other?"

For the first time since parking in front of Cat's quarters, Ryan felt his insides relax a little. He nodded. "We do, Mr. Heston." He looked at Tripp. "Pick three guys."

Tripp turned to face the room and the team immediately focused on him. "Tonto, Doc, and Bam-Bam." The three men stood and gathered together. "You ready to get Tiger back?"

"Hell yeah," Doc said.

"Really?" Tonto smiled. "You have to ask?"

Bam-Bam's eyes narrowed. "Do I get to blow stuff up?"

"Absolutely," Tripp, Ryan, and Heston said in unison.

Bam-Bam grinned, his face lit up like a Christmas tree. "I'll get my things."

Tripp shook his head and tossed Ryan a wry glance.

"Mr. Lee."

"Yes, Mr. Heston?"

"You're coming with us to the SF Command Center. We'll link up to your systems here so we can work together." Heston gave him a serious look. "You have anyone here who can do what you do?"

Lee thought about it for a moment. "Well, not as well as I can, but Burgess is a close second."

Burgess rose. "Hey!"

Lee grinned. "Relax, Burgie. He's your man, Mr. Heston. Give me ten minutes to get him up to speed and it's all good."

Heston pointed at Burgess. "Once we leave you're in charge here. You okay with that?"

"I'm more than okay, sir," Burgess replied. "I won't let you down."

"I know you won't." He looked at Ryan and Tripp. "All right, gentlemen. Let's do this."

***

Cat's breathing was labored, coming in sharp, shallow gasps, her muscles trembling. With her right eye now completely swelled shut her field of vision was limited, but she had no trouble seeing the body lying at her feet. After a moment of silent perusal, she looked up at her hands, which were bound with thick rope. She hung from a metal hook, and when it brushed against a length of chain dangling from the ceiling the sound it made was delicate, almost musical. Her feet barely touched the floor and thankfully she'd lost all feeling in her fingers. As she'd predicted, Hasan had decided to break them the second time around instead of simply dislocating them, four on her left hand and four on her right. Oddly enough, he'd left her thumbs intact again. Her hands were numb now but once she was released, providing she *was* released and not killed outright, the returning circulation would be agonizing.

"Abdul. Abdul, where are you?"

The voice was muffled, filtering through the narrow opening beneath the door. Cat braced herself for what was surely coming. The door scraped open and there was a brief silence before the man started shouting.

"Abdul!" He rushed in and knelt at his dead comrade's side. After checking for a pulse, he turned his gaze upward, his eyes alight with hatred and rage. "Bitch! You will die for this!"

He jumped to his feet and jammed the butt of his AK into her stomach, shouting and cursing at her. Her eyes welled with tears as he struck her again, putting considerably more effort into it the second time. She couldn't breathe, she couldn't cry out, and she couldn't get away, her body swinging like a pendulum as he rained his hatred on her. After half a dozen blows her ribs gave up the fight and a startled gasp escaped her burning lungs as she felt and heard the bones snap. Her vision started to go gray and she let herself fall, knowing unconsciousness would either bring death or a much-needed reprieve. At this point, she didn't care.

A gunshot split the air and her eyes snapped open. She looked to her left and saw Hasan standing in the doorway, a smoking pistol in his hand. Behind him were about half a dozen men, all armed, trying to peer around their leader's bulk to see what was happening. The man who had been beating her lay sprawled out beside his dead friend, bleeding but alive. Cat dropped her chin to her chest, too weary and in too much pain to hold her head up any longer.

"Take him to Mohammed."

Two men strode forward, shouldered their weapons, and grabbed the wounded man. As they dragged him out, another man moved to check the other body.

"He's dead." He paused and turned accusing eyes her way. "His neck has been broken."

The kneeling man jumped to his feet and Cat heard a click as he pulled a pistol and aimed it at her. Cat looked down the barrel of the gun for a moment and then closed her eyes.

"Put your weapon down."

"Did you not hear me, Tariq? His neck has been broken. She killed him."

"*Put your weapon down.*"

"She *killed* him."

"Had he obeyed my orders she would not have had the chance!" Hasan's voice thundered in the small, enclosed space. "You were all given instructions not to enter this cell without me present. Abdul disobeyed and has paid with his life, as it should be!" Hasan paused and took a deep breath. "Bury him, and let this be a lesson to you all."

The remaining men grabbed the second body and left without a word. Only the man holding the pistol and Hasan remained.

Hasan sighed. "Kareem, put the weapon down or I will shoot you myself."

"She must be punished!"

Hasan snatched the pistol from the man's outstretched hand and hit him with it. Cat winced as the man's forehead split open and blood ran in rivulets down his face.

"Did she cut her own shirt open?" Hasan demanded. "Did she try to remove her own clothing? She is *bound* and hanging from the ceiling."

The man pressed a hand to his bleeding forehead and looked at her. His eyes widened as he took in the state of her clothing. Her t-shirt had been sliced open up the front, her bra pushed up over her breasts, her pants unfastened and pushed down past her hips. A flush stained Kareem's cheeks and he looked away.

Hasan held out the pistol, butt first. "Abdul would have defiled himself and our cause with this infidel whore. It is right he is dead, but rest easy." Hasan turned a disapproving eye on her. "She will not go unpunished."

Cat's insides quivered but she kept her face impassive. They had been speaking in their native tongue. If Peter had indeed kept secret the fact she spoke their language, she didn't want to do anything to reveal she did.

"Go. Help them bury Abdul, and pass the word that the next man who defies my orders will meet the same fate, but at *my* hands."

The man looked at Hasan uncertainly for a moment then took his pistol, scrambled to his feet, and left the room. Too exhausted to lift her head, Cat looked at Hasan through her lashes as he faced her.

"You are more trouble than you are worth."

She jumped when she felt his hands at her waist until she realized he was pulling up and fastening her pants. Heat rose in her cheeks and she closed her eyes as he pulled her bra down. When he was done, he stepped back.

"You know, as much as Peter wishes it, I do not believe you will live much longer."

Cat said nothing. Hasan's dark eyes bored into hers.

"Before I deal with your treachery, I must ensure you will survive." He gave her a cold smile. "Rest while you can."

***

"All right, gentlemen, let's get this shit started." Commander Ferris gestured for the men to gather around the table. A wooden pointer in one hand, he tapped a spot on the large map. "We're going on the assumption Miss Beckett is here, in the mountains to the north. We will rally at FOB Kellerman, the closest forward operating base before we proceed. The base has already been appraised of the situation and are making ready for our arrival."

Heston stepped up. "Two Chinooks are being fueled for takeoff as we speak. Once we touch down at Kellerman we will wait for sunset, and then proceed to this point, five klicks south of the compound. From there you'll be on foot." He pointed at Ryan. "Lieutenant Heller, you will lead this particular mission. Lieutenant McCabe, aka Godfather, will serve as second in command, and Trippler will oversee the CIA squad. Details will be finalized once we get to Kellerman." He looked around the circle of men. "Any questions?"

A deep, somber silence fell. Ryan looked at the circle of men and that spark of hope burned a little brighter. He was surrounded by the best of the best. When he met Tripp's stony gaze the man smiled and nodded once. Ryan nodded back.

"Very good," Heston said. "Get your gear. Those birds take off at precisely 1300 hours."

Hushed conversation broke out as the men left the table and filed out of the room.

"Lieutenant Heller," Heston said. "A word please?"

Ryan nodded and stayed put. When only he, Commander Ferris, and Heston remained, the latter looked at him, his expression somber.

"I'm having some misgivings about you heading up this mission, son," Heston said.

Ryan crossed his arms over his chest. "Because of my relationship with Cate."

"You are awfully close to this one, Reaper," Ferris said.

"Which is why I'm the best one to lead it," Ryan replied, scowling.

"And if your emotions get in the way of your judgment, Lieutenant, you could get Miss Beckett, or yourself, or a member of your team killed." Heston flattened his hands on the table. "You need to be prepared for the worst-case scenario." He sighed and dropped his chin to his chest. "I doubt they'll be kind to her because she's female."

"I know." Ryan squared his shoulders. "She's American, she's female, she's CIA. Three strikes."

Heston gave him a pointed look. "Killing her may not be the worst thing they could do to her."

He'd already considered that and closed his eyes, pushing the mental pictures aside. "*Yes*, it is," Ryan said through clenched teeth. He looked at Heston. "Anything else she *can* recover from. *Dead* is permanent."

Heston lifted his chin and studied him carefully. After several long, silent seconds the man nodded. "You're absolutely right, Lieutenant." He extended his hand and smiled grimly. "Let's go get her."

Chapter Twenty-Six

Cold water jerked Cat back from the edge of unconsciousness and she gasped, her ribs protesting vehemently against the sudden intake of air. Another cascade rained down over her head and she nearly choked. With each cough the throbbing in her midsection expanded outward and a wave of nausea made her stomach clench. When her airways finally cleared, she held her breath and waited for the pain to pass. Once the agony receded to a tolerable level she slowly exhaled and then took several shallow breaths.

"Mohammed says your ribs are broken," she heard Hasan say from behind her. "More blows to your midsection could be fatal. He says if I *want* to kill you, I should continue what Fakhr started." There was a brief pause. "Oddly enough, despite what you did to Abdul, I find I do not want to kill you, not yet."

"Having too much fun, are you?" she asked, her voice little more than a harsh whisper.

Hasan laughed. "I had a horse like you once. Willful, stubborn to a fault, *refused* to be broken." He appeared in her periphery. "Eventually I had to put him down. It is one of the few things in my life I regret."

Blinking the water from her eyes she realized Hasan was now standing in front of her, his back against the wall, and her heart dropped when she noticed the jumper cables in his hands. Looking toward the desk she nearly groaned out loud when she saw the car battery sitting there. She gulped.

"Hmm." Hasan walked forward, hit the cables together, and smiled when sparks flew. "For the first time... I saw fear in your eyes."

She felt the tears stinging and tried to concentrate on her breathing, not too deep, not too shallow. Focusing on a spot over his head she ignored him, but when he touched the cables together again she jumped at the crackling and sparking. Hasan's smile widened.

"Have I at last found that which will break you?"

She ground her teeth together, welcoming the pain that radiated through her jaw and face. The throbbing and sharp twinges helped her focus on something other than her racing thoughts. "We'll... have to see now... won't we?"

Hasan sparked the cables once more and grinned. "Yes." He took two more steps toward her. "We will."

***

"What did Heston say to you?" Tripp asked.

Ryan shifted in the jump seat and sighed. "He thinks I'm too close to this."

"Are you?"

"Yeah," he replied, "but that won't keep me from doing what needs to be done."

Tripp smiled. "I didn't think so."

The co-pilot stepped into the cabin. "Prep for landing, gentlemen. We're on the ground at FOB Kellerman in five."

Ryan fastened his seatbelt and leaned his head back. They'd been in the air for nearly an hour, but those few words were the only ones either he or Tripp had spoken since taking off. Mack, Grady, and Voodoo were sitting with Tripp's men and McCabe's team in the back of the Chinook, talking quietly, their expressions serious. Ryan glanced at Tripp, but the man's face was as blank as ever. Knowing what was going through his own head, Ryan imagined similar thoughts were going through Tripp's.

"Tripp."

"Yeah?"

"You and Cate are as close as any two people I know." Ryan looked at him out of the corner of his eye. "How come the two of you never...?"

Tripp's expression changed and he focused on a spot on the opposite bulkhead. The silence stretched out and Ryan's brows rose. Tripp continued to stare at the wall, and Ryan sat up in his seat a little straighter.

"Wait." He leaned forward so he could look Tripp in the face. "Did you?"

A muscle in Tripp's cheek started to twitch. "Yeah... long time ago."

Ryan digested this piece of information. "So... what happened?"

"Nothing, Ryan."

Ryan couldn't let it go so easily. "Well... where did you guys meet?"

Tripp gave him a sidelong glance and lifted one black brow. After several moments of silent contemplation, he shook his head and looked away.

"Come on, Tripp. You can't make a statement like that and then drop it."

Tripp sighed and rubbed his eyes. "Fine. We met the first day of training at Langley." He gave Ryan a pointed look. "All the guys wanted a crack at her but she wasn't interested. I'd never seen anyone so... *focused.*" A wistful smile curved his mouth. "After graduation, we went out to celebrate, had a few too many drinks, and... one thing led to another. We tried to make a go of it, but very quickly realized we were much better friends than lovers." He looked at Ryan. "She's been my best friend ever since. I think of her as a sister I got to choose."

Ryan exhaled slowly. "Wow. Cate never said anything."

"We agreed to pretend it never happened," Tripp said. "I don't imagine you gave her a list of all your previous girlfriends." He shrugged. "Why stir up a hornet's nest if you don't have to? Cat and I have a history, but it's just that... *history.* We're friends, nothing more."

Ryan leaned back and let the revelation sink in.

"I love her, too, Ryan," Tripp said in a low voice. "Not like you do, but just as much, if not more." He ran a hand over his brow. "We have to get her back alive. We *have* to."

It was the first time Ryan had seen Tripp's veneer crack. The man was obviously worried, which, oddly enough, made Ryan feel a little better. Knowing he had an ally who cared as much about Cat as he did buoyed his spirits. He clapped a hand on Tripp's shoulder and met his troubled gaze.

"We will, Tripp. We will."

"And *Mitchell* is *mine*," he growled.

Ryan blinked. Tripp had gone from concerned to ferocious in a millisecond, a transformation even more stunning than what he had witnessed upon first meeting Cat. At that moment, Tripp looked every inch the cold, remorseless killer, and Ryan was glad they were fighting on the same side.

"You can have him, buddy," Ryan assured him with a nod. "He is *all* yours."

***

Cat tried to stop sobbing, her muscles still trembling and twitching. Back in her barren cell, she sat on the floor, arms wrapped around her knees. Her wet clothes were causing her core temperature to drop, and in addition to the leftover spasms from being electrocuted, she shivered with cold. Every inch of her ached, throbbed, or hurt, and even breathing was painful.

"C'mon, Cat," she said to herself. "Get it together."

Using her thumbs, Cat slowly and painstakingly unlaced her right boot. Once the ties were loose enough she used the toe of the other shoe to push the boot off. She tried to reach inside and sucked in a breath when the broken bones in her fingers ground together. Stifling a cry of pain, she paused and took several not-so-deep breaths, her mind working furiously.

She stared at the boot for a minute then placed the heel of each hand on either side of the back of the boot. Carefully, she picked the shoe up, turned slightly, and hit the sole of the boot against the wall. Pain shot up her arms and down through her fingers and she bit her lip to keep from crying out. Tears rolling slowly down her face, she hit the boot against the wall again, and again, until the detector finally fell out. Cat dropped the boot immediately and curled into a ball, weeping softly until the pain gradually ebbed. Then, taking slow, even breaths, she gingerly grabbed the device with her thumb and palmed it. Now, all she had to do was wait....

***

"Are we up, Mr. Lee?"

"Yes, we are, Mr. Heston. Linked in and ready to go."

"Good. See if you can get us any more intel regarding what and who is in that compound. Use whatever you need to."

Lee nodded. "You got it, sir."

"All right, gentlemen," Commander Ferris said. "Let's go over this one last time."

A map of the compound appeared on a large screen. Commander Ferris turned on his laser pointer and trained it at the monitor.

"After the helos drop you at the LZ, here, Reaper's team will proceed to this point, east of the tunnel entrance. Godfather will sweep west with his team, clearing the garage before proceeding to the main building. This is not a shoot-to-kill mission, but if you feel threatened or are fired upon feel free to light them up, gentlemen."

Heston approached the table. "While Lieutenant McCabe clears the buildings and detains the enemy combatants, Lieutenant Heller will find Miss Beckett. When she is safe, Mr. Brady, Bam-Bam, will rig the buildings and the tunnels." He leaned his hands on the table and looked at each man, his expression serious. "The only part of that compound I want left standing is the wall...." He paused and looked at Bam-Bam, "but if you have enough explosives, Mr. Brady, take that down, too."

"Out-fucking-standing, sir," Bam-Bam acknowledged with a grin. "One crater, coming up. I have some special charges already rigged, my own secret recipe. We just need to be *well* away from the compound before I blow them, if you know what I mean."

"Revisiting the mountain from last week, Bam-Bam?" Tripp asked.

"Nope." He shook his head and rubbed his hands together. "This will make the mountain look like *nothing*."

Tripp grinned and shook his head. "Can't wait."

Commander Ferris smiled. "A cas-evac with a full medical team will fly up to the LZ with you and wait there to extract Miss Beckett and any other wounded." His expression sobered. "Should you get into any trouble, you also have four Apaches on standby to assist. All you have to do is call and they will be overhead in less than five minutes."

Heston looked over his shoulder. "Mr. Lee."

"Yes, Mr. Heston?"

"Give it to us."

Lee typed quickly and an image appeared on the screen. "All right, guys. Satellite, infrared, and thermal imaging of the compound show roughly two dozen enemy combatants concentrated in the main building, and there is no evidence of anyone under restraint so Cat is most likely in the tunnels. We've had the area under constant surveillance for the past eight hours and the pattern is roughly the same. Three man teams sweep the compound every half hour and it takes about 15 minutes. Other than that, there is little movement. There are two hot spots here, and here, probably generators, and there are a couple of satellite dishes that weren't there the last time the military did surveillance, which was over three months ago. Also, there's quite a bit of electrical activity, which could mean computers and or servers. If you can get to them before they're destroyed, the intel on the drives could be worth *almost* as much as Cat."

Lee hit a few more keys. "Like I said, there's not much activity outside the main building, *but....*" He paused and zoomed in on the storage shed, "every few hours one person, accompanied by two armed men, leaves and enters the storage shed identified as the entrance to the underground tunnels. Facial recognition software confirms that one person... is Tariq Hasan."

Hushed whispers broke out among the SEALs.

"Do we have confirmation the package is actually in this location?" McCabe asked.

"No," Heston replied, "but this is the best lead we have, and you all know time is of the essence when one of our own is in enemy hands. We are going in under the assumption she is there. However, regardless of whether Miss Beckett is on the compound, the President has decided it's time to shut down this particular roach motel and take Hasan, alive if possible."

"Any idea if the package is ambulatory?" Voodoo asked.

Heston glanced at Ryan then looked Voodoo in the eye. "These people are savages, Lieutenant, so the odds are she is not. Take what you need to get her out." Heston looked at Ryan. "Lieutenant."

Ryan gave him a curt nod. "As Lee said, Beckett is most likely in the tunnels. We have no idea how big or complex the cave system is, or if there are more men down there, so we're going to wing it, go in blind, and look for her. Voodoo, you're with Godfather." He looked at Doc. "We also have no idea what kind of shape Beckett will be in so Doc, you're with me."

Doc nodded.

Ryan looked at Lieutenant McCabe. "Godfather, it's going to be up to you and your team to mop up topside. Keep it quiet. If she *is* there, we don't want them shooting the package before we can get to her."

McCabe nodded. "Roger that. We're in whisper-mode until the package is recovered."

"Tripp," Ryan said, "you and your guys are with Godfather until the facility is secured."

"Roger that," Tripp said. He looked around the circle of men. "And in case Reaper forgot to mention it, no one touches Peter Mitchell."

"We've gotten pictures of nearly two dozen men and Hasan," Lee said, "but not Mitchell." Lee hit a couple of keys and 23 pictures appeared on the screen looking oddly similar to a police photo array. "None of these guys are heavy hitters; most of them don't have any sort of record or reputation at all, not even locally." He paused and rubbed his chin. "I'll bet anyone here a million bucks Mitchell's there," Lee said, "but we haven't been able to capture an image."

"That means he's been careful and avoided the cameras," Ryan said with a scowl. "He knows we have eyes in the sky."

"I want him alive," Heston said.

Tripp lifted one brow. "I don't."

"Mr. Trippler," Heston warned.

Tripp rolled his eyes.

"Relax, Heston," Ryan said. "No one's shooting anyone in cold blood." He glanced at Tripp. "But we all know things happen in the field...."

Tripp smiled. "Exactly. Mitchell's safe... unless he does something that warrants a bullet. And knowing Mitchell, he's *going* to do something that warrants a bullet."

Heston didn't argue with that.

The silence stretched out for several uncomfortable moments.

"All right, gentlemen," Commander Ferris said. "Take another look at the intel reports and pre-mission briefing notes, get some chow, and then get ready to move. Once the sun goes down, we go in."

***

The door scraped open and Cat blinked as dim light fell into the otherwise pitch dark cell. Hasan's two bodyguards strode forward, put a hand beneath each of her arms, and hauled her to her feet. She gasped, her ribs sending stabs of pain through her abdomen as the two men dragged her out the door and into the tunnel.

The route was familiar now. Turn right out the door, down the tunnel about 20 meters, take another right, walk another 3 meters or so, and enter through the door on the right. Cat looked upward and counted the bulbs on the strand of electrical wire strung down the center of the tunnel, one roughly every meter. Eighteen, nineteen, and turn. One bulb, two bulbs, and door. It was already open and she was almost thankful when she saw the empty chair sitting in the middle of the room. At least she wouldn't be hung from the ceiling again, at least not yet.

The bodyguards sat her down in the chair and Cat winced, her ribs grating together. She heard the *riiiiiiip* of duct tape. The men grabbed her wrists, and then securely taped her arms to the chair. Once they had taped her ankles as well, the bodyguards left the room and closed the door behind them.

She couldn't see Hasan which meant he had to be standing at her back, or on her right side. She didn't bother to look around. Closing her good eye, she took a breath and waited.

"Do you realize you have been here almost 24 hours?"

Cat licked her parched lips, but it did little good. Her mouth was as dry as Afghanistan during the height of summer. "And yet it feels like so much longer," she croaked.

"Thirsty?"

She was parched, but she didn't bother to reply. She seriously doubted a tall glass of icy Pellegrino with a sprig of mint would be forthcoming any time soon.

"Hungry?"

She sighed softly and carefully tried to flex her broken fingers.

"Where is the ledger? Peter grows anxious."

She laughed and then whimpered, tears filling her eyes as pain throbbed through her ribcage. "Really? He's *anxious*?" She couldn't help but laugh again, tears sliding down her cheeks from the pain. "If I were him...." She paused and tried to take a steady breath, "I'd run for the nearest border... here it doesn't really matter which one... and high-tail it to a non-extradition country with a halfway decent standard of living and little or no relationship with the US. Someplace they wouldn't even send the SEALs."

Hasan sighed. "Have it your way." He appeared in her periphery on the left as he walked over to the desk. After perusing the various instruments lying there, he picked up one she hadn't seen, at least not since her last trip to the dentist. Retractors. She tightened her grip on the detector and fragments of pain shot up into her wrist. As much as she wanted to push the button she couldn't. She was afraid if she tried she would drop it, so she would have to get Hasan to do it for her, but she had to be careful how. He was suspicious by nature, and giving it up too easy would be an obvious red flag. She quickly decided on her course of action, and sent a silent prayer up that she could pull it off.

Cat resisted when he tried to put the retractors in her mouth, pressing her lips into a thin line and twisting her head away. Hasan backed off and then sent his fist into the side of her face, the sound of the blow echoing in the room. Lightning crackled behind her eyes and now she *knew* her jaw was fractured. Dazed, she tried to fight when he slipped the retractor into her mouth but the signal from her brain to her body got interrupted somehow. She screamed when he opened the retractor fully, the explosion of agony like a shockwave in her head. Her vision wavered and dizziness spun her, but when he picked up a pair of dental pliers her heart kicked into overdrive.

He loomed in front of her and Cat started shaking her head and crying out. Hasan paused.

"Do you have something to say?"

She nodded vigorously, and more lightning danced in her head. When he closed the retractor, it hurt just as much and she doubled over for a moment. After taking a few not-so-deep breaths, she slowly sat back up and lifted her eyes to his.

"What do you want to tell me?" he prompted.

She swallowed then said, "Start with the ones in the back, if you don't mind."

Hasan's face went black with rage. He backhanded her then punched her several times, cursing her as he did so. Cat clung to consciousness, despite how much she wanted to let herself pass out. She had to finish this.

When he reinserted the retractor, and opened it again she almost couldn't remain conscious as the pain seared through the lower half of her face with blinding intensity. She felt the cold metal of the pliers as he thrust them into her mouth and grabbed one of her molars. Silently begging for help from on high, she braced for what was coming. Hasan forced her head back, twisted the pliers, and pulled sharply. She screamed as her tooth came out with a snap. She tasted blood and gagged.

He didn't even wait. Moving to the opposite side of her mouth, he gripped the other molar. She stared up at the single bulb, tears obscuring her vision, gasping cries coming from her throat. When the second molar's roots released from her jaw, the pain was almost unbearable. Cat shrieked and started shaking her head again. Hasan, his face wet with perspiration and his breathing labored, released the retractor, took it from her mouth, and stepped back.

She doubled over again, spitting out mouthfuls of blood. Her stomach roiled dangerously and she vomited. When the spasms passed, she stayed there, her chest on her thighs, her head hanging past her knees, unable to move, her entire body on fire. Adrenaline pushed the blood through her veins at warp speed, which helped dull the throbbing, stabbing pains. She heard a soft wailing, and realized with some surprise it came from her own mouth.

Hasan fisted a hand in her hair and jerked her head upright. "Tell me what I want to know or I will remove every tooth from your mouth, and that will be only the beginning."

Instead of saying anything, Cat choked back a sob and opened her hand. The detector fell to the ground with a soft *click*. Hasan looked at the device, looked at her, and then looked at the device again. He released her and her head flopped down. She didn't have the strength to lift it. She saw his hand and his arm as he bent to pick the detector up, turned it over a few times, and then straightened.

"Where was it?"

She tried to answer, but her throat was so dry and raw she couldn't. Hasan obviously thought she was being stubborn again. Grabbing her by the hair once more he jerked her to a sitting position and then held the device in front of her face.

"*Where was it?*"

She licked her lips and tried to swallow, grimacing when all she swallowed was more blood. "In my... in my sh... shoe."

Hasan looked down and his eyes widened as he realized she was only wearing one boot. "Humph." He walked over to the door and jerked it open. She heard a scrambling in the tunnel. "My laptop. Bring it to me."

She fell forward onto her thighs as every part of her from the waist up throbbed and pulsed in an excruciating rhythm. Tears dripped from her lashes, plopping onto the earthen floor, but she couldn't stop the smile. It would all be over soon. One way or another, it would be over.

***

Lee's eyes widened and he jumped to his feet, the rolling chair shooting backwards and into the map table. Staring at the monitor in disbelief, he tapped several keys, and then spun to face a startled Commander Ferris. Heston stared at him from another nearby chair. When they saw the look on his face both men rose quickly.

"What is it Mr. Lee?" Heston asked.

Lee turned back around, his fingers flying over the keyboard. After less than five seconds he hit the enter key and then faced the large screen on the wall. "Satellites just picked up a large burst of electro-magnetic energy emanating from the compound. For a couple seconds the readings went off the charts, and then... nothing. Everything's dead up there."

"She's there," Heston said in a hushed voice. "She's there! Where's the team?"

Commander Ferris ran to one of the windows. "Just loading into the chopper."

Heston started for the door. "Mr. Lee, I want every available satellite focused on that compound and zoom in. I want to be able to see the pimples on an ant's ass inside those walls and record everything. I have a feeling all hell is about to break loose up there."

"What *was* that?" Lee asked.

Heston opened the door. "That was Miss Beckett confirming her location. Now get those satellites online!"

Ryan heard someone shouting something as he put a foot on the ramp of the Chinook. Being team leader meant he was the last one on, and he turned toward the sound. His heart dropped when he saw Heston racing toward him. The man was waving and yelling, but the helicopter's engines made it impossible for Ryan to understand him. Alarm racing through him, he jogged toward the older man.

"Lieutenant!"

"What is it?" Ryan shouted over the roar of the engines.

"She's there!" Heston grabbed his tac vest and pulled him close. "She's there. We have confirmation that Miss Beckett is at the compound."

Ryan stared at him, incredulous, and then exhaled sharply. Words escaped him, but Heston grinned and clapped him on the shoulder.

"Go get her, Lieutenant! Bring our girl home!"

Ryan shook himself then smiled. "Aye aye, sir!" He took a step back toward the chopper, then stopped and faced the older man. "Better put on some tea, Mr. Heston. She likes Earl Grey, two sugars."

Heston nodded. "Will do, Lieutenant. Be safe, all of you."

"Roger that, sir. Reaper out."

***

The tears had stopped for now. She hadn't moved since Hasan had picked up the detector, her chest on her thighs, her head hanging limp. She blinked when something crackled and she looked at the smoldering remains of the laptop. It was barely visible in the near pitch black and laying open on the floor where Hasan had thrown it after it nearly blew up in his hands. Sparks from the keyboard briefly illuminated the space, and then darkness fell again.

Cat shook her head and moaned when the pain ripped through her face and mouth. Broken glass from the exploded overhead light bulb fell from her hair, landing on the dirt covered floor with barely a sound. She wasn't sure how long she'd been alone, only that it was longer than a few minutes. He had taken the detector and left, probably to consult with Peter. That meant he'd be back any time now, and he'd be *really* pissed.

A chuckle escaped her. She'd put the detector on the highest setting and broken off the tiny wheel with her teeth so the setting couldn't be changed. Once Hasan had pressed the button, everything electronic within a football-field sized, spherical radius was dead. Then there was the added bonus of giving away her location. Hopefully the cavalry would arrive *before* the terrorists were able to clear out.

Suddenly the door slammed open, light invaded the room, and she recognized the characteristic hiss of a kerosene lantern. Cat didn't move. She wasn't sure she could even if she wanted to.

"Chain her."

One man cut the duct tape holding her arms and legs, slicing her arm in the process, while a second released the chain from its anchor on the wall. The first man then bound her wrists with thick, rough rope and pulled her to her feet as the second man maneuvered the large, metal hook around the ropes. She cried out when her arms were jerked over her head. One of the men pulled on the metal links until her toes barely brushed the floor then anchored the chain. Hasan appeared in front of her.

Without a word, he threw a punch to her midsection. Air was forcefully expelled from her lungs and pain mushroomed inside her. Apparently, Hasan had decided not to follow Mohammed's advice. He hit her again, and again, until she lost count and nearly lost consciousness. His breathing was heavy and ragged, and it was the only thing she could hear over her own heartbeat.

He stopped punching her to backhand her. Her head snapped to the side and she felt her cheek break open, warm blood dribbled down her face and dripped off her jaw. When another blow did not come, she opened her left eye and looked at him. He was staring at her, his hands fisted, brows drawn together. He was visibly shaking and clearly frustrated. It was obvious to her that hitting her with his fists was not nearly satisfying enough.

"Get me some rope," he said softly.

Cat closed her eyes. Tears squeezed out from beneath her lids. Her midsection was throbbing, and she was having trouble filling her lungs. She felt like she had a metal band tight around her chest, and it was all she could do not to panic as she struggled for air.

After a couple minutes passed she was finally able to draw a decent breath. She concentrated on inhaling and exhaling, but then she heard the sound of running footsteps and opened her good eye a fraction. Hasan sat on the edge of the desk, focused on her. She watched as his bodyguard entered the room and handed him a coil of heavy rope before withdrawing. Hasan took a knife from his belt, measured off about a four-foot piece, and quickly cut through the rough hemp.

A small smile curved his mouth as he tied a knot in the strand, roughly a third of the length from one end. Her pulse started to ratchet up as he unraveled the rope on the long side of the knot, leaving more than half a dozen smaller strands. He looked at her, and the glint in his eyes told her she'd finally pushed to the limit.

As he proceeded to tie knots along the entire length of the single strands, Cat knew exactly what was coming and closed her eyes. On the up side, the more time he spent on her, the more time that gave the rescue team, if one was coming. On the down side, the more time he spent on her, the higher the chance it would be a recovery mission and not a rescue. She said a silent prayer, asked for forgiveness of any sins she'd forgotten about, and thanked God for the life He'd given her. Then she pictured Ryan and her heart wrenched.

And thank you for giving me Ryan, she added to her unspoken entreaty, *even if it was only for a short time.*

Hasan tested his improvised whip. She heard the rope whistle as it cut through the air and felt the *pouf* on her face as it snapped and retracted in front of her. She instinctively shrank back, and he laughed softly.

"And now," he began, "let me show you how *I* destroy things."

"I hear you're good at that," she said, "*destroying* things, including your own family. Then again, I'm pretty good at destroying things, too... terrorists, electronic equipment... *truck bombs.*"

"What are you talking about?"

Cat met his dark, angry gaze. "Y'know, Ariahn has your eyes, but hers are full of life and love. Yours? Not so much."

His brows drew together and he hunched his shoulders, as if he was preparing to charge her. "How do you know my daughter's name?"

Cat smiled and welcomed the pain. "Who do you think rescued her and the rest of your family from that hovel before you tried to blow them up?" She switched into Dari. "You will never see them again, and that truly is your loss."

She heard the rumbling in his chest before the growl exited his mouth, and she couldn't stop the chuckle. He roared and the door swung open behind her, but one look sent his bodyguards scurrying back into the tunnel. Without a word, he moved to her side and raised his arm.

The first lash wasn't so bad, but her body jerked in response and she sucked in a breath. By the third her back was on fire, and it seemed Hasan was simply getting warmed up. Number five brought on a fresh rush of tears, but she bit her lip to keep from crying out. It was around number eight she found herself unable to choke back the scream, the knots acted almost like fish hooks as they dragged across her back in what seemed to be slow motion. She could distinguish each strand, identify where on her back they were hitting, and feel the flesh giving way beneath them. Thankfully, her world started to go gray, and by the time number twelve hit, it was over. Her head lolled forward and she fell into the welcoming arms of blackness with a hushed sob.

Chapter Twenty-Seven

Ryan crouched behind the wall to the rear of the storage shed and adjusted his NVGs. Peering over the mud barrier, he looked across the complex to the garage as Godfather and his squad took position. Using hand signals, he indicated for them to proceed. Godfather signaled back then he and two of his team entered the garage. Ryan saw faint flashes of light in the darkened windows, heard three soft *pops*, and then nothing. Glancing toward the main building he waited, but no one came out. Good. So far, they were undetected.

"Reaper, Godfather."

Ryan keyed his mike. "Go ahead, Godfather," he whispered.

"That weapons shipment that you guys went after? I think we found it."

"Leave Tonto and Bam-Bam. He can add that to the list of things to rig. Proceed to primary objective, get the enemy combatants rounded up, and retrieve whatever intel you can. We're heading down under."

"Roger that. Be careful, Reaper."

"Copy that. You, too."

"Gentlemen," Lee's voice said in their ears, "the three-man sweeper team is on its way out of the main building, copy?"

"Roger that," McCabe replied. From the door of the garage, he signaled for Ryan to wait until they had disabled the men, and Ryan signaled his agreement.

Ryan watched as five shadowy figures sprinted from the garage to the main building, moving so fast they were little more than a blur. He knew one of those figures was Tripp, and he was impressed a man of Tripp's size could move so swiftly.

The two-story structure was a plain cinder block affair, like most of the buildings built during the Soviet occupation. The windows on both levels were boarded up, but Ryan could see faint skeins of light between the boards. Several larger squares cut into the wood gave the impression of twinkling eyes, openings left for those inside to fire weapons through. His pulse sped up.

McCabe and his teammates would disable the men, then bind and gag them, unless they fought back. In that case the terrorists would still be disabled, but it would be a more permanent condition. Three men exited the building, and like ghosts materializing out of nothing the SEALs grabbed them from behind and vanished into the darkness. A few tense moments passed, and then his earpiece crackled.

"You're clear, Reaper."

"Roger that."

Ryan easily hopped over the five-foot barrier and flattened out on the back wall of the storage shed. Mack was next, followed by Grady and Doc. Mack moved to the opposite side of the shed on the hinge side of the only door, reaching across the thin panel to grip the metal ring. Ryan met Mack's eyes and then counted with his fingers. When the third finger rose, Mack jerked the door open and Ryan rushed into the shed, his weapon sweeping back and forth. Mack immediately followed. Doc came next, and Grady brought up the rear, closing the door behind him. The shed was roughly four meters square, barely big enough for the four of them, with only the one door and no windows. The hole in the floor in a corner was impossible to miss. He guessed the stack of crates centered on thick plywood that had been pushed into the center of the room would at one time have covered the tunnel entrance. He approached the opening cautiously, his weapon ready, but all he saw were stairs hewn into the bedrock descending out of sight.

He glanced at Mack, who nodded and flexed his fingers on his M4. Slowly, Ryan descended the stairs, crouching as soon as his head cleared the opening so he could see down the tunnel. It was empty. He took another step, checking carefully for any sort of trip wires or booby traps. The tunnel had apparently been carved directly out of the rock, so this was not a natural cave complex. He ran a hand over the wall, feeling the striations left behind by whoever had undertaken such a laborious job.

When he reached the bottom step he paused as something caught his eye. Broken glass. Ryan looked up. An electrical cable ran down the center of the tunnel with bulbs set every meter or so. All the bulbs were broken as far as he could see. He signaled Mack to stay to the side of the tunnel and pointed out the shards. Stepping on those would tell anyone in the tunnels they were coming. Mack nodded and silently passed the word.

Ryan proceeded down the tunnel on the right-hand side. Mack stayed back two paces on his left. After roughly 30 meters they followed the tunnel 90 degrees left. Keeping an eye out for glass, Ryan continued on. He counted four doors in this section of tunnel. Pausing at the first one he listened, hearing nothing other than his own heartbeat. He signaled for Mack to check the door opposite as he opened his and peered in. The small, narrow room was empty. He glanced at Mack, who shook his head. The next two rooms were also empty. Ryan ground his teeth together and signaled for them to move on.

Ahead, the tunnel T-d off and Ryan immediately held up a hand. The team froze. His NVGs were picking up light to the right, but it was dim and it came from farther down. The passage on the left was dark. Ryan signaled for Mack and Grady to explore the left fork, and for Doc to follow him. To his credit, the younger man had fallen right in with the SEALs, running where they ran, running as fast, without complaint, and seemingly without fear. He met Doc's eyes and Doc nodded.

There were two doors in this section of tunnel, both on the same side. Ryan indicated for Doc to stay back as he opened the first door. Frustration rose in him when he saw the space was empty except for a cot, an unlit candle, and a dirty, worn Koran. The door to the second room was already open and he stepped inside. His gaze swept left, then right and he froze, his heart dropping into his abdomen. In the far corner was a single boot. He bent to pick it up, and although he couldn't be sure, it looked like Cat's. The buoyancy of hope fought the riptide of despair in his chest, but he didn't have time to sort through his emotions. Putting the boot back exactly where he'd found it, he rejoined Doc in the hall. With a shake of his head, he continued down the passage.

Roughly 20 meters ahead the tunnel turned sharply to the right, and the closer they got to that intersection the brighter the light became. It wasn't bright enough to warrant removing his NVGs, but it was there. That told him there were also people, because rats didn't need candles or lanterns.

Ryan paused at the intersection and signaled for Doc to stay put. Taking a deep breath, he carefully peered around the corner. His heartbeat jumped a couple of points when he saw two armed men standing in the tunnel outside a door. In addition to light there was noise, noise he couldn't immediately identify. He knew he'd heard the sound before, but he couldn't put his finger on it. *Whistle, snap, crack,* pause.

One of the men in the corridor lit a cigarette, conversing quietly with his friend. *Whistle, crack, snap,* pause. The pause was longer this time, nearly a minute, and then a third man stepped into the hall from inside the room. He gestured for a cigarette and put it in his mouth. One of the others pulled out a lighter and in that brief moment of illumination the new man's face was spotlighted, the meager flame amplified by Ryan's goggles. He sucked in a breath. Tariq Hasan. The man's face, neck, chest, and arms were peppered with small, dark spots, but he seemed oblivious as he puffed vigorously on the cigarette.

Ryan turned to signal Doc as Mack and Grady appeared out of the darkness. Mack gave him a solemn look and shook his head. Ryan held up three fingers then mouthed, "Tariq Hasan." Mack's brows shot up and Grady looked at him in surprise. Doc's eyes widened.

Ryan peered around the corner again, his mind working furiously as his pulse started a slow climb. If Cat was in that room and he started shooting, one of them might have a chance to shoot her before he could stop them. An idea sprang to life in his head at the same time his brain finally analyzed the strange noise, a scene from a movie flashing briefly in his head. White hot anger flamed brightly in his chest, only to be snuffed out by a cold, dark wave of anguish. Ryan choked the competing emotions down and faced his men.

He signaled for Doc and Grady to backtrack and enter the room farther down the hall. He gestured for Mack to enter the room where he'd found Cat's boot. When they were safely hidden, Ryan took a deep, steadying breath then slowly and deliberately stepped on some of the broken glass. In the empty tunnels, the crunching noise sounded almost like firecrackers. He quickly stepped backwards into the room, hid behind the door with Mack, and waited.

When one of the men entered the room, Ryan snaked an arm around his neck, putting him in a sleeper hold as Mack grabbed the AK. The man struggled briefly before losing consciousness, and Ryan dragged him behind the door. While Mack bound him with zip ties and gagged him, Ryan resumed his original position. Less than a minute passed before their captive's absence was noticed.

"Azar? Azar?" The other guard's hushed whisper sounded like a shout, echoing down the narrow passage. "Azar!" He stuck his head into the room and Ryan went for him, but the man must have sensed something and the rifle came up. Before he could get a shot off Grady appeared behind him, grabbed the man's head, and twisted sharply. There was a sharp *snap* and the guard dropped like a stone. Ryan met Grady's eyes and nodded. Grady smiled grimly and stepped back into the hallway.

Ryan quickly left the cell and made his way back to where the tunnel turned to the right. He took a quick look around the corner. The passage was empty. On silent feet, he walked slowly and deliberately toward the open door. Careful to stay out of the rectangle of light falling through the doorway and onto the floor, Ryan maneuvered himself so he could see into the room without being seen himself.

Cat hung from the ceiling, her back to him. His heart nearly stopped. Something hot and malicious erupted in his belly and traveled upwards quickly, almost overriding his training and common sense. Fighting the urge to burst into the room and spray the terrorist with bullets, he took a deep breath and pressed himself against the wall, motioning for Mack to go past him to the opposite side of the doorway while Hasan's attention was focused on Cat. Since this wasn't a shoot-to-kill mission and they wanted Hasan alive, he couldn't kill Hasan unless Hasan threatened or shot at him. A grim smile curved Ryan's mouth. He had a feeling it wouldn't be hard to get Hasan to draw his weapon and sign his own death warrant. When Hasan sent his left fist into Cat's side Ryan decided he'd do whatever was necessary to ensure the man's death.

Ryan looked at Mack, and started counting with his fingers again. On three he swiftly and silently entered the room, moving from right to left, and Mack entered from the left moving right in a crisscross pattern. Their weapons swept the room in case there was someone hiding in a corner they hadn't seen from the door, and then Ryan aimed his M4 at Hasan. Less than two seconds had passed, and as Ryan's crosshairs found its target Hasan realized he was no longer alone. Hasan's eyes widened and he dropped the rope, reaching for the pistol holstered on his right hip. Ryan counted in his head as the 9mm came up, one one-thousand, two one-thousand. When the gun cleared the holster and started to rise, Ryan put his finger on the trigger and squeezed three times in quick succession, performing what was known in the military and law-enforcement communities as a "failure drill." Two dark spots appeared in the center of Hasan's chest, while a third darker spot appeared over his left eye. Hasan stared at him in disbelief for a second or two before his eyes glazed over and he fell to the ground with a thud.

Ryan exhaled sharply and then sucked in a huge breath of air, his heart vibrating against his sternum as the adrenaline rushed through his veins. He stared at the dead man for a moment, then closed his eyes and hung his head. Bracing himself, he pushed his goggles back and slowly turned to face Cat.

"Doc!" he heard himself say, though he didn't recall thinking the word before speaking it. Steeling himself he lifted his head to look at her.

"Oh, my God," Doc said in a whisper.

"Holy shit," was all Grady could come up with.

Mack stared at her in disbelief then looked at Ryan in anguish, his eyes unnaturally bright in the dimly lit room.

She looked more like a side of meat hung up to drain than a person. Her t-shirt was little more than a tattered, bloody rag, the top few inches of her trousers dark and wet from her own blood. The only thing that identified her as his Cate was the long fall of hair. It shone like a tangle of copper in the lantern's glow, disheveled and unkempt, but still red. Ryan's eyes stung and he blinked rapidly.

He couldn't see her face, but looking at what Hasan's improvised whip had done to her made his stomach turn. She seemed to be nothing but a canvas of cuts, lacerations, bruises, and abrasions from her fingertips to her waist, and her back looked like ground beef. He swallowed hard and took a deep, steadying breath.

"Mack, we don't have comms with the rest of the team down here," Ryan said, his voice oddly calm given the hurricane raging inside him. "Get up top and find out what's going on, and get that cas-evac here *now*."

Mack nodded and quickly vanished through the door.

"Grady, help me get her down."

Ryan purposely separated his emotional self from his professional self and put his emotional self, temporarily, in a box in his head. Moving to her side, he positioned one arm behind her knees and the other behind her back as Grady unhooked the chain from its wall anchor. Cat dropped into Ryan's arms, her head lolling against his shoulder as Grady slowly lowered her. When Grady had some slack in the chain he re-anchored it then removed the hook from the ropes around her wrists. Once she was free from the chain, he stepped back and shrugged out of his gear.

Ryan started to kneel but Grady said, "Hold up." Ryan paused and waited as Grady removed his pack and his uniform blouse and spread it on the ground. Ryan gave him a thankful look and Grady nodded. Slowly, Ryan knelt and gently put Cat's derriere on the ground then carefully eased her onto her back. When she was laid out flat, he took the knife from his belt and sliced through the rough rope at her wrists. Doc immediately moved to her side, dropped his pack, and bent over her.

That churning rage inside him bubbled closer to the surface as Ryan slipped his finger around her raw, bleeding wrist and lifted her hand. Her knuckles were bruised and swollen, her fingers obviously broken, her nails gone.

"Jesus, Cate," Ryan whispered. "What did he do to you?"

He put her hand down and gently brushed the hair from her face. He'd seen guys beat to hell before, but this took it to an entirely new level. Nearly her entire face was dark purple from bruising, her right eye completely swollen shut and a shade of burgundy so dark it was almost black. Between the cuts, the blood, the split and swollen lips, the deviated septum, and the bruises, she was almost unrecognizable.

"We have to get her out of here," Doc said in a hushed voice. "Her blood pressure is dangerously low, which could indicate internal bleeding, and I can hear bubbling on the left side of her chest, which means she probably has a punctured lung." He met Ryan's gaze. "If we don't get her to a surgeon, she's going to bleed out or drown in her own blood or both."

Ryan nodded, and slipped his arms behind her knees and back again. "Let's go then."

Grady stepped in front of him. "We have no way of knowing what we're walking into, Reaper."

"You two go ahead and find out what we're walking into." Ryan carefully lifted her against his chest and stood. The fact she neither moved nor made a sound concerned him almost as much as her obvious injuries. "I'll need to move slower so I don't hurt her any more than she already is." When the two men looked at him uncertainly, he frowned. "Unless one of *you* thinks you can carry her, *get moving.*"

"And if there are more enemy combatants down here?" Grady asked.

"Then I'll do what I have to do," Ryan replied. He was starting to get angry, and he didn't bother to hide it. "If we wait here and do nothing she dies."

"I'll stay back with Reaper," Doc said. "I'm not a SEAL, but I'm not a bad shot." He glanced at Cat and a pensive smile curved his mouth. "I learned from the best."

Grady looked between the two for a few seconds then nodded. "All right. Doc, you watch his six, you hear?" When Doc nodded, Grady met Ryan's gaze briefly then ran through the door, his rapidly beating footsteps echoing through the tunnels.

"Let's go, Ryan," Doc said, indicating for him to go first. "After you."

They were roughly halfway back to the stairs when the sound of running footsteps brought Doc forward, his rifle aimed down the narrow tunnel. Ryan paused, allowing Doc to go ahead a few paces. When Grady rounded the corner both men sighed.

"It's all good, Reaper," Grady said, not even a little breathless from his mad dash. "Godfather has everything under control. There's only one minor problem."

Ryan started walking again. "What's that?"

"They can't find Mitchell."

Ryan's steps faltered, and then he continued. "Are they even sure he's here?"

Grady nodded and fell into step behind Ryan. "Lee says their fancy equipment picked up a call made from a burn phone belonging to Mitchell roughly 15 minutes ago, and that the call was made from this location." He shook his head. "He's here, we just don't know where."

"Once Cate is safely aboard a helicopter we'll worry about Mitchell," Ryan replied. "Go back top-side and help Godfather get everything squared away."

"Roger that, Reaper. The cas-evac should arrive any minute." Grady jogged past him, going back the way he'd come.

Carrying Cat through the dark, narrow tunnel had been easy enough, but getting up the stairs was a little more difficult than Ryan had anticipated given the tunnel's narrow opening. He finally had to put her feet on the ground and encircle her chest from behind with his arms. He held her gingerly as he slowly backed up the rocky stairs, dragging her with him. Once he was off the stairs, he carefully lifted her into his arms and left the shed.

Moving away from the wooden shack a few paces, he turned and looked at Doc. "Let's put her down here. There's an emergency blanket in my pack. Grab it."

He stood still as Doc searched his pack and then Ryan heard the metallic crinkling as Doc opened up the thin, silver blanket. Once he'd spread it out on the ground, Ryan knelt and carefully lay Cat down. He shrugged out of his pack, removed his uniform blouse, and covered her with it, tucking it gently beneath her chin.

As he rose, her head moved and a low, pained moan escaped her. He was back at her side in an instant. "Cate? Cate, can you hear me?"

She took a shallow, hitching breath, and her left eye fluttered open. She looked around, dazed, and then she focused on him. She blinked slowly several times before a small smile curved her battered mouth.

"Ry-Ryan?"

Ryan felt his chest constrict tightly. He swallowed the lump in his throat and dropped his chin, squeezing his eyes shut for a moment. He reached for her hand, stopping himself just in time. Forcing a smile, he met her gaze. "It's me, babe. I'm right here."

She licked her lips, her breathing thin and raspy. "You... you came... for me...."

"Of course I did," he replied.

She chuckled shortly and winced. "I told you... Karma has a way of... of balancing the... scales...." Her voice died and her eye slowly closed.

Alarm raced through him. "Cate?"

Doc quickly pressed two fingers into her neck. "She's okay. It's weak and thready, but she's got a pulse." He glanced over his shoulder. "Where the hell is that chopper?"

Ryan felt his emotional self-pounding on the box in his head, demanding to be let out. Needing some space, he rose quickly and surveyed the compound.

The courtyard was a beehive of activity, enemy combatants were being rounded up and herded into a group near the garage. Bam-Bam was wiring the garage with explosives, Tonto was helping him. McCabe set up a large circle of flares to light the area and guide the helicopter in. SEALs walked in and out of the main building, piling up stacks of what looked like computer hard drives, weapons, and boxes of papers, books, and other miscellaneous items. Ryan took it in for a second then started walking across the compound toward the main building. McCabe caught sight of him and started his way.

They met in the middle and he listened as McCabe gave him a rundown of the dead and wounded. Thankfully only the enemy combatants had met their maker that day, and the two SEALs wounded only had minor injuries. When he was finished, McCabe asked, "How is she?"

"Not good." Ryan mounted the steps leading up to the main building. "Any sign of Mitchell?"

McCabe scowled. "No. Lee says he's here somewhere. We're searching for him, but so far... nada."

"Keep looking." Ryan ran a hand over his beard and looked around, doing a mental head count. "Where's Trippler?"

McCabe looked surprised, and started looking around, too. "He was helping search for Mitchell, but I haven't seen him in a few minutes. Maybe he's inside the main building. You want me to find him?"

"No." Ryan looked at the stack of computer equipment. "Find something to box this up with. The intelligence guys can sort through it later. That helo should be here any time, right?"

"Yep. Will do, Reaper."

Ryan stared up at the sky for a moment. His emotional self still demanded freedom, but the box had to stay shut for the time being. Closing his eyes, he took a deep breath and exhaled slowly.

"Cat!"

Ryan's head whipped around in the direction of the sound and he watched as Bam-Bam and Tonto ran across the compound to Cat's side. Even in the dark Ryan saw the anguish in Bam-Bam's face as he stared at Cat in disbelief. Tonto knelt at her side, his usually stoic features a mask of despair. Then the *whump-whump* of helicopter blades caught Ryan's attention. He looked into the south and a Blackhawk helicopter popped over the closest rise, the lights like beacons in the darkness. He heard the *pop-hiss* as McCabe lit a couple more flares and tossed them on the ground.

He glanced at Doc, who had found another thermal blanket and was shielding Cat with it as the chopper began its descent into the center of the compound. Ryan shielded his eyes with one hand as the dust kicked up into pinkish-beige rooster-tails beneath the whirring blades. When he heard the characteristic whine of the engine winding down to an idle he jogged toward the helo. The medical personnel on board quickly hopped off the aircraft, medical kits in hand. Ryan approached the man with the captain's bars on his collar. The name Blair was stitched over his pocket.

"Captain Blair," Ryan said, extending his hand. "I'm Lieutenant Heller. This way, sir."

The captain shook his hand firmly but said nothing, following quickly as Ryan walked over to where Cat lay. Doc and Blair immediately started talking in hushed tones as Blair pulled out a stethoscope and listened to Cat's chest then checked her vitals. Ryan stayed back a few paces, giving the medics room to work.

Blair looked up at one of his assistants and said, "Stretcher *now*. We need to get her to Bagram ASAP."

Ryan inhaled sharply. The fact the captain wanted to bypass FOB Kellerman made his abdominals spasm. He glanced at Bam-Bam and Tonto who stood several paces away. Bam-Bam thrust his fingers into his hair, clearly distressed, and Tonto clapped a hand on his shoulder.

"Come on, Bam," Tonto said softly. "She'd want us to finish what we're doing. Let's make sure not a single brick or tunnel of this hell hole is left standing."

Bam-Bam swiped at his eyes, then nodded and stalked off. He met Ryan's gaze briefly, and Ryan dropped his chin, not wanting to see reflected in Bam-Bam's eyes what he himself felt.

He was momentarily distracted as Grady and Mack appeared, the lone survivor from the tunnels walking between them. Mack said something to Grady, who grabbed the terrorist's arm and steered him toward where his fellow Taliban sat on the ground. Mack looked after him for a minute then approached Ryan, casting a wary eye at Cat.

"How is she?" he asked in hushed tones.

"They're taking her straight to Bagram, if that tells you anything," Ryan replied.

Mack looked him in the eye and put a hand on his shoulder. "She's going to be all right, Ryan. You *have* to believe that."

Ryan nodded once. "Yeah." He rubbed his forehead. "Go help McCabe get everything else ready for evac, and we still need to find Mitchell. I want that son of a bitch, preferably *before* Tripp puts a bullet between his eyes."

"On it, Reaper," Mack said. He squeezed Ryan's shoulder. "She's going to make it."

Ryan couldn't have replied had he wanted to. His throat was tight with anxiety as he watched the corpsmen lift Cat onto a stretcher. She was so still and quiet, her chest barely moving. The group of four carrying the stretcher moved toward the helicopter, Blair on their heels and Doc behind him. The younger man paused and looked at Ryan in silent question.

"Go," Ryan said. Doc nodded, handed him his uniform blouse, and then followed the medical team. Ryan watched until they were inside the chopper and he heard the engine start to ramp up. As he turned away, his earpiece crackled.

"Reaper, Command." It was Lee's voice.

"Yes, Mr. Lee?" Ryan asked, careful to keep his voice neutral.

"You may have a problem."

What now? Ryan cursed under his breath. "Explain."

"The call I tracked from the compound went to a village about five klicks north of the Tajik border. I tasked one of our spy satellites to take a look, and a convoy of four deuce-and-a-half trucks just left that town... heading south."

Ryan rolled his eyes. "Of course they are. Fuck."

"Given their speed, they'll reach the road leading to the outpost in roughly half an hour. If they get there before you're out...."

"We'll be cut off," Ryan finished for him. He squeezed his eyes shut. "I get it. Have those Chinooks spin up and get up here. We'll be ready to go as soon as they touch down. And tell those Apaches to stand by. We may need their help after all."

"Roger that. Command out."

Ryan stood there for a minute and looked up when he felt someone at his elbow. It was McCabe. "Yeah, Godfather? What's up?"

McCabe lifted his eyebrows. "I was about to ask you that. You don't look happy."

Ryan sighed. "Command is tracking a convoy headed our way, ETA three-zero minutes. If we don't get out of here before they reach the access road...."

"We'll have to call in the Apaches and shoot our way out." McCabe cursed. "Just when I was thinking things were going smoothly."

Suddenly, the crack of a gunshot split the air.

Chapter Twenty-Eight

The sound of the shot ricocheted off the valley walls, making it impossible to determine where it had come from. Ryan looked around in alarm but no one seemed to be injured. The SEALs were ready however, weapons up, postures tensed, eyes and ears alert. When he heard shouting and saw the medical team flee the helicopter, a sense of foreboding dropped over him. That foreboding turned to dread when another shot rang out. He did a mental head count, and realized Doc and Blair were not with the others as the corpsmen fled toward the nearest SEALs.

"Lieutenant Heller!"

Ryan's heart hit the ground as he recognized Mitchell's voice. Ryan stood at an angle to the aircraft, so he couldn't see directly into the cabin. He motioned for McCabe to lower his weapon as he moved slowly to the left. The SEALs silently closed in around the helicopter, and he signaled for them to stand their ground.

"Does anyone have a shot?" he heard McCabe ask in his earpiece. One by one the SEALs shook their heads.

"I just shot the pilot and Catharine's corpsman, so you better tell your men to lower their weapons, or the body count is going to double!"

Ryan eased sideways with slow, careful steps until he could see into the cabin of the Blackhawk. The glow from the flares barely illuminated the small space, but they provided enough light that Ryan could see Mitchell. He had a pistol to the back of the co-pilot's head, and he stood behind Dr. Blair, a knife angled across the man's jugular. Doc lay across Cat's legs, his head at Blair's feet, and he didn't move.

Mitchell had shielded himself well, wedged into a corner with the bulkhead of the cockpit on his right, and the bulkhead of the starboard side of the helicopter at his back. Only half his face was visible as he used the doctor for protection. Ryan scowled. *How the hell had he gotten into the chopper?*

"Ah, there you are." Mitchell smiled, as if he'd been waiting for Ryan to arrive so they could share a beer. "Now tell your men to drop their weapons and back off, or I kill the co-pilot and the good doctor here."

"You might get *one*," Ryan replied. "You won't get both before one of us takes you out."

"I *can* sever this man's artery and shoot at the same time," Mitchell sneered.

"Unlikely, but either way this is where you die," Ryan shot back.

Mitchell laughed. "If I die, Catharine dies."

"You're not *that* good a shot."

"I don't have to be. Didn't you hear me? I already shot the pilot. With the co-pilot and the doctor both dead, Catharine will die long before you can get another bird or medical team up here." He tightened his grip on Blair and Ryan saw the tip of the blade press into the doctor's throat. "Isn't that right, Dr. Blair?"

Blair looked at Ryan and nodded once, his expression grim and angry. Ryan ground his teeth together. He heard McCabe communicating in hushed tones with Command, but shut that conversation out.

"So, what happens now, Mitchell?" Ryan asked.

"The co-pilot is going to fly me out of here. I'll release him once Catharine and I are somewhere safe. The doctor will have to hang around a little bit longer, for obvious reasons."

"You do realize what part of the world you're in, don't you?" Ryan asked dryly. His insides were twisting, but he was too well trained to panic. "She'll die *long* before you get anywhere *safe*."

"*You* may not find safety in any of the neighboring countries," Mitchell said, "but I have cultivated quite a few relationships outside the borders of Afghanistan. In fact, *my* friends are only a short helicopter ride away."

"So, it's *your* friends who are driving those trucks headed this way?" Ryan asked.

Mitchell smiled. "Well, once I'm gone I didn't want you and your men to be bored. I know how SEALs *hate* inactivity."

Ryan saw Doc move and glanced at him. Ryan crossed his arms over his chest, his eyes moving unobtrusively between Mitchell and Doc. "Cate's taken out how many of your *friends* in the past few months, 15, 20, more? I wonder how friendly they'll be when they find out you're playing both sides against the middle."

"I find playing both sides is actually a fair proposition for all involved."

"Fair?" Ryan repeated, incredulous.

"Yes, fair." Mitchell shifted his position a bit, and the other half of his face became visible over the doctor's other shoulder. "I give the Taliban a chance to get their hands on a Special Forces team, and that top-secret equipment Catharine and her team have been testing. I also give Catharine and her team, and you Spec Ops gentlemen a chance to get away unharmed. Does that not sound fair to you?"

"Sounds like *treason*."

Doc's hand inched slowly across the floor of the cabin, toward an open medical kit. Ryan had an idea what the corpsman was up to, and he realized he needed to keep Mitchell distracted. He took a couple steps toward the chopper, stopping when the pistol swung around to point at him.

"No closer, Lieutenant," Mitchell said flatly, his brows drawing together. The gun moved quickly back and forth between him and the back of the co-pilot's head. "I don't *want* to shoot you, but I will."

Ryan held up his hands and stepped back as Doc's fingers slid into the medical kit. Other than that small, stealthy movement, the young man remained motionless.

"Okay," Ryan said. "I'm not moving." He put his hands down. "Why don't you let the doc go so he can take care of Cate? I don't think you want her to die any more than I do."

"True." Mitchell moved back to his original position. "However, sometimes sacrifices must be made."

Ryan swallowed his anger. "You went to a lot of trouble to get her up here alive. Why put so much effort into it if you're going to let her die? What was the point?"

"I wanted to give her the opportunity to choose," Mitchell replied, his expression darkening. "She chose *you*."

The glint of pink light on metal caught Ryan's eye and he resisted the urge to look. "Did you think drugging and kidnapping her would magically change the way she feels about you?" He dropped his head to glance at Doc. Massey had a scalpel in his hand, his thumb slowly and carefully working the protective sleeve off the blade. Ryan then met Mitchell's gaze. "After what you did to her, who did you think she would choose?"

"I have loved her for *five years*," Mitchell announced, his voice rising. "I've watched over her, kept her safe. I'm sacrificing my *marriage* for her. Doesn't that deserve some sort of consideration?"

Ryan's blood went cold. This guy was crazy, which made him even more dangerous. "You stalked her, you intimidated and terrorized anyone who tried to get close to her, and you *assaulted* her. Did you expect her to... *overlook* that?"

"That was an accident!" Mitchell shouted. "I never wanted to hurt her, but she made me so... *angry...!*"

"And now look what you've done to her," Ryan said. "Did you see her face?" He loosened his grip on his rage, just a hair. "Did you see her fingers, her *back*, you son of a bitch?"

"*I* didn't do that."

"Of course not," Ryan replied, his voice dripping disdain, "*you* wouldn't have the balls. But *you* gave her to Hasan, and that makes you just as responsible."

"All she had to do was tell me what she did with the ledger!" he argued. "That's *all!*"

Ryan planted his fists on his hips and dropped his chin to his chest for a moment, his lungs refusing to draw air. Cat was suffering because of an angry young woman and petty jealousy. It made him see red. He took several deep breaths, trying to get his anger under control. He had to give Doc time to work, so he resisted the primitive urge to storm the chopper and get his hands around Mitchell's neck.

"Problem with that, Mitchell...." He paused and lifted his head, meeting Mitchell's wild eyes, ". . . is Cate never had your fucking ledger. I'm assuming you're referring to the ledger Airman Avery stole from your desk?" His earpiece crackled.

"Ryan, it's Lee. Listen carefully...."

"Jessica?" Mitchell stared at him in disbelief. "She would never.... You're... you're lying."

Ryan shook his head. "No, I'm not." He crossed his arms over his chest. "She handed it over to us earlier today, and CIA code breakers have been going over it ever since. They asked me to give you a message." He paused and smiled. "Your assets have been frozen and will be seized, Ms. Emmerson, *all* of them including that fancy estate in Costa Rica. Forensic accountants are hard at work tracking down every dollar you spent out of those accounts." His smile widened. "You're officially broke, Mitchell. So, even if you make it across the border, you have nothing to grease any palms with. I doubt your *friends* are going to be very helpful if you can't reimburse them for their services." Ryan inclined his head. "The United States Government thanks you for your generous contribution to the Treasury."

Mitchell's face already looked pink bathed in the rosy glow from the flares, but Ryan saw his color deepen, his eyes taking on an enraged glint.

"You son of a bitch," Mitchell said under his breath. "You son of a bitch!"

Ryan's heart thundered in his chest as he watched everything unfold in slow motion. Mitchell took aim at the co-pilot's head at the same moment Doc's arm swung up in an arc. The corpsman jammed the scalpel deep into Mitchell's right thigh, then his arm fell to his side and he didn't move again. Mitchell screamed, inadvertently releasing the doctor as he reached for his leg. Blair jumped out of the helicopter and rolled out of the line of fire. The pistol went off, the round exiting the front canopy and smacking the ground not six feet from McCabe's feet. Ryan looked back at the chopper and another gunshot roared, but he knew immediately it wasn't from the pistol. Whatever weapon had just fired was a much larger caliber than the 9mm. He stared as a dark spot about the size of a nickel appeared on Mitchell's forehead above the bridge of his nose, and then Mitchell's brains and the back of his skull splattered across the bulkhead of the Blackhawk behind him. The man stood there for what seemed minutes, as if suspended by invisible wires, and then he fell, face-first, onto the floor of the helicopter. The gun skittered across the metal plates and landed in the dirt.

Ryan spun around, searching for the source of the shot as the Blackhawk's engines shut down. His eyes caught sight of movement on top of the garage and he shouldered his rifle, as did his fellow SEALs. He slid his finger onto the trigger and strained to see into the shadows. When Tripp appeared on the edge of the roof, the .416 in one hand, Ryan exhaled sharply and dropped his weapon.

"Game over," Tripp called. He hopped off the roof, straightened, shouldered the rifle, and walked quickly toward Ryan. "*Told* you he'd do something to warrant a bullet."

"I need some help here!"

It was Blair's voice. Tripp took a step toward the chopper. Knowing how close Tripp and Cat were Ryan grabbed his arm, worried how he would react when he finally got a glimpse.

"You don't want to do that." He met Tripp's incredulous gaze and shook his head. "Trust me, you really don't."

Tripp jerked out of his grasp, and Ryan sighed softly as he followed the taller man to the Blackhawk. McCabe and another SEAL were pulling Mitchell's body out of the cabin as the doctor hopped in and moved to check on the pilot. Tripp's face went white and he blinked slowly as he took in the extent of Cat's injuries.

"Captain?" Ryan called as he reached the chopper. "Sitrep."

"The co-pilot's wounded. It's not serious, but I don't think he'll be able to fly." There was a brief pause, and then a sigh. "Pilot's dead."

"Shit," Ryan said under his breath.

Blair appeared in the cabin and knelt at Doc's side. There was a dark, wet stain on the right front side of Massey's shirt, and he moaned softly. The doctor hooked his hands beneath the corpsman's arms and moved him so he lay alongside Cat, who was still unconscious. He examined the wound quickly and then started checking the younger man's vitals. He lifted his eyes to Ryan and gave him a grim smile. "It's a through and through, soft tissue mostly. He'll be fine."

Ryan heard the sound of running feet and turned as Bam-Bam and Tonto rushed up.

"Is everyone okay?" Bam-Bam asked, trying to look around Ryan. He caught sight of the blood and gray matter on the bulkhead and his eyes widened. "Who?"

Ryan nodded toward the rear of the chopper, where Mitchell's body had been covered with an emergency blanket. Bam-Bam's eyes widened in dismay.

"Relax, Bam," Ryan said. "It's Mitchell."

"Cat?"

Ryan looked at the doctor. Blair's expression was grim.

"We need to get her to Bagram," Blair said.

Ryan turned and stepped away a few paces. "Godfather...."

"Already done, Reaper," McCabe replied as he walked up. He looked at Bam-Bam. "I'm going to need your help, blastmaster, to clear a spot for the Chinook to land."

"Reaper, this is Lee."

Ryan watched as the doctor and corpsmen went to work on Cat and Doc. "Go ahead."

"Those trucks are 15 minutes out, Ryan."

He grimaced as the doctor swabbed an area on Cat's right side then made a small incision between two of her ribs. "Won't be enough time," Ryan replied, looking away. He'd watched field medics tend to wounded soldiers before, but watching the doctor work on Cat was almost more than he could stomach.

"I know," Lee replied. "Apaches are launching as we speak. Just wanted to give you a head's up so you're not surprised by the fireworks."

"Roger that."

"Um, Ryan?"

"Yeah?"

There was a brief silence. "Is Cat okay?"

"She's alive," he replied, his voice carefully neutral. "She's going to make it."

Another pause. "Are you saying that because it's true," Lee asked, "or because you *want* it to be true?"

Ryan swallowed the lump in his throat. "Yes." He heard Lee sigh heavily.

"Okay. Apaches are moving to intercept the trucks, and the Chinooks should be landing in five. We included a new set of pilots for the Blackhawk. The Sikorsky moves faster than the Chinook at top speed."

"Roger that, and thanks. Reaper out." Ryan looked at Tripp. The man hadn't moved, and Ryan saw the muscle twitching in his cheek. "C'mon, Ben. Let's give them room to work."

He walked Tripp over to the stairs of the main building, and sighed as Tripp eased down on the top step. Ryan knew Tripp was in shock, and wished he could commiserate. However, there were things that needed to be done first. He would commiserate later.

Ryan looked around, creating a mental checklist, and waved at Mack. Mack shouldered his rifle and jogged over.

"Yeah, Reaper?"

"Send a couple guys into the tunnels to retrieve the bodies, and then see if Bam-Bam needs any help." He scowled. "I want this place removed from the map, understand?"

Mack nodded once. "Absolutely." His expression softened. "You okay?"

"I'm fine."

Mack stared at him for a moment, then inclined his head and walked away.

"Fire in the hole!"

Ryan looked across the compound to the shed and watched as the wooden building blew apart into a million splinters. All that remained of the structure was the hole leading to the tunnels. Once the smoke cleared, the group of men disappeared through the narrow opening and a few moments later, a Chinook appeared over the rise and started its descent.

"Do you think she's going to make it?" Tripp asked in a low voice, almost as if he was afraid to speak the words.

Ryan glanced at him and eased down beside him on the step. "God, I hope so." He cleared his throat then asked, "Do you?"

"I don't know," Tripp replied. He pressed his fingers into his eyes for a moment then rose. "I don't know." Without another word, he walked across the compound and disappeared into the darkness.

The Chinook landed and a pair of men, the extra pilots no doubt, jumped out and made a beeline for the Blackhawk. He should've been relieved to see them. The end was in sight, but he was still pulled tighter than a high-powered crossbow. In this case *the end* might be just the beginning of a life he didn't want to imagine, a life without Cat. He squeezed his eyes shut for a few seconds and moments later the Blackhawk's engines ramped up. McCabe walked toward him and Ryan rose.

"Other Chinook's circling," McCabe said. "Once we get the wounded and the prisoners out of here, she'll pick you guys up." He glanced toward the Blackhawk as the engines whined. "Red's going to make it, Reaper. Just... hold onto that."

Ryan didn't reply. His eyes were on the smaller helicopter as Voodoo and Jigsaw, the two wounded SEALs, approached the Blackhawk. Jigsaw had been shot in the leg and Voodoo had taken a round in the arm. Voodoo paused before climbing into the aircraft, gave Ryan a solemn look, and then lifted a hand. Ryan nodded. About a minute later, the Sikorsky lifted into the air and turned south. Ryan watched until he could no longer see the lights. Once the cas-evac disappeared from sight, he looked at McCabe.

"Get the prisoners loaded so we can get the hell out of here." He glanced into the southeast, where the road from the compound met up with the main highway. "Those trucks should be making friends with some angry Injuns right about...."

As if to prove he had the gift of foresight, orange light burst upward into the night sky. The mountains were silhouetted by the fiery glow like an enormous campfire had exploded on the other side of the ridge. Then the *boom-boom-boom* traveled over the hills and into the valley. A few minutes later the Chinook's engines started to rev up and he watched it lift off, taking McCabe's team and the captured enemy combatants with it. McCabe gave him a wave from the ramp and Ryan lifted one hand in salute.

After the chopper disappeared from view, he and Mack started walking toward where the shed had been. Bam-Bam and Tonto were making final adjustments to the detonators they were using. They looked up as he approached.

"You guys seen Tripp?" Ryan asked.

Tonto frowned. "Wasn't he with you?"

"Until he walked off," Ryan answered. "The other Chinook should be here any minute. Once it lands we have to load up the salvaged equipment and the bodies, and then we're out of here."

Ryan heard the helicopter before he saw it, and as it appeared over the ridge Tripp appeared out of the darkness. His face was as blank as a freshly cleaned slate, and when he reached the group of men he looked at Bam-Bam.

"You ready to turn this little valley into the Grand Canyon, Bam?" Tripp asked.

"I'm always ready," Bam-Bam replied with a bleak smile. "Like Cat said, I really do enjoy keeping the geologists busy."

The men turned away as the Chinook touched down, filling the air with dust. One of the aircrew exited the aircraft and approached them.

"Lieutenant Heller?" he asked.

Ryan stepped forward. "Here, Captain."

The man smiled grimly. "I'll help you gents load up, and then we need to get the hell out of here."

"Why?" Ryan frowned. "What's going on?"

"Satellite picked up another convoy headed this way. Also, the Tajiks have scrambled fighters, so we had to pull the Apaches back. Command wants us home, ASAP, or we could have an international incident on our hands. We're awfully close to the border here, and the Tajiks aren't known for their understanding nature."

Ryan nodded. "Got it. Load up, everyone. It's time to get the hell out of Dodge."

After everything was safely and securely stowed, the team hopped in and the Chinook lifted off. The five men stood on the ramp, looking silently at the compound as they ascended.

"How far away did you say we had to be before you blew it, Bam-Bam?" Ryan asked.

After about half a minute, Bam-Bam gave him a solemn look and handed him the detonator. Ryan stared at it, then took it and faced out the back of the helicopter. Sliding his thumb to the button, he took a deep breath and pressed firmly. A few seconds later the garage and the main building exploded in a ball of sizzling flame and light, sparks shooting high into the air like fireworks. Then there was a rumbling he felt even over the vibrations from the chopper. He exhaled sharply as the ground of the compound itself started to undulate, like water after a pebble has broken the surface. Ripples moved outward from the tunnel entrance, and then the entire compound seemed to spring into the air, heaved upward by an unseen monster from below. Fire erupted from cracks in the hard, rocky ground and then engulfed the near acre where the compound had been with smoke, flame, and debris that mushroomed into the air. Ryan saw the shockwave as it raced over the earth and the Chinook dipped suddenly. It seemed hell itself spewed from beneath the old Soviet outpost, venting all of its brimstone and fury on the small, mountain valley.

Ryan whistled softly as boulders the size of trucks rained back to earth. "Patent that, brother," he advised as he handed the detonator back to Bam-Bam. "The military will pay you very well for destructive power like that, and you will never have to work another day in your life."

Bam-Bam frowned. "What would be the fun in *that?*"

Once the flames burned out and darkness reclaimed the valley, Ryan faced the others.

"All right, gentlemen. Take a seat. I don't know about you, but I'm ready to go home."

Chapter Twenty-Nine

Ryan burst into the medical center, Tripp and the rest of the guys on his heels. Ignoring the startled look from the woman at the reception desk, he stalked past her toward where he knew the operating rooms were. God help anyone who got in his way.

An armed security guard approached them as they approached the doors that read "Authorized Personnel Only." The name Perette was stitched over his pocket, and he held up a hand.

"I'm sorry, gentlemen, but you can't go back there."

Ryan frowned. "Get out of my way, Sergeant, or as God is my witness I will go *through* you."

The sergeant returned the frown and put a hand on his sidearm. "I'm sorry, Lieutenant, but I can't let you do that."

Ryan took a deep breath and fought to reign in his anxiety. The closer they'd gotten to Bagram, the tighter his chest had become. Now that the mission itself was over, all he had to focus on was Cat, and the thought of her sent his emotions seesawing wildly. On one hand, he was overjoyed they'd gotten her back alive. On the other hand, he was terrified he was going to lose her anyway.

"Sergeant," he began slowly, his teeth clenched, "my fiancée and several of my team members came in on a med-evac little more than an hour ago, and I need to know how she is... how *they* are." He met the sergeant's eyes and saw the man's expression soften.

"I don't know anything other than she's in surgery, sir," Perette said in a low voice.

"How do you know that?" Tripp asked, taking a step forward.

"It's been a quiet day. At least it had been until they brought *her* in. The rest of your team is still in the Emergency Department, but her...?" He sighed and let go of his weapon. "They took her straight in." Perette met Ryan's eyes and Ryan saw the sympathy in his gaze. "I'm sorry, Lieutenant. I don't know anything else, but if you and your friends will have a seat in the waiting room I'll see what I can find out."

"Thank you, Sergeant Perette." Ryan glanced at Tripp. "We'll be in the ER."

Perette nodded. "Roger that, sir. As soon as I know anything you'll be the first to hear."

Ryan nodded and he turned to Tripp. The two men exchanged a glance then started walking back the way they'd come. Mack, Tonto, and Bam-Bam followed a few paces behind.

"Fiancée, huh?" Tripp asked.

"If I'd said 'girlfriend' the guy wouldn't have given me the time of day."

Tripp shook his head. "You sure that's a word you want to be throwing around so casually?"

Ryan was quiet for several seconds, his heart fighting to beat against the barbed wire tightening around it. "There was nothing casual about it." He swallowed hard. "If I thought she'd say yes I'd have already asked her."

Tripp stopped in his tracks. "You serious? You've known her just over a week, Ryan."

Ryan kept walking. "I'd never joke about something like that." He glanced at Tripp over his shoulder. "And I feel like I've known her my entire life."

"Both hands, brother," Mack said softly. "Both hands."

***

Ryan stared at Digger and took several deep breaths. After checking on Voodoo, Jigsaw, and Doc and making sure they were all going to be fine, his mind had returned to obsessing about Cat. He tried to think about something else, *anything* else, but his brain was singularly focused and refused to be reset.

He made his way back to the waiting room, and was surprised to find it nearly full. The entire team was there, as was Commander Ferris, Heston, and a man who could only be Cat's brother. He wore desert digitals, and the patch on the front had the Force Recon insignia with his name and rank below it. Major Charles "Phoenix" Beckett. It didn't hurt that he had flaming hair like his sister and the same green eyes. As soon as Beckett looked at him Ryan nearly lost it. With a muttered

"Excuse me," he'd turned on his heel and walked quickly away. After wandering the halls for a few minutes and trying to get control of his emotions, he had found himself outside Digger's door.

It was late, nearly midnight. Ryan eased down onto the chair at Digger's bedside, orange light from the outside street lamps filtering through the one window. Leaning his elbows on his knees Ryan stared at the floor. Tears obscured his vision and he tried to blink them away, but more took their place. He pressed his thumb and index finger into his eyes and took a shaky breath.

"Hey, Reaper," Digger said softly. There was a soft whine as the head of the bed slowly rose. "What's going on, my man?"

Ryan ran a hand over his face, thankful that the lights were off. "Hey, Dig. I'm sorry. I didn't mean to wake you." His eyes had adjusted to the darkness, and he saw Digger frown.

"Don't give me that shit," Digger said flatly. "What's going on? And why are you here this time of night? Not that I mind, but if the nurses find you here we're both going to get in trouble."

It felt like a rock the size of his fist was lodged in his throat and he could barely breathe around the obstruction. Ryan squeezed his eyes shut briefly and rested his head in his hands. "It's Cate."

Digger's expression immediately changed, his eyes lighting up. "Hey, how's your girl?" he asked, smiling. "She comes by to see me every day, did you know that?"

"No," he ground out. "I didn't know that."

"I haven't seen her in a couple of days, I know she's probably busy, but before that...." He chuckled. "Even if it's only for a few minutes, she stops by, says hello, and asks me how I'm doing. On Tuesday, she snuck me a caramel macchiato from Green Beans. Mm, mm. I *love* those things."

The cold, pervasive despair in Ryan's chest swelled until he nearly choked on it. He bit back the sob trying to escape his throat, holding his breath as he fought to keep the emotions down. He couldn't stop the tears however. Digger flicked on a light, and when he saw Ryan's face his expression immediately sobered.

"What is it, bro?" Digger asked. His eyes narrowed. "Talk to me, Ryan. A mission go south or something? The boys okay?"

Ryan couldn't mentally reconcile the fact the mission had been successful, but Cat was still on an operating table fighting for her life.

That was *not* his definition of success. The images of her hanging from that hook were forever branded into his mind, and they flashed behind his eyelids like a gruesome home movie. His shoulders started to shake as the dam finally burst, and the anguish inside him escaped. He leaned over and laid his forehead on the edge of Digger's bed. When Digger's hand clamped down on his shoulder, he officially lost the battle.

"Whatever it is, Ryan," Digger said softly, "it's going to be okay. I'm here for you, brother, and I'll help you through it." He squeezed gently. "*Whatever* it is."

Ryan put a hand on Digger's arm and wept.

***

It was after one in the morning when Ryan left Digger's room and closed the door quietly behind him. He leaned against the jamb for a minute, then sighed and made his way back to the waiting room. Mack stood outside in the hall conversing with Tripp in hushed tones. The two men looked up as Ryan approached.

"Ryan," Mack said, walking toward him. "We were just going to look for you." His sharp gaze wandered over Ryan's face. "You okay?"

"I'm fine." He nodded. "I went to see Digger. Any news?"

"Perette said all he could find out was they were still working on her," Tripp replied with a scowl. "Seems like a lot of people are being really hush-hush about what's going on with Cat, and it's starting to piss me off."

Ryan rubbed his brow. "Nothing we can do about it. Might as well take a seat and wait it out."

He walked into the waiting room and his eyes were immediately drawn to Charles Beckett who looked so much like his sister it hurt. The man stood up and looked at him. The two stared at each other for a moment then Beckett walked over and extended his hand.

"Lieutenant," he said. "I've seen your picture, but it's nice to meet you in person. Cat's told me a lot about you."

Ryan shook the man's hand. "Likewise, sir."

"Please, call me Charlie."

"Only if you call me Ryan."

Charlie smiled. "Deal." His hand dropped back to his side and his smile faltered. "They tell me you're the one who found her." When Ryan nodded, Charlie continued. "Um... how bad?"

Ryan met the man's anxious gaze then dropped his chin. "Bad."

"Is that....." Charlie's voice died and he plucked at the sleeve of Ryan's uniform. "Is that... blood?"

Ryan looked down at his sleeve and blanched. How had he not noticed that? The right sleeve of his uniform blouse was nearly black from the wrist to the middle of his upper arm, and his chest was similarly colored. He gulped and took a deep breath. "Yeah."

"I don't care what time it is! I want to speak to someone in charge! Now get out of my way and get someone in here who can answer my questions!" The voice carrying through the halls had an edge and steel that matched Commander Ferris's. Ryan's head snapped around and he heard necks cracking all through the waiting room as people looked toward the sound.

"Shit," Tripp said. "Just when I thought the day couldn't get any worse." He stalked to the windows, turning his back to the room.

When Charlie groaned, Ryan glanced at him. "You know that person?"

Charlie only nodded and walked past him as an older gentleman with rigid posture, sharply creased slacks, and perfectly groomed hair appeared in the doorway. His hair was silver, and he was fit and still trim even though he had to be at least sixty. Somehow Ryan knew this was Colonel Frank Beckett, Cat's father.

"Charlie," the man said, as if he was addressing a platoon of troops up for inspection instead of his son. "Who is in charge here?"

"That would be me," Commander Ferris said, approaching with one hand extended. The men shook hands. "I'm Commander Doug Ferris. You must be Colonel Beckett."

Heston strode forward and shook Beckett's hand as well. "Good to see you, Frank. It's been too long."

Beckett ignored the remark, fixing Heston with a sharp stare. "Where is my daughter, Mike?"

Once a Marine, always a Marine, Ryan thought. Colonel Beckett had the same air as if he was still an active-duty Marine Corp officer with all the power and influence that came with his rank. Ryan crossed his arms over his chest and watched the three men, Charlie standing silently at his side.

"She's still in surgery," Heston replied. "There's been no word yet."

"Get me whoever's in charge of this hospital and I'll *get* word," Beckett said flatly.

The Commander frowned. "Unless you plan to strong-arm an emergency room doctor, you won't get any farther than I did." Commander Ferris paused and added, "*Sir.*"

Beckett colored slightly, but other than that he looked completely unflappable. "The hell I won't, Commander. Show me where—"

"Sir," Ferris interrupted, "last I checked you are no longer active-duty, and this is not D.C. With all due respect, Colonel, I think you should take a seat. The hospital personnel are busy tending to your daughter, and once she is stable I am sure their next stop will be here. Unless, of course, you'd like me to provide you with an escort to the BOQ so you can settle into your quarters... *sir.*"

Ryan fought the smile as Beckett and Ferris stared at each other. Neither seemed the least bit intimidated, but Commander Ferris had rank and active-duty status on his side.

"Dad," Charlie said as he stepped forward and put a hand on his father's arm. "Come on. Let's sit down."

Beckett stared at Commander Ferris for another second or two, then nodded crisply and walked to a row of padded chairs against the far wall. Charlie shot Ryan and the Commander an apologetic glance before turning to his father. Ryan watched them for a moment then approached Commander Ferris and Heston.

"That was... *interesting,*" Ryan observed quietly.

"No." Heston sighed. "That was Colonel Franklin "Rampage" Beckett. I haven't seen him in several years, but apparently age and retirement haven't softened him at all."

"Well-deserved moniker," Commander Ferris said. "I'm surprised he didn't demand an audience with General Mason."

Heston lifted one brow. "Had you shown even the *slightest* weakness, Commander, he would have. Frank is like a shark. He can smell blood in the water a *mile* away." He glanced at the two Beckett men then chuckled. "I'd better go soothe some ruffled feathers. This may not be D.C., but all it will take is one phone call." He took a step, then paused and looked at Ryan, his expression grave. "Excellent work out there, Lieutenant. I'm sorry for doubting you, but you proved me wrong, young man. You did yourself and your unit proud." He clapped Ryan on the shoulder then walked slowly toward the Beckett men.

"I'll second that, Lieutenant," Commander Ferris said. He glanced around the full waiting room then met Ryan's eyes. "I have an idea how difficult this mission was for you, son, but you performed like you always do. McCabe said you were rock solid from start to finish."

Ryan frowned. "Was he watching me?"

"They *all* were," Commander Ferris replied, "but not because I asked them to. Your relationship with Miss Beckett is no secret, Ryan, and I can't even imagine what you went through. Point is... you did your job regardless." He glanced at McCabe. "Godfather's exact words were, 'I don't know how he did it, sir. I don't think I could have done it if I was him.'"

Ryan nodded and looked at the floor. "Getting her out was easy, sir. It's *this* part that sucks."

Ferris sighed. "Might as well take a seat, Reaper. We're probably going to be here for a while."

He nodded and found a seat between Mack and Tripp. The three men exchanged glances then settled in for the long haul. Several hours passed, but none of them spoke, each lost in their own thoughts.

"Lieutenant Heller? Lieutenant Ryan Heller?"

His heart jumped and he rose in one fluid motion. A woman in her forties dressed in scrubs stood there, looking around the room. He took a step toward her. "I'm Lieutenant Heller."

She looked at him for a moment, her expression unreadable. "I'm Doctor Rhoades. Come with me, please."

"Excuse me, Doctor," Beckett said, rising. "I'd like a word."

The woman's face never changed. "I'm sorry sir, but I need a word with the Lieutenant. If you'll wait here, someone will be along shortly to brief all of you."

She glanced at Ryan and inclined her head toward the door. Ryan nodded and followed as she walked away. Once they were in the hallway, he fell into step beside her.

"What's this about, Doctor?" he asked, almost dreading the answer.

"Miss Beckett is out of surgery," Rhoades replied. "And she's asking for you."

Ryan let out the breath he'd been holding and felt tears sting. Blinking rapidly, he sent a silent prayer of thanks heavenward.

"She's in critical condition," Rhoades continued, "but she's stable for now. As soon as she woke up in recovery your name was the one thing she kept saying." The woman looked at him out of the corner of her eye. "I hear you're the one who got her out."

"It was a team effort, but yes, ma'am," Ryan replied.

She paused at the very door he'd been turned away from earlier. "And just in time."

He rubbed his eyes. "How... how bad is she?"

Rhoades sighed softly and pushed through the door. "Whoever worked her over really put some effort into it." She shook her head. "She has eight broken fingers, and because of the abnormal swelling at the joints I believe they were dislocated, relocated, and *then* broken. Ten missing fingernails, four broken ribs, bruised kidneys, broken jaw, broken cheekbones, both orbital sockets fractured, two missing molars, a concussion, punctured lung, ruptured spleen, and the various cuts, abrasions, and bruises that go along with having the hell beaten out of you." She stopped walking and faced Ryan. "Then there are the electrical burns and the lacerations on her back, which will require a plastic surgeon to repair." She scowled and started walking again. "Tell me you guys got the bastard who did this to her."

"I put a bullet in his brain myself," Ryan said in a low, voice. His insides were vibrating with anger, his hands clenching and unclenching at his sides as they continued down the hall.

"Good." Rhoades stopped outside a door. She met Ryan's gaze and he saw the sympathy there. "If it's any consolation, Lieutenant, I think she's going to make it." She turned the knob and opened the door a few inches. "She's right inside, but her jaw is wired shut and she's still groggy from anesthesia so I wouldn't expect much. We'll have a private room ready for her in a few minutes."

"Will she have to be transferred?" Ryan asked.

The doctor nodded. "Yes, once she's stable enough to travel, which will be several days. She'll be flown to Ramstein but eventually she'll be sent stateside, probably to Bethesda for final recovery and rehabilitation."

"Um, was she... sexually...?"

"No," Rhoades answered. "There *was* some bruising on her breasts, looked like fingerprints so someone might have tried. Thankfully, there's no indication they succeeded."

Ryan sighed as relief washed over him. After a moment, he held out his hand. "Thank you, Doctor. Will you send someone to brief everyone else, please?"

Rhoades smiled and shook his hand firmly. "Of course. I'll do it myself." She took a step then paused. "I'm guessing the gentleman with the silver hair and commanding tone is Miss Beckett's father?"

"You guess correctly," Ryan replied. "I think he's forgotten he retired from the Marine Corps."

"Great." She shook her head and started walking. "I'll see you in a bit, Lieutenant. Oh." She paused, turned to him, and reached into her pocket. "We found this on Miss Beckett when she came in. I thought you'd want to have it."

Rhoades held out a creased, rumpled piece of paper. Ryan took it from her, and his heart thumped when he realized it was a photograph. He opened it and looked at the image of the two of them. Tears stung his eyes when he saw the bloody lip prints. He refolded it. "Thank you."

"You're welcome." Rhoades put a hand on his arm for a moment then walked away. When the sound of her footsteps disappeared, he glanced at the photo again before slipping it into a pocket on his uniform.

Ryan took a deep breath and faced the door. Slowly, he pushed it open and stepped into the room. It was roughly 30 feet square, the walls lined with shelves and various pieces of medical equipment. Dim light came from a single fluorescent lamp on the far wall that cast a pale rectangle on the floor. He walked up to the end of the only bed and waited for his eyes to adjust. He didn't realize he'd been holding his breath until his lungs started to burn.

Exhaling slowly, he watched her sleep, and he couldn't decide if she looked worse or better than when he'd found her. What wasn't covered with bandages was purple, swollen, or stitched. Moving to her left side he pulled up a nearby metal chair and sat down. Rage and sorrow welled inside him and he wished Hasan was still alive so he could kill him again.

He reached out and slipped his fingers beneath her splinted hand, his thumb rubbing softly back and forth. She stirred and he leaned forward. After a moment, her left eye fluttered open and she looked around, blinking slowly. When she saw him, a faint smile curved her mouth.

"Ryan."

Her voice was barely above a whisper, but hearing it sent relief rushing through him. He smiled. "Hey, babe."

"I thought...." Her voice trailed off and he saw the convulsive swallow. "I thought I was... imagining you."

He shook his head. "Nope. You didn't imagine anything."

The machine at her side beeped and he glanced at it as it administered another dose of morphine.

"Thank everyone... for me... and... thank you," she said.

"For what?"

"For saving me." Her eyes closed briefly. "I guess this... means... we're even now."

He hung his head as a wave of guilt crashed over him, even though he knew it was ridiculous. He had nothing to feel guilty about, but logic didn't figure into his emotional process at the moment. Seeing her battered, bruised face, the IVs, the ligature marks around her wrists, and her bandaged, splinted fingers made him sick to his stomach. He felt responsible, and as if he'd failed her somehow.

"*Don't.*"

He looked up at her, surprised by the vehemence behind that one word. As he watched, the morphine took effect and her eyelids drooped. She struggled to open her eyes, and when she finally did the tiger's stare was clear.

"This is *not* your fault," she said. "This... this is *my* fault."

"Cate...."

"I didn't expect... to make it out." Her expression softened and he saw the shine of unshed tears in her eyes. "The one thing I wanted... wanted more than... *anything*... was to see... your face again...." Her eyes closed and the tears slid down her cheeks. "I... love you...."

Ryan gulped and closed his eyes against the tears forming there. "I love you, too, babe."

There was a soft knock and a moment later Dr. Rhoades poked her head in. She looked at Cat first, then met his gaze and smiled. "You okay, Lieutenant?"

He nodded.

"We have a room ready for her." The doctor rested a hand on his shoulder. "Room 157. Give us a few minutes to get her settled, and then you can join her there."

"Thanks." He stood.

"Staff Sergeant Perette tells me Miss Beckett is your fiancée."

He should have denied it, he should have set the record straight, but he didn't. He nodded once and walked through the door.

Rhoades sighed and shook her head. "That must have been... *awful*." When he didn't reply, she gave him a sympathetic look. "I'll have them move a convertible chair into her room. It lies flat so you can sleep in the room with her."

His guts were cinched in a vise and he could barely draw breath. Between the gratitude he felt towards the doctors who had saved her life, the uncertainty gnawing at him because he could still lose her, the anguish that threatened to drown him when he looked at Cat's battered face, and the lie that was more truth than not, it was all he could do to whisper, "Thanks."

"You're more than welcome," Dr. Rhoades replied.

When he entered the waiting room five minutes later everyone rose and looked at him expectantly.

Tripp left his position at the window. "Well?"

"The doctor didn't brief you?"

Tripp approached him. "I want to hear it from you. Did you talk to her?"

"Briefly." He sighed and rubbed the back of his neck. "She's sedated, but she said to tell all of you thanks. They're moving her to a private room now."

"I want to see her."

It was Colonel Beckett's voice. Ryan met the man's gaze and was surprised at what he saw there. Instead of concern or fear the older man's eyes glittered with anger. Beckett looked at him as if he was royalty gazing on a peasant, with arrogance and barely concealed disdain. Ryan bristled.

"The doctor said to give them a few minutes," he said, "and she's asleep."

"You *will* take me to her," Beckett said flatly.

Ryan frowned and took a step toward the man. "No, *sir*, I *won't*."

"I'm her father."

"And I'm the man who's going to marry her, if she'll have me." Ryan fisted his hands. "And before you ask, I'm fully aware of what she does and I'm not the least bit scared of her." Beckett looked surprised and Charlie's brows drew together. Obviously, Cat's brother had not been privy to the conversations between his sister and their father. Ryan took a breath and reigned in his anger. "I mean no disrespect, Colonel, but your daughter has been through absolute hell, and what she needs right now is rest. Perhaps you and Charlie should head to the BOQ and get settled in, come back in the morning."

Beckett bristled. "I suppose *you're* going stay with her?"

"I am. She *asked* for me."

Charlie gave him an apologetic look and put a hand on his father's shoulder. "Come on, Dad, let's head out. It's late and Cat needs to rest."

Beckett looked at his son, incredulous, and then turned that sharp gaze on Ryan. "I just flew thousands of miles to see my only daughter," he said. "I want to see her, *now*, Lieutenant."

Before Ryan could respond Charlie did, and Ryan realized Cat had inherited her tiger-like stare from her brother.

"It's not about you and what you want," Charlie growled, scowling, "it's about *her*. We'll come back in the morning when there's a chance she'll actually be awake and able to talk, but right now, we're *leaving*."

Heston stepped forward. "I have a car outside, Frank. I'll drive you and Charlie over."

Beckett looked at Ryan mutinously for a moment, then nodded and followed Heston. Charlie hung back a bit. When his father had left the waiting room, he approached Ryan.

"Sorry about that," he said. "Colonel Frank Beckett is accustomed to getting his way."

Ryan chuckled. "Runs in the family apparently."

Charlie laughed softly and nodded. "Yes, but at least *she* doesn't expect people to bow and scrape." He extended his hand and Ryan grasped his fingers firmly. Charlie gave him a solemn look. "Thank you for saving her." He turned and looked at each man in turn. "Thank all of you." He shook each man's hand, repeated his thanks, and then quickly left the waiting room.

"Nicely handled, Ryan," Commander Ferris said. "I guess you listened when Heston talked about not showing weakness in front of the Colonel."

"Not really, sir." Ryan shrugged. "He just pissed me off."

Ferris laughed. "That's the Ryan I know and trust." The older man put a hand on his shoulder. "The doctor said Miss Beckett will be here for the next few days, so you are officially off-duty until she's transferred."

Ryan gaped at him. "Sir, that's not necessary."

"I know," Commander Ferris replied. "But, I know how I'd feel if my wife...." His voice trailed off and he took a deep breath. "I know how I'd feel if I were you."

"Sir...."

"That's an *order*, Lieutenant."

"And if a mission comes up?" Ryan asked.

Commander Ferris crossed his arms over his chest. "I *do* have more than one SEAL team to choose from, son. You and your men have been *very* busy the past week, so it's time for all of you to stand down for a few days."

"Yes!" Grady said. When he saw he had the attention of both men, he colored and added, "Sorry, sir, Reaper."

Commander Ferris shook his head and chuckled. "All right, gentlemen. It's been a very eventful day for all of you. Head back to the compound and get some rest. You can visit Miss Beckett tomorrow, or later today actually." He gave Ryan a pointed look. "I mean it, Lieutenant. I don't want to see you at the compound unless you're sleeping, showering, or changing clothes. We clear?"

"Crystal, sir."

Mack walked up and smiled. "I'll run and get you a change of clothes and your shaving kit," he said. "Wouldn't want Red waking up in the morning to your dirty mug."

"Thanks, bro," Ryan replied. "For everything."

"You bet."

Mack walked away and Ryan stood there as the rest of the guys filed out, each pausing to clap him on the shoulder or say a few words as they passed. Soon, the only other people left in the room were Tripp, Tonto, Bam-Bam, and Lee. Ryan looked at the four men who were seated on the same couches he and his team had occupied the first night he'd met Cat. All that was missing was the beer, the Coke, the pizza, and her. He shook off the memory and approached them.

"Hey, guys. You all should probably head back to your quarters, too. They've got her on a morphine drip, so she'll probably be out the rest of the night."

"I want to see her," Tripp said.

"Me, too," Lee said.

Ryan looked at Tonto and Bam-Bam. "You guys, too?"

"Absolutely," they said in unison.

"Once we see her, we'll head out," Tripp said.

"Okay, gentlemen." Ryan started walking for the door and gestured for them to follow. "Let's go."

Minutes later all five men stood in Cat's room in a half circle around the end of her bed. The room was dark, but there was enough outside light coming through the window that they could see her. Bam-Bam seemed the most upset and left first, swiping at his eyes as he did so. Tonto rested a hand on her arm for a moment, said something under his breath Ryan didn't understand, and then exited silently. Lee looked at her in disbelief and Tripp was as expressionless as ever.

"Jesus," Lee whispered. "It doesn't even *look* like her." He moved to her side, gently took her splinted fingers in his, and held her hand for a few moments. He glanced at Tripp then Ryan, then released her and stepped into the hall.

Ryan watched as Tripp stared at her and that crack in his veneer widened a little. A muscle twitched in his cheek, and his eyes were unnaturally bright. He took a deep breath and exhaled slowly. After several minutes of silent contemplation, he rested a hand on the top of her head, leaned over, and brushed his lips over her brow.

"I'll be back in a few hours, sweetheart," he whispered. "Don't go anywhere." He kissed her forehead again, then straightened and put his poker face back on. He met Ryan's gaze. "Take care of her until I get back."

Ryan nodded. "Will do, big man. See you soon."

Tripp looked at her again then left the room without a word.

Chapter Thirty

"Get out."

Ryan came awake with a start and bolted upright in the chair. Sunlight streamed through the windows and he blinked against the glare, one hand moving to shield his eyes.

"Cat, what's wrong?"

It was Charlie's voice, and a split second after he spoke Ryan realized Cat's brother was standing on the other side of her bed. Ryan looked at her, but she wasn't looking at Charlie. She was struggling to shout despite the fact her jaw was wired shut, her brow furrowed in pain and her cheeks flaming. Following the direction of her gaze, Ryan's eyes came to rest on Colonel Beckett who stood at the end of the bed.

"I said... *get out.*"

Beckett looked surprised. "Catharine...."

"*Don't* call me that!"

Charlie looked completely confused. "Cat. *What* is wrong?"

Ryan rose, pushed the convertible chair back, and rested a hand gently on her arm. Her gaze never wavered. Her chin started to tremble and anger warmed his chest when a single tear trailed down her swollen, bruised cheek.

"You want to tell him, Dad?" she asked. "Or should I?"

Charlie's brows drew together. "Tell me what?"

Beckett's face was stony. "I don't know what you're talking about."

"Really? Because before he let Tariq Hasan torture me and then beat me nearly to death Peter told me all about... about the *arrangement* the two of you had." She took a hitching breath and paused, her brow furrowed in pain.

"Mitchell?" Charlie's eyes widened and he turned to his father. "What is she talking about?"

She paled and closed her eyes for a minute before focusing a blistering gaze on her father. "Ever since Baghdad, you have... called in favors and... pulled strings and... *manipulated* people to keep Peter stuck to my side like a... a *leech*." More tears fell. "Why, Dad? Afraid your cronies on the Hill might find out... your only daughter is a better shot than you... that I have more... confirmed kills than you do?"

Beckett frowned. "Don't be ridiculous."

"Then *why?*" She stared at her father. "You... you *knew* how much I despised him, how much he... *hurt* me...." She paused, her chin dropping to her chest as one hand moved to her side.

"What the *hell* is she talking about?" Charlie demanded from between clenched teeth, standing toe to toe with his father.

Ryan brushed the hair from Cat's brow then looked at Colonel Beckett. At last there was a shadow of emotion on the older man's face. If Ryan hadn't been so angry, he could have sympathized with the regret and pain that shone in Beckett's eyes. But, once again, he was resisting the primal urge to strangle someone. A soft beeping drew his eyes and he glanced at the monitor to Cat's left, alarm racing through him when he saw her blood pressure rising.

"I... I wanted someone to... look after her," Beckett finally said. He grasped the rail at the foot of the bed. "There's so much you don't know, Charlie."

"Like what?" Charlie demanded. "What could I *possibly not* know that would make you think Peter Mitchell, the man who has *stalked* and *harassed* her for five years, was the right person to look after her?"

"I wanted to protect her!" Beckett exclaimed.

"*Protect* me?" Cat's tear-filled gaze was incredulous. "Out of all the people on the planet, he was the one I needed protecting *from!*" A whimper of pain escaped her, and small beads of sweat broke out on her brow. "*He* did this to me, Dad, and you... you *handed* me to him, like a lamb on a platter!"

The machine started to beep again, faster and louder, and Ryan exhaled sharply when Cat's eyes rolled back in her head and her body went stiff. He immediately ran to the door, jerked it open, and raced into the hall.

"Doc!" he shouted.

Apparently, the machine was hooked up to a nurse's station, because Dr. Rhoades and several nurses were already running toward him.

"What happened?" she asked as she raced past him.

"I think she's seizing," Ryan replied, following her into the room.

Rhoades did a cursory examination. "All right, everybody out." When nobody moved, she gave each man a pointed look. "Now!" Rhoades went to work, speaking to the nurse at her elbow. "I need 3 milligrams of Ativan...."

Ryan stood in the middle of the hall, his hands on his head as the door closed behind them. Beckett walked down the hall a few paces, leaned one shoulder into the wall, and covered his face with his hands. Charlie walked the opposite direction, casting furtive, angry glances at his father every few seconds. Ryan could almost smell the pending explosion. He didn't have to wait long.

Charlie strode to his father, spun him, and pushed him against the wall, his eyes blazing. "What the *hell* were you thinking?" His brows drew together. He looked at his father as if seeing him for the first time, and he obviously didn't like what he saw. "Cat told me how Mitchell assaulted her, and then spent less than 24 hours in the brig. That was *your* doing, wasn't it? You're the one who got him out!" Charlie backed up, his eyes wide. "If you had left him where he was... *none* of this would have happened."

"I didn't know!"

"*Bullshit!*" Charlie clenched his jaw. "I remember you sitting at the same dinner table as me while she talked about never being able to get away from that guy." He looked at Beckett in disbelief. "You *knew* what he was doing to her; you *knew* she wanted to get away from him. For *five years*, you knew. All that time, Dad... and still you let it continue. You *helped* him do this."

Beckett's stony expression was gone. Tears filled the older man's eyes, and he looked genuinely distraught. "I wanted someone close to keep an eye on her, to keep her safe and watch her back. He said he loved her, so I thought...." He paused and pressed his thumb and forefinger into his eyes. "All I wanted was for her to be safe. I'm her father and...."

"Oh, *now* you want to be her father?" Charlie sneered. "After Mom died you didn't slow down for *one second* on your meteoric rise through the Corps. You left it up to me and Matt to take care of her." He got in his father's face. "I put off OCS for *two years* until Matt was old enough to look after her, and then *he* put OCS off for two years until Aunt Bethany moved in. Where the *hell* were you?"

Beckett covered his face with his hands. "I'm sorry," he whispered, his voice thick with emotion. "I'm so sorry. God forgive me."

"God will," Charlie said flatly, "and Cat might." He backed up a step and looked his father up and down. "I don't know if I can."

Turning on his heel Charlie stormed down the hall, nurses and orderlies looking after him in silent question. Beckett watched him go then shuffled slowly toward the end of the hall, weeping softly. Taking a long, deep breath, Ryan leaned against the wall and closed his eyes.

He had no idea how long he stood there before Dr. Rhoades left the room and approached him, her expression solemn. Ryan straightened.

"Is she okay?" he asked, his stomach lurching.

"She's stable," Rhoades replied, pulling the cap off her head, "but her pressure was so high she almost had a stroke. Want to tell me what happened in there?"

Ryan rubbed his forehead. "It's... complicated."

"So, simplify it for me, or I'm going to have to restrict her visitors." She studied his face. "Now, I *know* she wants to see you, so which of the other two do I have to bar from her room?"

"My father," Charlie said.

Ryan and Dr. Rhoades looked at him as he stood a few feet away.

He sighed. "I have to return to base tomorrow morning anyway, so I'll be gone."

"You're not staying?" Ryan asked.

Charlie shook his head. "My commanding officer isn't as understanding as yours, Ryan." He gave Ryan a small smile. "But knowing you'll be here makes me feel a little less guilty."

"Okay, then," Dr. Rhoades said. "No more excitement for Miss Beckett, are we clear?"

"Yes, ma'am," Ryan said. "Can I...?"

Rhoades smiled. "Go on, Lieutenant. She's probably asleep, but I'm sure she'll be happy to see you when she does wake up." She glanced at Charlie. "You too, Major. Just... *no* yelling."

Charlie nodded. "Of course, ma'am."

Ryan walked toward the door, stopping when Charlie grabbed his arm. When he saw Charlie's expression, he turned. "What is it?"

Charlie looked at him for a moment, obviously uncertain. Finally, he hung his head and took a breath. "What... what was she talking about in there?" He lifted his eyes to Ryan's. "Better shot, confirmed kills? Tell me you know what she meant."

Ryan rubbed his jaw, unsure how to respond. "I do."

The anguish was clear in Charlie's eyes. "Tell me it's not what I think it is."

"I can't say anything, Charlie." He gave Cat's sibling an apologetic look. "I'm sorry, brother."

"That's okay, Lieutenant," a familiar voice said from behind them. "I can answer your questions, Charlie." Heston smiled grimly when they faced him. "I ran into your father in the waiting room. It seems there have been some fireworks this morning."

"That's an understatement," Charlie said dryly.

"Well, why don't we head to the chow hall for some breakfast and full disclosure?"

"As long as it's just the two of us," Charlie replied. "I can't even *look* at my Dad right now."

"Not a problem," Heston said. "Your dad was pretty upset, so I had my driver take him back to his quarters. It'll be just you and me." He glanced at Ryan. "We'll be back in a while, Lieutenant. Keep her company for us."

"I will," Ryan replied with a nod. "See you soon."

***

Cat yawned as cobwebs of sleep gently fell away. She kept her eyes closed and did a body check, like she'd done for the past two days. From the waist down things were great, but from the waist up... well, she wasn't quite as sore as yesterday, but it seemed like everything hurt when she moved. The upside was that things could only get better from here. Taking a deep, slow breath, she opened her eyes.

The first thing she saw was Ryan. He sat in the same chair he'd used ever since she'd arrived at the base hospital three days ago. His head lay on the edge of her bed, his face turned toward her, and he was fast asleep. He had one hand on her arm, the other on her leg, and she smiled when he stirred. She reached out to touch his hair, frowning and pulling back at the sight of her splinted fingers. There would be no gentle touch today, or tomorrow, or at any time in the next few weeks. With a small sigh, she laid her hand over his.

God, she loved looking at him. Waking up to his face the past couple of days had been the best part of her morning. "I could get used to that," she whispered, blinking back tears. As she continued to watch him sleep her heart swelled until she thought it would explode. She loved him so much, and that made her decision to break it off even more painful.

She remembered her brothers putting their lives on hold to take care of her after her mother's death. Charlie had almost lost his commission and his career, and Matt had had to give up his dream of being a military pilot to keep his commission. Her heart twisted at the memory. Her brothers had never once made her feel guilty or as if she was a burden, but even as a young girl the regret had weighed on her. None save her father had had a choice. Now she stood at that crossroads and *she had* a choice. No matter how painful it was she had to put Ryan's interests first. Given what she was facing over the coming months, multiple surgeries, rehabilitation, and her eventual reassignment to who knew where, she couldn't, in good conscience, tie him down. She couldn't ask him to wait for her when she had no idea how long it would be until they saw each other again, *if* they saw each other again. For his sake, she had to let him go. Cat picked up the device connected to the morphine dispenser at her side and pushed the button. Within moments she felt the narcotic work its magic.

"I love you, Ryan." She blinked and a single tear trailed down her cheek. "I will *always* love you, no matter what."

***

There was a light tap on the door and Ryan looked up from his book. He glanced at Cat, who was sleeping, then marked his page and rose. As he did, the door slowly and silently swung inward, and he blinked when he met Yasmeen Hasan's dark eyes. He walked toward her as she entered the room followed by Michael Heston and a woman he didn't know.

"Yasmeen," he said. "Asulam Alaykum."

"Alaykum Asulam, Ryan," Yasmeen said in her soft, lilting voice. A frown furrowed her brow. "Caterina?"

"Oh." Ryan shook himself, smiled, and gestured toward the bed. "She's sleeping but come on in. I know she'll be overjoyed to see you."

Yasmeen listened to the stranger as she translated then smiled, walked past him, and stood at the end of the gurney. She gasped softly and he saw the sheen of tears in her eyes as she covered her mouth with one hand. Ryan moved to Heston's side and looked at him in silent question.

"She became concerned when Miss Beckett missed several of her daily visits," Heston explained in a low voice. "When I said she was in the hospital, Mrs. Hasan insisted on seeing her."

Ryan glanced at the stranger. She was tall, a couple inches shorter than Cat he guessed, and thin with fair skin, dark hair, and pale blue eyes. "And the translator?" he asked.

"Name is Wells. Brought her up from Kabul yesterday. She's on loan from MI5."

Ryan nodded and moved back to Yasmeen's side. The woman blinked and two tears slid down her dusky cheeks. When she spoke, her voice was barely more than a whisper and Ryan listened as the interpreter translated.

"Mr. Heston told me my husband did this to her."

Ryan was momentarily taken aback and glanced at Heston. "Yes," he said. "He did."

Her brows drew together. "I knew my husband was a monster, but I did not realize he was capable of... *this*." She wiped her cheeks. "Mr. Heston also said you were the one who rescued her."

"Yes."

A slight smile curved her mouth. "It is fitting." She sniffed softly and more tears fell. "Did you kill him?" When he didn't immediately reply, Yasmeen looked at him. "Did you kill my husband?"

Ryan looked at Heston and the man shrugged. Taking a deep breath, Ryan squared his shoulders and faced the woman. "Yes." She didn't reply, her eyes fixed on Cat, and he hung his head. "Yasmeen, I'm sorry."

"No." The woman shook her head as she turned and took his hands in hers. "*No*. Do *not* apologize. He deserved to die and I am glad it was you. He hurt the woman you love. It is right you avenged her." She gave him a sad smile and pressed a hand to his cheek. "You are an honorable man, Ryan. I wish you and Caterina much happiness."

Ryan heard Cat stir and turned as she opened her eyes. He moved to her side and sat down, gently taking her hand. She blinked slowly several times then gave him a sleepy smile.

"You don't have to live here with me," she said, "but I do enjoy seeing your face every time I wake up."

"I'm glad to be of service," he replied with a quick grin. "You have a visitor." He nodded toward the end of the bed.

Cat's eyes widened and she smiled. "Yasmeen."

"Caterina." Yasmeen's eyes filled with tears. "I... I am so sorry...." She took a hitching breath and covered her face with her hands.

Cat met his gaze. "Could you give us a minute?"

"Of course." He leaned over and kissed her cheek. "I'll go get something to drink. Want anything?" He thought he saw something in her eyes, a shadow of something he couldn't immediately identify, but it was gone so quickly he was sure he had imagined it.

"I'm good," she replied. "Thanks."

"You bet." He rose and turned to Heston. "Shall we?"

Heston nodded then looked at the translator. "They won't need your services," he said with a small smile. "I'd appreciate it if you'd stick around though, in case I do."

Wells nodded. "Of course, Mr. Heston. I shall be in the waiting room if you have need of me."

The two men followed her into the hall and watched as she walked away.

"Where are the girls?" Ryan asked absently as he started walking toward the cafeteria.

Heston fell into step beside him. "At the detention facility," he said. "Yasmeen wanted to bring them, but I told her I didn't think they should see Miss Beckett yet."

"Yeah." Ryan stuffed his hands in his pockets. "Probably not a good idea."

They walked in silence until they reached the cafeteria.

"They've decided not to leave," Heston said as they approached the coffee machine. "With Hasan dead, the major threat to their lives is gone. Mrs. Hasan decided she'd rather return to her family than try to start a new life in the US."

Ryan opened a nearby cooler, grabbed a bottle of water, and tossed a few dollars to the cashier. "I can understand that, but they *could* still be in danger here. Terrorists have long memories and aren't known for their forgiving natures."

"I've informed her of the risks," Heston said as he added cream and sugar to his cup. "However, chatter is already circulating that the SEALs and the CIA were responsible for the death of Hasan and the destruction of their outpost. I doubt AQ or the Taliban will waste valuable time and resources on a low-value-target like Yasmeen Hasan when there are so many servicemen and women in country they can vent their rage on."

Ryan snorted derisively. "*That's* reassuring." He walked over to a table and sat down in one of the metal chairs.

Heston chuckled. He sipped his coffee and looked at Ryan over the rim of the cup. "Have you decided what *you're* going to do?"

Ryan lifted one brow. "I don't make those decisions, or aren't you familiar with how the military works?"

"I meant about you and Miss Beckett."

That surprised him, and it took him several seconds to find his voice. "Um, haven't really thought that far," Ryan replied. "Cate and I decided to take our relationship one day at a time, so that's what we're doing." He frowned. "Why? Do you know something I don't?"

Heston shook his head. "No, but she's flying to Germany at 0600 tomorrow. You still have a couple months on your tour here. By then she'll be stateside, maybe even back to work."

Ryan felt a dark cloud position itself directly over his head and a chill slithered down his spine. "I know." He took a swig of water. "Why are you so interested?"

The older man shrugged. "I don't know you very well, but what I do know I like." Heston sighed heavily and looked at his coffee. "Long-distance relationships are extremely difficult, Ryan." He met Ryan's gaze. "Given your... *diverse* careers, *any* kind of relationship would be hard, if not impossible to maintain."

Anger ignited in his chest. "Well, it's not really something either one of us has been thinking about the past few days."

Heston's brows rose. "I may not know a lot about *you*, but I know considerably more about Miss Beckett. Regardless of what state she's been in physically since you pulled her out of that hell hole, *she* has been thinking about it... *trust* me."

Ryan remembered the shadow he'd seen in Cat's eyes and wondered if the man was correct. Shaking off his apprehension, he rose. "Perhaps, and forgive me for saying so but it's none of your business. Now, if you'll excuse me I think I'll go pay my other friend a visit before I go back to Cate's room."

"How *is* your teammate?" Heston asked.

"Good." Ryan looked over his shoulder. "He should be released within a week or so."

"Glad to hear it." Heston gave him a small smile. "Thanks for the coffee."

Ryan stared at the man for a moment, then nodded and walked away.

***

Cat looked through the window, her mind spinning, her heart heavy.

She and Yasmeen had said a tearful goodbye a while ago but Ryan hadn't returned yet. He was probably visiting Digger. Knowing he would come in smiling from time spent with his friend made her feel even worse than she did, because he wouldn't be smiling for long once he came back to her. Dread, uncertainty, and anguish swooped inside her like diving, angry birds and for a moment she thought she'd be sick. A throbbing started in her temple and she reached for the button to dispense more morphine. Before she depressed the plunger, she stopped herself. To say what she had to say would require a clear head, which meant she'd have to wait for her next dose of pain medication.

"Hey, sweetheart," a familiar voice said from the doorway.

Cat blinked back the tears stinging behind her eyes and forced a smile as she looked toward the sound. "Hey, Ben. I didn't think I'd see you again until tomorrow morning right before take-off."

Tripp shrugged and sat down on the edge of the bed. "The guys offered to finish packing your hooch up so I could pay you a pre-transfer visit. They send their love, by the way." He gently sandwiched her hand between his. "How are you feeling?"

"Better than yesterday."

His brows drew together and he studied her. "You don't *look* any better."

Cat rolled her eyes. "Thanks."

He grinned. "You know I'm joking... sort of." He gently touched her cheek. "Soon the bruises will fade and you'll be back to your old self. All of this will be nothing but a... a distant memory."

You have no idea how right you are, she thought. *I will be back to my old self, my old alone self and Ryan will be nothing but a distant memory.* "I know." She took as deep a breath as her broken ribs would allow. "It's going to take time." *Time... that's something I wish I had more of.*

He must have seen something in her expression because his brows drew together. "You won't do this alone, Cat. We're going to be there for you, all of us. And although Ryan might not be there *physically*, you know you've got his support 100%, right? We'll keep him updated and the two of you are going to stay in touch until you can figure this thing out."

The pain in her heart raked its claws across the inside of her chest. It took everything she had to keep her face impassive when all she wanted to do was throw herself against Tripp and sob. "Right." She closed her eyes. "We'll figure everything out."

The door swung open and she knew it was Ryan. She could sense him.

"Hey, Ben," he said quietly. "Is she...?"

"No," she replied. "I'm just resting my eyes." She looked at him and smiled, and her heart nearly broke when he smiled back.

Tripp rose and moved to the end of the bed. "You tired? We can go get dinner or something and come back later if you need to rest."

Cat shook her head. "No. I'm fine." She sighed softly and met Tripp's gaze. "I do need to talk to Ryan alone for a few minutes... if that's okay."

She groaned inwardly when she saw the narrowing of Tripp's eyes. He looked at her for a moment and his expression turned stony, which told her he had a *good* idea what she was about to do. He clenched his jaw, a muscle in his cheek twitched, and he nodded once.

"Of course," he said in a neutral tone. "I'll be back in a little bit."

Cat was relieved he hadn't said anything, but she knew he would eventually. Once the door closed behind his large frame Ryan sat down on the edge of the bed and reached for her hand.

"So, what is it?" Ryan asked, still smiling. "You tired of seeing me?"

She wished Hasan had chosen another appendage to break, because she *really* wanted to touch him. Her gaze wandered over his face, the face that no doubt left many a female heart beating faster, and when their eyes met she nearly lost her nerve. Tears welled.

"Oh, God," she said softly, "I'd never get tired of seeing you." It was as if he read her mind. His smile vanished, as she'd known it would, and his expression sobered.

"Cate. Don't. Whatever you're going to say... don't."

"You already said it." A pained smile curved her mouth. "About a week ago, remember?"

"I was wrong."

"No." She shook her head slowly. "You weren't."

His brows drew together. "Yes, I *was*."

"*We* were wrong," she said, her chin trembling, "for thinking this thing between us could be anything other than what it was."

"And what *was* it?" he asked, releasing her and getting to his feet.

The pain in his eyes sent daggers into her heart and lungs and she could barely breathe. "A beautiful week," she whispered, tears trailing down her cheeks, "one I will remember as the happiest in my life." She fought a sob. "This is your final stop, Ryan. You have to get off the train now."

He shook his head and swiped at his eyes. The stare he leveled on her was disbelieving. "I *love* you, Cate," he said from between clenched teeth.

"And I love you," she replied. "It's not a question of *love*. It's just... sometimes *love* isn't enough."

"Why not?"

She'd already known he wouldn't make it easy on her, but she hadn't expected it to be *this* difficult. The only advantage was now the emotional pain overwhelmed her physical pain, making morphine unnecessary. Cat took a hitching breath and closed her eyes.

"A relationship needs more than love," she argued. "It needs... *tending*. It needs... *proximity*." She looked at him through her tears. "In a couple months, the military will send you somewhere and the Agency will send me somewhere, and the probability of those two places being even *remotely* close to one another is almost zero."

He sat back down and leaned toward her. "I didn't say it would be *easy*."

"But is it supposed to be *this* hard?" She heard a beeping but ignored it. When Ryan looked at the machine she pressed a splinted hand to his cheek and forced his eyes back to hers. "And what happens when you meet someone closer to home? Someone who makes it easier?"

Ryan pulled away from her and stood up, his eyes wide and incredulous. "Do you think I go around giving my heart to any woman with pretty eyes and a nice ass?"

Her heart started to pound, and she had a feeling it had nothing to do with her emotional state. "No. But I also don't think you should put your life on hold for me."

"I'm not putting *anything* on *hold*," he shot back, a spark of anger in his eyes. "When you love someone you... *adjust* your life to accommodate them and they do the same. That's how it's *supposed* to work."

Tears spilled unheeded and she shook her head slowly. "Please, Ryan. Just go."

"So, that's it?" He backed away a couple steps. "You're... giving up?" He exhaled sharply, as if someone had punched him in the gut, and then dropped his chin to his chest for a few tense, silent moments. When he finally looked at her, what she saw in his gaze made her want to shrivel up and die. "Out of all the things I know you are, Cate... I never imagined *quitter* was one of them."

He watched her for a few more painful moments, then turned and left the room. When the door closed, Cat reached for the morphine dispenser and hit the button as tears continued to stream down her face. Unfortunately, the narcotic did nothing for the ache surging through her, and those claws that continued to rip at her heart were also unaffected by the drug.

Tripp appeared a moment later. "What did you do?" he asked, his brows drawn together.

"What I had to do."

"Cat... *why?*"

She felt her heart shredding. "It would never work, Ben."

"Ryan *loves* you."

"Like I told him, it's not a question of love." Tears streamed down her face. "He deserves better."

Tripp speared her with a hot, angry gaze. "Jesus, Cat. You fought harder to get us the weekend off than you did for him." Without another word, he jerked the door open and stalked out of the room.

Cold liquid anguish welled up inside Cat's chest cavity and escaped her mouth in great gasping sobs that echoed off the walls. She stared at the door, suddenly wishing she could rewind time and undo everything she'd done. Stabbing shards throbbed through her face and torso, the discomfort increasing with every increasingly rapid beat of her heart. The blood pressure monitor went off again and Dr. Rhoades appeared moments later, a nurse on her heels.

"What happened?" the doctor asked.

All Cat could do was shake her head and cry.

***

Tripp pushed through the front doors of the hospital and scanned the parking lot. When he spotted Ryan opening the door to his Humvee, Tripp broke into a run.

"Ryan! Ryan, wait!"

Ryan paused and watched him approach, his expression guarded. Tripp walked up to him and slowly closed the door of the vehicle. Ryan crossed his arms over his chest and leaned against the side of the Humvee.

"Ryan, whatever she said in there... disregard it."

Ryan pressed his thumb and forefinger into his eyes then exhaled slowly. "Easier said than done, Ben."

"Come on, man." Tripp stuffed his hands in his pockets. "She's in pain, she's on... *drugs*, and she's been through something that would break most *men*...." He met Ryan's gaze.

"She sounded pretty sure of herself to me."

Tripp hung his head. "Ryan... you have to understand something about Cat. She...." He paused and sighed. "She blamed herself for Charlie and Matt having to put their lives on hold for her, she still does." He leaned against the hood of the car and stared into the darkness. "At the academy if anyone needed help, whether it was on the obstacle course or on a test, Cat was there. But, don't *ever* try to return that favor." He looked at Ryan out of the corner of his eye. "She'll give herself to others all day long, but she can't handle others giving to her."

Ryan sighed. "So, what am I supposed to do?"

"Nothing." Tripp faced him. "Just... don't give up on her, not yet. I know you'll regret it if you do, and so will she." He put a hand on Ryan's shoulder. "I've known her for five years, bud, but I never really saw her happy... not until she met you." He saw the clenching of Ryan's jaw. "Unless... you *want* it to be over."

Ryan glared at him.

Tripp gave him a grim smile. "Then trust me. I've got your back, Ryan, and I'm going to fix this."

Ryan's expression turned incredulous. "How?" A short, sharp laugh escaped him. "If what you say about her is true, how are you going to change who she is?"

Tripp lifted one brow. "I'm not." He chuckled. "She doesn't know it, but she's already halfway there. I'm going to nudge her across the finish line."

"And until then?"

"Until then...." Tripp's expression sobered. "Wait for my call."

Chapter Thirty-One

Cat's feet padded rhythmically on the sand near the water line, but no matter how fast she ran she couldn't get away from herself. Despite the blazing turquoise water, the rugged volcanic peaks in the background, and the lush tropical jungle, her mind seemed capable of focusing on only one thing. The breathtaking vistas of American Samoa paled in comparison to the image of a dark-haired, blue-eyed man playing over and over in her head. She stopped and rested her hands on her knees, taking in deep, even breaths.

She had no idea where Ryan was, though it would have been easy enough to find out. It had been nearly eight months since he'd pulled her out of hell; nearly eight months since she'd put herself *back* in hell by sending him away.

"That was your best time yet," Tripp said from behind her as he checked his watch. "You're still not as fast as you were in Afghanistan, but you're getting it back." He handed her a bottle of water and a towel. "Then again, maybe if you concentrated on your running you'd carve off a few seconds."

She looked at him. "What is that supposed to mean?"

He walked into the surf and splashed his bare torso. "Nothing," he replied. "You just seem... preoccupied." He faced her. "Your mind is not on what you're doing."

Had it been anyone else making that observation Cat would've let the tiger out, but Tripp wasn't anyone else. Her throat tightened and regret swelled coldly beneath her heart. She wiped the sweat from her brow and took a drink. "I know."

"Want to talk about it?"

"No," she said, a bit too quickly. To his credit, Tripp's expression never changed.

"The scars on your back look better," he commented. "Those surgeons really know what they're doing. Can barely see them."

"Really?" She scowled. "You're supposed to be *watching* my back, not *looking* at it." As soon as the words were out, she wished she could retract them. Again, Tripp's expression remained neutral and she looked away, shamefaced. "I'm sorry, Ben. I didn't mean that." The silence stretched out and she searched for something to break it. "Have you heard from Tech or the guys?"

"Techno called right after you started your run," Tripp replied, moving to the shade of a group of coconut palms. "He and the guys are back in D.C., and he said they miss us already."

"And he's sure his parents don't mind us staying?" she asked.

Tripp looked at her for a moment, then smiled and leaned against one tall, smooth trunk. "Tech specifically told me to tell you his mom and dad think of us as their *aiga*." When she looked at him strangely he chuckled. "Their *family*, Cat. And I talked to Grace this morning. She said she's thrilled we're here."

Cat nodded and hung the towel around her neck. "Okay then." She grabbed Tripp's wrist and looked at his watch. "I think I'll hop in the shower. You're cooking dinner, right?"

Tripp grinned and rolled his eyes. "Yes, dear. Have some tuna steaks marinating now."

She smiled and walked toward the two-bedroom bungalow that sat on the stretch of private beach owned by Techno's family. The main house sat farther back from the water, close to the base of a looming mountain. As she approached the front door of the white-washed cottage she saw a woman sitting on the porch of the main house and waved. Techno's mom, Grace, waved back and smiled so widely Cat could see her teeth from where she stood. With a chuckle, Cat pushed through the screen door into the cozy living room.

When she entered her bedroom, her eyes were immediately drawn to the framed photograph sitting on the nightstand. She stutter-stepped and her heart plummeted to the floor. It was the photo Mack had taken of her and Ryan, and it hadn't been on the nightstand when she'd left for her run. The 8X10 had been in the second drawer of the dresser, underneath her socks. Slowly, she approached the picture and although she didn't want to, she picked it up. Tears stung and she blinked them back. Tripp had been right. She *did* look different. She looked *happy*.

A hot, pulsing ball of anger blossomed to life in the center of her chest, and when she heard Tripp enter the house it grew. He was her closest friend so he was allowed more leeway than the rest of the team, but this pushed the boundary even for him. Turning on her heel she walked back down the hall and followed the sound of his footsteps to the kitchen. The refrigerator door was open and he was waist deep in the appliance, but it wasn't Tripp that caught her eye. On the table behind him his laptop was open and on, and the desktop background sent her heart through the floor. It was a picture of him with Ryan, and from the seriousness of their expressions she had a good idea when it had been taken. It had been bad enough having Ryan in her mind all day, *every* day, but this was too much.

"What the hell's going on?" she asked, holding the 8X10 against her chest.

Tripp straightened and closed the refrigerator door with his foot, his arms full of food. His brows drew together and he put his armload down on the counter. "I'm... making dinner?"

Cat held up the photograph. "Why was this on my nightstand, Ben?"

He leaned against the counter and looked at her strangely. "Because you put it there?"

She stood toe to toe with him. "This wasn't on my nightstand, it was in my drawer."

"Which is an even stranger place to put a photo than a *nightstand*," he replied dryly.

That ball of anger expanded again. "This isn't funny."

Tripp stared at her for several seconds and his eyes narrowed. "I'm sorry, Cat, but I have *no* idea what you're talking about."

She gaped at him. "*Why* did you take this out of my drawer?"

"I didn't."

"There's no one else here!"

He scowled and crossed his arms over his chest. "Except Hanna. She was putting away laundry. I told her not to bother, but you know how she is."

Cat blinked. Hanna was the Kealoha's housekeeper, and she seemed to truly enjoy waiting on people. The dark-haired, dark-eyed woman was always flitting about and usually humming, and Cat had never once seen her without a smile. It made perfect sense that if she saw a picture like that she'd naturally think it should be displayed. That angry ball shrank a bit and she put the frame on the counter.

"Okay, well what about *that?*" She pointed at the laptop.

Tripp glanced over his shoulder and his scowl deepened. "You mean *my* background on *my* laptop? I didn't realize I had to get your approval for what pictures I put on *my* computer."

"But why *him?* Why *now?*"

He made an exasperated sound. "I've had it there for months. You've just never seen it before now." He tossed her an annoyed glance. "There are very few people in this world I call friend, Cat, but Ryan is one of those people whether you like it or not. Just because *you* dumped him doesn't mean *I'm* going to."

The anger evaporated and tears welled. That familiar pain, raw and savage, tore through her again and she covered her face with her hands. Not only had she pushed Ryan away, now she was doing the same thing with her last true friend. Tripp had always been there for her, had always been faithful, and she had just accused him of deliberately trying to hurt her.

Cat dared a look at him, and the expression on his face nearly sent her over the edge. He was angry with her, and hurt, and he had every right to be. Self-loathing nearly choked her and she backed out of the tiny kitchen. "I'm sorry," she whispered. "I'm *so* sorry." Turning on her heel, she ran for the front door as if Hasan was back and chasing her with his whip in hand.

Tripp watched in dismay as she fled the bungalow. "Cat, wait!" he called out. The screen door slamming was the only answer he received. Leaning his hands on the edge of the counter, he sighed and looked down at the photograph. The woman in that picture was beautiful, in love, and happy, a polar opposite of the woman who had just run from the bungalow. Her features were the same, but the light was gone. "I hope this works, buddy," he said to the picture. "I really do."

He walked outside and headed toward the water. A quick scan of the beach told him she wasn't there, which meant she was probably headed for the waterfall. He glanced into the west at the setting sun and scowled. "Damn it." There was about an hour of sunlight left, if that, and he would need every minute. He returned to the cottage, retrieved his hiking pack and a satellite phone, and started out.

The route to the waterfall wasn't particularly dangerous during daylight hours when one could see the turns in the trail and the sheer drops. It was a different story at night. Even as sure-footed as he was, Tripp had no desire to traverse the twisting, often dangerously narrow path after dark. Hopefully, if he got to her soon enough, they'd be closer to the bottom of the mountain than the top when the sun went down, and they could come home instead of being forced to camp out until dawn.

Unfortunately, by the time he saw her again he was at the base of the falls and the sun was gone. He glanced at the towering cascade, the free-falling water echoing like thunder off the rocks as it dropped more than a hundred feet into a clear, deep pool. He glanced at Cat. She looked so small sitting on a large boulder near the edge of the mist, her arms wrapped around her knees. Tripp sighed and moved to sit next to her.

"You were concentrating," he said. "Made much better time on that run, and uphill no less." He glanced at her. "You running from me... or you?"

She sniffed and wiped her cheeks. "I'm so sorry, Ben. You didn't deserve that." She looked at him out of the corner of her eye then hung her head. "I don't know what's wrong with me."

"I do." He pulled the satellite phone from his pack and held it out to her. "Call him." Cat looked at the phone for a few moments and tears slid silently down her face. He saw the pain in her emerald eyes and said it again. "*Call* him."

"I can't," she said at last, squeezing her eyes shut.

Tripp was losing patience. "Why the fuck not?"

"He's probably moved on, so why rip the scab off that wound?"

"Jesus, Cat. Would you let someone help *you* for a change?" Tripp resisted the urge to toss her in the water. "That man loved you with *every* fiber of his being. If you think he's moved on after only a few months you're nuts."

Cat put a hand on his cheek and turned his face to hers. "I appreciate what you're trying to do here, but it won't change what happened." Her hand fell. "I broke his heart. I sent him away, and now I get to live with that."

Tripp sighed heavily and put the phone away. "If you could go back, would you change it?"

"Absolutely," she whispered. She closed her eyes and nodded slowly. "In a heartbeat."

When she met his gaze the pain he saw tore at his heart. Tripp moved closer to her and pulled her onto his lap, wrapping his arms around her as she wept softly. He kissed her temple then rested his chin on top of her head.

"God, I miss him," she said between sobs. "What the hell was I thinking?"

"Don't worry, Cat," he said softly. "Everything's going to be okay. I promise."

***

Tripp ducked under the makeshift shelter he'd set up and checked on Cat as the waterfall rumbled in the background. She was fast asleep. He ran a finger over her cheek, then stepped back into the open air and walked to the opposite side of the pool. Taking the satellite phone from his back pocket, he dialed and waited patiently. After three rings the person on the other end picked up.

"Hello?"

"Hey, bud." He glanced over his shoulder toward the shelter, then looked into the moonless, star-filled sky and smiled. "It's time."

***

Ryan stood in the doorway, his eyes adjusting to the darkness, but he'd recognize Cat's silhouette anywhere. It had been three days since Tripp's call, and his stomach had been in knots from the moment he'd recognized his friend's voice. His chest tightened as she sighed softly and rolled onto her back, her face soft and untroubled in sleep. There was a small, crescent shaped scar barely visible on her left cheekbone and she was thinner than he remembered, but other than that she looked as beautiful as the first time he'd seen her.

Ryan tried to take a deep breath, but he couldn't. He could barely believe he was here and she was so close. Part of him wanted to rush to her and take her in his arms, but another part was wary, uncertain.

You're a fucking SEAL for Pete's sake, he chided himself. *Get moving.*

He slowly approached the bed and sat down on the edge of the mattress. She stirred again, her eyes moving quickly back and forth beneath tightly closed lids. A frown flitted across her brow and her expression shifted. Suddenly, she was neither untroubled nor peaceful.

The transformation was immediate and terrifying to watch. His eyes stung as the ghosts from her recent past revisited her with a vengeance. She started fighting. Her hands clenched and unclenched as she struggled against ropes only she could see, and the pained whimpers made his heart twist. When she screamed he jumped, startled. The tears slid down his face. He reached for her instinctively but jerked back when she started kicking and shrieked again.

Tripp had warned him about the nightmares, but hearing about them and seeing it happen in person were quite different. At that moment, his training took over. He knew very well how to subdue someone, but he had to remember this wasn't some armed terrorist hopped up on hate and *jihad.* He quickly removed his shoes and tackled her, wrapping her in his arms from behind. She started to kick harder and he threw his leg over hers, effectively immobilizing her. He was surprised by how strong she was, but it was her terrified cries that ripped at him. Goose bumps broke out on his arms and shuddering apprehension wound its way slowly but tightly around his spine. Everything inside of him said to run from her chilling wails, but instead he tightened his embrace and rested his chin on her shoulder, his lips near her ear.

"It's me, Cate," he whispered, desperately hoping she'd stop screaming. "It's okay, baby, it's me. I'm right here and no one is ever going to hurt you again." He closed his eyes and ground his teeth together when his name was torn from her lips in a pained, strangled cry. "Ssh, babe, it's all right. It's me. It's Ryan, Cate. I'm right here and I swear on my *life* no one will *ever* hurt you like that again."

He felt the warmth of her tears on his arm and fought his own, but as he whispered to her, her struggles slowed and finally stopped altogether. She was gasping from the exertion but he continued to speak in a low, soothing voice. Gradually her breathing evened out and deepened and he knew she was asleep. He exhaled slowly, his gut in knots as he prayed to never, *ever* hear that sound again.

Suddenly it didn't matter what had happened, that she'd broken his heart and sent him away. She was alive and she was in his arms again. When she murmured his name, turned to face him, and tucked in under his chin the ice that had built around his heart since their breakup melted. And then he saw it, the photograph on the nightstand. He vividly remembered that day, remembered that that night had been one of the last times he'd held her before she was kidnapped. Ryan closed his eyes and pressed a kiss to her brow.

"God, I'm glad to have you back."

Cat sighed softly and snuggled closer.

***

Cat couldn't remember the last time she'd felt like this. Oh, wait. Yes, she could. As she lingered in that twilight area between sleep and wakefulness, she realized she *did* remember. The last time she'd felt this safe and warm and content was the last time she'd been with Ryan. It was then she remembered the nightmare.

It hadn't been any different than the others, at least in the beginning. The change had come when Ryan had somehow entered her prison and released her from her bonds. Cat swam closer to consciousness but fought it. She didn't want to wake from whatever dream she was having now. It was *so* real. The pain of reliving her torture had been replaced with the strength and safety of Ryan's embrace. In fact, she still felt his arms around her, the gentle rise and fall of his chest as he breathed. His warmth seemed to penetrate her, relaxing every muscle and soothing every fear. She didn't want to wake up. She wanted to stay right where she was.

Unfortunately, the birds arguing outside her window were unaware of her desire to stay in dreamland. She tried to ignore them and pull the edges of the dream back together so she could stay in its peaceful embrace. The sounds of the birds faded as she focused on the rhythm of his breathing. She snuggled closer, looked up, and smiled. His beard was gone and his hair was cut in the familiar military style, accentuating the rugged planes and angles of his face. She reached up and touched his stubble-covered chin. His eyes opened.

"This is a nice dream," she said softly. "Too bad it has to end."

He smiled back. "It's not a dream, babe."

Cat frowned and blinked. "But...."

He grinned and lowered his head. Her eyes closed as he covered her mouth with his. Her body immediately responded and it hit her. She jerked away and scrambled to her knees.

"Oh my God," she said in a rush, staring at him. "You're... you're *real*, and you're... *here.*" She shook her head and backed away, an emotional tidal wave rising inside her. It swirled around her heart and lungs, crushing them beneath its weight. Joy flared like fireworks at the same time anguish threatened to smother it. "You shouldn't... you shouldn't be here."

His expression sobered as he sat up and reached out to tuck a stray curl behind her ear. "Ask me to leave and I'll go... no arguments and no looking back."

Panic vaulted into her chest. "No!" Tears welled. "No." She bit her lip and shook her head again. "I sent... I sent you away once. I... I can't... do that again." Her chin trembled and she hung her head.

"Cate...."

The sound of her name from his lips broke the thin hold she had on herself and the tears started to flow. When he put a hand behind her neck and pulled her to him she didn't fight. She pressed her face into his chest and clung to him as if her life depended on it, because it did. Having him in her arms made her realize with excruciating clarity how wrong she'd been.

"I'm so sorry, Ryan," she whispered. "As soon as you left I wanted to take it all back. Can you ever forgive me?"

"I forgave you as soon as the door closed behind me," he replied.

"I never wanted to hurt you."

"Hey." He pulled back and framed her face with his hands. "We said one day at a time, right?" Cat sniffled and nodded, and he smiled, his thumbs stroking softly over her cheeks. "So, that was one bad day. Let's just... *not* do that again. *Ever.*"

Cat rested her hands on his chest. "You got it." The sound of dishes clattering in the sink distracted her momentarily, and then she looked at Ryan and smiled. "Would you wait here a minute, please? I need to talk to someone."

Ryan kissed her quickly, then released her and lay back. "Don't be too hard on him."

"Oh, don't you worry about him." She got off the bed and walked to the door. "He's a big boy. He can take care of himself."

"*Cate....*"

She paused in the doorway and gave him a wink. "Relax, Ryan. I'm not going to shoot him if that's what you're worried about."

Cat walked down the hall and pasted a neutral expression on her face. Tripp was at the sink, rinsing dishes and putting them in the dishwasher. When she appeared, he stopped what he was doing and looked at her. She stared at him and his brows drew together. At this point it wasn't hard to cry, and when he saw the tears his eyes widened.

"Cat...."

Cat walked up to him and punched him in the stomach, not hard enough to hurt but hard enough that he grunted and hunched over. He looked at her in disbelief, and when she grabbed his head and kissed him his eyes got even wider. Then she threw her arms around his neck and hugged him tightly.

"Thank you," she said, tears continuing to flow. "Thank you for not listening to me and saving me from myself."

Tripp's arms wound around her and he lifted her against his chest, her feet dangled above the floor. "You're welcome, and that *is* my job, isn't it?"

She pulled back and met his gaze. "I love you, Benjamin David Trippler."

He grinned. "I love you, too, sweetheart." He put her down, turned her toward the hall, and gave her a light shove. "Now get back in there. You two have lost time to make up for."

Cat tossed him a grin over her shoulder as she ran back to her room. Once inside, she closed the door, then slowly turned and faced Ryan. Her heart skipped a beat when his eyes met hers and she sucked in a breath. All the questions spinning in her head vanished.

"God, I've missed you," she whispered.

He sat up and held out a hand. "Come here."

Cat walked toward him and slipped her fingers into his. He leaned back and pulled her against his side, his arm slipping around her shoulders as she stretched out beside him and nestled in beneath his chin. "How long do we have?" she asked softly.

"The rest of our lives."

She pulled back and scowled at him. "Ryan."

He chuckled. "Well, that's something we need to talk about." He must have recognized her concern because he smiled, brushed his lips over her brow, and pressed her head back down against his shoulder. "Relax, Cate." He enclosed her in his embrace and sighed softly. "I'm on leave for the next 30 days. Do with me what you will."

She was almost afraid to ask, but she did. "And after that?"

"After that... I report to my next permanent duty station." He paused. "In San Diego."

Cat leaned up on one elbow and gaped at him. "San Diego?"

He smiled and toyed with her hair. "Yep. Mack and I join the team to start training the next generation of SEALs mid-October."

A spark of hope came to life in her chest and she dared to let it burn a bit. "So, you won't be...?"

"Deploying?" He ran a finger over her cheek. "Not unless the entire world goes to shit, no." His expression sobered. "Your turn. Are you going back to the Agency?"

"I don't know," she said in a low voice. She sat up, dropped her chin, and wrapped her arms around her knees, familiar ghosts whispering in her ear. She closed her eyes. "I don't think I can do what they want me to do anymore."

He sat up and leaned toward her. "You don't have to." He watched her for a moment then pushed her hair back over her shoulder so he could see her face. "I read the report, Cate. I know what happened." He sighed. "It's different when you're face to face, isn't it?"

"Yeah." She glanced at him. "A scope brings you up close and personal to your target, so it's different than traditional warfare, but still.... You can't... feel someone struggle or hear them gasp for air... or hear the snap of bones through a scope." Her throat tightened and she grimaced as the memory surfaced. "When I saw the life leave his eyes... I swore to myself he was my final kill."

"Then don't go back," he said quietly. "With your skills, you can find a job... shit, *anywhere*." He rested his chin on her arm and smiled. "Even in sunny San Diego."

Cat smiled and moved toward him until no more than a hair's breadth separated their lips. "Well, then. You'd better get aboard this train before it leaves the station. Can I see your ticket, sailor?"

Instead of replying he kissed her, his arms snaking around her and his fingers fanning out over her back. Warmth blossomed inside her, invading even that part of her she'd kept so closely guarded. As his mouth moved over hers she gave herself completely to him and a great sense of freedom engulfed her. The sadness, the soul-crushing loneliness, the sense of isolation she'd always felt were gone, as if they'd never been there. For the first time in her adult life, she felt full and complete.

He kissed her deeply, leisurely, and her heart pounded a rhythm against her breastbone. When he finally pulled back she took a ragged breath and Ryan gave her a wicked grin. With one quick move, he tossed her onto her back and covered her body with his. Cat smiled.

"Sorry, ma'am, but I don't have a ticket," he said. He nuzzled her jaw, then her ear, then her neck. "However, I really, *really* need to get on this train." He nibbled her earlobe. "Do you think there's some sort of... *arrangement*... we can make?"

Desire sizzled through her and she gasped softly as his lips feathered over her skin. "What... exactly... did you have... in mind?"

"Whatever you want."

"Hmm." She ran her fingers over his hair as he pressed his lips to the pulse racing in her throat. "That sounds fair."

Ryan grinned. "Outstanding. Let's get started, shall we?"

Epilogue

"Gentlemen! Line up!"

Ryan crossed his arms over his chest as the BUD/S candidates scrambled into formation. Once they were where they were supposed to be, he smiled.

"Today you're going to learn a skill most SEALs are not often called on to use, but it's a skill you will learn and master nonetheless. Firing line, now."

He, Mack, and the other instructors trailed behind the younger men as they double-timed it to the firing line. Cat and Tripp were already there, both prone, Cat with her eye to the scope of Charlie, her .416 rifle. She and Tripp were speaking softly, and when she heard the shuffle of footsteps she glanced over her shoulder, rose, and faced the group. Tripp gave him a grin as he gained his feet.

"At ease, gentlemen," Ryan called out. "Gather round." He waited until the men were in place. "Allow me to introduce you to Cat Beckett and Ben Trippler. I think you can guess which is which." A chuckle went through the group. "Ms. Beckett is an intelligence officer and the head of firearms training and linguistics. Mr. Trippler is also an intelligence officer, and they both work for an agency that will remain nameless." More chuckles. "They are our guest instructors for this phase of your training."

"Afternoon," Tripp said. "Now, before we get into it, Cat and I thought a little demonstration would be in order. With the help of your instructors here we have set up three incendiary targets down range, one at 800 hundred meters, one at 1600 meters, and the final one at 2000 meters." He gave Cat a knowing grin. "Shall we?"

Cat nodded. "Absolutely."

"Grab a pair of ear muffs and binocs," ordered Walker, one of the other instructors. "And pay attention."

When Cat took her position at the rifle Ryan heard the whispers start and smiled to himself.

"What's she going to do, take the first one and let the other guy do the rest?" he heard someone ask.

"She can squeeze *my* trigger anytime," another man said. Several others snickered at the remark.

"Hey!" Mack shouted. "If I want to hear any talking I'll ask you a question or speak to my fellow instructors. Otherwise... *you* need to zip it!"

Silence fell like a stone and Ryan gave Mack a quick grin.

Cat glanced at Mack and winked. "All right, boys," she said. "The key to hitting long-range targets, in addition to a working knowledge of ballistics, a first-class spotter, and a well-honed weapon, is breath control." She glanced over her shoulder and smiled. "But I'm sure you already knew that. Muffs on, gentlemen."

Ryan smiled as she turned back to her rifle and it seemed everyone was holding their breath. Tripp did the calculations and she adjusted the scope with the lithe efficiency of someone who really knows their way around a gun. He watched as she moved her finger to the trigger, inhaled, then exhaled and held her breath. Her finger barely moved and the .416 clapped like thunder. The first target exploded almost simultaneously with the shot and Ryan heard several surprised murmurs. Cat didn't miss a beat. After cycling the bolt, reloading, and adjusting the scope for the next target she fired again. The second target immediately sent flames and smoke into the sunny Southern California sky. As she took aim at the final target the tension was palpable.

The .416 boomed and the 2000-meter target burst into flames roughly two seconds later. Cheers broke out among the candidates and Ryan fought a smile. Cat cycled the bolt to eject the spent cartridge from the .416 then rose and faced them.

"Any questions?" she asked.

Hands shot up and the men gathered closer around her and Tripp. Ryan and Mack and the other instructors stood back and watched.

"She hasn't lost her touch," Mack said under his breath.

"No, she hasn't," Ryan agreed. He looked at Mack and grinned. "Oh, wait. Are you talking about her *marksmanship?*"

Mack chuckled and bumped Ryan's shoulder. "Don't gloat. Just because you get to go home to her every night...."

Ryan looked down at the gold band on the fourth finger of his left hand then looked at his wife. Cat met his eyes briefly and winked.

"Yes, I do," Ryan said, winking back.

"Is it true she saved your ass in A-stan?" Walker asked.

He looked at the younger man and saw a reflection of himself at that age: sure, cocky, and bulletproof. "She saved a lot of people's asses in A-stan," Ryan replied. "But me? She saved more than my ass, Greg. She saved my *life*."

Walker crossed his arms over his chest and watched as Cat and Tripp worked with the candidates. "Nice. Where can I find a girl like that?"

"Not sure, just... be prepared. Sometimes they come armed." He chuckled and shook his head. "I don't know where they make 'em, buddy, but if you think you've found her I have one piece of advice for you."

"What's that?" Walker asked absently, his gaze still focused on Cat.

"Do what I did. Grab her with both hands, don't look back, and hold on *tight*." Ryan glanced at his wife and grinned. "It'll be the ride of a lifetime."

The End

About the author

Leslie has been writing since she learned to write, and her mother still stores boxes of handwritten stories in the attic. Her debut novel, Accidental Affair, was published in 2012. She is a veteran of the Gulf War who served with the U.S. Navy, and she was among the first groups of women to work the flight deck of an aircraft carrier. Leslie lives in California with her husband and has three sons.

Also by Leslie McKelvey

Accidental Affair

Jack Vaughn is sure his life is over as he tumbles down the wooded hillside onto the deserted two-lane stretch of asphalt. Years of work ended with a single gunshot. Yet, it's not over.

A good Samaritan stops to help him, despite the danger he poses to her

Laine Wheeler knows better than to stop for strangers on the rural Montana highway near her home, but her conscience won't allow her to leave an injured man behind.

What she doesn't know is the man is an undercover ATF agent tasked with infiltrating a domestic terrorist group. His cover has been blown and helping him will put her life in danger.

Though there is an instant attraction, Jack knows that beginning a romantic relationship with Laine would be both unfair and unwise. Yet the farther they run, the harder it gets to ignore the feelings that are surging between them.

Right Place, Right Time

While shooting pictures of a mama bear and her cubs in Rocky Mountain National Park, wildlife photographer Beth Drummond witnesses a murderous shootout and the violent deaths of four men. When those responsible realize they've not only been seen but also photographed they give chase, determined to tie up loose ends. Praying she can outdistance her pursuers Beth dashes headlong through the woods, intent on nothing but reaching safety.

When Special Agent Bear Bristol, on leave from the FBI, hears gunshots and sees the woman running for her life, he knows he must intervene. He recognizes those who are chasing her and realizes that things are much worse than they seem. A vicious cartel with a mole at the FBI has put a target on Beth's back, and there is no one they can trust. Unable to call for backup, Bear must keep Beth safe until they can figure out who the inside man is.

As they struggle to stay one step ahead of both corrupt law enforcement and the killers they learn to trust one another, and realize there is more between them than just friendship born of necessity. Can they overcome the obstacles they face, or will they win the fight to live only to lose the battle to love?

Her Sister's Keeper

Juliet Hall has the perfect life. She lives in a gorgeous little cottage with her sister, Cassie, whom she adores, she's a principal ballerina with a small but prestigious dance company in Seattle, and the beach is only blocks away. Then a madman takes away that perfect life, her career, and her sister. When the man comes after her she bolts, trying to get as far away from Seattle and the scene of her sister's murder as she can.

It's just an average day for Sheriff Grant Donovan as he patrols the long, mostly deserted roads around Evergreen Springs, Montana. Until he comes across a stranded motorist, a motorist with the most beautiful blue-green eyes he's ever seen. He finds himself losing his heart to the newcomer, and discovers there is someone else who also wants her heart. Someone who is willing to kill her to get it.

Runaway Heart

Lindsay Davenport has it all: a handsome, wealthy husband, a life of seeming ease, and everything money could buy. But what do you buy when you live in hell? After seven years of marriage, seven years of abuse and violence, she changes her name and flees to a remote town in Alaska, determined to escape her husband's cruelty and start her life over. Life, however, has other plans…. Ross Devlin loves his bar in Cooper's Ridge, Alaska. He loves being a bachelor, being a pilot, and playing hockey. Then a quiet woman, with a shady past, walks into his life. As time passes he realizes he doesn't love anything as much as he loves her, and his bar, his plane, and hockey are not as important as protecting her from an ex-husband who plans to make the phrase "Till death us do part" a reality.

See a full list of our titles at
www.blackvelvetseductions.com

Come and like us at
Black Velvet Seductions on Facebook
and follow BVS Books on Twitter

www.ingramcontent.com/pod-product-compliance
Lightning Source LLC
Chambersburg PA
CBHW051540250626
47157CB00001B/130